Devil's Den

A Journey from Darkness to Light

3

Devil's Den

by

Randall Lane

One evening an old Cherokee Indian told his grandson about a battle that goes on inside of people.

He said, 'My son, the battle is between two 'wolves' inside us all. One is Evil. It is anger, envy, jealousy, sorrow, regret, greed, arrogance, self-pity, guilt, resentment, inferiority, lies, false pride, superiority, and ego.

The other is good. It is joy, peace, love, hope, serenity, humility, kindness, benevolence, empathy, generosity, truth, compassion and faith.'

The grandson thought about it for a minute and then asked his grandfather: 'Which wolf wins?'

The old Cherokee simply replied,

'The one you feed.'

-Native Proverb

foreword

August 21st, 2017. The day the Sun and Moon aligned to showcase a majestic beauty which so few are fortunate enough to see in one's lifetime. A complete Solar Eclipse, the first to visit the United States, in particularly the Southeast, in over forty years. Wanting to get the best view possible to experience such a beautiful display, my family and I travelled two hours south to Mount Pleasant, South Carolina. Passing through Georgetown along the way.

It was on the way back when dealing with such atrocious traffic from all the onlookers, that we were forced into a standstill right in the heart of Georgetown. It was here, I began to take in all the sights and sounds that presented themselves. It was here my creative wheels began to turn.

Being a writer, I never go anywhere without a notepad. I'm always observing, whether I realize it or not. Being behind the wheel that day, I had my mother retrieve one of my notepads stashed in the glove compartment, in which she went on to jot down some of the ideas jostling through my mind.

I brainstormed from August 2017 to February 2018, building off the notes my mother was kind enough to record for me while passing through Georgetown. I began writing March 5th, 2018 and finished my first draft of

Devil's Den: A Journey from Darkness to Light, on February 5th, 2019.

The subtitle reflects my own journey while developing this story. I felt a deep urge to dive deeply into the theme and idea of evil. The original title idea I had was An Evil Within. I wanted to explore the deep darkness that manifests itself in such individuals as Franklin Ethan Thompson. The overall thought, being that if such evil can exist, then like everything else in the world, there must also be a polar opposite. One must not look far to see, that true evil does exist, it'd take only a glance through the news to see it. That being said, it wouldn't take you long to see the opposite as well. If there is evil, there must be good? Right?

I set out to shine a light on darkness so to speak and show that no matter how dark the darkness is, the light is always brighter. No matter how evil the evil is, the good is always greater.

With this thought and my experience that day in Georgetown, along with much prayer and research, Devil's Den: A Journey from Darkness to Light, was born.

It is my hope that as I attempt to show just how dark the darkness is, that you will also see its polar opposite and all the good things of life in a whole new way. So, sit back and enjoy the ride as you join James, Rebecca, and Ethan, on this thought-provoking journey from darkness to Light. And remember, no matter what darkness you may find yourself in, the Light within is always brighter.

—Randall Lane

April 14, 2019

Matthew 5:14

"You are the Light of the World."

Prologue

June 1981

Yellow and orange danced in the misty retinas of the gazing boy clothed in a stained white tee and worn-out jeans. The flame crackled, licking the wood and dry stubble with a hiss. His face flush, his blood pulsing, beads of sweat trickled down his forehead. His blistered hands grip the wooden end of a shovel, upon which rests his chin with his eyes glued to the Devil's Den. The Sun blushed at such a sight, quick to tuck its face behind a graying cloud. Darkness covered the earth as it caressed the boys back with a glancing stroke. The inky blackness crawled past the young lad and enveloped the fiery barn. An icy breeze trailed not far behind, neither did the smell of burnt hair and flesh.

A glance skyward to the towering pines, showed even the limbs shuddered at the display below. A trio of crows rummaged about, spreading gossip of the mischief. While the reeds took notice as they bowed in reverence to such an austere presence.

A pack of coyotes yipped and cackled, scrambling along the wood line just outside the bent reeds reach. It was as if they were reciting the words to a religious rite the boy had been forced to memorize along with his nightly prayers. The saying juggled in his mind with a flowing cadence: *All sin begins within and there is no cure without atonement. A sacrifice must now be made to ever ease the pain.*

If he listened close enough, he thought he could screaming.

A flood of memories washes over the boy and he struggles to stay focused. His head swims with voices and screaming. He squints his eyes and grinds his teeth.

The faint sound of growing sirens breaks the boy from his trance. The fire in his eye reflects the flame within. As much as he'd like to believe he'd ended such torture, somehow the boy knew by the burning in his gut and the chanting in his ear, it wasn't the end.

It was only the beginning.

1

1989

Georgetown, nestled between Myrtle Beach and Charleston, is not that different than any other town you'd find along the coast of South Carolina: Spanish Moss draped in Live Oaks, nice breeze, smiling faces. But that of course all changed after the summer of 1981. It's as if the town was visited by an omen, who decided that instead of passing through like the many tourist each year, it would linger and infect the town with its sin. A thick line was drawn between good and evil that day. On one side, you'd find yourself constantly looking over your shoulder to avoid any drug crazed mugger. Due to its proximity to the paper mill, this side of town reeks of burnt pinto beans and pig manure. But it also seems darker on that side, as if the Sun just doesn't shine the same. The other side of town is a polar opposite. Less stench, more salty air, beautiful old coastal homes built in the seventeen and eighteen hundreds, Live Oaks draping over the streets creating tunnels to pass through in route to the marsh. Original churches that'd been rebuilt and refurnished for appearances sake. Doing their best to not look like the other side of town. The polarity here, is obvious. As if you could literally step out of heaven and into hell within just a few steps. It seemed to require less steps to do so with each passing day as the darkness creeps in like an evening tide under a full moon.

With the missing boy, and a murdered family, everyone knows, things will never be the same. The line has been drawn. This is Georgetown. Now and forever. The tide has turned and has no plans of going back, unless visited by a savior.

††††††††††††††††††††††††††

A DREARY overcast covers the town, as a low-lying fog creeps across the busy four lane road. Meandering along, taking its time, passing in front of crawling cars and trucks as the burning of their headlamps cut into it.

Hot on its trail, the signature odor greets each commuter. There was no need for signs, you'd know by the smell when you crossed the town limits. A stench so strong, you'd swear it could seep through your flesh. In fact, the paper mill was cautious enough to install pressurized water spouts for each vehicle to pass through on the way out. Careful not to carry off any chemicals. No one objected to the new rule put in place in 1982. Seemed to help the conscience, something about passing under the shower felt like the cleansing of one's soul before entering the darkness among the street in route to the light. People felt more prepared to meet death after such a cleansing. Some even said a prayer as the water beat upon the shell of their vehicle, in case they were to come face to face with the business end of a loaded gun. Times are rough and people on this end of town can be quite desperate when faced with too many bills or an itch for another high.

Unseen to the natural eye, a trio of lofty wanderers cloaked in black, stood atop a weathered brick building which wore cobwebs and graffiti with pride, forming dark silhouettes against the wispy gray sky. They stood firm, arms crossed, lips stretched tight, wearing crooked grins as their gaze towered over the hustle and bustle of the morning commuters below.

Under the foes glare, a red 1982 square bodied Ford pickup maneuvered its way through traffic. A gravelly voice from the staticky radio muttering out highlights of the previous night's NBA games in between classics of Tom Petty, Greg Allman and the like.

For at least a half mile stretch, hundreds of beady red eyes glared back through the windshield. The soft rumble of engines, honking horns, and squealing brakes, all added to the stark tune of tires hissing away their tread against the wet asphalt.

Gulls squawked as they floated in the breeze, gathering in a nearby parking lot, seeking to scavenge their next meal.

Seated in the passenger seat, a middle-aged man attempted to lighten the mood as he reached for the knob and turned up a rhythmic tune from John Fogerty. The two screeched out lyrics to the last verse, keeping in harmony with Fogerty's trademark guitar twang and steady beat.

James Randolph couldn't help but laugh.

"Dang Jerry... you could've been another Chuck Berry."

"Psshh...yeah I wish. That be one way of getting out of this town. I don't know if there could ever be another colored folk as talented as him. At least not with the guitar that is."

"I don't know man...you were keeping up with Fogerty pretty good there. Might just be the raft that gets you off the island."

Jerry scoffed and wagged his head.

Coming into town along North Fraser Street, James glanced into the Piggly Wiggly parking lot in time to catch a flock of grouchy gulls hopping along the pavement in search of a crumb.

Ocean air wafted through the window. The dense saltiness lighted upon James' lips, causing him to reach for the bottle of coke next to his right thigh.

A glance to the right would reveal a paint chipping mural that attempted to show the old town. Written on a swirly scroll in the middle were the words,

Welcome to Historic Georgetown

The small clock on his truck's dash showed the big stick attempting to brush upon the seven, with the bony other kissing the one. The date rested just beneath, Tuesday, March 6, 1989.

"This town just has a way of keeping ya, you know. It's like a rip current, before you realize what hits you, you done been swept outta sea and tha harda you try and break loose from its grip, the furtha it takes you out. Then before long, after all those years of fightin it, it just spits ya up on shore. You get picked over by the gulls and nudged by a few passer byers to see if ya still kicking...all the while that ghostly current searches for another victim. There's got to be a better way man. I don't want to be another old man washing ashore, wishing I'd gotten out."

The cab of the truck grew still, except for the ticking of a turn signal as they waited to make a right down a ragged street which led to gravel parking lot. Jerry had always been the thinker and when he got to talking like that, you'd best listen. It helped that his voice had that powerful, yet soothing tone of Morgan Freeman. He favored him too. James had even heard a few folks claim the two were brothers. Knowing Jerry, James wouldn't find it all that surprising.

After a few cars pass through the intersection, a gap presented itself. James eased on the gas and made the turn, hitting a pot hole as he entered the street. Some of the houses wore trash bags for windows, they waved at James and Jerry on the way by as a breeze brought them to life. Others were boarded up, likely condemned from drugs or black mold. Trash littered the yards: a shredded Styrofoam cup, an old McDonald's bag and a queen's crown made with the golden arches. Bear bottles in all sizes tossed here and there. People on their porch having a smoke and eying each car that crossed the line in route to work. Coming to the end of the street, James rolled to a stop sign, to the left an AME Zion church which had seen its fair share of funerals through the years. They'd been robbed, vandalized, and covered with graffiti more times than James could remember. Though they never ceased with their efforts to brighten the streets. For that he commended them. He'd been at the mill for eight years now and it never failed to see a full parking lot on the Sundays he worked overtime. He just hoped they could make a difference before their flame grew dim like so many other churches on this side of town.

James scrolled through the crossway, over a bumpy entrance, passing a wooden sign which read,

Georgetown International Papermill

The brakes squealed as the tires crunched over the rock. White smoke billowed skyward from the old mill. The dark canvas of a thunder cloud served as a passing back drop before it grumbled and griped its way to the Atlantic with sass.

Jerry was saying something, "...you know James...this town used to not be like this. No sir. We used to be a happy little town. The Sun seemed to never set, weather was always right. We were a light in a dark world. Like a cozy fire after hard day's work in the cold. People used to come here to feel alive again...to feel free...to be refreshed. We used to be together. You know what I mean?"

James nodded.

"But man, ever since what happened to the Mooreland's...it just feels like it kind of locked everybody in a state of depression or something. Like we've been cursed by that boy's sin. Everybody's so burdened down with the thought of one day getting out, that they forget how to live in the here and now...and before they know it, they're another one of those cold...empty souls rolling ashore."

James shifted the gear stick, killed the engine, and took a deep breath before sighing it out.

"Yeah...I know what you mean Jerry. I often feel that burden myself. That's why me and Rebecca are saving for a house. We're hoping to be moved out of here within the next year or so. Trying to have a plan in place while watching out for that current," James gave a side grin that Rebecca had told him resembled Dennis Quaid's.

"Well...that's good. As long as you're both aware of it. I wish I'd took notice of it a lot sooner. But hey, better late than never, right?"

James tightened his lips and nodded as he opened the door and planted one foot followed by the other onto the gravel. He stretched and groaned before leaning into the truck to grab his metal lunch box.

Oh, the bliss of making a living. If only one could live while doing it.

✝✝✝✝✝✝✝✝✝✝✝✝✝✝✝✝✝✝✝✝

PEERING DOWN FROM the roof of an adjacent building, the three figures eyed James and Jerry until they disappeared into the mill. The larger of the three took a deep breath, scoffed it out, then marched away from the building's edge. A long bony finger and thumb to its chin, just below a tight grin. The other two strode behind the crusty, scaly feet of their master.

2

Upon entering the break room, James and Jerry were met with rumors of Dale hiring some new guys to help with the deadline. The men embraced the opportunity and indulged themselves with a moment of chatter and gossip. It wasn't long before a soft knock came to the door.

"Come in," James replied as he sat his coffee down on the counter next to him.

The door creaked open to reveal two men dressed in hand me down work uniforms, at least one size too big.

"Good morning guys...I'm Walter Avery," the lead man said as he shook James and the other three's hands.

Walter turned and looked at a young man that had followed in behind him,

"You said your name was Ethan, right?"

The man mumbled as he trained his gaze toward the floor with wandering eyes.

"Yeah, Ethan...Ethan Thompson."

"Well, it's nice to meet you Ethan. I'm James Randolph...this here is Jerry Turner, Billy Ross, and Hank Norton," he said going down the line.

The men nod while Ethan continued to look at the floor tiles, as if searching for faces and shapes, stealing glances toward the men only if necessary.

He was a scruffy young man, maybe a little over six-foot, a hundred and seventy pounds, with rough cut hair that may have been trimmed by a blind man. It proceeded over his ears like a waterfall. Mingled in with infected acne were several warts on the side of each nostril that seemed to grow the longer you stared at them. His face unnaturally elongated, his chin ending in a sharp point. And his shoulders were wide and flat like a book shelf.

"Just how old are you boy?" Jerry asked.

"I'm-I'm ni-nineteen."

"Yeah, I thought you were young. You graduate school?" Ethan nodded.

"Where did you go to high school?" asked James.

"I was actually homeschooled."

"Oh really?"

"Mm Hmm."

Having made more mistakes in his life than he'd like to admit, Jerry never hesitated to share what he'd learned with young folks like Ethan, so he went for it.

"Well boy, let me tell ya, you got a long road ahead of ya and you better make the most of it. Find you a good job, whether it's here or somewhere else and work your tail off. Don't be happy just staying where you're at but do what the job requires and then some more on top of that. Earn that promotion and climb the ladder, so when you're an old weasel like me, you can be thinking of retirement, instead of having to earn another paycheck. You feel me?"

Ethan's lips tightened as he dipped his head.

"Dang, somebody grab a tissue, that was good Jerry," Hank joked as his braided pony tail dangled along his shoulder. A faded skull tattoo wore a smirk on his forearm.

"Yeah Jerry, maybe you should retire now and become one of those travelling speakers," said Billy with a head full of curly blond hair, also known as "Bo" due to his resemblance of John Snyder from The Dukes of Hazzard.

James was thinking.

"Now he's got a good point there fellas. This kid needs to hear that. I wish someone would have told me that when I was younger. It'd be nice to move up the ladder and retire young. Heck, maybe even start your own business and be someone else's boss for a change."

"Yeah, keep dreaming Jimmy boy. Long as Dale is here, I don't know if any of us will be doing much climbing. At least not up, that is," Hank said with a scoff.

Upon the mocking, a piece of machinery fired up in the back, giving off a resounding roar. James had to speak up so the men could hear him.

"Well, I reckon it's time to get to work. You guys follow us, we'll take you out here to Kurt. He'll probably stick you with one of us for the day," James said as the men head out to the open floor lowering their protective glasses and squishing in some ear plugs along the way.

Outside the leisure and safety of the break room, men swarmed about like bees. Darting here, rushing there. The big machines roared, tumbled and wailed as they obeyed the orders of the men behind the controls. Glistening blades rushed to cut another sheet. And the smell...whew...the smell. Like stepping into a pigpen filled with boiled eggs, beans, and ammonia. The place crawled with Hydrogen Sulfide, which was used to strip the trees of their hardiness, softening them up before heading to the slaughter.

Walter and Ethan meet Kurt Burns, the leading supervisor of the mill and Dale Pennington's right-hand man. By the time he'd finished with them, he was about near shouting to make his words audible. There was a reason workers were required to have ear plugs. The wailing machines did their best to cover Kurt's words. Ethan gets placed with James and Jerry as Walter is stationed with Hank and Billy.

"So, have you worked anywhere before Ethan?" Asked James as he leaned in, only inches from Ethan.

"Yeah, I used to deliver the morning paper."

"Oh really? How did you like it?" James asked as he and Jerry placed new paper onto a large roller.

"It was good."

"Ah uh. Now you see what me and Jerry just did? You put this on here and make sure its fastened down, then just come over and press this here button," James demonstrated.

The machine started up. Joining all the others. The roller began its turn, pushing paper forward to a cutting press.

"Now once it gets here, it's your job to man the press. Someone will be here making sure the paper continues along the conveyor belt. Now, if the paper were to jam, the guy here will raise a fist, signaling for you to shut it off. Okay? Now you give him time to get the jam out, he'll give the thumbs up and you start it up again. Got it?"

"Yeah."

"All right, well let's give it go."

Ethan pressed a button as the roller entered a revolution, moving paper toward the press. James hovered Ethan's shoulder as Jerry stood by the reflective blade.

"All right, send her down and remember...*watch* for Jerry."

The paper passed under the large blade that resembled a medieval guillotine as Jerry tugged it through in about foot long pieces. It had cut off a dozen or so sheets before James had Ethan shut it down. The machinery whined and hummed before coming to an abrupt end.

"See, easy as pie, right?" said James, giving Ethan a slap on the shoulder.

Ethan nodded as the two of them shared a smile.

His deep, dark eyes whispered of a unique story and it'd take a lot of digging to hear it. James had always heard that the eyes are the windows to one's soul, and by the look in Ethan's eye...he knew it was true. For a reason he couldn't explain...he felt a connection with those eyes. Like they knew him. He had the feeling this boy would be quite the enigma

3

At Georgetown High School, students were antsy as the clock approached a quarter to three. The words of the teacher fell mostly upon deaf ears, except for the few who were engaged in the science lesson.

"Now class, can anyone tell me why an object will continue to move in its intended direction until acted upon by another force?"

Mrs. Randolph received a room full of blank stares, but the two with their hands held high, seemed to know.

"Yes, go ahead Rachel."

The blonde headed sophomore cleared her throat and said, "It's due to the force of inertia. Which is the basis for Newton's first law of motion."

"That's right. Very good, Rachel. Inertia is that force that causes us to lean to the side of our car when we go around a curve. Or like when we slam on the brakes, but our bodies continue to move forward. Basically, inertia is quite stubborn. It wants to continue moving in the same direction it was traveling. It doesn't like to be changed or redirected. As we will see during tomorrow's lecture, it plays a big role in the function of our tides here at the ocean."

With over a decade of teaching under her belt, Mrs. Randolph had mastered the art of ending her sentence just as the bell was inching toward its piercing ring. Less than a breath after the word "ocean" it did just that. The second it did, those who had already packed their things in anticipation of the bell, bolted from their seats and headed for the door. Those who hadn't yet, did so now. Note books slammed shut, as pencils and sheets of paper scraped across the desks before being shoved into book bags. Zippers rushing along their tracks.

The students stampeded for the door as they each had plans for a better day, none in which included Mrs. Randolph's homework assignments as priority.

But there was one student who was in no rush to leave the room. It was Rachel Fuller. In fact, if it were up to her, she'd probably allowed the lecture to continue another half hour or so.

She seemed to enjoy Mrs. Randolph's science lectures and for that matter enjoyed most any lectures that taught her something new.

As Mrs. Randolph finished gathering her things, she noticed Rachel was placing one last book in her bag. They were now the only two left in the room.

"Great job answering the inertia question Rachel. Most students don't get that one on the first try."

"Yeah, well I try not to be most students," Rachel replied with a gentle smile.

"I always try to stay ahead with my reading. I feel I learn more if I read the chapter I know you will be teaching from beforehand. It just reinforces what I've read and anything I didn't understand from the reading, you'll usually go over it in class. I feel that's the way I learn best."

"Well...whatever you're doing young lady, keep it up, because it shows. Your hard work will pay off. Trust me."

"I know. Thank you, Mrs. Randolph, see you tomorrow."

"Yes ma'am, you take care Rachel," she said as Rachel headed out the door and into the hallway.

"That child is going to be something one of these days. I can feel it."

††††††††††††††††††††††

HAVING ARRIVED at the local grocery store, Mrs. Randolph found herself near the produce section turning over tomatoes.

After some thorough searching, she found a few that suited her. As she reached for a bag to put them in, she noticed a familiar gentleman rubbing his chin and peering into the beer fridge.

He was an older man who had seen his fair share of a hard day's work. He wore a ragged pair of overalls that looked to have accompanied him during most of those days. His worn straw brimmed hat gave it away.

Mr. Mooreland?

As Mrs. Randolph questioned her sight, the man reached in the fridge and pulled out a twelve-pack of beer. She couldn't help but feel sorry for the old man. She couldn't imagine what he must be going through.

"Rebecca?" A whiny voice blurted from behind.

It startled her so bad, she dropped the ripened tomatoes to the floor. One of them splattered, as it couldn't withstand the impact.

Dang it. All that searching for nothing.

"Rebecca Randolph, that is you," the woman said with a big grin.

Rebecca rose from picking the dropped tomatoes off the floor and turned to give one last look toward the fridge, but he was gone.

"Hey Misty, how have you been? It's been a while hasn't it?" she said as they gave each other a quick hug.

"I know...it has. So how are you and James?" Misty asked pulling back.

"We're good. James is still at the paper mill and I'm still teaching at the high school. How about you? How are things with you and Jack?"

"Things are good. We just bought a new house on Holden Beach. It's so beautiful up there. I love the small-town feel. We should be moved in, in just a few weeks."

"Well that's good, I'm happy for you two. I will have to talk James in to visiting once you guys are settled. Hey...not to change the subject, but...did you happen to see the old man over there with the beer?"

"I saw him, but I didn't think nothing of it. Why? Was he bothering you or something?"

Misty was a stout girl and would have no problem giving the man something more to handle.

"Oh no-no. But...I...I think it was Old Man Mooreland," Rebecca leaned close, careful with the volume of her words.

"What? That was Mr. Mooreland?"

"I believe so. It looked like him, he had a pair of worn out overalls and the same straw hat that he likes to wear."

"Oh my gosh, you're right, that was him. Why is he buying a pack of beer though? He never drank."

"Well, I guess he does now. And after what happened, I mean you can't blame him."

"Wow, that's terrible. I wonder if he's still a deacon at church?"

"I don't know, he didn't seem to try and hide it, so he might not even go to church anymore," said Rebecca with wrinkled brows and a finger to her bottom lip.

"That's so sad. I just can't fathom how someone could do what that man did to that poor family. Mr. Mooreland is lucky to be alive."

"I know. I believe if it hadn't of been for him playing dead, his grandson would have killed him too."

"Yeah, you're probably right Rebecca. That man is lucky. I hope he's all right though and not drinking himself to death."

A moment passed.

Rebecca clicked her tongue against the back of her teeth and wagged her head.

"Yeah, I hope so too, but he didn't look so good. I know James was good friends with his nephew when he was younger. I might see if he could reach out to him and ask about his uncle."

"That would be good. Well, it was nice talking to you Rebecca. Come visit sometime. Here is our new number, it should be working in a few weeks once we're moved in."

"Okay will do. Take care Misty, nice seeing you," she said as they hugged once more before parting. Rebecca stole one last glance toward the beer fridge, then scanned each aisle she passed in route to the register. But Mr. Mooreland must've been in a hurry, because he'd vanished like a vapor.

††††††††††††††††††††††

IT WAS JUST after four o'clock that evening and the Georgetown Paper Mill looked a lot like Georgetown High School with all its busyness.

Inside, the men moved like disrupted ants as they each grasped for their jackets and lunch boxes before scurrying out the doors. The parking lot was no less busy. Engines cranked and revved as mufflers puffed out smoky pollution while the mill workers drove over gravel in route for US-17.

Second shift was beginning as big rigs loaded to their limits with supplies or shipments passed each other like stock traders on the streets of Manhattan.

"Man, J.R. really put it to Gary last night, didn't he?" said Jerry.

"Yeah, them Ewing brothers are always going at it on there," James replied.

Following behind the two men was the newbie, Ethan Thompson.

"Say kid, you ever watch Dallas?" Jerry asked turning to Ethan.

He wagged his head and continued to follow the men across the parking lot.

"Man, you don't know what you're missing. It's a good show. I never thought I'd like it much, but my wife's done got me hooked now."

"Yeah, I know. Rebecca got me watching it a few years ago. It ain't half bad to be honest."

"Well...take care James, appreciate you showing me that breakfast joint this morning. I'll see you tomorrow. See ya kid," Jerry wiggled the keys from his jeans and headed for a black Camaro.

"No problem man, see you tomorrow."

Assuming the reason Ethan had followed the men out to the parking was to bum a ride, James asked, "Needing a ride?" as he unlocked his truck.

"Yeah, if it's okay with you. I live about twenty minutes down the road. I'm working on my truck now, hoping to have it done in a few days."

"Yeah, it's no problem, I'll give ya a lift. Hop on in."

"Thank you."

James unlocks the driver door, gets in and leans over to unlock the passenger. Moments later they were cruising down the road in an awkward silence. In effort to change the mood, James clears his throat and asks, "So...you from the area? Or?"

Ethan nodded, "Uh huh, born and raised."

"I see. You have any siblings?"

"No, never had any brothers or sisters. Just me and my dad after mama died."

"Oh, I'm sorry to hear that. Were you close?"

Ethan took a breath.

"Oh yeah. It was tough."

"How about your dad? Are you close with him?"

"No, I haven't seen him in about three years, he moved off after mama died. I lived with my Aunt and Uncle until last year. I stay at the house my dad left behind now. Since I'm working though, I'll be able to get the power and water turned on."

"Wait, you mean you been living there with no power and water?"

Ethan bobbed his head.

"There's a creek in the back I make do with and I just bundle up in my sleeping bag at night. It's quite comfortable actually. It took me a bit to get used to the dark, but it grows on you after a while."

"Man…I hate you're having to live like that. If you ever need somewhere to stay for the night, you're welcome at my place."

"Nah, it's all right. I appreciate it though. I reckon I done got accustomed to being by myself. Although the coyotes and crows offer company with all their yapping and cawing. Especially at night."

A moment passed.

"Like I said, now that I'm working, I will get everything turned back on."

"All right, well the offer stands, so just remember that."

"I will, thank you," Ethan points ahead, "You're going to want to take a right at the next stop sign up there."

After following a few directions, James found himself in a quiet neighborhood of old and mostly vacant homes. In the front yards of those that weren't, were small signs staked in the ground that read "Bush & Quayle 88," with others reading, "Dukakis & Bentsen 88."

"You can take a left here."

Making the left, he later pulls onto a slab of aged pavement where numerous weeds poked through with at least a dozen cracks snaking this way and that. The pavement led downward to a small two-story home which sat on the corner of Morris and Becker. The house wore rugged cedar shakes and flaky shingles that could use some repairing. Not to mention the grass a good mow.

Three crows that seemed blacker than usual stood atop the ridge, their heads tilted to James with twitchy eyes. They cawed their displeasure of his presence. One spread its wings to cool itself with the gentle breeze.

Ethan opened the door of the truck and stepped onto the driveway.

"Thanks for the ride James. Like I say, I'm working on that truck over there, so as soon as I get it running, I'll be good," he said pointing towards a baby blue Chevy Suburban with a hard-shell camper attached to the back.

"That's nice. Is that a k20?"

"Yeah my mom left it to me. It was hers when she was around. Hoping I can get it running, just have to change out the fuel pump and a few other small things."

"What year is it?"

"1980."

"The box truck yours, too?"

James noticed it tucked behind the Chevy. It may have been a 1960's model. Its ragged and rusted exterior reminded him of the truck from the movie Duel with Dennis Weaver, only half the size.

"Yeah, my uncle gave it to me. Thought I could live in it if I had to. Maybe one day I'll convert it into a RV or something."

"I hear ya. Well, I guess I better get going, my wife's probably got supper waiting for me. You done good today at the mill, keep up the hard work and remember what Jerry told you. If you need help with your Chevy, let me know."

"Thank you, I will."

"Do you have a ride for the morning?"

"Yeah, Walter said he could take me. He has to pick his kids up from school after work, so he can't bring me home, but he can give me a ride in the mornings."

"Well, I can take you home, it's no big deal."

"Okay, thank you. I'll see you tomorrow."

"You got it big guy, take care."

James rolled the window up, shifted the gear stick and watched Ethan as he backed up to the street's edge. The kid scrolled with an odd gait, his head dipped below unnaturally wide shoulders, his feet skimming the pavement.

James stopped at the top of the driveway, the hitch poking into the road. Ethan's demeanor reminded him of someone, but he just couldn't put his finger on it. He watched as Ethan reached the door, took a glance to his right and left, breathed deep, inserted the key and pushed it open. He entered, and the enveloping darkness swallowed him whole. The door eased shut behind.

The cawing of the crows gave James' heart a start. He blinked, swallowed hard, then checked for traffic. As he worked his way out of Ethan's neighborhood, trying to get back to US-17, his gut began to call for feeding. If he tried hard enough, he could smell Rebecca's cooking.

4

The sizzle and crackle of hot oil could be heard

throughout the home. Trailing the sound was an array of spicy aromas. A hint of paprika, a pinch of cayenne pepper, a teaspoon of cumin, a few flakes of parsley and some taps on the ole bay container could make for a fine meal if left in the right hands. Cajun boudin, pronounced boo-dah, is a delicacy in the southern parts of Louisiana and to most would look like an ordinary piece of sausage, but when left to a Cajun, was anything but. Most were made with pork, but Rebecca made hers with crawfish. A recipe she learned from her Mother. When she wasn't filling casings full of crawfish boudin, she was stirring a pot of gumbo with a free hand.

After she achieved a break, she went on to slice a nicely picked tomato she had bought from the store. And no, it wasn't the one she'd dropped, this was a good one, firm with a little squish and full of juice.

With the tomato in her left hand and a knife in her right, the front door creaked opened. Peanut, the couples young Yorkshire Terrier, bolted towards the door, barking and growling, before stopping on the other side of the couch for cover.

Stepping in was James Randolph.

"Hey boy, you were going to eat me up, weren't you?" he says shutting the door and bending to the pup. "See, I'm not so bad."

Peanut relaxed and unleashed a fury of licks upon James' hands and ankles.

"Hey honey," a voice calls from the kitchen.

"Hey babe. What you cooking in there? That smells a little Cajun, am I right?" James said with a playful southern twang at the end.

"Yep, cutting some of deem fresh maters now," came her reply.

James chuckled, stepped into the kitchen, wrapped his arms around his wife and gave her a kiss.

"Missed you babe. How was your day?"

"It was good. Classes went well. Introduced inertia a little bit."

James smiled, leaned against the counter and crossed his arms,

"Oh gosh, all that energy in motion and Newton's law kind of stuff?"

"Yeah, that kind of stuff. Remember Rachel Fuller, the smart blonde girl I was telling you about?"

"Yeah, I think so."

"Well, she already knew the subject. She actually reads ahead like I ask them to, so when she comes to class, she can better understand what I'm teaching."

"Really? Dang, that's some determination there."

"That's what I said. I told her she keeps putting in all that hard work, its going pay off one of these days. I can tell, she's cut from a different cloth than the rest. Oh, and guess who I saw at the supermarket today?"

"Uh, let me guess...your brother?"

"No, he's still in Washington state with that girl, last I checked," Rebecca scoffed. "Guess again."

"Uh...Misty and Jack?"

"Dang, that's pretty good. I did see Misty, right after I was trying to spy on *old man Mooreland*," she said with a tilt of her head.

"Hmm?"

"Yeah and guess what he was buying?"

She waited a moment as James gave it some thought the said, "A twelve pack of beer."

"What?" James chuckled.

"Yeah, he didn't look so good. I was picking through the tomatoes when I saw him over in the beer fridge grabbing a twelve pack. Then Misty scared the bejesus out of me when she almost screamed with that little whiny voice of hers, 'Rebecca? That is you.' I jumped and dropped my tomatoes to the floor, the dang things splattered right there at my feet."

James couldn't help but get tickled at his wife's expressions as she told her story. That was one thing he always marveled about her, her sense of humor. Along with her beauty and slender frame of course.

"It was good seeing her though. Said her and Jack just got a place on Holden Beach."

"Really? Good for them. They deserve it. I hate that about Mr. Mooreland though. That's sad. He's probably drinking himself away."

"I know, that's what I'm afraid of. Do you still have Everett's number?"

"I might...I don't know, I will check though. If I can find it, I'll give him a call."

"Yeah, I would just be curious how they're holding up. So how did your day go?"

"It went good. We had a few new guys we had to show the ropes. Me and Jerry took a guy, while Hank and Billy took another."

"Really? You think they can help get the new order out in time?"

"No...I don't know what Dale and Kurt are thinking. They should've got help weeks ago, instead of waiting until two days before it supposed to be done. They're crazy if they think we can do all of that."

"Yeah, well just keep being the good worker that you are, somebody will see it. How was the new guy?" she asked as she turned her attention to the fridge in search of some onions.

James sat down at the kitchen table as he began.

"He was good. He's a little different, but he done good. I had to give him a ride home. He's working on getting his truck up and running. He's staying in a house over near the uh...umm...Crow Creek neighborhood. You know...off Morris and Becker. The place doesn't have any power or water, the poor kid has to use a sleeping bag at night to stay warm."

"Yeah-yeah. Oh, my goodness, that's horrible. Did you offer him our spare room?" she asked with a muffled voice as she combed through the fridge.

"Yeah, I told him he was welcome to stay with us until he got the power and everything on, but he said he was good. He's been like that for a few years now, the way I understood him. His mom died, and his dad left him to live with his Aunt and Uncle for a little bit. Then I guess they must've made him move on. It's sad. But like I said, he done good today, he's just a little strange, but I mean I guess you can kind of understand why."

"Yeah, that's horrible. How old is he?"

"He said he was nineteen. Old enough to take care of himself I guess."

"But if he's a little slow, he's probably got the mind of a child." She found the onions, straightened, and shut the door.

"Nah...he's not that slow...he's just...weird...you know?"

"Yeah. Well, just keep a watch on him and make sure he knows he's welcome here if he needs a place to stay."

"Yeah, I'll keep an eye on him. How about we get ready to dig into some boudin and gumbo? Sitting here smelling all that is about to drive me crazy."

"I thought I was the only one that drove you crazy?"

"Yeah, you're the only woman that drives me crazy, but your gumbo and boudin..." he whistled and craned his neck. "...now that's a different story."

"Oh, hush it. You know you love me," Rebecca said with a playful backhand across his chest as she crossed to the sink.

James caught her before she got there.

"You got that right. You're my girl, Becky," James said giving her a good squeeze around the waist. How much could a man love a woman? James still hadn't found the answer. Just when he thought he couldn't love her anymore, he found himself falling deeper and deeper into her warm embrace. He could stay here forever.

5

It's dark now. The Sun has tucked itself away. The creatures of the night are fully alive. Cicadas screech, treefrogs scream, and coyotes yap in the woods. The stark silhouette of an old rugged home stands out like a hooded mugger in an alley way. Behind the home, a jagged grove of pines stretches towards the moonless night. Beyond them, an open field and the remnants of an old barn taken by a flame long ago. The home has a wide porch just like so many here in Georgetown. The wooden banisters are ragged and home to an array of splinters just waiting to prick another victim. The decking boards are soft with rot and creak each time they're used. Crows caw somewhere from the yard as they hide beneath the cover of darkness.

A shadow passes by the window missing a pane. Inside a small candle flame dances with the breeze.

Beyond the door comes moaning and chanting. With all the creatures chatter and the sounds coming from within, it wouldn't take much for one to believe they'd entered the halls of a mental institute. Not to mention the sound of finger nails scraping along the wall and the tolling of a small bell.

Inside, the home reeks of bleach. Strong enough to burn one's nostrils, but not those of the man who lives here. A glance to the right would reveal the kitchen. In the center is the table, upon it, the dying candle flame and beside that there is a pack of raw hamburger meat which is stamped with a Piggly Wiggly logo. The burning candle serves as the only light in the house.

The chanting is growing now. The stairs creak and moan as the sound of footsteps can be heard going up and down them. The bell ringing, the man still chanting. There. His feet appear. Big boots. Likely a thirteen or larger. Thud...thud...thud. His knees now. Thud...thud. His waist. Thud...thud. His chest and look at how wide those shoulders are.

He reaches the bottom of the stairs, waving his hand up and down, he's tolling the bell. He's only a silhouette. Too dark to see his flesh. But there is no doubt who this is.

He snaps his head around so quick, most would wince in pain, but not Ethan Thompson.

The bell has stopped. He's looking straight ahead. Here he comes. The floor creaks under those big feet.

He's edging closer, his feet sliding across the floor to keep it from creaking. He knows he's not alone.

Now just inches away, his hot sulfurous breath rolls out. What's he doing? Sounds like a hiss. It's his tongue. He's trying to gather a scent. He's sniffing now, leaning closer. If someone's here, he will remember their scent forever. Tucking it away deep within his dark, cold abyss of a mind.

Ethan steps back, turns and marches down the hall. Lifting the bell, it begins to ring.

So, here's the man in all of his splendor. In his natural habitat. Ethan's den so to speak. But what would it be like to visit the deep, dark chambers of Ethan's mind? Only one way to find out. Come.

††††††††††††††††††††††
PACING THE FLOORS and mumbling a chant, Ethan has been tormented since sundown. It's just after two in the morning. Prone to such episodes since his youth, for the past few weeks, this has become a nightly routine. He could only hope it'd soon end, but he honestly couldn't see an end in sight. The voice he'd become accustomed to since that day at the Mooreland's was relentless.

Marching to and fro among the home, walking up and down in it, the stairs creak and groan each time he uses them.

A raspy voice whispers in his ear. He can't allow himself to hear it. He'd promised he wouldn't listen to it. He knows how it can connive him into doing anything *it* wants. *Its* tone echoes off every wall at once. *It* can speak forward and backwards with a flowing cadence and *it* knows every secret sin with perfect recollection.

Using his bell to block out the voice crawling about his skull, he just can't seem to wave it fast enough. With the other hand, he picks at hot warts along the side of his nose. There so irritating. Oh, how he wished they'd just go away. The voices too. If he wasn't picking at the warts or scratching on the wall, then he was chewing a thumb nail, which had seen enough damage to draw blood. He could feel his heart beat where the nail should've been.

The voice means well. He's just at times too stubborn to listen. But there are other times such as this, when he feels the need to stand up for himself. He's done a lot for the voice over the years and it should respect his labor for the greater good. If he needs a break...well...by devil's hell, he's going to take one. He deserves it. And if he wants an early retirement...what's the worst that can happen? Right?

Ethan darts his eyes about the darkened home as if searching for a pesky fly, "Leave me alone Kirkland! I don't want to do this anymore! You're not real! You're not real!" his words taper off, his mouth fills with an unnatural amount of saliva. He snorts through clogged nostrils and wipes a cheek with the crevice of an arm.

"OH, BUT I AM. I'M VERY REAL INDEED. TO YOU FOOLISH HUMANS' DEMISE, YOU CLAIM WE DON'T EXIST, BUT OH...HOW WE DO. WE ARE MORE REAL THAN YOU COULD EVER IMAGINE AND WE ARE MANY. YOU OF ALL PEOPLE SHOULD KNOW."

Ethan slams his eyes and wrinkles his face, swallowing hard and breathing quick through his nose.

An eerie hush follows.

The home moans as a howling wind thrust itself against the cedar shakes, shifting it among the foundation.

"WHY FIGHT, WHEN YOU KNOW DEEP DOWN, YOU'LL NEVER WIN?" the voice ends each syllable with a sharp hiss as it pokes at Ethan's emotions like a cat with a wounded rat.

"No-no-no! I'm not falling for it again. You're lying. Shut up! You're not real...you're not real!" he spits and spatters. His eyes are beady with an inky blackness and glazed film. He tries to control his tongue, but he loses the grip, allowing it to slither out between his lips.

What is that? A new scent. Ethan's senses are always on high alert when dealing with Kirkland. Nothing new there. Maybe the neighbor switched to a new shampoo or something.

If he stayed strong, the voice would pass and maybe he could have his break.

More voices, more chatter. Like being tossed into the middle of a large crowd. So loud. So many.

Inside, a fire rages on, causing him to tear his shirt in two, screaming incoherently at the ceiling. The bell has to ring louder. It has to work, it always has. Mother's pain will only grow worse, she'd soon need feeding. She will soon be calling.

The bell rings with break neck speed in his right as he claws on the wall with his left. Old wall paper falls to the floor like snow.

"FINE. HAVE IT YOUR WAY, BUT DON'T EXPECT THIS TO GET EASIER. IF YOU TURN DOWN MY NEXT ASSIGNMENT, THINGS WILL ONLY GET WORSE. IF YOU THINK THIS IS BAD, JUST WAIT FOR WHAT'S TO COME," Kirkland says through what sounds like clinched teeth.

"Wait...wait. What assignment are you talking about?"

"OH...YOU'RE WISER THAN I THOUGHT. WELL...LET'S JUST SAY IT INVOLVES A LITTLE CREATIVITY FOLLOWED BY A...LACK OF SYMPATHY. HMM?" Kirkland muses at the thought.

Maybe it won't be so bad this time, besides Mother needs feeding and she'll soon be calling. If he were to carry out the assignment, he would need his strength. He'd need protein. Just the way he likes it, raw and juicy. If he'd quit spending all his money at the Piggly Wiggly he might could afford to have his power turned on. Oh, stop it, Ethan Thompson doesn't need no light. He likes it in the dark.

Off to the kitchen. He can already taste the meat. So fresh. He touches his bicep, checking its size. He would check again after he was finished. Raw meat builds muscle. Raw meat gives him strength and he would surely need it to carry out Kirkland's plan. Mother needs him. he can't let her down. He devours the pack of hamburger meat and converses with the voice for another half hour, before collapsing to the floor in exhaustion, just as he has done numerous nights in the past.

Weds
4/25/81
After school today, me, Frankie, and Will
went over to the old Moorelands home.
Something weird happened while we were
there.

We broke in through the back window after
Will busted it out with a big rock. We brought
along a new board game that Will had
stolen from his brother. I think its called
a Wiji board or something like that. It
might be spelled with an O, but you say
it like its a W.

Anyway, they claim you can talk to the
spirits with it, so we thought we'd test
it out at the Moorkland's place, since
what happened there a few years ago.

So, we sat down in one of the back bedroom's
and started playing the game. We each had
to help hold a glass circle thing over a
bunch of letters and numbers. Nothing
happened at first, but then Frankie started
saying he heard whispers. Me and Will thought
he was messing with us, but he kept saying
he heard someone whisper. It kind of started
creeping us out a little bit... →

Then all of a sudden, Frankie screamed and grabbed his arm. We looked and could see the indention of a hand squeezing his arm. He then started shaking as he went into like a trance or something. His eyes rolled back as he jerked his face toward the ceiling and started growling. Kind of like a cat when its about to fight. It scared me and Will to death.

Frankie started gagging and choking on something. He finally hacked up this black ball looking thing that was wrapped in black cobweb looking stuff. Some of it hung out of his mouth like cheese from a pizza slice.

He started coughing as he tried to catch his breath. So me and Will got closer to see what this stuff was. It looked like some kind of eggs, but they were already hatched open.

Frankie eventually settled down a little and just stared at the floor. When we did finally raise his head to look at us, his eyes were solid black. They just weren't right. →

His eyes were so creepy and just the
way he looked at us. It gives me the
willies thinking about it.

He then asked us what was wrong
and why we were staring at him. He acted
like nothing ever happened.

Then all of a sudden, a door slams shut.
It scared the crap out of us. We all
jumped up and ran out of there as fast
as we could. Will even left the game
lying there in the floor. I sure hope his
brother never finds out.

Frankie was quiet the rest of the
day and just didn't act right. We all
promised with an oath to never go back
in there or play an Wiji board ever again.

I wonder how Frankie will be tomorrow?

Daniel Hoffman

From the journal of David Hoffman

Wednesday

April 25th, 1981

Age 11

6

It was a quarter to seven and outside a car horn blasted

like an alarm clock. Ethan awoke with a start, kicking and squirming, he busted out of his sleeping bag. His breath in short gasps.

"Oh crap! Dang it! Dang it! Dang it!"

He hurried to unzip and jolted to his feet, the horn still honked in the driveway.

"He's going to wake the whole dang neighborhood."

Digging through a bag of clothes lying in the floor, within seconds he had most of the bag scattered about the tiny room. He managed to find his work uniform they'd given him the day before and quickly threw it on before bolting out the door, while still slipping an arm through a sleeve. Waiting in the driveway was Walter Avery.

"I told you to be ready by six-thirty. It's almost seven now!" Walter bit off as he dipped his head to glare out the passenger window.

"I know. I'm sorry, it won't happen again," Ethan reached for the door handle.

"You dang right it won't happen again. If it does it'll be the last time you get a ride from me."

The Dodge pickup roared backwards up the driveway, it stopped with a sudden jerk, Walter checked for traffic, once clear, he backed into the road, slung the gear shift to drive and sped away through the neighborhood, not letting go of Ethan's tardiness.

"What did you stay up all night or something? Cause let me tell you if I catch anything from Dale or Kurt about me being late, you're going to get it."

Ethan wagged his head and stared at the floor board, occasionally stealing glances out the window at the speeding houses, mailboxes and trees.

"You know I just don't get kids like you nowadays."

Ethan turned to see where this was going.

"I mean you search for a job, finally get one, then you end up screwing it up with crap like this. You know it takes half an hour to get to work from our town, not counting traffic and yet you don't come out until five to seven?"

Ethan returned his attention to the window as he did his best to take the scolding.

"I mean this is our second day on the job and this isn't exactly starting out on the right foot," Walter glared at the side of Ethan's head.

Ethan had no need to turn and face him, he could feel Walter's icy eyes stabbing his spirit. Walter continued the rant as his voice now became a faint whisper compared to the voice inside Ethan's head.

"WHO IS HE TO THINK HE CAN TALK TO YOU THIS WAY? NOBODY TALKS TO YOU LIKE THAT, HE'S NOT YOUR PARENT. KILL HIM! KILL HIM! KILL HIM!"

Yeah...who does he think he is? Does he even know who is talking to?

His gut burned so hot, he thought he may have caught the faint sound of a crackling flame. Then again maybe he was imaging it. That was one thing Ethan had, a wild imagination, which led to an exciting reality.

Ethan jerked around causing his neck to make a loud pop, "Shut up! All right, I get it! Just shut up already!"

"Hey! Chill it kid, you deserve this. This is the real world, this ain't school. You might could get by with being late or skipping a day with them, but not here. Not in the real world."

"Just drop it all right? I've done told you it won't happen again."

"It better not or else."

"Or else what!" Ethan snapped. His jaw set, eyes black and bulged, nostrils flaring with huffed breaths.

Walter seared him with his icy eyes once more, sighed through his nose and wagged his head. The two hardly spoke the rest of the way to the paper mill. Though Ethan caught him cutting his eyes to him more than once.

††††††††††††††††††††††

LEAVING THE break room while taking the last few sips of his coffee was James Randolph.

"Aww man...another day in paradise...right Jerry?" James said as he tossed his empty cup in the trash.

"Yeah, but where's the yacht and palm trees?"

The men chuckled at the thought and made their way to the cutting press.

"Oh, look...they showed up," said James as he pointed a thumb to Walter and Ethan who were in a rush to drop their lunches off by the break room.

Two machines on the assembly line fired up with long, rising howls before settling into constant roars.

"I thought they may have gotten enough yesterday," said Jerry, having to speak over the roars.

"Huh?" James asked leaning in and squinting his eyes.

Jerry repeated himself.

"Yeah...well they better not make a habit of showing up just in time to get started. That won't last long."

"Huh?" Jerry asked holding a plug next to his ear.

"I said, that won't last long."

Jerry raised his brows and nodded, returned the plug and slipped on some glasses. James did the same as he manned the press. It howled and roared like the others, before the slow-moving conveyor belt full of oversized paper rolled toward Jerry with the guillotine like cutter.

A few minutes passed, and Ethan was making his way over to the men. James stopped the machine for a moment and waved to Jerry. It whined down, then huffed what sounded like a backfire.

"Sorry, I'm a little late. It won't happen again."

"It's all right, just don't make it a habit. You want to take this over and we'll do like we did yesterday?" said James.

Ethan nodded, lowered some protective glasses and pushed in his ear buds. The press howled and roared once more, the conveyor belt glided to Jerry and James. Jerry handled the cuts as James separated them into different stacks.

One stack for the good and another for the bad.

As Ethan busied himself with pressing the button to send the blade down, he replayed his morning ride with Walter. Over and over and over again.

††††††††††††††††††††††

LESS THAN A hundred feet away, Walter Avery, Billy Ross and Hank Norton ran a similar press. Only this one made larger cuts that were passed down to James and his crew to trim down to normal 8.5 by 11's.

Billy had controls of the blade, just like Ethan did at the other machine down the line. Walter placed the paper under the cutter before passing the cuts off to Hank, who

46

then separated them into two stacks. One for the good and one for the bad.

"If I'm not careful, that kid might end up costing me my job," Walter thought, "I probably shouldn't say anything to Kurt just yet, you don't want to come across as a whiner or something.

"What if I just made it hard on him? Maybe he'd quit, and I wouldn't have to worry about him," Walter mumbled as he continued pushing cut pieces of paper on down the line to Hank.

†††††††††††††††††††††††

NOON HAD MADE its appearance for the day and the men gladly welcomed it. They headed to the break room to find their lunch boxes or grab their keys to search for lunch elsewhere. Either way, they had an hour before they were expected to be back on the job.

Inside the break room was Ethan, Walter and Hank.

"So, what's with your house man? It get handed down from your great granny or something? Cause god knows it sure looks like a granny," Walter said with a cheek full of sandwich and scoff.

"Huh?" Hank asked with crooked brows.

"Yeah man, you should've seen this dude's house this morning. Looked like an old shack."

"It was left to me after my mama died," Ethan mumbled before taking a bite of his turkey and cheese.

"See man, that's why you don't pick at stuff unless you know the full story," Hank wagged his head.

"Well...at least she left you something I guess...just looks like you would take a better care of it."

Ethan sat there not saying a word. All the while the flame grew within. He chewed the bread and turkey with a grind, his muscles quivered, the room felt hot and void of oxygen. He leaned back in the chair, crossed his arms and ate the sandwich out of a firm right hand. Mayonnaise oozed onto the back of his hand as he'd squeezed too hard. Too bad it wasn't Walter's neck he was squeezing, and instead of mayo, the jelly substance from an eye. That'd sure cool him off.

James and Jerry had just walked in the room and caught the tail end of what Walter said.

"Take better care of what?" asked James

"That shack of a house he lives in. You've seen it haven't you?"

"Yeah, but it's not that bad. I mean at least he has somewhere."

"I reckon. I guess if he had anything more comfortable, he wouldn't wake till noon," Walter cut his eyes to Ethan.

Ethan ignored him and continued chewing as the voice whispered, "IN TIME, IN TIME, BE PATIENT. YOU'LL GET YOUR REVENGE. PERHAPS TONIGHT?"

"Oh...so that's why you both were late this morning, huh?" James asked with a smile, "you stay up late last night?"

Ethan in a daze. Walter leaned over and snapped his fingers just in front of his nose. Ethan shook away the voice, his eyes darting about the room. He swallowed and said, "Yeah...I was thinking about my truck and how to fix it. Couldn't get it off my mind."

"Well...you said it's just a fuel pump, right?"

"Yeah, but I think there's something wrong with the starter now, just isn't acting right."

"Really? Well, if you want, I can talk to my wife and make sure we don't have plans, and maybe stay for a bit when I drop you off, to see if we can figure something out.

"Jerry here knows a thing or two about cars, maybe we can talk him in to joining us," James said with a grin and wink as he pointed a thumb to his friend.

"Yeah, I've got a boring evening planned. I could swing by and take a look at it."

Ethan nodded, "I'd appreciate it fellas."

"Well good, maybe you'll get it running, so I don't have to worry about running late for work," said Walter in mid chew.

††††††††††††††††††††††

HOURS HAD PASSED, and James found himself in Ethan's driveway. Jerry wasn't far behind.

The men plant their feet to the cracked pavement and head for the Chevy.

"So that's the ole rascal that's giving ya trouble, huh?" Asked Jerry as he cupped his mouth and lit a cigarette.

"Mm hmm."

"Dag gummit Jerry, don't you know them things are going to kill you?" James said as he snatched it from his fingers and grinded it into the dirt.

"Hey! Man...let me be. Whatever's done, done. It ain't gonna make no difference now anyhow."

"C'mon man. Don't talk like that."

Jerry wagged his head, "Shoot. I'd be worse off without the darn things," as he slid another cigarette from the pack, lit it up and coughed out the smoke.

"Seriously though, you need to can it."

Jerry rolled his eyes and ruffled his brows, wearing a smirk as the smoldering killer draped from his lips.

As the men walked towards the baby blue Chevy, James carried a bag of tools that must've weighed thirty pounds with all the wrenches and sockets. He sat the bag down beside the truck, causing the metal to clank and rattle.

"Why don't you try turning it over and let us hear it?" asked James.

Ethan retrieved the keys from his pocket, found the right one and stuck it in the ignition.

Clank-Clank-Clank-Clank.

Jerry wrinkled his face and waved him to stop, the noise dug at him like nails to a chalk board.

"Sounds like the flywheel to me. You sure it's the fuel pump?" asked James

"Well...I just replaced that yesterday evening, but I'm trying to figure out what this noise is."

"Right-right. Well...it sure sounds like a flywheel to me. What do you think?"

"Yeah, that's definitely the flywheel. Let me crawl under here and see if we can pull it out," Jerry took a drag on the cigarette, sat it on a stump next to him, squatted and made his way under the truck. Blowing out the smoke along the way.

A moment passed.

"Can you get me a 5/8's socket? That's what it looks like."

James fumbles through his bag, clanking metal here and there.

"Here ya go."

Within ten minutes the flywheel was off, and Jerry was back on his feet.

"Look at that. No wonder it was making all that racket. You've got cracked flywheel my friend." Jerry held it up to show Ethan and James.

"If you want, we can ride up to Carl's, I'm sure he would have it in stock. This is what an 80 Suburban?"

Ethan nodded and said, "Yeah. That'd be great, I'd appreciate it."

"Oh, you got it brotha. Well, let's ride up here and see if Carl has it. Won't take long to put it in, if he does."

†††††††††††††††††††††††

WITHIN TWO HOURS, the men were back at Ethan's and finishing up the flywheel. Jerry and James tighten the last few bolts before crawling out from under the truck to dust off.

"Well…give it a go boy. See what she's got," said James.

Ethan climbs in the driver's seat and turns the ignition. The engine fired up and grumbled as the muffler puffed out a gray cloud. A half grin slid across his face, his eyes followed the slow movement, looking to James and Jerry. His head was the last to slide. It turned to the men like an owl. He nodded.

"Hey now, say that sounds a lot better, huh?" Jerry asked him with a smile. Ethan bobbed at a steady pace, killed the engine and climbed out of the cab.

"I appreciate you guy's helping. How much I owe you?"

"Man don't worry about that. We're just glad we could help you out," said James.

Jerry agreed while wiping his hands clean of grease.

"Well thank you, I sure appreciate it. I guess you don't have to worry about giving me a ride now."

"Yeah and neither does that ole fart, Walter. I'm sure he'll be happy."

Yeah…Walter.

7

The Sun had settled in for the night, a cool breeze filled the air, as did the blackness that accompanied it. Cruising through a darkened neighborhood in his baby blue Chevy Suburban, Ethan went to his ever-preserved and well-watered memory to visit with a conversation he'd had with Walter yesterday when they met.

"He said 'Amity Drive' I know that's what he said." Ethan leaned over the steering wheel searching for Walter's Dodge pickup. His skin tingled at the thought of finding it.

"YOU HAVE TO DO IT TONIGHT. HE DOESN'T DESERVE TO SEE ANOTHER DAY, NOT AFTER THE WAY HE TREATED YOU. HE DESERVES TO DIE." Kirkland in his ear.

Like a million maggots crawling beneath the flesh, his muscles contracted as he gripped the steering wheel with grinding teeth. A thought caused his gut to tighten, which was a rare occurrence.

"But what if I get caught Kirkland, then what?" Ethan glanced to the passenger seat where a small boy sat with ashy skin.

"SO, WHAT IF YOU DO, IT'LL BE WORTH IT. JUST LIKE IT WAS WORTH WHAT YOU DID TO WILL."

"Shut up! I told you not to talk about him."

"SORRY, FORGOT HOW SENSITIVE YOU WERE ABOUT IT. AFTER ALL, YOU HAD TO DO IT." Kirkland with a matter-of-factness about his tone.

"Just drop it all right? Help me find Walter's house."

"TAKE A RIGHT ON THE NEXT STREET. IT'S THE SECOND TO LAST HOUSE ON THE LEFT. THERE'S A PLACE YOU CAN PARK A FEW BLOCKS DOWN THE ROAD. NO ONE WILL EVER NOTICE IF YOU CUT THROUGH THE WOODS."

Ethan squinted his eyes and peered out the window. Scrolling through the neighborhood just a few ticks below the 25mph speed limit, the brakes squealed as he came to a rolling stop. He'd found it.

"That's his truck!" His eyes widened, his brows furrowed, the corners of his mouth rose as if hooked with a string.

"All right, so where do I park?"

"TAKE A LEFT AT THE STOP SIGN THEN TAKE THE THIRD ROAD ON THE RIGHT. THERE'S A DRIVEWAY TO AN ABANDONED HOUSE NOBODY LIVES IN OR AROUND. YOU CAN PARK BEHIND IT AND WALK THROUGH THE WOODS, RIGHT TO WALTER'S BACK YARD."

Ethan nodded with the same expression he wore when James and Jerry fixed the flywheel. He killed the lights and eased behind the old house. He put the truck in park and took a deep breath.

"You sure we should do this?" Ethan turned and asked the passenger seat, which was now empty.

"YOU HAVE TO. IF YOU WANT OUR BLESSING THAT IS?" Kirkland's voice, a deep raspy tone.

Ethan shut his eyes and nodded. A rush came over him as his whole body quivered with energy, he couldn't wait to release it. He leaned over and opened the glove compartment where he'd stashed a .44 revolver, packed with six rounds. He spun the silver cylinder to be sure. He leans up to conceal it in the back of his pants, steps out of the truck, grabs a large hunting knife he'd hidden under the seat, and places it next to the revolver.

"All right, let's do it."

"WITH PLEASURE. FOLLOW ME."

After trudging through the woods for five or ten minutes, Ethan could see the kitchen light hiding behind the limbs and branches.

"JUST A LITTLE FURTHER. LET'S WAIT BY THE WOOD LINE UNTIL THEY GO TO BED."

"Well how long will that be?"

"MAYBE AN HOUR OR SO. JUST BE PATIENT. TIMING MY FRIEND. TIMING."

They make it to the edge of the woods and peer through the branches, the kitchen and living room shown with clarity as the vast darkness without gave strength to the light within. The back of Walter and his wife's heads rested next to one another on the couch. The TV busy at running re-runs of Dallas.

He'd already seen this episode. Not at his house of course. He didn't have the luxury of a television. He'd watched it through the Montgomery's window a few months ago, just prior to the place being sealed off with yellow caution tape. Mr. Montgomery was a weak man. An easy taking. It was a joy to take him last, that way he'd be forced to watch as his wife took her last breath. That was Mother's last feeding, and she was growing weaker by the hour, she'd soon be calling. She needed feeding. It is here, Ethan would wait.

Kirkland continued for the next hour whispering in Ethan's ear. His voice began to mix with others, sounding like a horde of tree frogs chattering into the night.

Movement. Walter and his wife stood to their feet and turned off the lights.

"WE'RE GETTING CLOSE, NOT MUCH LONGER."

Another hour passed before the order to advance was given.

Ethan retrieved the revolver and pulled back the hammer, curved his spine and tiptoed through the brush. He emitted like a plane from a cloud, into the Avery's back yard. He crossed to the back door.

Living in a small neighborhood, it wasn't uncommon for people to leave the dead bolt unlocked. Hopefully the Avery's were the same.

Ethan stood at the door and rested his balmy hand upon the knob. It was locked, but if he was lucky, the deadbolt wouldn't be latched. Oh, how many would still be alive if only they'd slid the dead bolt home. An unlatched deadbolt was too inviting to ignore.

He grabbed the hunting knife wedged behind his back and wiggled it in the crease of the door. After a few tries, the door gave way with a soft pop. Ethan entered.

He eased through the home. a dark figure glided next to him. In the light, Kirkland often appeared as a small boy with a striking resemblance to Will Abercrombie, but in the darkness...he'd change. Black and deep-set eyes with a black mouth that draped open as if in the middle of a silent but anguished scream. Kirkland trudged alongside him, not saying a word.

With a cocked revolver in hand, Ethan slid his feet across the living room floor towards the bedroom. Less chance for creaks and pops this way. Though he almost tripped over a little pink dollhouse on the floor next to the coffee table. Probably a seven or eight-years-old by the looks of the toys. A Tonka truck rested in the hall. A boy and a girl. Just like Walter had said.

The bed room door open, Walter and his wife asleep. Ethan slides his feet into the doorway and stands there admiring the offering. Mother will be pleased. His head cranes side to side, his pupils growing without the rays of light. He narrowed his gaze, the corners of his mouth lifting to each ear, he raised the revolver.

A horde of blackness, so thick it affected Ethan's breath, hovered around him. Sweat trickled passed a bulging and pumping vein on his neck.

Wh-Wh-Whaaaa...whaaaa...whaaa.

Darting away from the doorframe, he hid in the hall with his back pressed firm against the wall. The shadows vanished like smoke.

"Dang it!" He mouthed with a firm jaw.

The cry of a baby stung Ethan's flesh.

He couldn't remember Walter mentioning having a newborn.

The Avery's moaned as the baby's cry forced them from their slumber. By the time Mrs. Avery had picked herself up from the cozy bed and attended her precious baby, Ethan was easing out the back door, leaving as he came. He heard her sooth the baby as the door latched. Its cries hid the sound.

Stuffing the revolver in the back of his pants, guilt and frustration washed over him as he trekked back into the dense patch of woods.

"Dang it, Kirkland! They almost caught me."

"SO? YOU SHOULD'VE DONE IT ANYWAY. JUST KILLED THEM ALL AND GOT IT OVER WITH. BUT...I GUESS YOUR WEAKER THAN I THOUGHT."

"Shut up!" His jaw tight, hands balled into fist, dangling at his sides. Ethan took a deep breath and allowed it to roll out of his nostrils.

Chatter broke from the sidewalk just on the other side of the woods. A grin stretched across Ethan's face.

"I'll show you."

He popped out of the wood line and onto the sidewalk about a hundred feet behind what sounded like a young guy and girl. Ethan pattered up behind them.

"Excuse me. Excuse me."

The two spun around, startled by Ethan's presence.

"Hey, I'm sorry, my car's needing a jump, the dang battery died on me. I was just about to start knocking on doors, but I kind of hate to at this time of night. Are you going to your car?"

"Yeah, we're parked just right up here. Where's your car at?" the guy asked.

"Aww, just a few streets over. You wouldn't mind giving me a lift over there would you? Wouldn't take a second to jump it off, I have a pair of jumper cables in my truck."

"Yeah sure, it won't be a problem."

"Great! Thanks man. I'm Kirkland by the way, but you can call me Kirk."

††††††††††††††††††††††

HOURS HAD PASSED as the night crawled toward the morning. Almost finished with his shift under the moonless night, Ethan chugged along a wooded trail in his old box truck, singing along to the stereo as The Police were in mid chorus for *Every Breath You Take*. Beyond the rough rumble of the engine and crackling music, whimpers and moans emitted from the back.

The spike of a euphoric rush had declined, but was about to spike once more, which reminded him of a pleasure he'd forgotten about. Like after enjoying such a fine meal, you forget the dessert. He still had one last pleasure to indulge. Mother needed her feeding and she was sure to enjoy this one.

Ethan retrieved a bloody box cutter from his pocket, stopped the truck in the middle of the path, extended the blade and gingerly wiped it with a rag from the glove compartment. A bloody blade always seemed to rust quicker than a clean one. And giving it a good wiping, also cleaned his conscious a little, must've been what Pilate felt like after he sentenced Christ for His crucifixion.

Like a gnat appearing from nothing at the scent of fruit, a dark shadow manifested next to him. A familiar voice breathed in his ear,

"ALL SIN BEGINS WITHIN AND THERE IS NO CURE WITHOUT ATONEMENT. A SACRIFICE MUST NOW BE MADE TO EVER EASE THE PAIN."

More muffled moans from the back. Banging against the metal cab. It was a fighter. Mother would like this one. Its sacrifice wouldn't be in vain. Mother needed her strength and this one was sure to offer it. Oh, how he was glad he'd accepted Kirkland's assignment. See, Kirkland knew what was best for him and for Mother. He'd almost forgotten how much he enjoyed working for him. He could hardly wait to hear of the next assignment. Though he knew in his gut what it should be, he just hoped Kirkland had the same thoughts.

He usually did.

Mon
5/21/81

I saw Frankie at school today for the first time in about a week. I was getting worried about him. Every time I went over to his house, his mom or sometimes his dad would come to the door and say he was sick and were afraid I'd catch it and then spread it around school.

I noticed he had a light bruise around his eye and when I asked him about it, he said, "I fell and hit a chair one night when I got up to use the bathroom."

Something just doesn't make sense. He told me before that he doesn't like it when his dad drinks, but never said why.

He just doesn't act right. Ever since that day at the Mooreland's, he hasn't been himself. He gets angry super easy and always seems to be mad or sad about something. He's just not the same Frankie anymore.

He even flipped out on Will today, just because he called him a "Wuss", for not talking to Samantha during recess. He got mad and started cussing Will and told him to not ever call him that again, "or else"

I was worried an adult would hear us and get us in trouble, but luckily it was just us kids out there. I'm worried about him. Just the look in his eyes... its not right.

I think maybe between what happened at the Mooreland's and what's probably going on at home with his dad, he's starting to break.

I'm going to talk to mom about him and see what she says. Maybe she can call his mom while his dad is at work and see if she will talk.

I'm just really worried about him. I miss the old Frankie.

David Hoffman

Journal Entry of David Hoffman

Monday

May 21st, 1981

AGE 11

8

The Sun had peaked over the trees and began to flood the streets with its radiant light. Birds chirped and sang to each other as another spring day in coastal South Carolina had begun.

"You know what happened to that folder I laid on the table last night?" asked Rebecca from the kitchen.

"You mean that big thick one you said had the tests in it?" James' voice coming from the hall.

"Yeah, that one."

"I thought you placed it in your bag. Remember we were busy taking about Misty and Jack's new place on Holden?"

"Oh yeah, you're right," Rebecca headed for the living room and fumbled through her bag.

James walked in, still working on a blue button up work shirt. He had his right arm through a sleeve and was about to stick his left through the other.

"Don't forget, we have left over gumbo and boudin you can take to work with you."

"Yeah, how can I forget that. It was amazing as always babe," he passed Rebecca on his way to the kitchen, but not without giving her a kiss.

"Aw ah! Got it. Whew, had me worried for a second."

"Yeah I remember seeing you put it in there. How did they do?"

James retrieved a coffee cup from the cabinet, it clanked against the others on the way out.

"Overall, they done pretty good. Rachel and a few others got their A's, while the rest got B's and C's. Only had two with D's."

"Oh, well that's not too bad."

"Yeah, I was happy with the grades. This test was a lot tougher than the last two."

Rebecca sat down at the kitchen table with about ten minutes before she'd be on her way to Georgetown High.

James had the fridge open as he stuffed his lunch box with his wife's Cajun cuisine.

"I'm glad your parents believed in the importance of preserving your roots and teaching you the family recipes, because I'm telling ya, your cooking deserves to be in five-star restaurant."

"Oh, thank you honey. I'm glad they did too, I don't know what I'd do without my Cajun roots. I can't wait to teach our kids the Cajun traditions," she said with a soft smile and dreamy gaze.

"I know honey. It will happen, we just have to be patient. One of these days, we're going to have a house full of youngins and all you're going to hear are those little feet pattering across the floors.

"Then one day, we're going to be out on our front porch swinging in our chair watching a yard full of little grand babies running around the yard, playing hide-n-go-seek and using us as base. You wait, it's going to happen. We just have to keep believing. But in the meantime, let's enjoy each other while it's just us," James said with a grin.

Rebecca smiled as her heart warmed at the thought of James' prophetic imagery. If she closed her eyes and allowed her mind to wander, she could hear their laughter. Her eyes became watery as her heart overflowed with a hope and desire for that house full of kids. Then a thought hit her.

"James...what if it takes too long? What if it doesn't happen within the next few years? I mean we are not getting any younger. I'm thirty, you're going to be thirty in just a few years. They say it's dangerous to have children after thirty-five."

"Well...if thirty-four rolls around and we still haven't had any kids of our own...then maybe we can adopt? I mean it's not the end of the world if that happens...right?

A moment passed.

"Think how we could help someone and give them a shot at becoming something in life. There's a lot of kids out there in those adoption agencies, that if the right couple doesn't come along, they won't stand a chance."

"I know James...but I want children of our own too. I mean I would love to adopt a child and give them a second chance at life...but I want to be able to feel our precious baby kick and squirm within me, and to be able to hold them tight as they open their eyes for the first time and see their mother and father staring back at them with unconditional love."

Now James' eyes were strained with streaks of red as he closed his lunch box and grabbed a day-old egg and cheese biscuit from the fridge. James continued as he poured him and Rebecca a cup of coffee. He sat down at the table and slid his chair next to Rebecca's. He reached out and took her hand in his with a gentle touch.

"Baby...with your heart and the kind of desire you have for a family and believe me I'm right there with you...I don't see how the universe could withhold giving you the greatest gift on earth. And if there is a God up there," James paused and turned his gaze to the ceiling.

"Then I don't see how or why he would either. Because I know with everything within me, you'd be the greatest and most loving mother this world has ever known."

They sniffled and held each other until it was time for them to head to work. Neither wanted to let go, but they knew they must. For they had a future to work for and their children depended on it.

†††††††††††††††††††††††

RIDING ALONG IN his Chevy Suburban, Ethan was only minutes from arriving at the paper mill. He fidgeted with the knob on the radio, checking each station.

His anxiety eased just a little when he had trouble finding anyone talking about two missing teenagers.

It should take a little bit for them to be found, which would give him enough time to think things through.

He stole glances toward his reflection in the rear-view mirror. Two warts. They'd moved in right beside the other ones he'd grown accustomed to since his youth.

They were painful and hot. At every red-light he'd peer into the mirror and pick at his new guest.

Not again. C'mon.

Ethan gripped the wheel with a greasy left and tuned to a rock station with his right. His heart palpitated at the end of each song, hoping his favorite would be next and play before he reached the mill. His hand had taken to the shakes again. All would be okay if he'd could just hear his song.

Kirkland smirked as he rode shotgun. Choosing to be silent and let Ethan's mind wander.

Yellow sulfurous breath rolled out of Kirkland's nostrils as he peered straight into Ethan's soul.

He belonged to him now. But he wasn't satisfied, he wanted more. More of his heart, mind and soul. He wanted everything Ethan had or could ever have. He wanted him, all of him.

"If I call for help and bring in the big boys, he could really be something. A prodigy perhaps?" Kirkland snickered at the thought.

"Although..." he thought for a moment and tapped a bony finger to his chin. "...that may not be wise. Maybe I shouldn't pressure him too much just yet. I may just have to speak with Lucifer himself about this one."

Kirkland sat in the passenger seat with his gaze locked on Ethan thinking of more devious assignments for his project.

††††††††††††††††††††††

PULLING INTO the parking lot at the papermill and crunching over the loose gravel, was James's red F-150. Just a few minutes behind him was Walter in his Dodge pickup.

"Doggonnit! Wake up already!" Said James as he gave his right leg a good shake.

It had been giving him trouble over the past few days with a tingling and numbing sensation. Seemed to always be asleep for some reason.

"Morning Walter. How you doing?"

"Aww...doing pretty good. How about yourself?"

James was busy studying and massaging his leg as it slowly regained the feeling.

"I'm good. I guess you got to sleep in a few extra minutes this morning, didn't ya?"

Walter tiled his head.

"You know, not having to pick up Ethan."

"Oh yeah-yeah. I know, I'm glad you and Jerry were able to help him get that ole jalopy of his running."

65

Walter and James began the journey inside and as the two were about ten yards from the front door, James' leg gave out and down he went, lunch box and all.

"Dad gummit! Stupid leg!" he huffed as he lay in the dirt and gravel.

Walter extended his hand to help him to his feet, "Dang man! You all right?"

"Yeah..." James grunted while in mid-sentence and on his way up, "...I'm good. My dang leg is still asleep."

He dusted himself off the best he could, while Walter was kind enough to dust his back.

"Dang...does it do it that much?"

"Nah...it comes and goes. Just been giving me a hard time this morning for some reason."

"You might want to go get that checked out man."

"I know. If it doesn't get any better in the next week or so, I just might."

James limped the rest of his way into the building.

††††††††††††††††††††

MINUTES LATER, Ethan pulled in with a trail of dust and debris behind him. It was about a quarter after seven. Fifteen minutes before his shift started.

After having checked every radio station one last time and not hearing of any news about the gruesome discoveries that were sure to take place any moment, he allowed himself to relax for the time being.

He parked the truck, got out and made his way inside to the break room, where James, Walter, Jerry and a few other men chatted their usual morning buzz by the coffee pot.

"Aww, speak of the devil, there he is," said Walter with a snicker as he took a sip of coffee.

Ethan nodded. His eyes low and wandering, not making an effort to look at the men.

"Morning bud. Truck running good?" asked James.

"Yeah. Running fine." Ethan said sitting his lunch down on the counter as one of the men had to scoot down just a bit.

"Well, that's good. I bet it feels good having her running again, huh?"

"Oh yeah. You just don't know."

"What about that old box truck? You planning to get it running anytime soon?" asked Jerry.

"Nah, I'm not in no hurry to get going. Not like I really need it now anyway."

"Well if you ever want to get it running, just let me know, I'll give it a look and see what I can do."

"I appreciate it, Jerry. I'll let you know if I change my mind."

Ethan walked out towards the restroom.

"Man, that kid's right pitiful, isn't he?" Jerry said as he wagged his head and took a sip from a cup of coffee.

"Yeah," James said, "he's had it rough."

"He told me yesterday, that his dad spent some time in prison for third-degree murder. Said he didn't get to meet him until he was about seven or so." Said Kevin, one of the new guys. The one Ethan forced to slide down the counter.

"Dang, really? He say what happened?" asked James.

"Something about he killed his sister's boyfriend and claimed it was self-defense. Served about five years but was originally sentenced to ten."

"Man...must've had a good lawyer."

"Huh." Walter grunted, crossing his arms and rolling his tongue around the bottom of his teeth.

"Yeah...that's something to know," added Jerry.

James stole a glance to the clock above the door as the skinny hand nudged the five.

"Well...I reckon we should head back there and get started."

The men nod and each took one last sip of coffee before forming a line for the trash can.

"Keep talking to him, maybe he'll give you more information. I'd be interested as to what he has to say. That kid's a mystery to me man," Walter said to Kevin as he held the door open.

Kevin dipped his head and said, "I know...we'll do," on his way out. Walter and the others followed behind as Ethan stood waiting by the machine him, James and Jerry had run the previous day.

††††††††††††††††††††††

LESS THAN an hour later, Walter Avery got a tap on the shoulder from the big man himself, Dale Pennington. Walter's heart skipped a moment passed as he took a hard swallow at the sight of him. Thoughts rifled across his mind.

What have I done?

He pulled out an ear plug and aimed his head toward the man. With a blank poker face, Dale motioned for Walter to follow him with a slow, stubby finger.

Walter's palms dripped with sweat as one bead began a trek down his face. He tried to control his breathing as his heart felt like it could jump out of his chest and grip him by the throat any second.

Dale made his way into his office, where the only reason an employee would be invited here was one of three things, a) You're fired! b) You're promoted or c) There was an emergency at home.

He knew he wasn't going to be promoted that fast, so there really were only two options and neither would be good.

Walter entered the office behind Dale as he turned and waved for him to shut the door. Walter shut it slowly, it creaked before latching shut. Locking him in, with what could be a caged Lion.

"Your wife is on the phone, she's fine, but she says it's important she speaks with you."

Walter let out a breath for the first time since Dale tapped his shoulder.

"Yes sir."

Walter lifted the phone from its cradle, causing it to jingle from his shaky hand.

Dale reclined back in his chair and fiddled with different grips on a foul ball he'd snagged at a minor league game a few years ago.

"Hey Mary. Is everything okay?"

"Walter! You have to get home. They've found a body at the Henson's old place. They don't know who did it."

Sounded like she'd been crying.

Silence filled the other end for just a moment as Walter tried to process what she'd just said.

"Wait. What? You mean Evelyn and Tim's place?"

"Yeah."

"Well, what happened? I mean what did they find?"

"They found a young man with his hands..."

She paused to gather herself.

"*Okay?*"

She took a breath and let it out in a just a little more than a whisper. "...with his hands tied to the steering wheel by his own shoestrings..."

Walter's heart sank to the office floor

"...and his throat slit wide open."

"Dear God."

"Walter, you have to come home. I'm scared," she said as her voice was choked with sniffles.

Walter coughed, craned his head and rubbed his throat at the thought of the poor man.

"Okay. Yeah, I will be right there. I'm leaving now."

Dale turned his attention, lowered his head and raised his brows.

Walter felt the glare but didn't care. He comforted his wife. told her he loved her and ended the call.

"Well, what happens to be so important it must require your immediate attention. Please tell me, I'm intrigued."

"They found a man murdered less than a hundred yards behind our house and the killer is still out there. The poor guy had his hands tied to the steering wheel of his car by his own shoelaces and his throat sliced opened."

Dale stared back at him with that blank expression of his, for what seemed like an eternity. Then with a hard flash of his eyes and rub of his face he said, "My apologies...please...go be with your wife. Don't worry about today, just give me a call tonight before eight and let me know how things are going."

"Thank you, sir. I will."

Walter shook Dale's hand and rushed out the door to go tell his buddies.

Dale, busy now with flipping stations on his small television set, trying to find the news. After a few tries, he found it and sure enough it was live coverage of detectives and CSI members loading a gurney supporting a white body bag into the back of an ambulance.

9

James heard someone yelling and when he raised his vision, he saw Walter rushing past Hank and Billy, pounding closer.

He began to yell again as he rushed past them, "Some dude was murdered behind my house and they don't know who did it. Check the news it'll probably be on there."

James only caught half of what he said through the thick ear buds and roaring machines but made out enough to catch, "...dude murdered behind my house...check the news."

James signaled with a clinched fist for Ethan to shut the cutting press off. The machine came to a halt as the men pulled out their ear plugs.

Jerry yelled, "Whaddayasay?"

"Check the news," Walter hollered back as he rushed into the break room to grab his things.

"Did he say what I think he said?" asked James.

"About the dead body?" Jerry asked to be sure.

James nodded with scrunched brows.

"Is that what you heard, Ethan?" Jerry turned and asked.

He nodded his signature nod, heart pounding like a subwoofer. Without him noticing, a finger nail had found its way to his mouth, where it was being clipped off like paper under the guillotine cutter.

"Let's take a quick break and go talk to Dale or Kurt and make sure everything's all right," said James.

Jerry and Ethan agreed.

†††††††††††††††††††††††

"WHAT DO YOU think may have happened?" Ethan, still chomping on a nail, as he followed behind James and Jerry towards Dale's office.

"I don't know but must be pretty serious for him to get off of work. Dale's usually pretty strict about stuff like that." said James.

As they approach the office, they can see Dale through the glass window, glued to the TV screen. Hank and Billy stood next to him. They looked like kids on a Saturday morning watching looney tunes.

James drums three quick knocks with his knuckles, then pushes the door on open as Dale welcomes them in.

"So, what's going on boss? Everything okay with Walter?"

Dale wagged his head and turned to face the men, still working his different grips on the foul ball. The slider was the one he could never remember and in times like these, he always groped for the feel of it.

"They found a guy behind Walter's house, tied to the steering wheel of his car with his throat slit." Dale pointed to the tv screen.

"Dear God! Is his wife and kids okay?" James asked.

"Yeah...they're fine. The wife is scared to death as would be expected. Cops don't have a clue who did it."

"Dang that's scary," said Ethan as he stood there with one hand in a pocket with the other busy picking at new warts. He had so many mixed in with the acne, he was the only one to notice.

Hank and Billy turned and nodded.

"Man...I hate that, I hope they find whoever did it. Sounds like a nut case to me," added Jerry.

"Well...we just wanted to check and make sure everything was all right. Walter hurried out, saying something about a dead body behind his house, we didn't know what was going on," said James as he scratched the back of his neck.

"Yeah...well...you boys get back to work, you can catch the news later when you get home. And tell the others while you're back there, cause I'm sure they're wondering too."

"Yes sir, you got it," said James as they showed themselves out of his office.

"Dang that's crazy isn't it?" James asked.

There was that tingling sensation again. It rifled down his leg, beginning at the right hip and running all the way to his right pinky toe.

His whole leg went numb and down he went. Smashing an elbow and knee in the process. Jerry and Ethan tried to catch him, but it was too late.

"Dang man! You all right?" Jerry asked extending a hand.

"Yeah-yeah...I'm good."

"What happened?" asked Ethan.

"Ahh...it's my dang leg, been going to sleep on me for some reason. Does it off and on."

"Man, you might want to get that checked out. As much as you on me about my health, I'm gonna get back on you about this one."

"I know. If it hasn't gotten any better over the weekend, I'll try to plan a trip to the doc at the first of the week," James said rubbing his knee and elbow.

"Well you need to man."

"Hey, you think we can knock out our quota for the day?"

"I don't see why not. Just as long as this here slacker picks up his pace," Jerry said with a toying glare towards Ethan.

Ethan stared back. No emotions.

"I'm just picking with ya kid. You're doing great, keep it up." He slapped on the shoulder which knocked a smile out of him.

The men headed back to the cutting press where Ethan fired up the machine. It began its routine once more. Pull paper off the giant roller, push it down to Jerry, who wiggled and moved it around to get it just right, then with the push of button by Ethan's thumb, the sharp metal blade came crashing down, severing the remnants of a once tall oak.

††††††††††††††††††††††

AFTER FINDING Steve Rickles tied to his car on Thursday morning, detectives found themselves with little to no leads. It wasn't until after talking with his family that they learned his girlfriend Melissa Berkley should've been with him. But where was she?

The neighborhoods of Georgetown were quiet and ghostly that night and the following. Which was odd. A Friday night in Georgetown was not your typical quiet evening.

Everyone was talking and spreading gossip and rumors about all the weirdos in town. Everyone had their own speculations and rightfully so.

Paternal instincts were in full affect as parents wouldn't allow their kids outside after dark and some even made pallets in the living room floor where the whole family slept for protection.

Moms were sure to dead bolt every door and lock every window while not standing by the phone hooked to the wall. Chatting with other mothers while stealing glances toward their children, as most had a habit of twirling the cord with a finger.

Dad's doubled checked their guns either leaned in a corner behind a bedroom door or stuffed high on a shelf in some closet. Mostly depending on the age of the children, regarding where the gun was placed, but never the less it was somewhere convenient, loaded and ready for any would be intruder.

†††††††††††††††††††††††

ON SATURDAY MORNING an old John Deere tractor grumbled, puffing out a black ball of smoke as it made its way down into a large cornfield.

Manning it, was Mr. Kirby Mooreland. A man who had seen his better days and had no hope for any in the future. He held a beer can in one hand and gripped the wheel with the other.

He towed a large plow behind, as he had plans of tilling up the cornfield which had seen its better days as well. He figured he'd till it up today and use the Sabbath to sow the seeds. That seemed to work in church when the usher came by. Sow on Sunday, reap on Friday. Or something like that.

As he made his way down a big red clay hill, passing his old barn, he couldn't shake the feeling of being watched. He even glanced to the heavens a time or two to be sure God wasn't shaking a fist at him for taking a liking to his new sudsy friend. He burped and glanced to the wood line more than once and turned to look over his shoulder more times than he could remember. Something just felt off. As if an army of banshees leered at him from the cover of trees. The cornfield now in clear view, or what was left of it.

Something stood out to him though. He applied his foot to the break, took off his coke bottled glasses, wiped them with a handkerchief, put them back on and tried again. Whatever it was, it was still there. He just couldn't make it out.

He mumbled and cursed, blaming teenagers for pulling a prank on him.

Continuing closer to the odd arrangement in his field, the tractor puffing out more of the same black pollutant.

"Why son-of-a-motherless-goat! Somebody done put a dad blame scarecrow in my cornfield."

As he got closer, a lump formed in his throat as the hair on the back of his neck stood straight. His skin turned to gooseflesh.

A fear he hadn't felt in years, suddenly gripped his heart with an iron fist. His heart knocked hard against his rib cage.

The scarecrow seemed awfully human and just too real to be fake.

He killed the engine and climbed down. By now the wind had shifted and was blowing right in his face, confronting him with a horrible stench.

"Oh, sweet Jesus, what have they done?" he said covering his face with the neck of his shirt and moving closer to the foot of the cross.

Melissa hung like a martyr, as her flesh had entered the decaying process. Her head was covered with a potato sack, her hands and feet tied to wooden four by fours.

"Judas priest! I have to get back to the house and call the cops."

His veins felt as if they'd just received a transfusion of ice.

Mr. Mooreland angled for the tractor, stealing glances to the woods, then the girl, then woods, then the sky.

Beady eyes were everywhere, he just couldn't see them. But they were there, he could feel them. He hoped and prayed he'd never feel them again, but here they were.

He climbed back onto his fifty-year-old tractor and headed for the house, which must've been about three-quarters of a mile away but felt more like twenty.

His palms were soaked, he was hoping against all odds his heart could bear the pressure. He stole glances along the tree line, waiting for someone or something to pounce on him like a hopeless fawn on some National Geographic show.

Surely the woods were full of soul thirsty devils.

The tractor just wouldn't go fast enough for his liking. It chugged along as if caught in slow motion.

"They may still be out here and their probably right on my tail. I've fallen in a dad blasted trap. I'm toast. Come on boy...get me back to the house."

The old man was sucking in air faster than his lungs could keep up. He didn't know which would go first, his heart or his lungs.

He'd be lucky to survive the trek back to his house. Either the killer and his devils would catch up to him or his heart would attack him, but one thing for certain, he'd be a victim.

It was like a dark, choking smoke had entered his body, stealing his breath, as each felt like it could be his last.

The stench of rotten eggs slapped his olfactory glands.

"Whew! What the heck?"

The stench was so bad, he was forced to cover his nose again.

††††††††††††††††††††††††

ALL THE WHILE, Kirkland rode on the finder with a crossed leg and long fingernail to his god forsaken mouth, wearing a crooked grin.

10

It was Saturday afternoon, the tenth day of March and by now Mr. Mooreland's corn field was buzzing with cop cars and delicate Crown Victoria's like an army of wasps.

The coroner pushed a gurney out to Melissa Berkley's body which still hung upon the cross. Numerous police officers and CSI personnel were scattered about the surrounding field.

Lieutenant Randy Callahan and detective Ann Marshall were busy questioning Mr. Mooreland.

"So, have you heard or seen anything unusual in recent days?" asked Marshall with a notepad in her hand.

Callahan stood by with his hands to his hips but gave his attention to Melissa hanging lifelessly upon the cross, a potato sack covering her head, hands and feet nailed with six-inch spikes to the wood four by fours. Officers and CSI worked with grace to pry the nails loose, one using a hammer and two others using a flat crow bar.

A foggy vision of teenagers each with a beer in one hand, and a joint in the other, laughed and mocked the cries of the girl as they hurled insults and jealous remarks toward her.

They vanished like a vapor and a ritualistic tribe of cult members arrived. Each wearing black robes and chanting some unknown language that hell could only recognize, formed a makeshift circle and danced in efforts to please their master. They vanished too.

Leaving, a lone, perhaps often misunderstood soul, standing there admiring his kill as a rush of dopamine and adrenaline sped through his body. A rush that was just as addictive and deadly as the most desired drug on the street.

But he too disappeared as a fog lifts off a body of water during a cool moist morning.

After popping the nails loose, causing a metal tinging sound to ring out, Melissa was free. The officers and CSI worked her down and along with the coroner loaded her onto the gurney.

Callahan came to in time to hear his partner's next question.

"If you haven't heard or seen anyone recently, how you think they got down here?"

"Well...I don't know, but I have had trouble in the past with people coming in my cornfield by the old logging road in the back. It's a long and rough haul, but it eventually leads out to the main road. I put a fence up a few years ago to keep those young-ins out. I haven't been back there in about a week, so you'd probably want to check that out."

Bingo! Now they might be getting somewhere.

"Okay...thank you Mr. Mooreland, hang tight right here for a second, I'm going to pass the information to an officer, so they can go have a look."

"Yes ma'am," he said with a tilt of his old straw hat.

Marshall turned and gave a brow lifted look to Callahan who was stepping closer to give Mr. Mooreland some company.

"So how have you been holding up?"

"Well...to tell you the truth...I haven't. These past few years have been rough, but I reckon I make do the best I can."

The old man leaned against a patrol car, chewing a wad of tobacco in one cheek and collecting the juice in the other. He emptied his stash of juice with a well-practiced sound effect as it landed on some unfortunate innocent weeds, which if could talk, would be giving Mr. Mooreland an earful.

"I know it must be tough...I can't imagine going through that. You're stronger than most people and I admire you for that. I really do."

"Well, I appreciate that, Randy. So, what are you thinking with all this?"

Callahan crossed his arms in front of his chest.

"I have different feelings about it," Callahan said taking a breath, "it may be out of revenge...you know maybe the killer was cheated on by one these two or wronged in a deal...who knows? But whatever happened...it ignited something in our killer, that not only wanted them dead, but wanted them to suffer in the process.

"Which makes me think of three different scenarios: 1) This was a group of teenagers who felt they had been wronged by these two and decided it was time for justice, 2) It's a cult and this was a sacrifice to appease whoever it is they serve, likely Satan himself, I guess...but that leaves me wondering why the guy was left in the car and not dragged out here with the girl. Also makes me question what the inscription of "The Reaper's Helper," is all about. Lastly, 3) which is the most disturbing for me...is...we're dealing with a psychotic serial killer, who did this simply for the thrill and joy of it. Those are the types that cause me to sleep with the lights on at night."

A crow cawed overhead, glaring down at the scene below with a twitch and tilt of its head.

Mr. Moreland lowered his head to Callahan who watched as the crow landed in a tall Pine to the left and said in his deep gravelly voice.

"And he's not done."

Callahan forgot about the crow and focused on Mr. Moreland who stood with his rump against the police cruiser wearing tight lips and narrow eyes.

11

With particles of quartz, mica, magnetite, along with bivalves and clams disguised as sand stuck to their feet and toes, James and Rebecca were taking a stroll just above the swash zone. Various sized footprints going this way and that, just to the left of them. Sandcastles, both new and old, were scattered about, names drew here and there.

Their hands interlocked as remnants of waves crawled close enough to splash their feet and give them a good rinsing from the sticky sand.

Gulls squawked above. The cool ocean breeze confronted their faces. A Pelican fell from the sky like a dive bomber, beak first into a school of menhaden just behind the breakers.

They were passing a surf fisherman who'd just finished baiting his hooks and was about to catapult them into the deep. The aroma of shrimp was so strong, Rebecca claimed she could taste it.

"Aww, c'mon. You can't really taste that can you?" Asked James.

"I can too. Reminds me when my grandpa used to take us kids to catch shrimp in the marsh. The smell was so strong, I could taste it. We'd come back to the house and have a big Cajun broil. They tasted a lot better with his secret seasoning."

"Oh, I bet. If his shrimp was anything like yours...whew," James whistled and tilted his head.

"It was. He's the one who taught me how to make gumbo for the first time."

"Really? I didn't know that."

"Yeah...well...he taught me how to make it, but it was grandma's recipe," she said as a surfacing dolphin diverted her attention, "oh look!"

"Wow! He's pretty close. Must be after those pogies," James said referring to the school of Menhaden the Pelican was after.

"You know, I can't get that poor boy off my mind."

James turned and gave a puzzled expression,

"That boy they found behind the new guy's house."

"Oh, yeah I know. Crazy isn't it? I hope his girlfriend is all right."

"That poor girl."

Rebecca lowered her head and gazed at the passing sea shells.

"I mean it's scary enough to think someone could do that, then to know their still out there...that's horrifying," she said looking to James.

"I know honey...but don't worry...I'm sure the police will find him pretty soon. I mean it's hard to get by with stuff like that nowadays."

He squeezed her hand with a gentle grace.

"Yeah...I sure hope so. I just hate it for the family. Think about what the parents must be going through."

"I'd rather not...I can't imagine."

They continued their scroll in silence for a few steps then find a nice spot to rest. Rebecca places a sheet on the sand and the two of them sit next to each other. Rebecca leans into James' left breast as he pulls her close.

"So how you think all the new guys are doing at the mill?" Rebecca asked.

James cleared his throat and gently brushed a strand of hair from her face.

"Well...not bad, I mean their holding their own I guess you could say. Dale is ticked since we didn't get the order out, but Kurt said he talked to him and explained our side of it. He feels he might understand the situation a little better now. So, we'll see I guess."

He kissed her head.

"But as for Walter and Ethan...they've done a pretty good job so far and I've heard good things about the others. I think with time, we could really get rolling."

"That's good...I'm glad Kurt was able to get through to Dale, maybe he'll be a little more reasonable."

"Yeah...I hope so."

"Say...how about the Ethan kid? How's he doing? Does he have his power on yet?"

"No...he said it gets it turned on this Monday. But he's doing good though. He can be a hard worker when he wants to be."

"Yeah...what do you think about inviting him over for Sunday dinner? I'm sure he could use a good home cooked meal."

James gave it some thought.

Rebecca pulled away looked at him with those innocent brown eyes that melt the heart of the vilest criminal.

"I guess...yeah. It'd probably do him some good. We could stop by on the way home and ask."

"Good. I wonder if he likes Cajun food?"

"Shoot, who are you kidding? Even if he doesn't, it'd have to be a cold day in hell before someone turned down your cooking."

James placed his arm around her shoulder and gave her a good squeeze.

"Aww, thank you babe."

Rebecca wrapped her arms around him and gave him a peck on the lips.

He pulled back.

"I love you, Rebecca Randolph. You're my girl."

††††††††††††††††††††††

JUST AFTER three o'clock on Sunday afternoon, a phone jingled in its cradle on the wall.

James was finishing a laugh as he sat at the dinner table before his wife Rebecca and coworker Ethan Thompson. He dabbed the corners of his mouth and swallowed the small remains of an A1 covered steak, before saying, "hang on a second."

He scooted the chair back and angled for the phone in the kitchen. He reached it just as it finished a ring. He placed the phone to his ear. There was breathless static at first.

"Hello?"

More static.

"Hello?"

"Is this James?" a masculine voice asked after clearing a phlegm

"Yeah, this is James. Who is this?"

"Hey man, it's Walter from the mill."

"Oh hey, what's going on?"

"Uh, well I was wondering if you'd heard the news lately?"

"I don't believe so, it depends, I guess. Why do you ask?"

"Well, they find that boy's girl."

"What? You mean the guy they find near your place?"

"Mm-hmm."

"So, they found his girlfriend? Well, how is she?"

"She's dead."

That breathy static returned.

"Dang man. Really? What happened?"

Heavy breathing.

Rebecca being curious made her way to James, leaving Ethan at the table alone. He busied himself by chewing on a nail.

"Man, tell me, what happened?"

"They found her looking like a scarecrow out in a cornfield. Said she was nailed to a cross like Christ and that she had her throat slashed open just like her boyfriend."

James paused as the information needed time to settle. Rebecca heard it through the receiver, gasped and cupped her mouth.

Walter continued, he knew James was there, because he heard Rebecca's response.

"They found her in some old farmer's cornfield near Graves. Said she'd most likely been there since Wednesday night and they just found her yesterday."

"Who found her? Was it the farmer?"

"Yeah...the poor old man found her while he was down in his field on his tractor."

"Did you catch the man's name?"

"Um, yeah I think it was uh Kirby something. I want to say Kirby Mooresville. If you hadn't of asked."

James placed the phone on his shoulder and whispered to Rebecca.

"You there man?"

"Yeah, I'm here. Did you mean Kirby Mooreland?"

"Yeah-yeah, that's it, I knew I was close though. You know him?"

"Well yeah, I grew up with his nephew. We were good buds back in the day. You've heard about what happened to him haven't you?"

"No, what happened?"

"Huh, well his wife and daughter were murdered, and he got cut up pretty bad when they tried to cast a demon out of his grandson about ten years ago. You never heard about all that?"

Ethan stopped biting his thumb nail, his eyes grew wide. He was taken back to the day when he and two friends tried out a "wiji" board for the first time.

As the flash flood of memories rifled through his mind, he had to dry his palms on his pants leg. He stole a glance towards the kitchen where Rebecca was clinging tightly to her husband's arm as they both leaned into the receiver.

Ethan moved on to his index finger. Each chomp being more powerful than the last.

Chomp...chomp...chomp. The nail was quickly disappearing. A numbing, burning sensation set in. It took the taste of Iron slapping Ethan's taste buds to get his attention. He retrieved his finger and examined the damage. The nail was down to the raw meat as blood oozed down to his first knuckle.

"Dang it!" Ethan said through clinched teeth.

"Well...if you hear anything else before the morning let me know. Thanks for calling...okay...all right...see ya."

James hung the phone back in its cradle as he and Rebecca stepped further into the kitchen. Their voices in whispers, low enough for most not to hear. But Ethan wasn't most. He'd been deciphering whispers for a while now. he heard every word with perfect clarity.

"My goodness." Rebecca's voice sounded strained.

James sighed.

"Man...I hate that. Especially for Mr. Mooreland."

"This is beginning to scare me James."

It sounded like he pulled her in close.

"Don't worry honey...I'm sure they will catch the guy in no time. I mean their professionals, you can't get too far, right?"

"Yeah...I guess you're right. I just hope they catch him before he does it again." Her voice against his chest.

"Honey...don't think like that. I'm sure this was just an isolated incident. They may have owed the guy drug money, or maybe it was a love triangle or something. Don't go to thinking about all the horror movies and crime shows now."

"Yeah...well...I sure hope so."

"Don't worry about it baby. I'm here, I'll protect you. Now let's remind ourselves we have company and get back in there."

It sounded like they kissed.

The two make their way back into the dining area where Ethan awaited.

He sat there with one hand across his chest and tucked under an armpit while the other was balled into a fist with a finger in his mouth.

"Everything all right?" he asked.

James went on to tell everything he and Rebecca just learned from Walter.

Ethan did his best impression of being surprised and pulled it off with masterful technique. He showed all the right expressions and asked the right questions.

After a few hours of discussing the murders proceeded by some small talk, Ethan glanced at a grandfather clock which showed the short hand aiming for the six.

"Well...I guess I better get going. I appreciate the dinner Mrs. Randolph, best I've had...all day."

That got the trio chuckling.

Rebecca nudged James foot under the table. He knew what she was implying.

"Well...Ethan your welcome to stay in the spare room for the night. I know it's supposed to get quite chilly out there."

Ethan thought about it.

"You sure you wouldn't mind?"

"Nah, not at all. It'd be our treat," said James.

Rebecca nodded with a soft smile.

"Well...I sure do appreciate it. Like I said, I'll have my power turned on this week, so I won't have to worry about the cold nights anymore."

"Don't worry about it, Ethan, we're just glad we can help you out."

With that, they chatted a bit more before settling in for the night. The Sun was down, and the voices were starting. It'd be a long night at the Randolph's, he hoped he could control his impulses. Kirkland had hinted about the next assignment but had yet to announce it. He knew what it should be, but he had to wait for Kirkland. If this was it, Rebecca done a fine job of preparing him a pre-ritual meal. He'd need his strength and he could already feel the proteins working in his muscles as euphoric rush jolted across his body, almost causing him to spasm.

It will be a long night indeed.

12

The air was dark and cold. A strong breeze brushed by as cornstalks bowed in honor. The sound of iron ringing against iron beat at the eardrums. The thudding continued with each muffled scream.

Storm clouds methodically rolled in bringing with it the usual occupants. Within minutes the ground was soaked. Thunder drowned out the agony.

An unforgettable sight in the distance. A cross stood erect high above the corn. Something was nailed to it. Or someone? Could it be...?

A dark figure glared up at the victim.

Who is that?

The figured must've heard the question. Just as they were turning, a bolt of lightning fell from the sky with a crash.

The witness turned and jolted away. To where? Who knows, anywhere but here. The man fell to the ground as his lower half went numb. Crawling was the only remaining option. Breathing was hard and labored. Footsteps crunched over the cornstalks, rushing ever closer.

Crunch! Thud! Crunch! Thud!

They were gaining ground much quicker than the rate of a belly crawl. They would reach their destination in a matter of seconds.

A darkened silhouette rushed closer like a giant wave of rage ready to overtake anything in its path.

"You did this James! This is all your fault!" The voice bellowed through the darkness.

"God help me!"

A flash of light filled his view followed by a booming crack of thunder.

†††††††††††††††††††††††

SOAKING WET, his heart pounded harder with each breath, James gasped for air and sucked in a room full as he forced his body to form an L. He tossed the sheets onto Rebecca.

What is that?

His mind had to be playing him? Or did it?

A dark shadow stood in the doorway leering in. James rubbed his eyes and the shadow was gone, but its presence remained with the sound of footsteps creeping down the hall.

By now Rebecca was waking as the bed had suddenly felt like it had been moved on board a ship lost at sea. Drenched in sweat and rocked about. Her husband's panting startled her.

"James, what's wro..." Before she could finish, James had already called out.

"Ethan! Is that you?"

A moment passed. He glanced at the bright red numbers beside the bed, they read 3:33.

James was about to ask again but didn't need to.

A faint voice answered, "yeah. Sorry, I drank too much water before bed. I'm sorry I woke you."

"It's all right bud, just making sure."

James took a deep breath, placed his hands to his face and rubbed them down to his chin.

91

The lamp flicked on, such sudden light was painful for the eyes.

"Honey what's the matter?" asked Rebecca.

James let his breath out and said, "nothing. Nothing. Just a bad dream, that's all."

"You sure? You're soaking wet."

She gripped his arm and wiped sweat from his forehead. The toilet flushed.

Rebecca offered him a glass of water that sat on her nightstand. He happily obliged. He lowered the glass and passed it back to her.

He fell to his pillow with one hand tucked behind his head and the other along the side of Rebecca as she snuggled up close.

"I saw the girl."

Rebecca squinted her eyes, didn't say a word but her gaze did.

"She was there in the cornfield and the killer saw me and started chasing me, but I couldn't run, my legs just wouldn't work. I tried to crawl, but it was no use."

The bathroom door opened, followed by footsteps. But they were just like crickets in the night at this point. All James could see and hear was that poor girl nailed to a cross in that cornfield.

Ethan's shadow passed by the half-cracked door.

"Sorry again. Goodnight y'all," said Ethan as he headed back to the bedroom room.

"No worries, just get you some sleep."

††††††††††††††††††††††††

KIRKLAND WAS furious as Ethan crashed on the bed.

"YOU WORTHLESS PIECE OF FLESH! ARE YOU GOING TO LET THIS MOMENT PASS? YOU'RE MORE PATHETIC THAN I THOUGHT!"

"Hush! Not now, some other time," Ethan said with tired eyes.

"SOME OTHER TIME? SOME OTHER TIME? ARE YOU KIDDING ME? THERE MIGHT NOT BE ANOTHER TIME! YOU MUST TAKE ACTION...NOW!"

"I have to take care of Walter first. We've never left a job unfinished. You know that. Besides, I just don't think it'd be a good time to take James and Rebecca. Mother wants Walter, then these two, not the other way around."

"WHAT AN INSULT! WHY YOU PIECE OF SCUM. STILL TAKING ORDERS FROM YOUR MOMMY. YOU'RE NOT WORTHY TO EVEN BE IN MY PRESENCE."

"But here you are."

"WATCH IT!"

The smell of rotten eggs filled the room.

"WILL YOU BE THE ONE TO CARRY OUT THE MASTER'S PLAN OR SHOULD I SEEK ANOTHER?"

"Calm down. I told you I'll do it."

"THEN GET YOUR ACT TOGETHER! OR I WILL TURN YOU OVER TO HER. YOU THINK I'M TOUGH?"

"No...no...please! No! Not Lucinda. I'll do it, I promise, just not now." Ethan said in a foamy whisper.

"WHEN?"

"I will make it happen, I'll come up with a plan and take care of it."

"THEN YOU BETTER SEE TO IT...OR ELSE."

Kirkland vanished like a black ball of smoke. Ethan shut his eyes and set his jaw. He could still sense a presence. Though all he saw now was a red darkness from the back of his eye lids, he knew they were there.

Out of instinct, not desire, he opened the windows to his soul. The room was full of them. Dark figures stood beside the bed, at the foot of the bed and one even hovered right over his face, nose to nose. Black eyes and a black mouth wide like a python.

There must have been a dozen or more of these silhouettes. Each chanting with a deep voice straight from the pits of hell itself, "DO IT FRANKIE...DO IT FRANKIE...DO IT FRANKIE!"

Ethan slammed his eyes and squinted with enough force he thought they might pop under such pressure. It gave him a headache. He peaked through an eye lid and saw the room was empty.

They were gone, and the chanting had stopped. For now.

He rolled over to his side, the fear ebbed away.

A few minutes passed, and the sound of rubbed bed sheets was enough to bring the fear back like a ram's head to the gut. His heart pounded harder and faster with each beat.

He squinted one eye open to see the sounds origin. Right in front of his belly was an enormous snake that took its time slithering to his face with a smooth hiss.

His heart was pounding before, but now it had leaped from his chest and left him in the room to fend for himself.

He swatted at the blackness as it disappeared in a puff of dark smoke. Ethan sighed and glanced about the room, Kirkland liked the corner shadows and was likely in one now. Ethan couldn't find him, but knew he was near. He rested his head back down to a stiffened and barely used pillow. James and Rebecca must not have many night guests. Wonder if they'd notice if he decided to hang around?

He tried to fall back to sleep as he lay on his side with one hand under a pillow and the other hanging off the bed.

As he was beginning to doze, he felt two fingers gently walk from the palm of his hand to his forearm. The sensation was enough to make his skin crawl as his blood had turned to a cool slush.

He gasped for breath, jolting awake. Eyes wide.

Standing beside his bed, right in front of his face was a young boy, perhaps maybe ten or eleven in age.

"Hello Frankie!" Said the little boy with such a sweetness and cuteness in his voice that would've made any grandma's heart burst with infatuation.

"I didn't mean to startle you," he said with a cute dimply grin and giggle, covering his mouth with little ashy pale hands.

Ethan was cemented to the bed. His heart pounded. his lungs labored for each breath. His teeth chattered as each breath escaped with a puff of steam.

The boy was silent as the two stared at one another for what must've been all of ten seconds, but for Ethan felt like an eternity.

The boy cocked his head to one side as his eyes pierced Ethan's soul. His brows narrowed downward in sharp angles as he said in a deep mechanical voice that ended each syllable with a growl, "WHAT'S THE MATTER FRANKIE? DON'T YOU WANT TO PLAY?"

Ethan squeezed his eyes as hard as he could. His head pounded as his heart beat was now in his brain. Tears strolled down his cheeks. Sharp talons of fear ripped him to shreds as if he were fresh pray for a hungry vulture.

An eerie laugh echoed off each wall before dissipating into the shadows. The darkness lifted after a few terrorizing minutes.

All that was left was that same red darkness from the back of his eye lids. He was too afraid to check the room for any guest, he trusted his gut. He knew the evil had retired for the night. Just like countless nights before.

He rested his head into the stiff pillow, he'd need another to ever be comfortable here. He breathed deep and soon entered another world.

The only place where if he was lucky enough, peace might be present.

Mon
5/28/81

I talked to Will at school today. He got me off to the side and started telling me what Frankie had told him.

There is some really weird stuff going on with his dad. For starters, Frankie told him that his dad has found religion and is no longer drinking like he used to. He said he's now a Jesus Freak.

But he's a different kind of Jesus Freak. Said he's talking about how the government is always watching us and that the Battle of Armageddon is coming. Something about there's going to be 144,000 warriors that'll rise up and fight. Supposedly, Frankie and his family are a part of the 144,000.

He even said his dad has a way of asking God and getting an answer on the spot. Said he'll grab a pen and piece of paper, then go into a trance and start talking in some crazy gibberish before writing down "The voice of God."

Frankie claims they already have about a dozen followers, who say they believe he is a prophet for being able to call down "The Voice of God."

Said they believe in animal sacrifice, like in the Old Testament, and that "If Abraham did it, then we have to do it." I guess that explains where Sylvester went, I'm assuming Frankie has done figured that out.

He said they have really strict rules now too. Like no T.V. or newspaper or any other kind of connection to the outside world. Frankie told Will that his parents are going to pull him out of school and start homeschooling him.

I've been wondering why he's seemed so down lately. I think this explains it. I'm going to ask him about all of this tomorrow, and just see what he says.

I'm glad his dad quit drinking, but I
don't want him brainwashing Frankie into
some cult either.

I'm going to talk to mom about it
too and see what she says. She talked
to his mom the other day, after I told
her of his dad's drinking and possible abuse,
But his mom just brushed it off and
denied everything.

I'm curious though... I'd like to see
the man call on "The voice of God."
Reminds me a little of that day when
Frankie flipped at the Mooreland's.

Anyway, I'll talk to him and mom
tomorrow.

David Hoffman

Journal Entry of David Hoffman

Monday

May 28th, 1981

AGE 11

13

After failing to get a good night's rest, the morning came hard for both James and Ethan. They each had their reasons however different they were.

James couldn't get the picture of the poor girl in the cornfield out of his mind. Her screams and the ringing of the hammer against the nails, sent shivers down his spine.

While Ethan couldn't overcome the darkness that had invaded his room. It was thicker than ever and tried its best to choke the life out of him.

He also couldn't get the snake out of his mind either. The thought of having a six-foot snake cuddled close beside him under the bed sheets, was enough to keep him wide eyed for most of the night.

But regardless of how they both felt, the morning had arrived whether they were ready for it or not. At six-thirty, James found himself sitting at the edge of the bed, rubbing his face and trying to wipe the vile images of the girl from his mind.

He crossed to the closet and pulled a shirt off its hanger, it swung like a pendulum after losing its cover. He slipped the shirt over his head, passed the kitchen and wandered towards the guest room.

This better not be hard.

He gave a few soft knocks and said, "You up man?"

A voice moaned back, muffled under the sheets,

"Yeah...I'm getting up."

James mumbled under his breath before heading into the kitchen where he busied himself with preparing a fresh pot of coffee. He did a 180 and headed for a cabinet to retrieve the filters when his right leg left the room.

Numbing, burning, tingling sensations shot from his hip to the floor as his leg crippled under him like a toothpick supporting a cinderblock.

He crashed with a thud.

Rebecca bolted out of bed and was in the kitchen by the time James was just getting comfortable.

"What happened? Are you okay?" she asked going to her knees beside him with one hand on his chest and the other behind his head.

"Oh, I'm great. Just thought I'd take a trip to floor-da, always wanted to see the ever-dazed," he said with a straight face.

Rebecca cracked and so did James. They shared a laugh together as she helped him to his feet.

"You're crazy. Now seriously, what happened? Are you sure you're okay?"

Ethan entered the room to see what all the commotion was about.

"Yeah-yeah, I'm fine. My foot must've caught the corner of the island. I'm good though, I caught myself pretty good."

"Dang...you all right man? I thought I heard you go down."

"Yeah, I'm good. Well, I guess that's one way to get everybody awake." James grinned.

He went on to fix the pot of coffee as they each enjoyed a fresh cup with homemade biscuits Rebecca had made the previous morning. A short time later, they each were off on their way to work.

Ethan went ahead as James had to stop for gas.

"Dang man, $1.04! It's going to be $1.50 by the end of the year," James said as he whipped his F-150 into a Citgo, the only gas station on the way to the mill.

He finished pumping and stepped back inside where he checked his watch. 6:55. Good. With current traffic he should be there by 7:10.

He pulled out of the station and got on US-17. Must've drove a mile before a sudden flood of brake lights flashed ahead. Someone was turning left into a Food Lion parking lot.

James saw the lights with plenty of time to spare, he went to apply the brakes.

Nothing.

His leg had fallen asleep and was lifeless on the gas pedal. Panicking, he glanced at the speedometer.

48 mph.

The brake lights must've been forty yards away but rushed closer with every Nano-second.

No matter how hard he tried, his leg and foot just wouldn't budge.

Twenty yards. 48 mph. Bright red.

The brake lights reflected in his eyes. Three cars sat motionless only seconds away.

He reached down and grabbed at his pants leg, he swerved in the process.

Ten yards. 48 mph. Bright red.

He managed to force his foot to the brake. He slammed it as hard as he could and hoped for the best.

Oh God.

Ten feet. Tires screeched as the speedometer needle fell from 48 mph to 40 mph.

An explosion of crinkling metal bit through the air.

14

Loose gravel crunched in the mill parking lot as the tires of Ethan's 1980 Chevy Suburban pulled in.

It was 7:05, the earliest he arrived yet at his new job. He toted a lunch box alongside of him as he headed into the mill to start another week.

He entered the break room, where Jerry, Hank and Walter conversed in hush tones with cups of coffee in hand. Walter filled them in on what he knew so far about the murders.

They paused and greeted Ethan. He nodded back and said, "morning."

"I guess you heard about the girl?" Asked Jerry.

"Who?" Asked Ethan.

"You know...the guy they found behind Walter's place. His girlfriend."

"Oh yeah-yeah...I heard. Do they think they know who did it or what might have happened?"

Jerry pointed a thumb to Walter.

He cleared his throat, crossed his arms and said,

"Well...they did find some tire tracks along an old logging road that leads into the field, but they say it's not clear enough to get a good impression. And they said they found something carved into the cross the girl was on. 'The Reaper's Helper.' I heard they found the same thing carved into the dashboard of the guy's car. But as far as I know, that's about all they've gotten."

Ethan looked to the floor and wagged his head, his skin crawling, it took all he had not to chomp on a nail. Something about chewing one down to the quick, made him want to go even shorter on another one. He had enough tape to help with the pain afterwards.

"What did you smash your thumb or something?" Asked Walter.

Ethan's heart flatlined.

"Huh?"

"Your thumb. What you got it all bandaged up for?"

Ethan looked at it, not sure of an answer. He hated being asked something on the spot like that.

"Uh...uh...yeah...I was messing around with my box truck, had to change the brake calipers. The wrench slipped and sent my thumb into the disk. That's all."

There, hopefully that'll do.

"Oh...well what's got you here so early?"

What's with the dang questions?

"What are you talking about?"

"You're ten minutes early. Thought you didn't show up till twenty after?"

"Well I guess I felt a little ambitious this morning."

"Ambitious? I didn't know you could say such big words," Walter said with a chuckle as he raised a coffee cup to his lips.

"Yeah well...a man can go from peasant to king with a passion for reading. You should try it," Ethan said with a wink.

"Yeah well...we're not in the medieval days anymore either, so I think I will stick with a hard work ethic. That usually seems to do the trick. Besides...I don't have to time to read and never much cared for it anyhow."

Jerry and Hank just stood back listening to the whole squabble, waiting for their chance to chime in.

That moment came when Ethan and Walter paused to catch their breath.

"Ethan's right. A habit for reading can make for a smart man," said Jerry sipping his coffee. He dipped his head toward Ethan with a soft grin.

Hank nodded.

Three to one.

Walter's face flushed. A vein along his neck bulged.

"Well, if you ask me, reading just creates a hunger for the truth that a man can never know or truly satisfy. I'd rather not light that fire."

A moment passed.

"That sounds so sophisticated...yet so stupid. I think that calls for a new word...stuphisticated," Hank said as he and Jerry got a good laugh.

Ethan lost in thoughts, Kirkland's voice louder than the others.

Walter simmered as he tried to concoct a comeback. He snarled his nose as the best he could muster was, "Well...take your chances...just make sure when the fire gets going...you have the strength to put it out."

The other three stared back at him as if he were speaking another language.

They each broke their glares and looked to each other before bursting out in laughter.

"Oh...that's a good one man. That's stuphistication at its finest right there," said Hank as he slapped Walter's shoulder on his way to discard his coffee cup, before heading out the door, snickering and wagging his head.

Walter glanced at the clock, not doubt ready to end the whole ordeal.

Ethan followed his glance, 7:17

"Well...I'm going to head out here...we can finish this some other time."

"All right man. I'll be back there in a second," said Jerry as he turned to Ethan, "I wonder where James is?"

Ethan shrugged his shoulders, "I don't know but he shouldn't have been too far behind me. He'd stopped to get gas, but I figured he'd be here by now."

"Oh really? How close do you live to him?"

"Well I live about fifteen minutes or so away, but they invited me over for dinner yesterday and I ended up spending the night with them."

"Oh...well that was nice of them. They're good people, aren't they?"

Ethan nodded.

"He'll probably show up any minute. Must've got caught in traffic. It can be a real booger at times. Well...let's get started, shall we?" Jerry said with a pat to Ethan's shoulder as he went for the door.

† †

HAVING JUST began writing on the chalk board and lecturing on Archimedes principle and his eureka moment with isostasy, Mrs. Randolph was interrupted with a few knuckle raps on the door of her classroom.

Rebecca stopped her writing about where the S met the T in isostasy and turned to see Ms. Tates who stood in the doorway.

She gestured for Rebecca to come see her.

"All right excuse me just for a moment. If you have your textbooks, I want you reading the introductory for chapter twelve while I'm gone. I'll ask questions when I get back."

She sat the chalk down on the cliff of the black board as it gave off that familiar chalky thud. She dusted her hands and approached the waiting Ms. Tates.

"Yes?"

Ms. Tates turned and began a scroll down the hall.

What is this about?

"Rebecca, James was just in an accident. He's okay, but he is at Georgetown medical being treated."

Rebecca stopped their migration dead in its tracks and flooded the conversation with her obvious questions.

"What? What happened? What are you talking about?" she asked as panic, fear and a numbing pain got the best of her.

"He crashed into the back of someone as a car in front of them was turning left into Food Lion. You need to get to the hospital. I can take your class for the day."

"Oh, my goodness."

Her mind in a rush, she turned to walk away, then turned around and hugged Ms. Tates, "Thank you-thank you."

Within minutes she was turning the ignition over in her red convertible Fiat and leaving the parking lot of Georgetown High.

The little engine under that red hood roared as it was put under a stress unlike it had ever known.

††††††††††††††††††††

AN HOUR HAD PASSED as Rebecca now sat close to James's bedside clutching his hand in hers.

His head wore a bandage covering a gash along the front side of his head. His knee was banged up and bruised, but other than the small cuts and bruises, he had nothing to complain about so far.

"James, why didn't you say something about all this?"

"Well...I just didn't want you worrying about me. I'd planned to give it a few more days and if it hadn't changed, I was going to tell you and make an appointment with the doctor."

"That's why you tripped in the kitchen this morning wasn't it?"

James shut his eyes and nodded.

A set of knuckles drummed the door.

They turned to see a large middle-aged dark-skinned man dressed in a white lab coat with a clip board in hand. He dipped his head, cleared some phlegm and pulled an extra chair out of its place and sat next to them.

"Hi James, I'm doctor Santini," he said extending a hand.

"And you must be Mrs. Randolph?"

"Yes sir, this is my lovely wife, Rebecca."

She smiled and shook his hand.

"So how do you feel?"

"Well...I feel like I've just been in a car wreck, but other than that...I'm good," James grinned.

Doctor Santini smiled sheepishly and said, "Well...I figured that much.

"I wanted to ask some questions about your 'sleepy leg' as I believe you stated for the cause of the accident. Could you please explain that to me? What exactly do you mean by 'sleepy leg?'"

Rebecca gave her husband the look of "If you don't tell him I will," and that was enough to get James going.

"Well...it just hits me out of nowhere and sends a numbing, tingling sensation from my right hip all the way down to my pinky toe until I eventually can't feel my leg anymore. Then it just gives out, like its dead."

"Like its paralyzed?" Santini offered.

"Yeah. Like I've just lost all feeling in it."

Santini busied himself with jotting down notes, before tapping a pen to his chin and glaring at the ceiling tiles. His eyes cut to James,

"How long do these episodes last?"

"I don't know, a few minutes, I guess. Usually by the time I'm picking myself up off the ground, the feeling is back enough for me to get walking again. It was scary this morning though, because I didn't realize it was doing it until I tried to lift my foot off the gas and onto the brake. I mean I had to physically grab my pants leg and force my foot onto the brake."

Rebecca cupped her mouth with her hand as tears formed in her big brown eyes.

"Wow...yes, that can be frightening. I tell you what, I'd like to run a few neurologic exams such as, magnetic resonance imaging and a evoked potentials exam . Just to be sure I'm covering all the bases. What you're telling may be something as simple as a pinched nerve, and with these tests I will be able to determine what is causing these episodes and be able to find the correct solution. Okay?"

James took a deep breath, let it out through puffed cheeks and said, "Yeah, sounds good."

"When will we get the results?" asked Rebecca.

"Umm...soon. Usually within a few hours, I can give a confident diagnosis."

Santini rose to his feet.

"Okay. Thank you doctor."

"So just sit back and relax, a nurse will be by shortly to escort you for the testing. Okay?"

"Thanks doc," James said as he shook his hand once more.

†††††††††††††††††††††

IT WAS JUST after ten o'clock at the papermill and Jerry and Ethan were struggling to make up for James's absence. They'd been informed about his wreck minutes earlier as Dale had come out and relayed the message he'd received from Rebecca.

They could use a third person. Maybe Hank and Billy could spare Walter for the day.

Oh, how nice would that be? Seeing Walter reach under that shiny blade. Ethan's muscle's quivered at the thought.

Jerry raised a fist.

This is it.

Ethan shut it down. It whined and huffed.

Jerry took out his ear plugs as Ethan did the same.

"I'm going to go see if I can steal Walter to help pick up the slack. Just hang tight, I'll be right back."

Ethan nodded, doing all he could to restrain that twisted grin of his. He watched as Jerry forced himself into a quick jog over to Hank, Billy and Walter about a hundred feet away.

His pupils widened as his tongue narrowed. He had to keep it tucked behind his teeth, couldn't let anyone see it. Though, he did allow the tip to poke out between his lips. He shut his eyes and trembled. Not out of fear, but out of anticipation of what was to come. He could already smell the blood.

Yeah. Bring Walter over.

†††††††††††††††††††††††††

AFTER UNDERGOING the numerous tests, James found himself back in his room with Rebecca by his side, waiting for Dr. Santini to deliver the results.

It must've have been two or three hours since the test and after having a bland hospital style lunch, James and Rebecca were in the middle of enjoying a well needed afternoon nap.

The knock to the door startled them both as they came to attention. James rubbed his eyes and glanced to the clock.

11:52

Rebecca fixed the recliner back in its normal sitting position with the lever along the side. She rubbed her face, scooted closer to James and squeezed his hand.

Dr. Santini showed himself to the same chair as before, with the same clipboard in hand, but this time with new information.

"Sorry to have woke you. My apologies."

James waved him off with, "No...it's no problem. Don't worry about it."

"So, what did you find?" asked Rebecca, knowing that by Santini's countenance and body language, he had something to share, but struggled to convey it.

Santini took a deep breath and began by saying, "Well...I have good news and bad news. I'm afraid."

"Go on." James said as he swallowed hard and scrunched his brows, sending three wrinkles across his forehead.

"We've discovered that you are in the beginning stages of Multiple Sclerosis. That explains the episodes with your leg."

Rebecca gasped as tears formed and scrolled down her cheek. Her grip to James's hand tightened.

James took a deep breath and rubbed the back of his neck, "So what's the good news?"

"Well...the good news is...that it appears to be that of the relapsing-remitting type. Which means it is not acute or fast acting, but is rather chronic and can take some time for the severity to set in. The symptoms will come and go with flareups. Some can last for weeks or months and if it's a bad one, maybe a year or two. We can offer treatment that can help to offset and prolong these symptoms. And there are many experiments and test being conducted each day to help find a solution to this disease.

"So, there is always the possibility we find a cure."

Rebecca crashed into James chest and sobbed as the tears soaked his gown.

James patted her back with his right and rubbed his eye with his left palm. He swallowed the lump that had formed in his throat and started a question, but it was too hoarse to be coherent. He cleared his throat and tried again.

"How long before the symptoms worsen?"

"It depends. Seems to vary with each patient. On average...ten to fifteen years. However, as new medicine is developed...hopefully longer or not at all. A good thing is...you're young which gives your body a much better chance of fighting it. I would not be surprised if you lived a rather normal life, other than the symptoms you've experience with your leg...for another twenty years...before the flareups became more frequent."

Twenty years? Flashes of himself crippled in a wheelchair flooded his mind.

It can't be? He can't be crippled by fifty, can he?

††††††††††††††††††††††

WALTER HAD settled in as he took Jerry's job of placing the raw paper under the cutter before passing it off to Jerry who separated the cuts like James would.

Ethan manned the cutter and with each press of a button, dropped the razor-like blade, slicing...cutting...shredding fibers as he watched he tear away paper...piece by piece.

Ethan glanced at the clock.

11:55

Do it. Now is your chance.

DO IT. DO IT. DO IT.

A voice echoed in his mind. It sounded like Kirkland, but he wasn't sure.

The blade dropped and sliced, as it tore away at the paper fibers.

It raised as Walter reached under and pulled the sliced paper through.

A process they'd done for the past two hours.

DO IT. DO IT. DO IT.

Ethan marinated the thought.

They'd take a lunch break at noon. He'd have to do it before break.

He stole another glance at the clock.

11:56

His heart began to flutter as his palms rung with sweat. He could just picture Walter under the blade as it came crashing down. If he listened hard enough...he could hear his screams. He quaked as such euphoria was too much. Mother would be so pleased. She was sure to enjoy this one. It'd give her even more strength than the last one.

A bead of sweat rolled down his forehead, passing a few whiteheads and warm warts along the way. It stung as it landed in his left eye. He blinked and wiped it with the back of his hand.

The blade returned to its position above the paper, with only one purpose, to tear away at whatever laid below it, whether it be paper or...human flesh.

The paper jammed.

Ahh...such providence. It's truly meant to be.

Walter stretched under the blade as he wiggled and wrestled the paper loose.

This wasn't the protocol, but he was new, and Jerry had his back turned as he separated the cuts into their destined bins. One for the good. One for the bad.

NOW!

Ethan slammed the button.

The blade dropped.

Jerry was turning around as he caught the horrific view before him.

Walter fully underneath the falling blade.

"Look out!"

15

Dale Pennington, reclined in his office, feet propped on his desk, with a crooked neck as a phone was sandwiched between his ear and shoulder.

In his hands was that same foul ball that he could never find the slider grip on. He rubbed it up as if he was about to make a pitch.

On the other end of the line was an unhappy client with a major newspaper press. She squawked at him about a late arrival of material. No paper equaled no newspaper. Bad deal.

Dale could barely get a word in, as a few times he even removed the phone from his ear and wagged his head in disgust. Anger tore at him like a garden tiller, but he had to keep his cool and remain polite. Which for him, could be hard to do. He never was one to willingly keep his cool. Something he was still working on.

He heard a scream in the back but shrugged it off and figured it to be the guys fooling around.

The screaming didn't stop. It sounded like someone in mortal agony.

Other voices piped up over the roar of machinery which was beginning to quiet down with a soft hum.

What in the devil is going on back there?

Dale turned his attention to a monitor high in a corner that showed a four-square surveillance of the mill.

Men were congregating somewhere in a hurry. A few bolted passed his glass window.

"I'm sorry Miss Carrolton, I'm going to have to get back to you, something has come up here at the mill. I have to go, please forgive me. I will get back to you shortly."

The high-pitched squawking never lost pace and continued even as the phone was resting into its cradle.

Dale grabbed his hat off a rack near his door and gripped the door knob the same time Billy Ross did on the other side.

In a panic, almost hyperventilating, he managed to force out, "Call 9-1-1! Quick! It's Walter. The cutting press. Not good."

Dale's eyes bulged at the thought as his mind raced as quick as Miss Carrolton could spit out insults. Which had to of competed with the speed of light.

He hurried to the phone on his desk, yanked it from its cradle and pounded out the number.

16

An ambulance was on the way and with Dale's sense of urgency, they would hopefully be there before Walter had drained of blood.

Dale ran toward the crowd which must've have been fifty yards from his office. He passed through like a salmon swimming upstream.

After moving a few men aside and peering in between heads that looked on in horror, he could now see a pair of dirty pant legs and work boots writhing on the ground.

Gut-wrenching screams filled the air.

He could hear Jerry, Hank and Kurt's voice as they offered comfort and applied pressure to the wounds. He made his way to the front but hadn't prepared himself for the scene before him.

The grey concrete floor was now splotched a shiny red. The smell of Iron was strong.

Walter's body quivered as he screamed and squirmed. His color turning paler by the second.

Jerry, Hank and Kurt were now painted the same shade of red as the concrete floor and so was Walter.

Ethan paced to and fro a few feet from the three with a hand to his hip and the other to his head.

Dear God! Dale knelt at the feet of Walter and tried to keep him still.

"Someone needs to put his arms on ice!" Jerry screamed as he applied pressure with his shirt just below the tourniquet. Hank did the same. Kurt was ripping off his shirt and was about to apply pressure where needed.

Dale had seen two red stained figures about the length of a guitar's neck, out of the top of his peripheral moments ago. But it didn't dawn on him what they were until he heard Jerry's words replay in his mind.

It was now that he realized Walter was missing both his arms just above the elbows. He raised his vision and there were Walter's bloodied arms as each hand curled as if clutching a foul ball. One hand even looked to have gripped a slider…or was it a cutter?

The sight and thought were enough to send his stomach tumbling. He stood and made it about fifteen feet before curling over and losing his lunch.

Lettuce, tomato, cheese, strands of packaged turkey meat and stomach acid now covered the cold grey floor as it competed with the red stain behind him.

Walter's screams were so loud and immobilizing, Dale could hardly think.

Billy was emptying a trashcan outside the break room. He disappeared back inside. Ice could be heard clanking to the bottom of the can. Here he comes, sprinting out of the break room, toting the ice filled trash can.

Dale coughed and hacked a few times before finally straightening his spine.

He knew what it was for but couldn't bear watch as Billy put it to use. Instead, he squatted back down near Walter's feet. Glanced at his watch and wondered how much more time he had left.

It'd been four and a half minutes since the 9-1-1 call. By his estimation, it should take eight to ten minutes for them to arrive.

"The bleeding has slowed, but he's still leaking. We just have to keep him awake, can't let him doze," said Jerry.

"Yeah, I know. I need another shirt...mine's soaked," said Hank.

Dale unbuttoned one of his favorites, slid it off and passed it on to Hank, who quickly removed the old one and stashed Dale's at the bloody nub.

"How long before they get here?" asked Kurt, his words spewing fast.

"Should be close. We need to move him to the parking lot, so we don't waste time when they get here. He needs to be ready, the second they pull in," ordered Dale.

The men agreed.

"All right guys, we're going to move him to the parking lot so we can get him on the ambulance quicker. We're going to need some help," said Dale.

Kevin Gantz, Ethan Thompson and a few others stepped up and helped get Walter in the air as they rushed him toward the door.

Ethan gripped Walter's right pants leg near the knee as he stole glances towards Walter's hazy eyes.

"I hope you die...you sorry rascal. No one messes with me without paying a price." Ethan mumbled to himself.

They're eyes met.

"You son-of-a-." Walter blurted a handful of times with the derogatory slang for a female dog at the end.

Ethan turned his attention toward the door they were aiming for.

"Sshhh...Walter...calm down now," said Jerry.

"You did this to me! You killed me! You sorry son-of-a—" Walter screamed as his eyes were so full of rage they flooded with tears.

Ethan ignored his banter as it continued all the way through the door and into the parking lot.

Jerry and the others tried to calm him, but just couldn't get the thought off his mind.

Billy followed behind them carrying a trash can full of ice and arms. The hands stuck out the end as one of them still had a grip that resembled that of a cutter.

After only waiting for about two minutes according to Dale's watch, the siren howled in the distance and before long the ambulance was roaring into the parking lot, throwing up dust and gravel.

It swerved up next to the men carrying their dying co-worker. The passenger and driver jumped out and rushed to sling the back doors open.

An EMT awaited in the back.

The men hoisted Walter up on the gurney as the passenger and EMT began their work. He still screamed his insults as he glared at Ethan until the ambulance door blocked his view.

Sirens blared and the engine roared, as dust flew behind the tail lights. The men sighed and wiped their brows as they watched the ambulance disappear toward a crowded US-17.

Maybe they will have a flat on the way there. If it wasn't for Jerry, Walter would be missing a lot more than just his arms. So close. Dang Jerry.

Dale squinted and rubbed his eyes with his forefinger and thumb, "Alright. Everyone listen up. Get your things and call it a day. Be back in the morning, eight o'clock. We'll meet outside my office and...I'll...give updates and...further instructions. Okay?"

The men nod.

Dale turned to Ethan and said with piercing eyes, "I'll see you at seven sharp in my office, if you ever expect to earn a paycheck from me, that is."

Ethan lowered his gaze and bobbed his head.

Regardless if he lost his job, it wouldn't matter, he'd eased Mother's pain for the moment. It'd be enough to get her to the next feeding. Which would be soon rather than later. Gosh, how he loved working for Kirkland. His tongue slithered around the back of his teeth, feeling each line as a strong iron flavor sat on his taste buds.

Mother will be so happy and hopefully Kirkland will be too.

17

Later that morning, Ethan eased into his driveway as the brakes of his Chevy Suburban squealed. He killed the engine, dangled an arm out the window and rested his chin in his right hand.

"Now what?"

He waited for the voice. It'd show up. It had to, didn't it?

A few moments passed. Silence.

"Now what?" he demanded.

"GET OUT OF DODGE! THAT'S WHAT!" Kirkland's voice crackled with a fiery tone as it resonated throughout the walls of Ethan's mind.

He squinted and twitched his eyes. Then took a deep breath.

Relieved that the voice was back but also secretly fearing his presence, whether Kirkland knew it or not. He probably did, as it was fear that seemed to fuel him.

"What do I take? The Chevy or the box truck?"

"YOU GOT TO DITCH THE BOX TRUCK, YOU IDIOT! YOU CAN'T BE SEEN DRIVING AROUND IN THAT. GET RID OF IT. PAINT THE CHEVY AND DISAPPEAR."

Ethan nodded as his hot breath escaped his nostrils and flowed over his knuckles.

"BESIDES...I THINK YOU'LL LIKE WHERE I HAVE IN MIND. LOT OF POTENTIAL FOR YOU THERE. EVER HEARD OF PALM SPRINGS?"

He gave it a thought then wagged his head.
"PALM SPRING, CALIFORNIA. I THINK THAT'LL DO."

"California! You expect me to drive across country!"

"UH, YEAH. YOU'RE A BONA FIDE MURDERER, WHO JUST CHOPPED OFF ANOTHER GUY'S ARMS. THAT'S KIND OF WHAT THEY DO." Kirkland said with a smirk as his voice seemed to come to him from all angles, as it travelled through different octaves.

A moment passed.

"All right. I'll do it. I'll get out of town."

"GOOD...THERE IS JUST ONE THING I NEED OF YOU BEFORE YOU GO," the voice like a howling wind, thrust against Ethan's eardrum.

A chill ran down his spine. Kirkland knew the tone could manipulate him like a puppet.

Ethan gathered himself, cleared his throat and asked,
"What is it?"

18

Four hours had passed since Walter's dismemberment and James's diagnosis. Both were in stable condition. The emergency doctors were able to stop the bleeding and provide enough transfusion to spare Walter's life, but he would have to go on without his arms. At least from the elbow bones down that is.

As for James, he was resting in his hospital room with Rebecca by his side. The doctor said it'd be best for him to stay overnight and get the well needed rest. He would be free to leave in the morning.

Soft knocks drummed the door. James forced his eyes open, gave them a few good rubs and then glanced at the clock.

4:23

Rebecca awoke with a yawn.

"Come in," said James as he expected to see Dr. Santini or another nurse.

The door cracked open enough to reveal a African-American man, who held his cap in hand, wearing a familiar work uniform. Jerry Turner

"Hey there strangers."

"Jerry. How's it going man?" James said as Jerry gave him and Rebecca a hug.

"Oh, I'm good-I'm good. So how are you doing?"

James nodded trying to find the right answer, if there was one.

"I'm doing pretty good. A little banged up, but I'm good," He said as he glanced towards Rebecca.

Jerry noticed the look between the two.

"You sure?" he asked with a grin.

James started to speak, but Rebecca spoke for him.

"The doctor believes he may be in the beginning stages of MS."

"MS? Multiple—"

"Sclerosis," James and Rebecca said together,

"Oh Lord have mercy. I'm sorry. Are they sure?"

"They're pretty sure. They did an MRI and some other tests...everything points towards it. Said it explains the problems he's had with his leg giving out on him."

"Yeah, like the other day when you went down at the mill. Dang man." Jerry said lowering his gaze and wagging his head.

"What? You fell at the mill too?"

James admitting his guilt, tightened his, closed his eyes and nodded.

"How long has this been going on?"

"It's been off and on for the past few months, but the last week it became more frequent."

The room got quiet.

"Well, have you heard about what happened at the mill today?"

James shook his head.

"Huh...Walter Avery...the man got his arms cut off by the cutter. Ethan accidentally pressed it as Walter was trying to loose a paper jam. I had my back turned and didn't see what he was doing until I heard the blade coming down."

"What!"

Jerry nodded. "It was bad. The whole floor was covered in blood in just a few seconds. Luckily me and Hank were able to throw some tourniquets made from our belts on him until the ambulance arrived."

Rebecca cupped her mouth, "Oh my word, that's horrible."

"How is he? Is he all right?" James asked rubbing his forehead.

"He's good right now. He's stable. They weren't able to save his arms though. He lost them both right around the elbows. He's lucky...I'm telling ya, because when I turned around, he had his whole upper body stretched under the blade reaching for the jam. I thought it was going to cut him in half. I really don't see how he pulled back in time."

James shook his head and rolled his eyes, "it's all my fault. If I'd been at work today, he wouldn't have been under that blade. This would have never happened. If that was you, you would've known better."

"Now James, you can't think like that man. It was a freak accident. It could've happened whether you were there or not. Don't start thinking like that man. You have enough to think about as it is."

"He's right honey. You can't blame yourself. You didn't press the button, Ethan did."

That rose both their brows as they unlocked their gaze from one another and turned to Jerry.

"How's Ethan?" their voices in harmony.

"He's okay...I mean considering the circumstances. I'd really be surprised though, if he sticks around after this. He'll probably never come back or even if he does, I don't see Dale forgiving him. I heard him tell Ethan to meet him in his office at seven sharp tomorrow. You know how he is."

"Man...this is awful," James shook his head, "I tell you what, if he doesn't show up in the morning, give me a ring. I want to go by there once I get out of here. Just call my room."

"Honey, I'm not so sure that'd be such a good idea."

"What? Why not?"

"Well...I mean, maybe give him a little time to cope first, you know."

"I just think it could do him some good, if we swung by to check on him. Let him know somebody cares. I mean the poor kid doesn't have anybody."

Rebecca thought about it, then gently nodded.

"Yeah maybe you're right, I guess it won't hurt nothing."

19

Our Lady of the Reformed. a nice little Catholic church nestled like an egg in a bird nest under Spanish moss-covered live oaks on the good side of Georgetown. Father Louis Vendetti, an Italian immigrant who'd come to America to escape the evil invading his land during the war, had served the community of Georgetown for the past twenty years. He was what you'd imagine a priest to look like, white hair, clean shaven, black wire glasses and of course his black suit and white collar. Not to mention the white hair crawling out his ears and nose like spider legs. Father Vendetti was well liked and so was Our Lady of the Reformed. The reason Ethan was here.

He stood on the sidewalk looking up at the brick structure, a bell tower with a crossed steeple. A dark cloud passed behind. Next to the church was a small lot, bordered in with corrode and ivy covered brick and black iron fence. Inside, were old slate cross monuments honoring the dead.

A crow cawed in the oak above him. Ethan raised his head and locked eyes with it. Footsteps pattered along the pavement. Keys jiggled.

"Can I help you sir?"

Ethan lowered his gaze.

Father Vendetti was even smaller up close.

"Would you have a moment to talk?"

A moment passed.

"Sure. Follow me. I'm Father Vendetti by the way and you are?"

"Kirkland. Kirkland Luender."

"Nice to meet you Kirkland."

Father Vendetti found the right key and opened the door to the church. They stepped in.

"Come on in."

The musky smell of freshly cleaned carpet greeted them. Beyond the aisle of wood and red velvet pews...a large wooden cross held a life-size Christ.

Ethan couldn't remove his eyes from it. He was glued to the floor. His mind filling with the voices...the chanting. Father Vendetti now realizing he was no longer being followed, was half way to his office when he turned and asked, "Ahh...yes...it's the eyes isn't it?"

Ethan blinked away his glare, "Huh?"

"The eyes of Christ. They know the very depths of who are yet love you fiercer than any mother or father on earth. They've stopped me in my tracks more than once too."

A moment passed.

"So, what brings you here?" Father Vendetti said as he pushed his office door open and held it with his back to it, motioning for Ethan to enter.

"Thank you," Ethan said in passing, "Well...I have a friend that I'm really concerned about."

Ethan scooted a wooden chair across the maroon carpet and sat with grace, his eyes locked on the crucifix mounted to the wall next to where Vendetti would sit.

"I see," Vendetti shut his door and crossed to his chair, "Well, what has you concerned?"

Ethan cleared his throat and crossed his leg and folded his arms, "Uh. Well, you see I think my friend may be experiencing something paranormal. Um. You know, perhaps something evil."

Father Vendetti interlocked his fingers across his groin and gently nodded with a firm jaw, "Go on."

Ethan wiped his face with his palm and said, "He's uh, saying he hears voices at night and feels like someone's watching him. You know, like the eerie feeling you get when someone sneaks up on you and watches over your shoulder? That kind of thing."

"I see."

"What should he do?" Ethan's eyes bouncing between the father's and the crucifix.

Vendetti craned his neck around and looked to the cross above him. He peered at Ethan out the corner of his eye as he began, "What's your friends name?"

"Frankie."

"Hmm. Is Frankie a believer?"

"No, not really. I don't know. Hard to say."

"Mm hmm. Tell him he needs to pray the Lord's prayer with rosary beads and say his hail Mary's each night before these episodes begin," he said as he bent low and fumbled through a file cabinet. He pulled up and slapped three pamphlets on the oak table between him and Ethan. Instruction manuals for prayer and protection from evil.

"And if he likes, tell him he's welcome to come here for prayer. I can bless and anoint him to rid the evil. How old is your friend?"

"Nineteen."

"And how long has this been going on?"

"Since he was eleven."

"Really?"

"You think it could be uh, you know, like a haunting or something?"

"Possession?"

"Yeah."

"Hard to say without me being there and not knowing your friend. It could possession if he's not a believer or it could be oppression if he is," Vendetti narrowed his gaze and swallowed hard.

Ethan's eyes were back on the crucifix.

"Perhaps we should pray for your friend? Would you be objected?"

A long beat.

The lights flickered as a cool draft brushed through the room. Vendetti stood and looked next to the crucifix at the window, he thought maybe was left open.

"As a matter of fact, I would," Ethan said in a deep, grotesque voice, not his own.

Vendetti froze as he stood by the window. The crucifix beside him on the wall.

"Dear God!"

20

The house was dark and cold as Monday night pressed into Tuesday morning. Ethan paced it's rotten remains, bell ringing in one hand as the other clawed at either a bedroom door or the scabby warts on his face.

Voices. Some deep, some shallow, some high, some whispering like a passing wind and others chatting away like chatter in a high school hallway.

They were everywhere, bouncing off every wall, floor and ceiling. Speaking in their unknown language, with others repeating the words of his father as they rapidly recited one of his sacred rites,

"ALL SIN BEGINS WITHIN AND THERE IS NO CURE WITHOUT ATONEMENT. A SACRIFICE MUST NOW BE MADE TO EVER EASE THE PAIN."

Ethan screamed as his mind swarmed with the infestation of voices.

"I can't do it Kirkland! I just can't! I'll do anything else, but not that!"

Dark blobs the size of people buzzed around the room like hornets in his peripheral but disappeared with every glance. The darkness was so thick, it seemed to smother every breath.

The house reeked with the smell of rotten eggs.

Ethan covered his face in his palms as he banged his head against the door. Tears seeped through his fingers and fell to the floor.

Silence.

Yet a presence still to linger.

A child's giggle suddenly echoed throughout the home. Footsteps pitter-pattered from the hall way and stopped right in front of him. The child's giggle was enough to chill his spine.

He turned and peaked through a gap between his fingers. He gasped and forced himself against the wall.

"What's the matter Frankie? Don't you want to play?" a child's voice. It sounded so innocent.

But it didn't come from a child's mouth, it came from a man who's head and face were ravaged with deep wrinkles that snaked their way around the eyes, mouth and forehead like the Amazon River. The face was droopy as the mouth hung open in a drawl. The man had a big head, big ears, big hooked nose with a few warts and small patches of gray hair that looked like weeds scattered across his scalp. It looked like Father Vendetti, but much older and pale.

The old man glared at him with a forced smirk, wearing only a pair of white underwear.

If he'd stood beside Ethan, his head would've barely come to his thighs. His body was that of a child. Pale skinned and weak.

If you'd just seen him form the neck down, you'd though it was a pre-pubescent boy until you saw the face.

The body and head just didn't match. It was an un-godly sight to behold. One that burned in Ethan's mind.

It was enough to freeze Ethan's back to the wall like a rat stuck in a glue trap.

He tried to scream, but nothing would form. His jaw was forced wide from the initial shock, as it grinded against the hinges.

But no matter how hard he tried to force a scream or even a flinch, nothing worked, except one thing...his senses.

He could see the old man/child staring at him. He could smell the rotten eggs. He could hear the old man's/child's voice. He could feel the darkness as his back pressed against the wall and his buttocks sat flat on the floor. And he could taste the sulfurous breath rolling out from the creature that stood before him.

His body began to tremble. The strong smell of urine mixed with the stench of rotten eggs. His groin felt warm. He'd must've wet himself.

The old man/child stood there, still wearing that same smirk that was enough to stop time.

"Well?" he asked in a deep tone. Much different from the boy's voice earlier.

They stared at each other in silence.

"Are you going to do it?"

Ethan tried to force his tongue to form the words, but it sounded like a doctor was checking his throat. His tongue just didn't work, it was like someone was restraining its strings.

"Hmm. I see. Well, do you want to play Frankie?" the man's voice tapered off to the boy's voice once again. He giggled, then bolted down the hallway.

Ethan's feeling and voice was slow to return.

With tingling and weak legs and arms that felt like rubber, he slid his back against the wall and forced himself up.

His blood was cold. A vapor escaped his mouth after each gasp for air. His heart gained speed with each pump of blood.

The voices returned as the child's giggle had faded in the background.

Ethan rung his little bell faster than ever as he jolted for the bathroom.

He entered and slammed the door behind him. The voices and blackness followed as they must have seeped under the door.

He cuddled into a corner of the tub, wrapped his arms tight around his knees and rung his bell.

He squinted his eyes as hard as they would allow him to. His chest aching with a heart thumping like a bass. He was covered from head to toe in gooseflesh as every hair on his body was fully erect.

Voices. Voices. Voices.

"All sin begins within and there is no cure without atonement. A sacrifice must now be made to ever ease the pain."

Their voice was mixed with that of a growl and hiss as they sped through the rite faster and faster.

"All sin begins within and there is no cure without atonement. A sacrifice must now be made to ever ease the pain!"

Faster and faster and faster.

"Stop it! Stop it! Leave me alone!" Ethan screamed, emptying his lungs of air.

Silence.

His shoulders began to shake vertically as he sobbed with his face buried in his arms that were wrapped with a death grip around his legs.

Thud! Thud! Thud!

Heavy footsteps approached the bathroom door.

No! No! No!

Thud! Thud! Thud!

"Kirkland! Make it stop! Please!" His voice now in a whimper as tears and snot oozed down his face.

"SORRY. I CAN'T STOP WHAT YOU'VE BEGUN." The voice rebounding off the walls.

Thud! Thud!

It stopped at the door.

A moment passed

Bam! Bam! Bam!

The door jolted with each blow.

Bam! Bam! Bam!

The door knob rattling, the hinges quaking.

The old door won't withstand much more. It can't, can it?

The deep roar and bark of a vicious dog gave Ethan a start, as he almost crawled out of his flesh, like a snake shedding its skin.

The dog turned his claws toward the bottom of the door.

Bam! Bam! Bam!

The scratching, clawing and barking continued.

"I can't do this anymore! I quit!" he screamed stretching the syllables as tears filled the tub.

"WELL...GET READY TO MEET LUCINDA. ENDER WON'T BE FAR BEHIND."

"Noooo! No! Please nooo!"

"TOO LATE MY FRIEND."

A voice pierced the air in the distance like a damsel in distress. It penetrated every wall and stabbed at his heart and mind like a dagger. He was poisoned with fear as the very thought of her was enough to make him sit up wide eyed for nights on end. Let alone her screams, which almost forced him to jab spikes in his ears once. Now, he wish he'd done it.

Bam! Bam! Bam!

The scratching and clawing would tear through any second. The dog's hot breath trickled under the door in a vapor.

Ethan's teeth chattered as frost covered the bathroom mirror.

Lucinda's scream crept closer.

The back of his head throbbed with a sharp pain. He combed his hair and found the spot with a finger. It was met by another, but not his own.

A bony finger had penetrated the scalp from within as a sharp finger nail scraped its way passed the flesh and gripped Ethan's finger with such a force, he thought he'd lose it as he yanked it back. It slipped from the woman's finger that had protruded out of his head.

Bam!

The door flung open.

Ethan jumped and faced his soon to be killer.

A black dog stood in the doorway with fangs bared and dripping with saliva as he growled with an intense glare that penetrated Ethan's soul.

Standing beside the canine was a woman wearing a potato sack as she carried a large crucifix, like the one Ethan had nailed Melissa Berkley to.

Ethan trembled in the corner of the tub like a child.

Lucinda must have entered the home as her scream sounded like it came from the living room

The dog lunged with a ferocious bark, as Melissa and Lucinda screamed so loud, Ethan had to cover his ears. He slammed his eyes belted out, "Jesus! Oh God! Help me Jesus!"

The name, always so foreign and useless, but at a time like this, it never felt of such value.

An eerie hush filled the room. The house was empty.
The frost on the mirror began to melt.
What just happened?

Weds
6/06/81

I can't believe it. I don't want to believe it. Will's gone. He never came home from school yesterday.

I knew he shouldn't have walked home alone. I tried to tell him to take the bus like usual, but for some reason, he didn't want to. I think it might have had something to do with Frankie.

I don't think he felt comfortable around him since his mom wouldn't allow him to hang out with him anymore. Ever since Will told her about Frankie and his dad's new religion.

I should've walked with him. Gosh! I'm so stupid. Why did I let him go alone?

I'm sorry Will. We're going to find you buddy and whoever did this is going to pay, I promise.

David Hoffman

Journal Entry of David Hoffman

Wednesday

6/06/81

AGE 11

21

Seven o'clock Tuesday morning came and went with a

no-show for Ethan. Which wasn't that surprising to Dale Pennington. Detectives and police had spoken with Dale and agreed to speak with Ethan right after Dale was finished.

So now, with it being ten after nine, detectives were on their way to a house in the Crow Creek neighborhood.

††††††††††††††††††††††

JERRY HAD spoken with James around eight-thirty and let him know Ethan never showed. Twenty minutes later and with a clearance from Dr. Santini, James and Rebecca gathered their things and were heading to Ethan's house.

††††††††††††††††††††††

JAMES AND REBECCA pulled into Ethan's empty driveway at nine-fifteen. Rebecca climbs out of her fiat and does a half circle around the front to get to James on the passenger side. With her help, he manages to get to his feet and move along with a cane and Rebecca's hand under his elbow until he was good enough on his own.

They make their way to the front porch, where they notice something white spiked to the front door.

Rebecca helps him up the steps. His knee and back ached, but he was curious what was on Ethan's door.

He gets to it and rips the white piece of paper from the spike and begins reading it to himself as Rebecca read it over his shoulder.

I'm sorry. I have to leave. I can't stay here in this town after what happened. I feel terrible about Walter and I can't bear to ever return to the mill after that. His screams and the bloodied mess will forever be etched into my mind. I have to get away and start a new life and move on the best I can, like none of this ever happened.

I'm sorry Walter, for what I've put you through. I'd do anything to take it back, but I think the best thing would be for me to disappear for a while. Maybe one day, we can work something out. But until then, I feel its best this way.

James and Rebecca: Thank you so much for being so kind to me in the short amount of time we got to spend together. I will never forget your kindness and hospitality. James you are a good man and someone I wish I could become one day if only my past would allow it...

The sound of tires easing over the pavement gained their attention. A black Ford Crown Victoria eased in just behind their fiat.

"Must be looking for him," said James.

He and Rebecca return to the note.

I hope that with time, I can bear to return to Georgetown and continue our friendship. But until then, I wish you guys all the best and hope to one day see each other again.

Ethan

"Hmm," said James as he sighed and looked at Rebecca who was wiping a tear away.

"Excuse me? Is this Ethan Thompson's residence?" a deep voice questioned as a man in a black suit and tie stood between the driver's seat and car door of the Crown Victoria.

James cleared his throat, nodded and returned with, "Yes sir, it is. I'm assuming you must be looking for him?"

The man motioned to the passenger who opened the door and stood to their feet. It was a black female detective

They make their way to James and Rebecca on the porch.

"And who are you?" asked the man.

"I'm James Randolph, a co-worker with Ethan and this is my wife, Rebecca."

"I see. I'm Lieutenant Randy Callahan. This here is Detective Ann Marshal."

They shook hands and nodded.

"So, I assume you know of the accident?"

James dipped his head.

"What happened to you?" asked Marshall.

"I was in a car wreck yesterday on my way to work. Found out I have M.S., that's what caused the wreck, I couldn't move my foot to the brake, so I slammed into the back of someone."

"My word...that's terrible. I'm sorry to hear that."

"Wow...I'm sorry," added Callahan.

He and Marshall then asked almost simultaneously, "So, what do you have there?"

James passed it to Callahan who read aloud for his partner.

"So, any ideas where he might've run off to?"

James and Rebecca wagged their heads.

"Well...James, you remember he did say something about having lived near Graves once."

That got the detectives attention as they both glanced to one another.

"Yeah...he did, didn't he?" said James.

"Graves?" asked Marshall.

"Yeah, you know, just right down the road."

"Yeah, we know where it's at. Its where we found Melissa Berkeley." Callahan said as he began jotting notes.

"Wait, you're not trying to say Ethan had something to do with that are you?" asked James.

Callahan finished his writing and glanced up from his pad, "Look...I'm a detective..." he raised his badge that hung low around his neck as a reminder, "...okay, I don't accuse anyone of anything, unless there's some facts that point their way. And right now...there's a few pointing toward Ethan Thompson. Now...I'm not saying he's guilty, but I'm not saying he's innocent either," he looked to Marshall and said. "Radio dispatch and tell them we want a warrant to search the place."

She nodded and headed back to the car.

"Now what kind of car did he drive?"

"Um, a uh, Chevy Suburban. Baby blue with a camper on the back. I want to say it was a 1980 model. He's got a box truck too. it should be around back."

Callahan nodded, then turned to Ann in the driveway who was speaking to dispatch on the radio.

"Put in a BOLO for a baby blue, 80 Chevy Suburban with a camper."

She nodded and spoke into the handheld radio as she stood in the crevice of the door.

"I want you two sticking around. Once back up arrives, me and Detective Marshall are going to search the house. Just hang tight with my officers once they get here, as I'll probably have some more questions about Ethan."

"Okay," said James as Rebecca nodded.

"So, did he talk about his relatives any?"

"Well, he said his mom died a few years back and that he went and lived with his aunt and uncle for a little bit, before moving back in with his dad here. Said his dad left him though. Been living here with no power or water for a while."

Marshall was heading back to the porch now.

"Hmm," Callahan scribbled and flipped a page, "what about school? He say where he went to high school?"

"Said he was homeschooled."

"Really? Hmm...okay...umm, Ann can you continue questioning them? I'm going to go check around back for this box truck."

"Yes sir."

He handed his notepad to her as he headed for the steps and then angled around the side of the house.

After answering a few questions from Marshal, Callahan came back around the house, "The box truck ain't here either."

††††††††††††††††††††††

WITHIN FIFTEEN minutes, back up had arrived. Two patrol cars and four officers. Two stayed with James and Rebecca as the other two followed Callahan and Marshall into the darkened home with guns drawn and flashlights gripped alongside their weapons.

James could hear the floor creak and pop as they combed the home, along with faint voices.

Couldn't have been more than five minutes, when the two officers came briskly out the front door, their faces drained of blood, eyes wide, breath in short gasps.

Callahan and Marshal weren't far behind, their faces in similar expressions. Marshal marched to the car and made haste to radio in to dispatch. Callahan crossed to James and Rebecca, wiping his brow with the back of his hand. In his other hand was what looked like a piece of paper.

What the heck did they find in there?

"Uhh…James…Mrs. Randolph…we've got a problem on our hands here." Callahan took a breath, looking at the paper in his hand as if he couldn't decide to show it to them or not. He finally turned it over with a reluctant sigh.

James' heart sank. Rebecca gasped.

It was four black and white photos of them walking about their home, taken from the cover of a wood line. They started in the kitchen, then headed into the living room with trays of food. The television set in the back ground showed J.R. Ewing wearing his suit and tie and cowboy hat from an episode of Dallas.

The last picture was of the back James' and Rebecca's head as they sat on the couch watching the program.

"That's not the only one either…there's more…lots more. Remember the Montgomery murders at the first of the year in Simmonsville? He's got similar pictures of them too."

A moment passed.

"Marshal is contacting forensics now."

James rubbed his face with his free hand, the other gripping the cane. Rebecca clung to his arm.

"What-what do we do? I mean…you really think he's after us? Why? What have we done to him?" James said.

Callahan sighed, "I don't know, but you need to be careful. I'll need to have a patrolman watch your place for a bit until we get all of this figured out. And I'll just say this," He stepped closer, "the Ethan you thought you knew, is not the Ethan that lived here."

A voice crackled from the car.

"Ann, can you get that?"

She nodded and went to the car.

Rebecca had the back of her fingers to her mouth, eyes shut, head wagging. James placed his arm around her and steadied himself with the other on his cane.

"Sir…we've got another body," came Marshall's voice.

"Huh? Who? Where?"
"Father Vendetti. Lady of the Reformed."

22

Police cruisers and black Crown Victoria's littered the road in front of Lady of the Reformed as if it held a hostage. An ambulance and coroner van sat on the curb in front of the doors. Two local news vans, Georgetown Times and The Sun News parked just behind them. Satellite dishes extended on top with numerous cords spiraling to the heavens. Most of the church was in a shadow as the Sun hid behind the clouds. The crow sat in the live oak, watching the people below.

Callahan and Marshall were stepping out of the car, their detective badges swinging below their chest as they hurried to the doors of the church.

An officer busied himself with rolling yellow tape around the perimeter.

Voices. Sirens. Reporters. Flashing lights. Dead leaves skittering across the pavement. A crow cawing from a slate tombstone in the graveyard.

"What happened?"

A man wearing collared shirt with the word, *SHERIFF* across his shoulder blades, stood in the doorway with his back facing the road. He turned and looked. His dark mustache rode up and down as he spoke, "Callahan. Marshall," he nodded, "The custodian found him like this about an hour ago. It's a sick man you've got on your hands Randy."

Callahan squinted his eyes and glared inside. It was dark, but he could hear people talking. A flash of light. A camera shutter followed by a loud hum.

What was that?

Flash. Shutter. Hum.

The body lit up.

No.

Flash. Shutter. Hum.

Dear god no!

Callahan and Marshall stepped into the darkness.

Flash. Shutter. Hum.

The pale body of Father Vendetti nailed to the cross like Christ flashed before their eyes.

He was naked just like Christ except for the loin cloth around his waist.

Flash. Shutter. Hum.

His head, wrist, and feet oozed blood.

Marshall gasped. Callahan placed his palm atop his head.

Flash. Shutter. Hum.

That's when the letters dripping in what looked like blood on the wall behind the cross popped out like a jack in the box.

†††††††††††††††††††††††

460 MILES southwest of Georgetown, travelling along I-10 in a dark green 1980 Chevy Suburban, missing the camper on the back, with classic rock blaring on the stereo was Ethan Thompson. Passing a bright green sign which read,

Tallahassee 4
Pensacola 193
Mobile 239

So far, he had travelled alone. No voices. No Kirkland. No Will, or any of the others he'd murdered.

He'd beat it. He must've, right? If not, then where were the voices? Where was Kirkland?

What he said back there must've scared them off.

The more he thought about it, the more uneasy he became. He didn't know what to think of being in his own company without the gnawing voices that scratched the inner chambers of his heart and mind.

What is this?

He felt a presence, but it was different.

He reached and turned the stereo knob to dim the music.

He listened and over the roar and hum of the tires, he could hear it.

It was his own heartbeat. He could hear it pumping blood through each vein and artery with perfect rhythm. He could feel the blood flow.

The feel and sound were nice. No voices were a pleasant change.

The first time since he was a child, he'd recognized his own presence.

Who are you? What have you become?

He remained silent as he let his own original, untainted thoughts process without interruption.

What are you doing? Why have you done this?

His heart picked up pace as the steering wheel greased with sweat. He never had enjoyed his own company.

He took turns drying his palms on his pants leg and before long he was chewing on a nail.

††††††††††††††††††††††

A BURLY ANGEL dressed in glowing white rode shot gun with him. He had been sent by the Great Spirit himself and was there to offer comfort after Ethan's request earlier that night. He rested a hand on Ethan's shoulder and did his best to quiet Kirkland and the others voices but was slowly losing ground. Kirkland saw a chance to flank and went for it. He called for backup and within minutes the Angel was forced to leave. He was outnumbered.

He conceded to losing the battle but would return to his commander with insight and a request for numbers to equal that of the rival. They would form a strategy and try once more.

For now, he'd done what he was sent to do and that was to offer comfort the best he could, if Ethan would receive it. He seemed to respond well, perhaps a little better than expected. There may still be hope.

††††††††††††††††††††††

HE NEEDED HELP. He can't do all this on his own.

The thought crossed his mind.

Ethan nodded, but remained silent.

He needed Kirkland. He'd get caught if he tried to do it on his own. Wouldn't he?

Kirkland had protected him this long, he couldn't forget about him now, could he? Ethan would rather suffer the long nights to himself than to be crammed in some cell with a lonely Leeroy.

Tears clouded Ethan's eyes.

"Kirkland. I need you. Can you please help me? I'm sorry. I don't know what I was thinking."

Surely, he would hear him.

"WHY HELLO FRANKIE...THOUGHT YOU MAY HAVE WRITTEN ME OFF," his voice sizzled as it resonated within the cab of the truck and Ethan's mind.

It startled him, but it was a relief from his own presence. He didn't know which was worse, being stuck in a cross-country road trip with himself, or having Kirkland in his ear with all the other voices. If he had to choose, he'd likely choose the latter.

He shut his eyes for a quick moment, swallowed the lump in his throat, wiped a palm and said, "I'm sorry for what I did Kirkland. But I need you, I can't do this without you. Can you please help me?"

"MY PLEASURE FRANKIE."

"Please...just call me Frank. For now, at least. Please."

"OKAY...I CAN DEAL WITH THAT. ANYWAY...NOW THAT YOU'RE BACK ON TRACK AND IN YOUR RIGHT MIND...I HAVE SOME BIG PLANS FOR YOU IN PALM SPRINGS."

"As long as it keeps me out of trouble, I'm willing to do whatever it takes."

"THAT'S WHAT I LIKE TO HEAR."

"And do you think the visits could ease down a bit?"

"WE'LL SEE. DON'T WORRY ABOUT THAT, JUST FOLLOW MY ORDERS AND YOU'LL LEARN TO COPE. THEY ALL DO SOONER OR LATER. YOU'VE GOT A LOT TO LEARN MY FRIEND AND I'VE GOT A LOT TO TEACH YOU," Kirkland smirked, "WHY YOU HAVEN'T EVEN HIT YOUR PRIME YET. YOU'VE GOT A LOT OF YEARS AHEAD OF YOU AND WE'RE JUST GETTING STARTED.

"I THINK YOUR MOTHER WILL REALLY ENJOY THE FOOD OUT HERE. CALIFORNIA HAS QUITE THE VARIETY. SHE'LL BE STRONGER THAN EVER BY THE TIME WE'RE FINISHED."

Thursday  March 16th, 1989

GEORGETOWN TIMES

Gruesome accident at Georgetown International Papermill lead police to possible suspect in local murders...

Horry County Sheriffs Office believed to have suspect in recent murders of Stephen Rickles and Melissa Berkely.

After a horrfic accident at Georgetown International Papermill, that cost a man both arms just below the elbows and nearly cost him his life, Ethan Thompson, a 19 yr old man who was recently hired at the mill was operating the cutting press that malfunctioned and severed Walter Avery's lower arms.

Horry County Detectives arrived Tuesday morning following the accident at Thompson's residence for questioning, but only to find the home vacant and a note left behind by Thompson, in which he expressed his need to "get away," in order to cope with the accident.

As if that wasn't enough for suspicion, what detectives discovered inside, was nothing short of that from a horror movie.

Claw marks riddled the walls, floors and back of doors, as most of the wall paper draped like shreded ribbons. Newspaper articles stretching from the 1950's to today, of missing people were spiked to the walls along with religious quotes and references as well as expressions of inner conflict scribbled in dried blood across the walls.

As detectives made their way into the kitchen, they discovered a refrigerator that was full of bleached white canine and feline skulls. Which along with the notes and writings of Thompson found in the house, lead detectives to...

Thursday   March 16th, 1989

GEORGETOWN TIMES

Continued from previous page...

...believe Thompson may be involved in a satanic or religious cult which practices animal sacrifice and possibly human sacrifice as well.

Causing more concern were the photos nailed to the wall of James and Rebecca Randolph which were taken from the cover of a tree line as Thompson snapped photos of the couple during their evening and nightly routine of enjoying dinner by the kitchen table and then retiring to the sofa for the night to watch their favorite television shows.

"I have been doing this kind of work for a long time now and believe me, I have had my fair share of weird and disturbing cases, which have caused me to lose sleep at night and I honestly have to say this one ranks right along top with them. I just couldn't believe what my eyes were showing me." Said Horry County Homicide Lieutenant of twenty-three years, Randy Callahan.

"It's crazy, I mean I knew the kid was a little off when I first met him, I just thought he was slow or something. I would have never imagined they would have found what they did in there. Heck, the kid just spent the night with us Sunday. My wife and I invited him over for dinner and offered him a place to stay for the night. It kind of makes my skin crawl to think this guy was at my house the other night and my wife and I invited him!" Said James Randolph, a co-worker of Thompson's.

GEORGETOWN TIMES

Continued from previous page...

Horry County Sheriff's Department is asking for your help in locating Ethan Thompson who is believed to be connected to the murders of Stephen Rickles and Melissa Berkely and advise to not approach or confront Thompson as he may be armed and dangerous

Due to the findings at Thompson's home, detectives have reason to believe he may not have travelled far and could still be in Horry County. Police ask that if you come in contact with Thompson, inform your local authorities immediately.

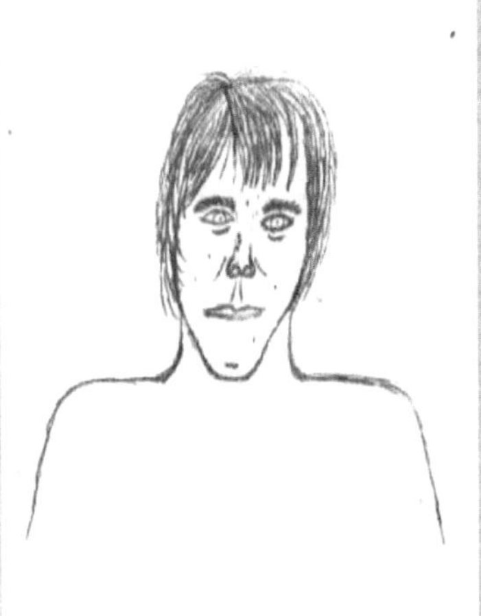

Description & Notible Characteristics:
Ethan Thompson, 6'2 175lbs, brown hair, squinty brown eyes, three warts along right side of nose, noticeable acne, scar across back of left hand, low lying neck and square shoulders.
If seen, contact your local authorities, immediately.

23

It was Wednesday, September 17th, 2014 and the fourth period world history class at West Brunswick High School was coming to a close as the clock read, *1:20*

Another ten minutes and the ringing would begin, sending the group of teens to find their way to the next class. For some it was Grammar and Rhetoric, for others it was Biology or Science and for a dreaded few it was Algebra or Geometry.

Whichever it was, most would rather skip and be on their way to retire to their room to play video games or arrange plans to hang with friends.

In the dimly lit room, the YouTube video Mr. McGaha played which documented the fall of ancient Rome came to an end.

"Could you get the light for me Jason? Thank you?" Said Mr. McGaha with his jet-black hair, red skin and sharp cheek bones.

Lee McGaha, a middle aged Native American man who traces his roots to that of the Waccamaw which belong to the Siouan Tribe, has taught at West Brunswick High School for the past twenty years. McGaha stays true to his roots and culture and never misses a meeting at the Waccamaw Tribal Grounds in Conway, South Carolina some fifty miles from Shallotte, North Carolina.

"All right, remember we will have a quiz on this next class. You can watch it again by going to the link I gave you, in case you need help refreshing your memory. Other than that, have a great rest of your day and I'll see you tomorrow."

The students hurried and packed their things and headed out the door for another lecture.

Jason Randolph was in the middle of the pack and was on his way to his Science class. One in which he enjoyed along with the company of two people close to him. He passes through the hall and comes to the entrance of room 112, meeting him there is his sister Lauren.

They give each other a smile and brief hug before entering the class room. They were usually the first two in the room and today was no different. They passed their teacher along the way as she had her attention to the white board where she was busy scribbling out notes to go along with her lecture for the day.

"Hey mom," said Jason and Lauren as they each gave Mrs. Rebecca Randolph a hug before sitting in their usual spots in the front row.

"Hey. How's your day been so far?"

"Good," said Jason.

"Okay...it was a little tough in Algebra today, but besides that, it's been good I guess," said Lauren.

Turning to her daughter she said, "Well remind me tonight and I'll help you with it," as students began to slowly trickle in.

"Yeah, I will."

Rebecca smiled and turned back to the white board where she finished sketching out what looked like a blank face of Mickey Mouse, with a bunch of positive and negative signs here and there and two capital H's along with one capital O. It was the structure of a water molecule.

She turned back around to a room half full of students as the rest had about five minutes before class would begin.

"So, how's everyone's day going? Got any big plans for the weekend?" Rebecca asked with a contagious smile that could brighten anyone's day.

The room was silent as most students thought about it and then wagged their heads.

"Oh c'mon...living at the beach, somebody's got to have something planned. Right?"

One girl spoke up and said, "Well, I think I might have some family coming into Wilmington for the weekend, probably going to hang out with them and maybe tour the battleship."

"Oh, that will be fun. Yeah, my daughter Lilly who is a senior this year at UNCW had an internship there her sophomore year. They say the place is haunted. She got to meet the night watchman, Danny, who has lived on the ship since the 70's, I think. You should hear some of the stories she's told us. Y'all remember all that?" Rebecca said as she turned and questioned Jason and Lauren who each gave a nod.

"Oh wow, really? I didn't know that. That's interesting," said the girl.

"Yeah it was pretty crazy. You'll have to get the guys book when you're there. If you're lucky you might catch him doing a book signing. He'll tell you some stories that'll make your skin crawl. He's a super nice guy though," said Jason as he twisted back in his desk chair.

"Yeah, she said she thought she might've seen something a few times, you know like a shadow passing by or something," added Lauren.

"Wow, I really want to go now. I've always had an interest in ghost and things. I'll let you know if I see anything," the girl smiled.

More students piled in and took their seats and after more small talk, it was time to get started.

The clock read *1:39*, but it was always a minute or two slow, so Rebecca began her lecture on the chemistry of water and other liquids. One in which she had taught so many times, she could probably maneuver through it in her sleep.

Another forty-five minutes and the day at West Brunswick would come to an end. Only one class stood between the students and the rest of their day and just one more day stood between them and the weekend.

† † † † † † † † † † † † † † † † † † † †

LOOKING OVER balance sheets and income statements, while marking them up with a pencil and jotting down a plethora of numbers was James Randolph. He was stationed out on the front porch of his and Rebecca's beach front home on Holden Beach.

He had a question about the cost of goods sold, so he dug the cell from his pocket and dialed the client.

The man answered on the fourth ring.

"Hello?"

"Hey Thomas, this is James with Randolph Accounting. How you doing?"

"Oh, hey James, I'm doing well how about yourself?"

"That's great, I'm good. Just had a quick question for ya. I'm going over your Income Statement now, I believe your Cost of Goods Sold might be off just a little. I ran all my numbers through but keep getting the same thing. You wouldn't happen to have that number, nearby would you?"

As James asked the question, the deep roar of a diesel engine neared the driveway followed by a releasing

PHOOSH sound from air compressors used for the lifts and brakes. The big yellow bus came to a squealing stop as the doors folded in, opening with a hiss.

James leaned his head over the railing and saw Kelly and Connor with their backpacks hurrying down the steps of the bus, both wearing big grins.

After a few squawks in his ear, he'd gotten what he called for.

"Okay...that's what I thought, that sounds more like it. I'll have it done and emailed to you by tomorrow afternoon. Appreciate it Thomas...have a good one."

He hung up and reached for the lever on his electric wheelchair. It surged forward as he crossed over the decking boards. The sound reminded him of the rumble strips on the highway. He passed through the opened sliding glass door and made it to the living room just in time for the front door to swing open.

Kelly and Connor, their nine and six-year-old daughter and son, burst through with smiles and laughter.

They'd evidently raced each other from the bus to James. They ran to him as Kelly just edged her brother. They hugged and squeezed their daddy tight.

James and Rebecca had adopted the siblings when Kelly was only three and Connor just an infant. Having always wanted a big family, it seemed the man beyond the kitchen ceiling that day, agreed with what James said about his wife and didn't withhold life's greatest blessing...family. A big one at that.

"Hey babies...y'all have a good day at school?"

"Mm-Hmm," said Kelly.

Connor gave a grin the size of the boarder of California and Nevada.

"Learn anything new?"

"No, not really," said Connor after giving it some thought.

Kelly chipped in, "We learned about fractions and decimals in math today. That was something new, but I didn't like it too much. Oh, we learned some about Lincoln in history. Did you know he was a famous wrestler?"

"Well, I don't know if I would say famous, but yeah he was pretty good. What else did you learn about him? Surely that wasn't the highlight for the lecture. Abraham Lincoln, world's famous wrestler." James said like a tv show host.

Kelly and Connor chuckled as they make their way into the kitchen. James followed behind, manning the controls of his wheelchair.

It'd been twenty-five years since his diagnosis, and he had fared better than most at this point. Doctor Santini was happy how he had adapted to the changes and how well he'd handled everything this new life was throwing at him. Not to say he hadn't had his lows, because boy, had he. He'd been so low, it took all he had at times just to reach and touch rock bottom.

From the waist up, he was just as strong and functionable as he ever was. Not without his occasional episodes where one of his hands or sometimes both if it was a bad one, would draw up and ignore his commands, just like his foot did when it decided to remain on the gas pedal that day. It'd remain cripple for days and sometimes weeks on end during a flareup. But besides the occasional episodes, James was in good shape, all things considered.

From the beltline down, now that was a different story.

He slowly began losing feeling in his legs about six years ago. Two years later, he was completely paralyzed from the knees down, which forced him into a manual wheelchair, which he hated with a passion.

Dr. Santini had hoped it was just another flareup, but this one didn't want to leave.

It wasn't until two summers ago he finally got the electric chair which allows him to motor around with speeds that could win a grandpa race any day of the week. It turns on a dime too, something the old one wasn't too skilled in. Through the highs and many lows of dealing with such a disease, James and Rebecca were faring the best they could.

Having always had an interest in budgeting money, James took online classes and was able to graduate with a degree in Accounting within three years and would go on to earn his CPA. Then after years of hard work, strict budgeting and saving, the two were able to purchase their dream home.

Holden Beach was a well needed change of scenery, not that Georgetown wasn't fine in its own right, but like Jerry had told him all those years ago, they got out before the current got them. Jerry on the other hand wasn't so lucky. He stayed at the mill right up until his death. All those years of smoking finally caught up to him. He passed a decade ago from lung cancer. Boy, Jerry was a good man.

Now, with a beach front home, James would be reminded of his words each time he saw the rip current from his balcony. Jerry would be proud to know he and Rebecca had gotten out.

The police said it was good for them to get away anyhow, less chance of Ethan finding them in a place like Holden Beach. Small town feel, everybody knows everybody. They couldn't feel any safer here.

"Do we have any jelly?" came a soft voice from the kitchen.

James blinked.

"Uh...yeah...did you check the pantry?"

"I got it." Said Kelly as she closed the closet pantry behind her.

Connor pulled out a bar stool and rested his elbows, forming a teepee with his hands.

"So, what else did you learn about Abe?"

"Oh yeah, well we learned about how he helped put an end to slavery by forming the Emancipation Proclamation in 1864, I think?"

"63."

"63. That's right, 1863. His wife's name was Mary and they had a boy that died at a young age. And John Wilkes Boothe assassinated Lincoln on the night of April 14th, 1865. Two other guys tried to kill Andrew Johnson and the Sectary of State William Seward that night too. They planned to do it all at the same time. The guy that was supposed to kill Johnson, chickened out and the other guy almost killed Seward as he cut him up really bad with a knife," she stopped to catch her breath as she struggled with the jar of peanut butter.

She finally gave in and passed it off to James.

"Wow, I'd say you learned a good bit. A lot more than him just being a famous wrestler," James said with a grin and wink as he twisted the lid off.

He handed the jar back to her and then proceeded to scratch his graying beard as Kelly continued telling of her day. While Connor sat anxiously waiting for his mid-day snack.

Oh, the sweet reward of family. James and Rebecca's long-awaited desire was worth every second.

††††††††††††††††††††††††

TRAVELLING ALONG I-10, listening to the stereo hiss out his favorite band, the man busied himself with wiping the blade to a box cutter. Guiding the wheel with his hairy, bony wrists. A tight grin stretched across his wart and hair covered face. Long salt and peppered hair, down to his shoulders, with a matching colored beard draping past chest. Wearing a gray polo shirt with a patch on the right pectoral that read, "*Spectrum Cable*" while on the left pectoral, a patch read, **Kirk**.

He just finished his latest assignment and had already changed back into his work clothes. His night shift was different than his day job of installing cable. Though the cable job did come in handy with his night shift. He was sure to make lots of notes in the deep chambers of his mind. The voice of a life-long friend always helped, in case he forgot something important. He'd stored the layout of at least three dozen homes in his mind over the last two decades. Life was good for Kirkland Luender. Though not his real name, it had plenty of significance to him. The last name he pronounced, Lain-der, as he cherished the spelling, insisting it include the two names of those close to him. To his wife Leslie, and friends, he was simply known as Kirk.

He looked at the dash, 9:24. She'd wonder what took so long. He'd just have to tell her the customer was a picky one and had a thing for all the extra channels, causing him to stay late.

Of course, none of that was true. Who does cable after dinner? Unless it was an emergency, not that many. He'd spent the last three nights working late, and after much planning and scoping, he finished it only hours ago. He was through with the Westfield's, Mother was full. On to the next one.

He had three cable installations lined up in Beaumont for tomorrow. Nice area. Good money there. Good food too. He was sure to find something of Mother's liking. Although, to be honest, she wasn't that picky. Big, small,

black, white, green, it didn't matter. As long as she got her
nutrition to ease the pain, all was well. He couldn't stand
to see her suffer and by devil's hell, he wouldn't allow it. He
had to keep her fed.

Though he knew she was with him in spirit, he missed
seeing her physical form. He knew the day would come
when it'd right to return home and give her the final
offerings, the last meals. The last supper. It wouldn't be
much longer. Maybe one more meal on the West Coast,
then perhaps a return back east. Mother would be happy
to see him.

24

Sandwiched in between the remnants of Mt. San Jacinto and Mt. San Gorgonio among countless humongous white windmills with flashing red lights, that never ceased to blink, was Cathedral City. Nice, but not quite as rich as Palm Springs. Similar taste and look though. Affordable for a cable installer and IHOP waitress.

Rolling into the driveway of a small single-story home with tan stucco walls and iron colored clay shingles, decorated with plenty of palm trees and pebble gardens full of cheap flower pots in effort to blend in with the surrounding beauty of Palm Springs, was the residence of Kirkland Luender. His wife of eighteen years, and seventeen-year-old son waited inside.

He climbed out of the vehicle and shut the door. Toting a red and white igloo cooler in his right, he adjusted his company hat with his left.

Looked like every light in the house was on. Wouldn't be the first time he returned to a house like this. The television spoke from within. Sounded like the news. She's probably all worked up about the San Bernardino Phantom again. Last he checked, that was the name they were still giving the mysterious murderer of over twenty-two bodies in the past fifteen-years. They'd only found those he wanted them to find. They'd never find the ones he kept for himself.

He opened the door, the television grew louder, must've been on at least thirty or forty. The two lamps in the living room were bright, the television flashed its light across the carpet in front of the couch where Leslie and Alan sat.

He saw her rise. She had that look. Oh boy.

"Where have you been?"

He didn't answer.

"Hey...where have you been? You know I don't like being here at night by ourselves. For crying out loud, there's a freaking killer on loose. Don't you get that! Don't you care!"

No, he didn't. Because he knew she didn't need to worry while he was gone, it was when he came home, she should be worrying. Not that he could tell her that though. He often wondered what it would feel like, to watch her take her last breath at his expense. No. Stop it.

C'mon, stay off my case, it's for your own good. Don't wake the devils.

"What have you been doing?"

"Working. What do you think I've been doing? Huh? Somebodies got to pay the bills. Right? Last I checked tips from IHOP don't keep the power and water on. Here I am out here slaving to provide a home for you two and this is what I come home to?" his brows furrowed as he looked around Leslie to their son Alan on the couch.

Not getting a response out of him was worse than him mouthing back.

Kirk marched passed Leslie, shoving her out of the way. That got Alan's attention, always did. He bolted from the couch, "Hey!"

"Hey what! You think you all big and bad? Huh? Why I ought to drag you out here and grind you in the pavement. Teach you a lesson. Think you going to buck up me? Why don't you go out there get you job, freaking grow up and get a life."

"Kirk, stop it! He hasn't done anything to you."

Kirk cursed, unleashing a dam of vile obscenities.

"I ain't listening to this," he flicked the lamps off and snatched the remote from the coffee table, turning off the television. He took two steps towards the bedroom, when he heard a lamp flick back on. He stopped and slowly turned around. his head craned like an owl. His eyes blacker than black, nostrils flaring.

"What'd you turn that lamp on for?"

"Cause we're not going to bed yet," said Alan.

That was it. He charged after his son, snatching him by the collar of his shirt, yanking him into his reddened face and began a series of spit and hate filled cursing.

"Kirk! Stop it!" Leslie screamed.

He eased his grip, but not without giving him a good shove into the couch.

Veins bulged from his neck, his eyes protruded from their sockets, his breath was like hot steam from an old worn out engine.

"Who do you think you are to disrespect me in my own house...this is my house! You hear me! My house! And you have the balls to flick that lamp back on, *after I just turned it off*? Who the hell do you think you are?"

Kirk eyed both of them with his piercing glare. He'd love to just slam both of their heads through the sheetrock.

"Kirk! Stop it! What is your problem?" Leslie yelled as she tried to get between her son and this rabid dog of a man.

"You! You are my problem! See what you've made me do! This is all your fault! My life is a living hell because of you!" Kirk screamed as spit emitted from his mouth like popcorn.

"Well if it's so bad, why are you still here?" Alan asked in effort to steal Kirk's anger from his mom.

Kirk huffed out a growling sigh and marched back down the hall, snatching his keys from the key rack on the wall. He barged out the door all huffy like a pouty three-year-old, slamming the door so hard, one of the hinges broke loose. The sound echoed throughout the home.

The engine to the truck roared.

He'd eventually come back, either repentant or still seething. All depends on whether he'd had his pills.

By the looks and sounds of it, he was off his meds and had been for the past week. Roaming through life like a mad zombie that would lash out at the slightest opposition, everything was an agitation.

Oh, and don't dare ask the man a question. That was a no-no. Ask a question and you were sure to get full fire and fury of a demon loosed from hell.

"Don't worry baby, it'll all work out. Just be patient, we will get through it and when the timing is right, we'll find a way out."

"The time is now! He's gone, let's get our stuff and get out before he comes back. He don't deserve us and he certainly doesn't deserve you and you don't deserve to be treated like this."

"We can't. We don't have anything in order, if we leave now, then we will be homeless."

As Leslie and Alan were discussing the matter, the sound of a revved engine filed the driveway.

The mad man was back.

"See I told you we should've gotten out," said Alan.

Leslie grimaced at her possible mistake and lack of action.

The two sat on the couch in the living room, as the front door flung open, smashing a hole in the sheet rock with the door handle. In an even deeper rage than before, his nostrils flared as he gave a soul cutting glare to his wife and son with icy eyes.

The look was filled with jealousy, pride and every wicked thing known to man.

He marched off into the bedroom as he feet pounded at the floor like bowling balls.

Alan knew in his heart it was time to act. His dad was up to something more evil than he could ever imagine, but just wasn't sure what.

Could his dad really do it? Commit a murder-suicide? He was evil, but was he that evil?

Alan knew the guns were in the bedroom closet and he had a picture in his mind of his dad marching right in, grabbing the 12-gauge, running into the living room and blowing him and his mom to smithereens.

The thought was like a punch to the gut and a two by four to the face all at once. It dazed him for just a moment, but the sound of rattling around in the closet crept through the sheet rock and into the living room, right into Alan's ear.

He's going to do. This is it.

Alan rose quickly from the couch, motioned to his mom to "get out!" Then reached down and grabbed their fifteen-year-old border collie, in fear of what the crazed lunatic might do and headed for the front door, as his mom snatched up Katie and Chloe, their two chihuahuas.

Out the door they went. Where? Anywhere but here.

They lived in a gated neighborhood that was surrounded by a popular golf course. Their home was the one on the end that bordered the wood line that fed onto the golf course which eventually led to a large parking lot, where the family kept their 28-foot C class RV as it was too large to fit in the driveway.

If they could manage to make it to the RV, which would be about a mile-long hike through the woods and across the golf course, then they would have time to think of their next plan. Right now, the biggest concern was creating distance between them and shotgun.

Luckily Alan was smart enough to grab his keys which had a spare to the RV. He wanted to load up in his jeep that was parked in the garage but knew that by the time the garage door raised behind them, Frank would have already filled them with pellets.

So, the next best thing was to trek through the woods and get to the RV. At least they would have cover. He figured when his dad realized they were gone, he'd search the neighbor's homes first, which would have been the easiest way of escape, but also the riskiest, as he just knew that would be where his dad would begin his search.

Alan wrestled with the thought to call the police. Part of him wanted to, but another part was afraid of what might not happen. What if they did come out, but his dad put on a facade, like he was such an expert at and fooled the police into thinking that Alan and his mom were the crazy ones. After all, they were the ones running through the woods and trekking over a golf course at ten o'clock at night.

They both agreed that if they could just make it to the RV, then it'd be their getaway.

They marched onward along the darkness of the tree line which felt like a blanket that covered them from sight. The golf course felt like a desert, sand pits and rolling hills centered in between the line of trees.

They moved from cover to cover seeking refuge from the tree line and when they had to veer from that, they'd hide behind a hill, to catch their breath and check the map on

Alan's phone, to make sure they were headed in the right direction.

He'd cover the phone's glare as best he could, as he would lay as close to the ground as possible and angle the light to the ground.

Then after verifying their location, he'd check a security camera that he and his mom had secretly hidden for such a time as this.

It was a live stream camera that glared into the living room and down the hall towards the door of Frank and Linda's bedroom. The camera lay hidden in a thick of flowers that rested in a vase in the corner.

One would have to be looking for it to ever find it, otherwise it'd go unnoticed, just like it had from Frank for the past year.

Alan and Linda watched his phone's screen for about 60 seconds, no sign of Frank.

He had to of left. For all they knew he could have been out in this field stalking them like a mountain lion. He could hide in the brush and pounce at any moment or maybe just step out from the tree line behind them and take his shots, it'd be like shooting fish in a barrel.

Katie sniffed in the air then let out an unsure yelp which was quickly muffled by Leslie.

She smelled him. He was nearby. He had to be, didn't he? He was crouching like a cat ready to make its move. Alan could feel it.

"We got to move," he whispered to his mom. She nodded with trembling lips and gasping breaths. She'd be lucky not to have a heart attack, though she'd never be considered overweight, living with his dad had done quite the number on her blood pressure and right now it was likely touching the night sky.

Alan rose from his knees ever slowly and peeked over their protective hill as he peered out across the golf course in the direction his dad would most likely be coming from. He tried to adjust his eyes to the dark. He felt just like a gazelle wondering out in a safari, waiting to be devoured. Surely his dad had vision like a cat and probably spotted him the second he peeked over the hill.

Alan swept the field and tree line for any movement. Nothing.

"I don't see—"

Emerging from the dark like a ship out of a thick fog, a dark figure protruded from the tree line about two hundred yards away.

It was him, it had to be, right? He saw them, he heard Katie's muffled yelp. He'd locked in on them like a heat seeking missile.

This was a mistake. They should've never wandered out here in the middle of the night. Why didn't they just go to the neighbor and call the police, at least there would be witnesses, right?

This was the stupidest thing they could have done. It was a trap, and they walked right into it.

"We got to go, now!"

25

Leslie knew by the tone in her son's voice, he saw him.

She shuddered at the thought of what was to come. Fear gripped her with a clenched fist and almost squeezed the life out of her. Her heart pounded so hard, she thought she would collapse right there and give up the ghost.

But she had to get a grip on herself and keep fighting, she couldn't give up now, not here, not like this.

The two grab the dogs, crouched low and headed for another hill in the direction of the parking lot.

They still had a long way to go before they would make it to the clubhouse. She could see the lights, but they seemed so far.

They'd come this far. they could make it if they kept at it. She had to find the strength to keep going.

Twenty minutes passed, they were still alive and creeping ever closer to the RV. It was now within clear sight.

"Let's make it to that tree line over there, then let's make a break for it. What do you think?" Alan turned and asked her. She nodded.

They crept closer, before stopping to gather their strength and breath to make one last surge for safety.

A few minutes passed.

"You ready?" asked Alan.

She took a deep breath and nodded.

Alan extended a finger, then extended another and another.

"Go!" he said with a horse whisper.

They bolted from cover, out into the light, pounded the asphalt, eyes darting, head ducked and tense, just waiting for a gunshot to ring out. They rushed to the door of the RV. Alan with the key ready, he slammed it in, unlocked the door, helped his mother in, then ran around the front, unlocked the driver door, hopped in and turned over the engine.

It fired up, Alan threw the gear stick in drive and forced down the gas pedal.

They left the gated community, that was supposed to keep people like his dad out, but it could never protect against a Trojan horse.

They made their way onto I-10 and travelled for half an hour before getting off on exit 101. She had found a KOA campground in the small town of Banning, which was about thirty miles west from here.

Alan filled out the night registration form, dropped it in the box and found their way to an open site near the back that rested just below Mt. San Jacinto.

It was here they would spend the night, surrounded by campers. The one beside them, apparently being a former Marine, going by the Don't Tread on Me and American flag draped across the front of the large fifth wheel camper.

The sight offered a small bit of comfort, in the hopes of the camper beside them being home to a hardnosed, good hearted American man who wouldn't put up with Kirk's crap. She felt safe here. Her mind spinning a million miles a second, one distant word kept pounding in her head...Phantom...Phantom...Phantom.

† Devil's Den †

†††††††††††††††††††††††
SITTING BEHIND a computer screen, face illuminated in the darkened lobby, Kirk's fingers twitched fast along the keyboard. He had checked into a Holliday Inn for the night and tried to get some rest, but after a few restless hours had passed, in which were spent arguing with Kirkland and himself, he couldn't get away from the thought.

Arguing was something he seemed to have a passion for, it was one thing he was good at, he could win an argument against the best lawyer any town had to offer. He had his way of manipulating even the strongest mind, something that was a gift from Satan himself. One in which he cherished like an only begotten son.

Memories from his childhood flooded his mind as he tried to go back to when everything was normal, and he actually had a clean conscience, something that Kirkland had stolen that day at the Mooreland's.

He adjusted his glasses and squinted at the keyboard and pounded one letter at a time.

D-A-V-I-D H-O-F-F-M-A-N N-C

The search came back with a dozen different answers. One in which was a Facebook profile. He gave a quick left click. his heart pounded as he waited for the page to open. It revealed itself like an unrolled scroll.

There he was.

It was David. Aged of course, but it was him.

His profile pic was him with his wife and two college aged kids it appeared. A boy and a girl.

The cover picture seemed odd though.

It was a picture of David with a microphone in one hand a Bible in the other.

A preacher?

David Hoffman...a preacher?

This couldn't be the right guy. But the picture said otherwise. Yes, it had been over thirty years, since he had last seen him, but make no mistake the man in the picture was David Hoffman, one of his best friends growing up, besides Will of course.

He glanced over to the left-hand side of the screen where it read, Preacher of the Gospel at the Good Shepherd Church of Shallotte.

"You didn't go far did you?" smirking as he reclined in the chair and brought his clasped hands up to his chin.

"I need to see you David and I need to see you soon."

But there was one name that kept ringing in his ear. Kirkland just wouldn't give it up. He typed it out.

He found the website for a small accounting firm in Holden Beach, called Randolph Accounting.

"Well James...looks like I'll be seeing you again too."

It would be like a family reunion, David, James, and Mother.

He could hardly wait to hit the road in the morning. Though with this much stirring in his gut, he might not be able to wait that long. Kirkland probably wouldn't allow him to sleep anyhow. He likes being awake at night, especially in the early morning hours. The cold, dark streets were a lot like his mind. Oh, and it was a new moon too, even better. More darkness. Perfect.

26

Darkness clouded his view as if he was trying to peer through a thick blind fold. A cold and damp breeze chilled him to the bone. The crunch of sticks and leaves filled the air as a deep graveled howl echoed in the distance. Crickets chirped in harmony with the croaking hoard of bull frogs.

He had to be near water. Most likely a small pond or lake. Bull frogs seemed to like it there.

A white object up ahead slowly pierced through the blackness. It was on all fours and was as white as snow. It stood out like chalk on a blackboard.

The canine snarled its teeth at the man and let out a low baritone growl as every hair along its back was fully erect.

The moon had just stepped into view as it was hidden by a passing cloud. Its light licked up shades of the darkness, enough where the man could see the ground in front of him.

Leaves and sticks crunched behind him. He did a quick 180 and glared into the darkness. He couldn't see anything just yet, but something or someone was approaching. He squinted his aging eyes and peered ahead. There, two red eyes appeared about a foot off the ground, followed by a deep growl.

The dog was so black, he hid in the cover of darkness. A crow squawked as it flew overhead, but the growls on either side of him, held his attention.

The red eyes stopped where the moonlight ended. It chose to retain its cover. The red dots went black just for a moment and then flashed back to red. A slow blink.

Peering into the darkness, locked on the red glowing eyes, more leaves and sticks crunched behind him. He glanced over his shoulder, keeping the red eyes in his peripheral, the white dog approached from behind. It stopped beside him, leering at the dog of darkness.

He was relieved at the thought of having a possible ally.

The growling stopped. The frogs and crickets hushed. Everything was silent, except for a slight breeze that tickled the tree leaves.

"I know who you are. You call yourself a child of God. You really think a Holy god would want to have anything to do with you?" the deep, mechanical like voice scoffed at the thought.

"You think your Faith and traditions can protect you from me? You need to mind your own business old man, before you hurt yourself and bring an evil that no amount of prayer or rituals can protect you or your people from. This is a war you shouldn't be a part of and if you try to stand in my way, I will squash you like the roach that you are. I'm coming and I'm bringing every demon I can muster with me, so unless you want to end up like your friends at wounded knee, I advise you to step aside."

The old man gave his answer some thought as he worked up enough courage to speak what was on his mind. The white dog still wore a snarl, remained silent, but was ready to attack if need be.

"I know who I am, and I know whose I am. I am a child of the Great Creator. The blood of His sacrifice gives me power over anything that would even dare stand in my way. You have already been defeated on Calvary. You are a powerless and weak demon who is nothing more than an ant biting at the feet of an elephant. The Great Spirit will crush your head like the week little ant that you are. You are nothing and you are worthless, I stand in the power and Grace of the Almighty Creator." The old man's words cut through the darkness like a searing sword.

"Well...we'll just see about that."

The sound of a hammer being pulled back by a thumb was the last thing the old man heard before the bang of the firing pen slammed against the butt of the cartridge.

A bright flash spread across the darkness, illuminating the man behind the trigger and black dog at his side.

The old man jerked and squirmed, twisting the bedsheets before jolting awake. His heart felt like it had yanked him up from his pillow.

His chest ached with each pound and thump as blood rushed through his veins. He sucked in a room full air, but it wasn't enough, so he had to do it again and again and then once more.

His bed was soaked. His hands trembled.

The room reeked of gunpowder, whether for real, or only his imagination, either way, his spine chilled at the thought. His blood felt like it'd been turned into a slush.

The loud bark at the foot of his bed was enough to have him leap from his flesh. He gathered his breath, gripping his heart with a clinched hand.

"Sshhh. Sasha, it's all right girl. Just a nightmare, that's all," the old native said to his full-blooded Husky which had come to the side of the bed to check on her owner.

The old man reached down and petted the husky's head as he stared into her beautiful blue eyes.

"I think I saw some one of your ancestors."

The dog wined and licked the man's forearm.

"Yeah, I did. He was right there beside me protecting me from the darkness."

The man took a deep breath and sighed it out, "One in which I'm afraid may be approaching like an evening tide. I have to tell the others. We must prepare for what's to come. Our people and this town must be ready."

The old man said as he rolled to his back with interlocked fingers behind his head full of long black hair. He stared at the ceiling, thinking of the vision or nightmare, whichever it was.

Sasha leaps onto the bed and lays beside the man's hip.

"A war is coming girl, and I'm not talking about no war like we've seen in the past. No, this one is different. This is a spiritual war and we got to seek the Great Spirit and ask for the Creator's help. There's a darkness coming, and we've got to be ready for it."

27

Lee McGaha struggled to get through the day at West Brunswick as his mind kept returning to a conversation, he'd had with his brother on the way to school that morning.

Lee's brother Clennon had called and told him that their uncle Wes, who is the Tribal leader at the Waccamaw tribal grounds, had a vision that he wants to share with everyone that night at seven.

It wasn't very often he called these sorts of meetings, so when he did, you best make every effort to be there.

††††††††††††††††††††††

IT WAS SIX that evening, and the Randolph's had just finished supper and were retiring to the living room for a family movie night. Lily had come home from UNCW to stay the night, as her only Friday class got cancelled due to her professor attending a Marine Science conference.

So that Thursday after class she headed home to spend the night with her family.

It was good to have them all together.

Rebecca made homemade popcorn for everyone and had just finished passing around numerous full bowls

The previews of new movies were busy on the screen, as they waited for the family comedy to play.

"Hey mom, did you know that Mr. McGaha's uncle is the tribal leader for the Waccamaw Tribe?" asked Lauren.

"Yeah...seems like I remember him saying something about that. Why?" asked Rebecca.

Lily had a mouth full of popcorn she finished with a crunch as she said, "Yeah...I forgot about that. He said his uncle Wes took it over after his dad died. Never had any kids, so him and his brother Clennon are like his sons."

"Yeah...I was just wondering. He said they had a big meeting tonight at seven. Said his uncle had something important he needed to share with them. Never said what though."

"Hmm. Maybe he will tell us on Monday. I know Lee is a big shot over there now. He showed pictures before with him and his brother and some others dressed up and dancing like they do. You know like a rain dance or something," said Rebecca as she cuddled up beside James.

"Really?" asked James as he wrapped an arm around her, "I didn't know that."

"Yeah...they have Pow Wows and all kind of stuff."

"Huh."

"That's pretty cool. I'd like to go see it sometime," said Lily.

"He said we were welcome to stop by. Said they have a get together on the second Thursday of each month and if I'm not mistaken, there is a Pow Wow coming up," said Jason.

"Yeah, we ought to do it. That would be something to see," Lily answered.

"Sshhh! The movies starting," said Connor with a finger to his lips.

"Yeah, guys we're going to miss it," Kelly in a daze as her eyes were glued to the screen.

"Sorry," Rebecca said with playful raised brows and a silly smirk.

Alexander and the Terrible, Horrible, No Good, Very Bad Day, began its opening scene and held the family's attention, demanding a good laugh once every few minutes.

A house full of kids and laughter. What wasn't to love. It just what James and Rebecca had always dreamed of. It was a fun night for the Randolph's and one in which they wished they could have more often.

††††††††††††††††††††††

ORANGE LIGHT danced across their faces as they formed a half circle around the fire pit. Just over a dozen to be exact, counting Lee, Clennon and their uncle Wes.

A lonely owl sounded off in the dense forest to the South of them. The tree frogs were loud and so was the crackling of wood as it was incensed by the flame.

Red embers floated skyward to the half Moon above, which peaked through the passing clouds.

Uncle Wes sat in the middle, dressed as you'd imagine a Waccamaw tribal leader would be. Tan hide jacket with tan hide pants and a head dress made from the head of a coyote, decorated with eagle feathers.

He played a relaxing tune on his flute that seemed to follow the bright embers skyward to the Creator.

It was a form of worship and thanksgiving to the Almighty Creator, the giver of life and everything in it.

The others swayed in rhythm with the tune as they shut their eyes and entered the presence of the Almighty.

With his heart now full of joy and gratitude, Wes eased to a stop.

The others opened their eyes, some which were glazed over with love and joy as if the Creator Himself had joined them and wrapped his arms around each one like a loving Father would with His beloved children.

"Father God, Almighty Creator, our Lord and Savior, I think You tonight for Your love and grace that has made a way for us to be one with You as You are one with us and in us. We are one in You as You are one in us.

"We have power and strength over the enemy, because You live within us and as You are, so are we in this world. We are Your sons and daughters, and nothing shall by any means harm us because we belong to You our King who is ruler of all the earth. Thank you, Father for Your love and grace. Thank You for the cross. Thank You for Your blood that was shed, which has made a way for us to be reconciled with You and be made whole and complete.

"We are Holy and righteousness just as You are, not because of anything we have done or will do, but because of You and Your finished work on the cross. We have the power to trample the enemy under our feet, because the same power that defeated Satan and death on the cross and raised You from the dead, now lives within us. Thank You Father. We give You all the glory and honor. Bless Your name Lord, In Jesus Name, Amen."

Uncle Wes took a deep breath through his nostrils and let it out through his mouth.

"I know you are all wondering what this is about. As you can tell, what I am about to say, is very important and something I believe the Creator revealed to me in a dream last night. Listen to what I have to say and take it to heart."

He goes on to tell them his dream of the two dogs and the man of darkness.

He waited a few moments to let it sink in before giving his interpretation.

"Now, here is what I believe the Lord is trying to tell us: The two dogs, I believe are the flesh and the spirit, just like the story I know you have heard me speak of so many times. I believe they represent the battle within, good versus evil, spirit versus flesh. The man in the shadows, I believe is Satan and the black dog is our flesh which he will use against us. If he can get us to live in the flesh and feed it with our own self-serving desires and lusts, then he will bring his condemnation and accusation to keep us in shame and guilt, and therefore smother our light and life. Chaining us to self-condemnation.

"Now, more than ever, especially in today's world with all the temptations and self-serving traps, we must starve this dog of flesh and feed our spirit, if we are to overcome and retain our power within that the Lord has granted us by His death on the cross.

"Satan knows he can never defeat us, much less even attempt an attack, as long as we starve our flesh and feed our spirit, but the second we throw a crumb to the old scavenger, we will find ourselves throwing another and then another, before one day, we realize that what once was a frail little pup, has become as strong and mad as a grizzly protecting her cubs.

"We must continue feeding our spirit and vow to not give even the slightest crumb to the old deceiver which is our flesh. We must stick together and rely on each other, we must pray together, fast together, and worship together. For a three-fold cord is not easily broken, as it says in Ecclesiastes.

"The Lord has placed it on my heart to call a five day fast beginning this Monday and I ask that each of you pray about it and find a way to join me on this fast. Do what you can, when you can, but I believe it is very important we defend our flanks and proceed to fire the first shot in this battle before it's too late.

"I believe an evil is coming and we must be strong in the spirit to fight and defend what we hold dear."

The group sat in silence as orange light reflected off Wes's face. The frogs still screeched, the owl still hooted, and the cicadas began their night song

A piece of wood fell in the fire, sending an army of embers skyward, lighting up the night.

Lee cleared his throat.

"Did you see what the man in the shadows looked like?"

"Aww yes, he was rough looking, just like you would imagine Satan to be. Long shaggy gray hair that has never seen a good shower, matched with a long gray beard which must've hung just past his chest. He was a big fellow, maybe six foot two or three, two-fifty probably. As strong and daunting as he appeared outwardly, I could see the weakness within. He's nothing but mouth, he doesn't have a leg to stand on, he's already defeated. His only weapon is a mouthful of lies, which he uses to twist our flesh in his direction."

"Hmm. You don't think this has something to do with the Georgetown killer, do you?" asked Lee.

His brother Clennon scoffed at the thought.

"What are you talking about? That dude disappeared a quarter century ago and hasn't been seen or heard from since."

Lee remained quiet, tightened his lips and craned his head to the side.

"Well, it is a possibility, though I wouldn't bank on it. I feel like it's the Lord's way of wanting us to be more aware of the spiritual battle that is taking place within and around us as this world draws closer to the end. But it is something to keep an eye and ear out for."

The fire crackled as a gentle wind pushed the flame and smoke in Wes's direction. He turned and covered his eyes, but they had already been stung by the warm gray cloud.

He coughed.

The wind shifted and allowed the smoke to return to its vertical form.

"Either way, we must prepare for war and be ready for any attack. Our fasting will call in the Angels to lead us in this battle as they fight alongside us. We must remain strong and cling to the Creator, for that is where we will find our strength."

†††††††††††††††††††††

DRIVING ALONG I-10 EAST just outside of Houston, Kirkland Luender AKA Franklin Ethan Thompson, was ready to call it a night. He glanced at his stereo and three green numbers shined back at him.

1:36

A big blue sign with bold white letters about fifty yards ahead, got his attention.

Exit 765

He eased onto the ramp and came to the stoplight. Brakes squealed in agony as all the padding had been worn off and the cross-country escape wasn't helping.

Leaving behind Palm Springs along with those two evil bats he called family, was the best thing he could've ever done.

After all, they were the problem. They were the reason for his anger, they were the ones who drove him to such extremes. Not him, not Frank.

He was his own man and he wasn't going to take that kind of crap anymore. He deserved his freedom to come and go as he pleased. After all, it was his life, not theirs. If he wanted to please a secret desire, well what was it to them, it was his desire not theirs.

After waiting for two cars to pass, he took a right at the red light. He continued down the deserted road, looking for somewhere to retire for the night.

"HEY FRANKIE!" the raspy voice crackled through the cab of his truck. His skin had to of leaped an inch off the bone. Every hair on his body stood fully erect as gooseflesh covered him head to toe.

His heart pounded as it had climbed into his throat and clung to his vocal chords. There's just something about that voice that always sends shivers down his spine.

A voice that sounds so innocent, yet so evil at once. It came at him from every direction, but he could never find the source, unless it chose to reveal itself. It could speak forward and backwards with perfect pronunciation. It was like backwards was a whole other language from a world never explored.

The voice knew everything about him. The good, the bad, and the sin that would make even the devil himself blush. And the voice had no issue spewing it all out, like a well-rehearsed presentation.

Frank slammed his eyes shut for a moment to gather himself. He swallowed hard, waited a moment, then slowly lifted his eye lids.

"Kirkland, I've done..."

An array of dark figures stood on the asphalt glaring at him, just beyond the headlamps reach. The sight was enough to force out a yelp, as he jerked the wheel causing the rear end to fishtail. He skidded to a halt as his tires screeched with melting rubber on the unforgiving asphalt His truck sat motionless as he straddled the double yellow line.

"C'mon man, get a grip on yourself for once."

He poked his head up as he glanced into his rearview mirror. An older, gray headed man with a long salt and pepper beard stared back at him, as he picked at one of the many warts along his nose.

He'd grown his hair out to aid in disguise. You'd never guess this was the same guy posted in the Georgetown

Times and any of the other papers published throughout the region.

He'd gone undetected for a quarter of a century simply by blending into the crowd in Palm Springs, Banning and Beaumont.

He shared his time, living on the streets, panhandling and on occasion doing odd handy man jobs when he could. It wasn't until he met Leslie at a downtown bar, that he decided to get his act together and begin a family.

Between handy man jobs, cable installation and his night shift, along with Leslie working as a waitress, the two were able to rent and live a mostly comfortable life.

"FRANKIEEEE." Kirkland taunted.

Frank snapped his head to the passenger seat and blurted, "What? What do you want?"

"YOUR HEART...YOUR SOUL...YOUR MIND...EVERYTHING THAT YOU ARE. I WANT YOU. FRANKIE, I WANT YOU AND YOU NEED ME. YOUR MAMA NEEDS ME."

Frank grabbed the gear stick and forced it into drive, applied pressure to the gas pedal causing the truck to lurch forward, back into the right lane.

"What do you want me to do? What's next?"

"THERE'S A GAS STATION ABOUT A MILE DOWN THE ROAD. I WANT YOU TO PARK THERE AND WAIT ABOUT AN HOUR. YOU'LL KNOW WHAT TO DO. JUST MAKE SURE YOU HAVE YOUR JUMPER CABLES READY, IF YOU KNOW WHAT I MEAN."

Frank took a deep breath, squinted his eyes and let the breath out slowly, as his knuckles turned white while he gripped the wheel. His heart began to flutter as a tingling sensation spread throughout his entire body, before landing and staying put in his gut.

He lowered his foot onto the pedal, the needle angled to sixty. The engine growled as the tires roared over the asphalt. A homemade bone cross dangled from his mirror as it danced to the rhythm of the inertia.

He reached over and held it softly with his right. Rubbed it between his forefinger and thumb.

"Don't worry mama, I'll ease your pain."

A smirk stretched across Frank's face as his piercing eyes glared at the road ahead.

Kirkland sat on his haunches in the passenger seat and busied himself with chewing on a pointy nail that attached itself to a long bony finger.

28

Waves crashed against the shore giving off their peaceful roar as the Randolph's home was darkened except for a dim kitchen light.

Tired from a long night of movie watching, everyone but James and Rebecca decided to sleep in the living room as they rested on make shift palates and beds.

Having always been a light sleeper, the pop in the floor was enough to wake Lily from her slumber.

A gentle rain and thunder conversed with one another in the darkness of night, interjected by momentarily flashes of lightning.

Lily rose from the couch, rubbed her eyes, blinked hard and glanced about the living room.

Lauren was nothing but a big ball of covers and was sound asleep on the opposite end of the couch. Lily leaned up to look on the other side of the ottoman where she remembered Jason, Kelly and Connor sleeping on a pile of covers.

Jason was covered up to his neck and lying on his side at the very edge of the palate. Kelly hogged most of it as she appeared to try and mock Leonardo da Vinci's Vitruvian man. Lily scanned passed Kelly and landed on the spot beside her. She blinked hard and adjusted her focus as she thought her night vision must've been failing her. She rubbed her face once more and refocused.

Connor's spot was empty.

The covers where he lay, were peeled back and thrown to the side. He must've got scared and went to mom and dad's room.

The sound of sniffles, at first seemed to have come from the low volume of the TV. But they didn't match the anti-wrinkle cream advocates from the late-night infomercial.

Lily scanned the room until her eyes landed on a small dark figure standing in the corner of the wall and entertainment center where the TV sat.

More sniffles.

She threw the covers from herself and stood to her feet. The figured continued to sniffle and was now scratching franticly at its elbow. Lily reached out and gently touched the back of an arm.

The small figure spun around, screamed and bolted for the front door faster than Lily could think. It was Connor.

He'd already twisted the dead bolt and swung the door open, before she could even take two steps.

If Connor's scream and feet trotting out the door wasn't enough to wake everyone, then the ear-piercing alarm would surely do the trick.

Connor sped down the steps and shot around the corner of the house.

Lily wasn't far behind him.

By now, Jason and Lauren were making their way out the front door as well.

Connor conquered the steps that led over the dunes, sand flying every which way. He ran at full speed, lungs fully exhaling.

She had to get there before he reached the water. He was about twenty feet from the swash zone, when she gripped his arm, spinning him around. He fought and screamed as if the hand was going to murder him.

"What's wrong? What's the matter with you?"

Lily gasped as she grabbed for her next breath.

Connor was staring right through her, mouth wide in a terrified scream.

She grabbed him by the shoulders and shook him, but it didn't help.

By now, Jason and Lauren were racing from the dunes. Rebecca topped the steps. The sliding glass door on the back deck slid open.

James rode over the hump and made it onto the deck. Kelly wasn't far behind James as she ran over and clung tightly to his arm.

Rebecca sprinted down the slope where Lily, Jason and Lauren tried to calm Connor, but he wasn't having it.

He fought off their attempted embraces and kept screaming something about a big man trying to get him.

Rebecca made it to the group and squatted down in front of Connor, one knee in the damp sand.

"Connor...Connor...its mama. I'm here baby...I'm here...I'm right here. It's okay...ssshhh."

Tears streaked down his face as snot hung from his nostrils and dripped onto his blue superman t-shirt.

He panted for breath. A dark spot stained his pajamas as it streaked from his crouch to his foot.

"The man...the man said he was going to get me. I saw him." He muttered out through a broken voice and more sniffles.

"What man? Where did you see him?"

"He was standing over us in the floor, watching me. He was big. He tried to snatch me up, but I hid in the corner beside the TV."

"What did he look like?"

"He had lots of hair and a long gray beard. He was big and mean looking. He pinched my elbow when he tried to grab my arm, but I got away and hid in the living room."

†††††††††††††††††††††

EXHAUSTED FROM his three-day drive, Frank had dozed off in the Citgo parking lot. His head rested against the window.

"FRANKIE!" Kirkland blurted as he yanked at Frank's arm with enough force to jerk his head from the glass. He gasped for breath. his heart thumping in his chest like a bass. He blinked and gave his face a rub down.

"What?"

"WE GOT COMPANY." Kirkland's said in a hushed tone, like a kid whispering in church.

Headlights eased into the parking lot and strolled over to the opposite side. Must've had the same idea as Frank. The SUV parked and dimmed the lights.

Frank peered at his stereo.

The green digits read,

1:12

He had lost two hours since leaving Palm Springs and still had one more to lose as he travelled back to Eastern Standard time.

Something he hadn't been in, in quite some time.

"TURN THIS UP."

Frank turned the knob to the radio and rested his chin in the crevice of his thumb and forefinger with his elbow stabbing into the cushion of the center console.

The tune brought back a lot of memories and it was just what he would need if he were to carry out Kirkland's plan.

Frank sang along to the lyrics of *Every Breath you Take* by The Police.

"ALL RIGHT...THIS GUY'S A LONER. IT'LL BE WEEKS BEFORE THEY EVER REACH HIS FAMILY. BY

THEN YOU'LL BE IN NORTH CAROLINA. DO IT FOR YOUR MAMA, SHE NEEDS HER FEEDING. IT'LL EASE HER PAIN."

Frank breathed deeply, glanced over at the jumper cables in the passenger seat, then reached for the glove compartment, opened it and retrieved a .38 caliber hand gun.

He snatched the jumper cables and pulled the hood lever under the wheel, releasing the hood with a pop.

He exits the truck. Walks to the front, raises the hood and rest it on the prop rod.

Whistling to his favorite tune, he cracked his neck angling it side to side. He could feel his muscles tingling as the euphoric rush of dopamine flowed from his brain like a water fall of milk and honey. So blissful, this feeling. Aw, he loved working for Kirkland.

His eyes locked on the SUV, his feet marched onward, pounding the asphalt with his size 13 boots. Jumper cables in hand and .38 stuffed behind his back.

29

The sound of knuckle raps against the glass, looked to have startled the man as he busied himself looking over the map on his phone.

A light rain had begun to fall.

The man cracked open his window.

"Can I help you?"

"Hey...sorry to bother you this late. My battery is dead and so is my phone. You think you could give me a jump?" Frank said as he held the cables in the air.

"Yeah man...sure. Is that you behind me?"

"Yeah, I'm just right over here. I'd sure appreciate it."

"Ahh no problem...just give me a second."

"Okay...thanks buddy."

Frank headed back to his truck and waited for the man.

The SUV fired up. the lights illuminated the trees in front of it. The man put it in reverse and did a 180 as small pebbles crunched on the pavement.

He pulled in front of Frank's truck, bumper to bumper with just enough space to stand in between.

Frank stepped between the two with the cables in his left and his right by his side.

He waited for the man to reach for the lever under the wheel, before retrieving his gun.

The man slid off his seat, stood on the asphalt, adjusted his pants and shut the door.

"So how long you been out..."

The loud crackle of a shot rang into the night as the slug lodged itself into the man's skull.

A .38 round to the head dropped him like a crumbling tower of Jenga blocks. He collapsed to the with his legs folding under his back.

He groaned and mumbled gibberish.

Frank straddled him, retrieved a pocket knife, lifted the man's right hand, made a few quick glances, then began cutting away at the pointer and middle finger. The man squirmed and moaned as his breathing became heavy and labored.

Cutting through flesh and bone took a lot of strength. Frank was glad he'd eaten that extra rare T-Bone steak at the Waffle House only hours ago. Raw and juicy always seemed to give him the most strength. Come to think of it, cutting fingers was sort of like slicing through a fatty steak.

The bone cracked as Frank finished his last cut. He placed the fingers in his pocket, bent down and got nose to nose with the dying man. He sniffed the man's breath. Dying breath smelled so good. his fingers quivered, his muscles spasmed, as the breath snaked along the cavity of his nostrils. Such a rush. He shook like a wet dog.

Frank rose, eyes black and bulging, steadied his aim. "ONE MORE OUGHT TO DO THE TRICK."

"Here you go mama, this should help."

He squeezed the trigger. Fire emitted from the barrel. the crack rang out. The man stilled, his body limp and lifeless, just like Mother liked it.

30

Gathered around the kitchen table, the Randolph's took turns questioning little Connor.

James and Rebecca looked over both of his arms but couldn't find any marks where he said the man had grabbed him.

He used to have night terrors when he was younger but hadn't had any in about three years.

It must've just been one of those.

It had to of been, right?

All the doors were locked, James had doubled checked and so did Rebecca.

There was no way someone could have snuck in without getting their attention or sounding off the alarm. James was a light sleeper. he would have heard an intruder.

It had to of just been another night terror.

Had to be.

†††††††††††††††††††††

LATER THAT MORNING, Rebecca awoke from her alarm at 5:45. She fixed breakfast and got Connor and Kelly dressed for school as well as herself.

If they left by 6:50, she would have time to drop them off at Brunswick Elementary before driving herself, Jason and Lauren to West Brunswick High.

James got up and ate breakfast with them before they headed out. Lily had plans to sleep in until 9, before making her way into town to pick up a few things for the weekend.

On the way to school, Connor rode quietly in the back seat as he stared out the window.

"It's been a while since he's had one of those, hasn't it?" asked Jason.

"Yeah...probably two or three years, I guess. I figured he grew out of them, but..." Rebecca glanced at Connor through her rearview mirror. "...I guess not."

"You don't think he really saw someone do you?" asked Lily.

"What?" Rebecca questioned with a soft laugh.

"Yeah...I mean what if he really saw someone last night? What if it wasn't a dream?" Lily continued.

"Hey, maybe it was a ghost?" said Jason.

Rebecca passed a quick glance at the two of them.

"Don't say that, now you're going to give me nightmares," said Kelly.

"See, now that is why I don't want you two talking about stuff like that. I'm sure it wasn't anything, it was just another night terror like he's had in the past. Don't make it out to be something it's not. Okay?"

Jason and Lily nodded.

They rode for a few moments in silence as the night before tumbled through their minds.

"He said he was going to kill us. He said he had to do it for his mama," Connor said as he watched the trees and mailboxes streak past.

Like someone jabbing a dagger in their hearts, a angry wave of fear crashed over them.

Rebecca swallowed the lump in her throat as she could feel her pulse quicken.

Jason rubbed his forefinger and thumb between the eyes as he tried to process what his brother had just said.

Kelly whimpered and threw her arms around Jason, squeezing as hard as she could.

Lily blinked, took a breath, then turned around from the front passenger seat, "You really believe you saw someone don't you?"

Connor turned his gaze from the window to his sister, "I know I did. He was big and hairy, wore glasses and was really mean. He nudged my leg, that's what woke me up. I opened my eyes and he was standing over me, looking down at me. He said he had to take me for his mama. That's when I jumped up and tried to hide behind the TV."

Rebecca covered her mouth with a trembling hand. Her face felt flush. The thought of an unknown man being in their house last night, tore deeply at her heart and mind. She needed a breath to gather herself. She glanced at Connor in her mirror and said, "Honey we searched everywhere last night, the house was empty, and we didn't see anyone outside either. I'm sure it must've been another night terror. It's just been awhile since you've had one, that's why this one was a little worse."

"I guess. It all just seemed so real."

††††††††††††††††††††††

HALF WAY THROUGH her second class that morning, Rebecca kept having the reoccurring thought of speaking to Mr. McGaha about Connor's episode. She couldn't get it off her mind, it nagged at her like a mosquito bite after having been scratched. Knowing how spiritual McGaha was, maybe he could offer an explanation.

After her last class before lunch, Rebecca made a point to speak with Lee McGaha and hopefully talk with him over lunch.

She made her way down the hall to room 127 where Lee taught world history 101. The door was open as she had just missed the stampede of hungry teenagers scurrying out. She gave a few gentle knocks as she noticed Mr. McGaha standing behind his desk, placing the day's quizzes into a folder.

"Hello Lee, how are you doing today?"

He glanced up from the folder, smiled and said, "Oh, hey Rebecca. I'm doing good, how are you this morning?"

His expression bore the question without him even asking, what can I do for you?

"I'm good. Hey, I was wondering if I could speak with you about my son, Connor?"

"Yeah...of course. Is everything okay?"

"Yeah...he just had a crazy episode last night. I believe it may have been a night terror, which he has had in the past, it's just been a while since he's had one."

"Really? Okay, yeah sure. Were you about to get lunch?"

"Yeah, I thought maybe if it's okay with you, we could talk over lunch?"

"Absolutely. Just let me gather my things here and lock up."

"Great, thank you."

Rebecca waited by the door as Lee finished stuffing folders into his shoulder bag, then turned off the projector he used for the PowerPoint, and headed to the door, flicking off the lights.

"So how old is your son?"

He asked as they stepped into the hall and began the trek for the cafeteria.

"He's six."

"Oh okay. So, tell me about this episode. What happened?"

"Oh boy...well...I guess I will start from the beginning."

By the time, the two of them made it into the cafeteria, Rebecca had told everything, other than the mysterious man's description.

The two grabbed their plates and stepped into line.

"Did your son ever say what the man looked like?"

Rebecca leaned into his ear and described the man exactly like Connor had in the car.

Lee looked as if he had just taken a sledge hammer to the gut. His eyes widened as he had to steady himself by gripping the counter. He rubbed his forehead with his right thumb and pointer.

"Lee...is everything okay?"

A moment passed.

"You're going to want to sit down to hear this."

††††††††††††††††††††††

TWENTY MINUTES INTO the conversation, Lee had told everything he knew.

Rebecca's jaw dropped more times than he could've counted, and her hands seemed to tremble each time she raised one to cover her mouth in a reflexive gasp. Her eyes misted over soon after he begun the story Uncle Wes had shared.

He paused to give her a chance to gather herself and to also give him time to delicately sort through the words coming to mind.

"Rebecca...I know this has to be frightening...but I want you to know you and your family are not alone in this."

She sniffled and dabbed a tear with a Kleenex she'd unearthed from her purse. She looked him in the eye and swallowed hard.

She nodded and gave a gentle smile.

"Thank you."

"Rebecca...we are here for you and the Creator and His Angels are too. Don't you forget that."

"Thank you. I just guess we've never really been the religious type, but it's good to hear that."

"Well neither are we. I mean of course we have our traditions that we keep in honor of our ancestors, but our Faith is just that...Faith. It's not based on a religious doctrine so to speak, but a genuine relationship with our infinite Creator."

That seemed like something new to Rebecca as she tilted her head, blinked her eyes and glanced to the ceiling as the words settled.

"Wow. I guess I've never heard it explained like that. That's refreshing."

"It is. Say what are you guys doing Tomorrow afternoon?"

She thought for a moment.

"Uh...nothing I don't guess."

"We are having our annual Pau Wau tomorrow. I think you'd all really enjoy it."

"Count us in. What time?"

"Three o'clock. If you will come a little early, I'll introduce you to everyone and make you feel right at home."

"Good. I will talk to James and uh...we'll make plans to be there."

Lee glanced at his watch. Ten minutes before the next period started.

"Well...I guess we better wrap it up. Fourth period will be starting soon."

"Oh yeah, I reckon we should, shouldn't we? Lee, thank you so much for talking with me and telling the truth about all of this."

"Of course, Rebecca. I'm glad to help."

They stand from the table, gather their plates and cross for the trash can. They empty their garbage and angle for the hallway.

"Say...you don't think this could have something to do with the Georgetown killer, do you?"

Her question seemed out of the blue but was perfectly appropriate given the circumstances.

He waited a moment before giving an answer, which gave him time to gather one in his mind.

He sighed, "You know...my brother asked the same question. I don't know, I hope not, but it does have its connections. Are you familiar with the details of the GTK?"

"Huh...well...let's just say that's a whole other conversation."

31

Driving along highway 38 just outside of Big Bear Lake about an hour drive north of Beaumont, California, a young couple stopped at a pull off to get a good picture of Deadman's Peak. Sarah being the artsy type, busied herself with squinting an eye as she peered through her Cannon camera lens. Mike, being antsy after having just drunk a large cup of freshly brewed coffee from one of the many gift shops they had the pleasure of visiting that day, was going to cause a flood if he didn't find a tree to water soon.

"Honey, I'm about to bust, you be all right for just a second?"

"Yeah, I'm fine." Sarah said without giving it much thought. The scene was breath taking and had her full attention.

Snap! Snap! Snap! Snap!

Mike headed off for the woods, as he attempted to create distance between himself and any passer byers along the highway. He went just far enough where he could keep an eye on Sarah through the limbs and branches but would take a good hard stare from the roadway for anyone to ever notice him. A faint stench greeted him as he steadied himself against a tree overlooking a ravine that led to what appeared to be an old creek bed. Blended in with the forest, he rushed to relieve himself. As he did so, he couldn't help but notice a big lump of plastic about 30 yards at the bottom of the ravine.

What the heck is that?

It was rolled up like a rug and had a few lumps here and there. One of those lumps suddenly found its way into Mike's throat.

He swallowed hard as he tried to calm himself, hoping away the fear of it being what his thoughts were telling him.

32

Detectives had arrived on scene at a gas station just outside of Houston. Numerous police cruisers and Crown Victoria's scattered about the parking lot of the vacant gas station. The Sun was setting. Shades of orange, yellow, and purple streaked along the horizon. The roar and hiss of the highway in the distance. A body dressed in a white sheet rested on the pavement in front of a green Jeep Cherokee. A howling wind, ruffled the sheet, causing it to flap more than once.

Harris County Homicide Lieutenant, Jeff Easley checked his watch before stretching on a pair of latex gloves and crouching beside the body.

6:49

He peeled back the sheet, revealing the man's face and chest. His skin a pale purple with dark veins snaking this way and that like a lightning strike. His nose was missing as a huge hole had replaced it. Another hole dug its way into his skull just above the left ear.

The body was stiff as Rigor Mortis had already done its work. The coroner report stated the man had been dead for at least fifteen to eighteen hours, judging by the thermometer technique he'd used. Making a small incision just above the liver before sticking what resembled a meat thermometer into the liver. This was always the most accurate way to check for core body temperature, which would give the best estimate of a time of death. For this man, it was likely sometime during the early morning hours of last night. Perfect time for a murder. Dark. Not many witnesses.

The way the man lay, told Easley, he was shot just after exiting his Jeep. He could tell by the way he'd crumbled to the asphalt, legs bent awkwardly under his back.

A pair of jumper cables sat next to the man. The hood to the Jeep had also been popped. Which meant either the battery was dead like the owner, or the battery of the one responsible for sending the slugs into the man's skull, was.

Easley pulled the sheet on down to reveal the body from the waist up. The first thing he noticed were the missing fingers. He lifted the hand and twisted it this way and that.

The fingers were forcefully removed with what appeared to be some type of blade as dull as a rock. Easley's eyes finished the scan of the hand and met the victim's glazed pupils. He could sense the terror in his bulging glare. Something just wasn't right though, besides his nose being blown clean off. The mouth doesn't look right, why is it fixed like that?

Easley placed his index and thumb to the man's chin and lower lip and had to apply a decent amount of pressure to pry open the man's crooked mouth.

It finally gave way with a crack. Easley swallowed and craned his neck, turning his attention to a line of officers behind some yellow tape as he tried to shake off the tingling sensation exiting his body like an electric shock.

He breathed deep and turned his attention back to the dead man's glare. Something was lodged in the man's mouth. Looked to have been a wad of paper.

He went to remove it, his heart picked up pace, his blood pumped harder. His palms sweated under the hot gloves.

As he was retrieving the paper, a large jumping spider streaked out of the man's mouth, and jolted up Easley's hand, sending him scooted backwards the pavement on his rear as he flashed his hand through the air.

"Geez! What the—?" Easley cursed.

An officer rushed over to check on him. Easley sat on his haunches, trying to catch his breath.

"Sir...are you okay?" the officer questioned, placing a hand on Easley's shoulder.

He swallowed hard and gathered his breath.

"Yeah...yeah. I'm...I'm good. A dang Spider crawled out of his mouth and shot up my hand, scared the day lights of me."

"Dang! No wonder you freaked out."

The officer offered a hand to get him to his feet.

Easley's face had drained of blood. He thought he'd puke any second, he bent at the waist to try and control it, but that only made things worse.

It was coming up rather he liked it or not.

He turned away in just enough time not to disrupt the crime scene. His lunch spewed across the pavement about four yards from the body.

He coughed and hacked a bit before retrieving a handkerchief from an inside pocket on his jacket. He wiped away the vomit, took some deep breaths and reassured the officer he was okay.

Easley dusted himself off and then unwrapped the wad of paper. A note. Hard to read, between the creases and ink smudging here and there from the man's saliva.

Easley read it to himself. This is what it said:

Dear Detective,

Hope this letter finds you doing well! Sorry we must meet this way, but I wouldn't have it any other way, if you catch my drift. Anyhow, the man from Whob Mouth just retrieved this, is by no means a targeted victim, he was randomly selected to ease my Mother's Pain. Like natural selection I guess. Survival of the fittest, or what have you. She will greatly appreciate the sacrifice, it will serve her well. I don't know why it has taken so long to give her a tongue, I guess the timing was just never right. But better late than never I reckon. So now I just need to give her some eyes & ears to complete her senses, don't worry I already have what I need for smell and touch, I just have to give her sight & hearing and she'll be complete. Then maybe she can rest in piece. So I guess that means another 4 victims. 1 offering from each. Well, good luck in catching me before you find the other 4, cause your going to need it and so are they. Believe me! perhaps once this is all over, I can relax, if Mother is pleased and Kirkland obliges. One piece of advice though: Don't get in the devil's way, or he may just stab you in the heart, then drag your limp body home to gut and eat himself, then mount your head on his mantle like the trophy kill you are.

So long... I'll be Watching!

GTK

Easley wiped his forehead and sighed.

"What's it say?" the officer asked.

"Put these on, then take a look for yourself."

The officer pulled on a pair of blue and took the letter from Easley's grip.

As the officer busied himself with the letter, Easley squatted back down in a search for the man's tongue.

Easley took a breath and let his eyes wonder across the rest of the uncovered body.

Then something demanded his attention.

It was what was carved into the flesh of the man's arm opposite of the missing fingers.

33

Reclined in a chair with his black wing tipped dressed shoes stacked on the desk, David Hoffman cradles a phone to his ear with a shoulder as he licked a thumb before using it to flip the pages of a magazine.

"David, I just don't understand why you want to spend so much time at the office. I know you have to study for Sundays, but can't you do that here? I mean can't we just make you an office here?"

"Honey, we've talked about this before, I just get more done when I'm here. Less distraction."

That was returned with the sound of silence and a bit of static.

"You there?"

A pause.

"Annie?"

"Yeah...I'm here," her voice muffled with tears.

Knock. Knock. Knock.

Who in the world could that be?

"Hang on a second honey, there's someone knocking on the door."

"What?"

"Yeah, just hang on, let me see who it is," David sat up, laid the phone down and hurried to stuff the magazine in a desk drawer under a pile of sermon notes.

He took a breath, adjusted his pants as his hands tugged at each hip, and rubbed away some wrinkles on his white button down.

He marched out of his office and into the foyer of the church, he could see someone standing on the other side of the swirly glass beside the door.

Must be another homeless person and it better not be the same one.

He cleared his throat and opened the door. The man had his back turned but was in the process of spinning around at the sound of the door creaking open. The man wore a long gray beard that stretched just below his chest and salt and peppered hair that hung below his shoulders.

Furrowed brows underneath a pair of glasses accompanied a sneaky grin beneath all that hair.

"Can I help you?"

"How you doing preacher? Yes...my name's Kirk. I was wondering if you had a minute to talk?"

34

Darkness had invaded David's office. he could feel it seeping through his flesh, snaking its way deep into his gut. After a brief introduction, that included exchanging of names, where you froms, and so forth, David showed Kirk to a seat in his office. A bead of sweat attempted to trickle down his forehead, but he caught with the back of his right hand just before it landed in his eye. He gripped the arm of his chair with a greasy left. He swallowed hard in effort to relieve the stress that was building in his throat and chest. His eyes were fixed upon the man seated across from him who could easily pass for Jerimiah Johnson.

"Now preacher...I know my presence must make you uncomfortable, especially at this time of night. I guess with my appearance I could make bought near anyone squirm in their seat, I know I ain't very easy on the eyes. But make no mistake about it, I didn't come here to do you any harm, I just simply need someone to talk to. The way I figure, you'd be the one," the man said as he stroked his beard.

David cleared his throat. "I understand...so uh...what's on your mind?"

"Well...you see I guess I never did have much of a family, reckon I'm a bonafide loner and wanderer of the streets. Sometimes the weight and heaviness this world places on you can be hard to bear if you have no one to help share the load. So, from time to time I sort of get weak in the knees from carrying too much on my own and well...I guess I just go searching for someone to help me out a little."

"I see. So, what exactly is this load that you speak of?"

"The load of sin. I just have too much to bear and quite honestly, I'm not sure the man upstairs wants to be bothered with so much garbage. I mean is a king really willing to get his hands dirty?"

David did his best to remain calm, but his nervousness showed as he fumbled for words before being interrupted.

"Guess what I'm trying to ask...is...do you think I'm too far gone?"

A moment passed.

"No. There is never a sin too great for our Lord. Just as it says in Romans, 'Where sin abounded, Grace did much more abound.' You see, you are never too far gone. And to answer your question about the king...yes. If your child were to fall into mud hole, would you not dirty yourself to help them out? Even if they were to willingly jump in the mud, would that cause you to disown them and leave them in their mess?"

"I reckon not. No."

"Well then, if that's the case for us mere humans, who's to say the Good Lord above wouldn't do the same?"

Another beat.

"Yeah, you got a point there preacher. Guess I never thought of it that way. I just hope I can keep mama happy."

"Are you close to your Mother?"

"Oh yes, we're very close. I take care of her and feed her and such. She's been through so much, even death itself can't hold her down. She's a fighter."

"I see. Is she in a rest home?"

"Yeah...something like that. Say...how about...someone being haunted?"

David craned his head.

"You know…like the movies."

"Possession?"

"Yeah."

"What about it?"

"You ever dealt with it before?"

"Yeah. I've been around it before a few times, but that was before I became a minister, so I was more of a spectator than anything. Why do you ask?"

"I was curious, because you see I have a buddy who thinks he may have something like that going on."

"Really? Can you give me any specifics?"

"Well, you know, hearing voices, feeling like he's losing control of his thoughts and actions. Being dictated by a higher being I guess. Weird thoughts, depression, that sort of thing. You reckon that could be…uh…you know—"

"Demon possession?"

A moment passed.

"Yeah."

"I'd say it certainly meets the criteria."

"What should he do?"

"The quickest way to find out would be to have someone pray for him. Demon's don't like prayer, or anything connected to God for that matter."

"I see. So how long you been here?"

"This spring will be 11 years."

"No. I meant how long have you been here today? Must not have a family. Awful late for a preacher to still be in church, isn't it?"

His words caught David off guard. He squirmed in his chair and concocted a reasoning.

"Well, trying to make sure I'm prepared for Sunday."

"I see. Something tells me you're hiding something." His words stopped time as they penetrated David's heart like an arrow.

"Excuse me?"

"Do you have a family?"

"Yes. A wife and we have a daughter and son at USC. Why? I don't see why that would be of your concern."

"It kind of is. I mean just doesn't seem right for a man with a family to willingly spend time away from the wife if he didn't have a dirty secret. Let alone a preacher. Seems to me you may be hiding something from the mistress. And if that's the case, I'm not so sure I should listen to your advice."

"Now buddy, you've crossed the line. I've done told you I'm here preparing for Sunday," David said standing as his face flushed with heat.

Kirk reclined in the chair, interlocked his fingers behind his head and wore a grin partially hidden by all the hair.

"That's it. Get out! Now!" David shouted with a firm jaw and stiff finger to the door.

"So, you are hiding something," the man said as he rose and made his way to the door, with David on his heels.

"It's the magazines you keep in that drawer. You think you have everyone fooled. The only one being fooled is yourself. The master has you right where he wants you,"

Kirk said with a chuckle as he started a soft whistle before passing through the door and easing down the steps onto the sidewalk.

David's heart pounded as each breath was a fight. How could this man know such a secret? Who is he?

"Boy, you got some nerves, you know that. Who are you anyhow?" David said with enough volume to reach the back of the mysterious man as whistled his way down the sidewalk about to vanish into the darkness of night.

"Thompson. Franklin. Ethan. Thompson," he said slowly, one name at a time.

It was like being hit by a train. David staggered as he groped for something to steady himself. His greasy palm found the jagged brick wall. The flood of memories and emotions were enough to make him queasy.

"My word...what have I done? That really was Frankie. I'm a dead man."

†††††††††††††††††††††

WITH KIRKLAND squawking orders over Frank's shoulder in the streets of Shallotte, the town would certainly have something to talk about in the coming days.

35

It was just after nine o'clock Friday night and James and Rebecca were still talking about what Lee had told her earlier that day during lunch.

"Do you really think this could be Ethan? I mean why would he wait all this time, why wait a quarter of a century?"

James struggled for an answer, so Rebecca answered her own question.

"Maybe he's been fighting it all this time and has finally just given in, or maybe he's been killing somewhere else and has decided to return where he started. My word."

She covered her mouth and wagged her head. Her gut shook like San Francisco during a quake.

James wrapped his arm around her and brought her in close.

"I tell you what, how about we all just sleep in the living room for the next few nights, until this thing blows over. We'll double check all the doors and windows, add extra locks if we have to, maybe even install some security cameras."

Rebecca didn't say anything, she just nodded her head against his chest.

"Let's get the kids in here and give them a rundown," said James.

Rebecca agreed.

He cleared his throat, "Hey kids...can you come here for a second?"

One by one they made their way into the living room. Lining up in front of the couch like they were waiting for a protected witness to pinpoint a crime.

"Sit down for a second...we need to talk about some things."

Jason and Kelly sat on the ottoman and Lauren and Connor took a seat beside Rebecca.

"Hey, listen...we all know about what happened last night, whether it was just a nightmare or something else, I want us to err on the side of caution and really take this thing seriously. Now your Mother was able to speak with Mr. McGaha today during lunch and he helped spread some light on what really may have happened."

James turned to Rebecca and gave her the floor.

She cleared and being careful with her words, she retold of what she'd learned from Lee. Being sure not to cause too much fear, but also being sure she got the point across to Jason and Lauren. Even though they didn't do anything wrong, they were basically grounded and put on house arrest until it felt safe to return to normal life. Lily would be informed of the same precautions as soon as she got home, which should be in another hour according to their last phone call about half an hour ago.

†††††††††††††††††††††††

AN HOUR PASSED before Lily walked through the door and was briefed on the news. Of all the kids, she understood the seriousness better than any, simply due to her being the oldest, she was able to recall her parents speaking more of Ethan and the GTK than the others. She had also heard her friends and classmates talk about it a time or two as well.

As they busied themselves with creating a palate in the living room floor, Rebecca retrieved her phone.

"Hello?"

"Hi Rebecca...it's me, Lee."

"Oh, hey Lee...sorry didn't recognize the number, haven't had a chance to put it in my phone yet."

"Oh, that's okay...so how is everything? You guys doing okay?"

"Yeah we're good...just making a bed in the living room for us all to sleep on. Just...you know...trying to be safe."

"Yeah...I know what you mean. We're all being cautious ourselves. Rather be safe than sorry."

"Exactly."

"Well, I won't keep you, I just wanted to check on you guys and see how you were holding up."

"Well thank you Lee, I appreciate you calling. So, tomorrow at three o'clock, right?"

"That's right, but remember, get there a little early if you can."

"Okay, sounds good...we'll see you then."

"Okay...be safe Rebecca."

"You too...bye now."

††††††††††††††††††††††

2,500 MILES WEST in Big Bear, CA, it was around 5:30 that evening as detectives and CSI busied themselves with uncovering the body wrapped in plastic down the ravine. Police cruisers and black Ford Crown Victoria's lined the side of the road. Mike and Sara stood on the opposite side leaning against the front of their car while being questioned by an officer.

The stench that welcomed the detectives, spoke of the severity of decomposition.

As detective Murphy peeled back a flap of plastic, the lifeless face of an elderly woman stared back in terror and pain. Her nose was sliced off and there was a deep carving into her forehead.

36

Just past midnight and well past Uncle Wes's bedtime.

Lost in a deep sleep, he found himself waking in another world. Crickets sang, as leaves above sounded like a tambourine with the gentle breeze. Burning wood crackled and popped. He raised his eye lids and discovered the flame, glowing embers billowing heavenward. Before him laid a feast fit for a king, that only those of high esteem could enjoy. Fruits and nuts, fish and fowl, milk and honey, platters of vegetables, gold goblets of freshly squeezed wine and crystal glasses of the purest of water.

As his eyes tried to take in all that was before him, he couldn't help but notice the glowing light across the flame. It grew stronger by the second. As he was peering in curiosity, a gentle yet strong voice spoke from the light.

"My beloved son in whom I am well pleased."

The love and warmth were almost overwhelming. A stirring of energy began deep within as a resounding hum filled the air. Wes tilted his head and glanced over his body, which was now beaming with a golden light. He held out his hands and noticed the blood in his veins that snaked up his arm had turned from blue to gold.

"There is royalty in your veins my dear son. Never forget that. You are of a royal dynasty and of great value and treasure. You have more

power and authority than you could ever imagine. You are mine, I am in you as you are in me. We are one."

"Great Creator, who am I to receive such an honor?" Wes questioned as tears tried to form but wouldn't.

"You are mine. You are my child, you are Holy, you are Righteous, you were bought with the price of my Son's death and you are precious to me. I love you more than you will ever know, and more than your earthly mind could ever fathom."

"That's right Wes, you are priceless. My blood which was shed for you gives you access to the same power and glory of my Father and his royal kingdom. All the power and glory of Heaven is within you. And my Angels and Spirit are ever with you. I will never leave you nor forsake you. I am in you and you are in me, we are one," said a man next to the light, dressed in a beautiful white and gold gown with a sparkling gold crown laced with glistening diamonds.

"Listen to my voice. I will lead you. I will guide you. I will never lead you astray. I know the way in which you should go and I will show you, you need only be still and wait for my voice," said a second beaming light seated next to the radiant man. This was surely the great Spirit of Truth.

"Thank you, Father. For you are good and your mercy endures forever," said Wes as love and gratitude filled his heart.

"Hey!!" a voice came from the darkness, hidden by the fire's light.

"Why don't you come out here and face me like a real man? What are you too fearful? Or better yet, are you too frail with age?"

Wes stood to his feet and crossed where the flame met the nights shadow.

"*Son, don't mind him, he is only a distraction.*"

Wes squinted and scanned the darkness. There he stood, proud as ever with his dog of blackness snarling beside him.

Wes's heart pounded at the sight.

"Father it is the evil man who has come to destroy us!"

"*Are you so forgetful my son? Have you already forgotten who you are? You are my son, nothing can by any means hurt you. For you are the Light of the World and no darkness could ever overcome this light, for it has already been defeated. This man and all evil that accompanies him is a mere dung beetle crawling before a mighty elephant. Have no fear for you are more powerful than you think. Remember all of Heaven is at my command, you are safe in my presence. You have no need to worry, only trust me. Do you trust me, my precious son?*"

As Wes turned his attention from the man and dog, gathered about the fire were beautiful winged Angels their height like that of a Grizzly on its hind feet. Clothed in gold armor and baring glimmering swords. They each in one voice said, "Do not fear, for we are with you and we are many."

"*Rest easy my son, for I am with you and I am in you. Continue to lead your tribe in this fast, for in so doing, you will strip this evil of its power and unleash the fury of Heaven upon its many dignitaries and princes. I will bless you and all those under your command and any who follow your leading. This is my battle, you need only rest and trust my plan. I am with you. you are my beloved son in whom I am well pleased. Remain in My light. I am in you and you are in Me. We are one. We are the Light of the World.*"

A bright flash caused him to cover his face with his arm. He lowered his arm and peaked, he found himself seating by a large fire where he was accompanied by his native ancestors. They each wore a proud smile as they showed their pleasure in the great leader Wes had become. That night went on to be the most restful and relaxing night Wes had ever received. The next morning, when he awoke, he felt as if he could slay a hundred giants and that he may very well do.

37

2:30 on Saturday afternoon, the Randolph clan arrived at the Waccamaw Tribal Grounds for the annual Pau Wau.

They wanted to go earlier as the gates opened at 11 o'clock, but with it being almost a two-hour drive from Holden Beach, North Carolina to Aynor, South Carolina, along with toting five offspring and a paraplegic, the late arrival was inevitable.

After getting James situated in his motorized wheelchair, they paid admission and made their way to where most of the crowd and noise were. A large circle of hay bales, with an outer circle of wooden planked benches must've seated a few hundred people.

Native American's dressed in bright colors with feathers, bells, and animal hide busied themselves with dancing in the center as the on lookers gazed at such a rhythmic display. At the West side of the circle was the Emcee and band. The Emcee told of the dance that was being performed, while the band kept the beat and rhythm with the drums along with singing in Native tongues.

The music itself was enough to mesmerize as it could penetrate and awaken parts within the soul that James otherwise never knew existed.

At the South side of the circle, sat what looked like the Chief. He wore a buffalo head, its horns stretching towards the heavens, his face painted black, red, and white. He sat with wide knees, clutching a large stick adorned with feathers and bells. Must be Lee's uncle Wes. He seemed to have a glow about him as he sat alongside others dressed in a similar fashion but not quite as radiant as he. Uncle Wes looked to be the only one with buffalo hide. The others wore coyote or bear it appeared. In front of the other men who were seated behind uncle Wes, were small signs which read: Cherokee, Siouan, Catawba, and Pee Dee. Four chiefs apparently.

Beside uncle Wes, was Lee McGaha and another who had to be his brother. They too were dressed in a similar fashion. Painted faces, tan hide pants and vest, feathers and bells.

Lee noticed James and Rebecca and gave a quick wave and gentle smile to acknowledge their presence.

The Randolph's found their spot just to the right of the East Gate.

"Wow...this is really something," said James.

The drums continued their beat, along with the chanting and soothing tune of Native's voices together in harmony.

Under a bright blue sky, a gentle breeze eased the intensity of the Sun's rays. It was such a beautiful September day.

As the Native's continued their dances, sweeping their arms towards the grass with bundles of Eagle feathers and tomahawks, a few cried out with a tongue of a banshee, just like you hear in the movies before they lead a charge against the gun wielding cowboys.

Then it all came to an abrupt halt, James had to glance about to see what had interrupted them. As he was busy looking over his shoulder, the crowd erupted into a thunderous applause

Lee leaned and whispered into the ear of his uncle before leaving the tent of elders and walking over to the Randolph's.

"Hey guys...good to see you all. Thank you for coming," Lee said as he shook each of their hands.

"Wow Lee...I've got to tell you this is amazing!" said Rebecca.

"Thank you, thank you. Yes, cherish our traditions and do our best to show respect and gratitude to our ancestors in all that we do. As you can tell, these Pau Wau's mean a lot to us."

"Dancers if you would, please leave the circle as we have our intertribal dance next. All intertribal dancers please report to the East gate," said the Emcee through the microphone.

"I must say...it's a lot more than I expected. This is really special," James said.

"It is, it truly is. Well how long do you guys plan to stay?"

Rebecca glanced towards James then to the kids.

"However long it last," James said with a grin.

"Great...well we'll be here until sundown..." Lee glanced at the Sun. "...which should be around sevenish.

"If you guys get hungry, we have plenty of food trucks around. A lot of good food here."

"Okay...yeah we may have to find us something. Say you don't mind if we get a picture with you do ya?" asked Rebecca.

"No, of course not. Hey, excuse me miss...would you mind taking a picture of us?" Lee said to a nice older lady seated at the end of the wooden bench. She looked to of had some sort of Indian heritage based on her complexion and appearance. Her husband looked more of an Irishman than an Indian when compared to her.

The lady agreed with a gentle smile and after getting a rundown of how to snap pictures with Rebecca's phone, took three shots of Lee and the Randolph's.

"Are you a real Indian?" asked a curious Connor.

That brought on some laughs among those who heard it.

Lee chuckled, then bent at the waste as to get to eye level with him, "I sure am. As a matter of fact, some say I'm a long descendant of Sitting Bull himself."

"Sitting Bull? Yeah, I learned about him in History class the other day. Remember me telling you about him daddy?" Kelly filled with wonder, turned and asked James.

"I sure do. You didn't know you'd get to meet one of his relatives today did you?"

She wagged her head as she and Connor both wore big grins.

"See History class ain't so bad. Right kids?" Lee asked with a wide smile toward Jason, Lauren, and Lily. They each grinned and shook their heads.

"Speaking of that, I think you all will really enjoy Ms. Suzy's stories. Ms. Suzy is a full-blooded Cherokee from Walhalla and has been gifted by the Creator in storytelling. She's good. Her stories are filled with a lot of wisdom."

"Well that will be interesting," said Rebecca.

"Hey, listen, I need to get back to my uncle for the next dance. You will see me out there after this one. But if you need anything just let me know and be sure to check out our vendors, we have a lot of neat handmade crafts and such. Pretty cool stuff."

"Thank you, Lee, we sure will," said Rebecca as they all shook hands again before Lee returned to his seat beside his Chief, uncle Wes.

††††††††††††††††††††††††

AFTER THE NEXT two hours were spent showing various dances, some which even included Lee, his brother

Clennon and Uncle Wes, another hour was spent on the teaching of Native survival methods. Everything from hunting, to fire starting, wood carving, harvesting crops, et cetera.

After that, the Randolph's found some food and finished just prior to Ms. Suzy beginning her story telling.

The crowd settled a bit as Suzy took to the center of the circle, seated in a chair, microphone in hand, with the lowering Sun in the distance behind her.

She began by telling and acting out a few jokes to gain the crowd's attention. Once she had achieved that, she introduced a new word for those who weren't accustomed to the Waccamaw language.

The word was, "Hobbu". Which simply means, "I'm listening, continue." She informed the audience that after each time she finished a story if they would respond with "Hobbu," she'd tell another.

So, she begins.

"Long long time ago, as the great Creator was far up in the sky and almost finished with His creation, he still had a little clay left in His bowl, so He grinded and spread the clay in the bowl and formed it into a long, slim piece of clay. That's when he realized he didn't have enough for arms or legs, so he decided to call this piece, snake.

"He said, 'Okay snake, you stay right here and don't you slither out of this bowl. I'm going to go down to the river and collect more clay. I'm not finished with you just yet. Wait here until I return.' So, the Creator marched down to the river and searched to pick the finest clay to add the arms and legs with. But as the Creator tarried in finding the perfect clay, the ole snake became antsy and began to squirm and slither around in the bowl as his impatience got the best of him. For the Creator was taking far too long for the snake's liking, so he decided to do things himself.

He slithered up the side of the bowl and after a few attempts jumped clean out of the bowl and thumped onto the hard soil below. Snake wiggled and shook off the pain, then slithered off into the forest.

"As he made his way deeper and deeper into the forest, Snake started thinking to himself, 'See this ain't so bad, it'll be all right. If I'd waited in that there bowl until Creator returned, why it'd be nightfall. At least doing things my way, I don't have to sit around doing nothing. Look at me I'm an explorer.' Snake boasted as he continued slithering through the woods. Not long after Snake escaped from the bowl, the Sun began to set, and the air became chilled. Snake having no fur began to shiver. It was then, the Great Creator returned from the river with two large clumps of the finest clay. To His dismay, He couldn't find Snake anywhere, so he began calling out for him, 'Snake! Snake! Snake! Oh Snake, if you'd just listened to me and waited for me, look what I could have done for you. For I had plans to make you arms and legs, and even some fur so you wouldn't be cold at night. But now because of your impatience, you'll have to go about the Earth crawling upon the dust and at nightfall you'll have no fur to give you warmth. Oh Snake...if only you'd waited for my return.' The Creator said with tears streaming down His cheeks, for the thought of Snake not being complete and having to suffer, brought great pain and sadness for the Creator.

"So, the moral of the story is: Be patient and humbly wait upon the Great Creator, though He may seem to busy Himself with some other task, make no mistake He hasn't forgotten about you and if you will just be patient, He'll give you all that He has planned for you, He won't leave anything unfinished. Hobbu?"

"Hobbu!" the crowd roared back.

"Okay, another story. This one is about a young Native boy by the name of Dragging Canoe. Some of you may have heard of him before.

"So, a long, long time ago, there was a young boy whose name was Attakullakulla, named after his father. Now I know what you're thinking, what kind of name is that? Well it's the Native name for "Little Carpenter." His Father was a small man but was known as a skilled craftsman who'd built most of the shelters and structures within the village. Anyhow, they lived with the Overhill Cherokee on the Little Tennessee River and according to Cherokee legend, the name Dragging Canoe derived from an incident in his early childhood. Wanting to join a war party against the Shawnee, his father told him he could stay with the war party as long as he could carry his own canoe. So little Attakullakulla tried and tried to heave the canoe up on his shoulder like all the others but was just too weak to do so. So instead he only drug it. Hence the name Dragging Canoe.

"Now the name Dragging Canoe wasn't given to him until after the war. Little Attakullakulla would go on to grow into a very strong young boy from dragging his canoe so much and become a great leader and warrior for the Cherokee and led them to great victory over the Shawnee. Now, in Cherokee tradition, we do not believe one has to live with the name they were given at birth, if one does something great and noble for his people, such as Attakullakulla, then that person has the right and honor to change their name. So, the elders of the Cherokee in a show of gratitude and honor, renamed Attakullakulla, Dragging Canoe to honor his determination and persistence and to show gratitude for his efforts in the war. This tradition is still around today, no matter what you've done in the past or who you are today, you can always do something great and noble for your people and earn the right for a new name. Hobbu?”

“Hobbu!” the crowd roared once more.

Ms. Suzy would go on to tell a few more stories in the next half hour that passed.

The Randolph’s stayed to listen to each one before finally rising form the wooden bench and making their way over to the vendors just before speaking to Lee on their out.

They give Lee their appreciation for inviting them to such a beautiful event, say their goodbyes and then one by one climb into the Dodge Caravan after carefully loading James through the sliding side door.

Rebecca turns the ignition and heads for the main road that’d take them back to 501.

“Wow...how about that? That was really something wasn’t it?” asked James.

“It sure was. That was really moving and so much wisdom...I mean it’s just hard to put into words the feeling that was in the atmosphere there,” said Lily as she turned to her daddy from the passenger seat up front.

“Yeah...you’re right. It was really special.”

Rebecca flipped her turn signal as she waited for the passing traffic to allow her onto to 501.

They spend the next 45 minutes discussing the Pau Wau and all the sights, sounds, feels, and stories that came with it. By now Connor and Kelly were out cold, Jason was dozing, leaving James, Lauren, Rebecca and Lily in full conversation.

They were just passing through Little River, the last coastal town in South Carolina before the state line. They were travelling along US-17 N, about to turn onto US-179.

“I think the stories from Miss Suzy is what will stick out for me. So much meaning and morals,” said Lauren.

“Yeah, I really liked the story of Snake and draggin—

James didn't finish his sentence, just as they were crossing through what appeared to be an empty intersection, a glimpse of bright lights filled his peripheral. The sound of tires screeching across the asphalt was followed by the crash of the impact.

A pickup truck clips the back-driver side, which sends the Randolph's van spinning across the black pavement before eventually rolling three times and coming to a halt upside down in the grass. The van's engine steamed as lights flashed in abundance.

†††††††††††††††††††††

THE TRUCK THAT ran the light sat about ten yards to the right. The driver door creaked opened as one large black boot thudded down onto the asphalt followed by another.

Moans and cries could be heard coming from the wreckage. The large black boots strode to the van. Followed by a soft whistle that kept a nice tune. His favorite. The boots stop at the driver door where Rebecca hung upside down, suspended by her seat belt, face bloodied with shards of glass. Look at her. Such a pretty woman, even after surviving a car wreck. Mother will be proud.

The man wore all black, easier to blend into the night that way. He held a cloth in one hand and a glass bottle in the other. He sloshed the liquid from the bottle onto the cloth, all the while continuing his whistle and stealing glances to his surroundings. This would be easier than he'd planned. He was so good at what he does. Kirkland should give him a promotion.

Rebecca moaned. She looked so helpless like this. He almost felt sorry for her. Stop it.

Frank forced the cloth to Rebecca's face, not putting up much of a struggle, she was out within a matter of seconds.

He retrieved his large blade and sliced the belt, dropping her limp body with a thud. He hooked his hands under her arm pits and drug her out before carrying her to his truck and binding her hands and feet along with taping her mouth and eyes shut with tight strips of duct tape.

Satisfied that Rebecca wasn't going anywhere, Frank returned to the van reaching behind his back as he did so. He retrieved a small revolver, checked the cylinder and chuckled. He reached the side of the van, busted the window with the butt of the pistol, shards of glass scattered across the pavement, revealing James, Jason, Lauren, Kelly and Connor, all bloodied and mangled. Kelly whimpered in pain, as the rest was out cold.

"Wow. You know James, we've waited a long time for this. Too bad it's taken this long. If only you would have had my back that day, then none of this would have had to happen. But hey...least you won't feel anything right?"

He raised the revolver, cocked the hammer, and with the slightest of movement from his finger, the hammer released...the shot rang out as fire emitted from the barrel followed by a trail of smoke.

† Devil's Den †

38

Tree frogs were in abundance and so were the Cicada

bugs with all of their screeching into the dark night. The forest was alive with all its inhabitants. A pack of Coyotes could be heard off in the distance, likely hunting their meal for the night.

A light mist had begun to fall, soaking the ground with its dew. The crackle and pop of a flame sounded off to the right. Next to it was a soft whistle.

Rebecca took her time opening an eye lid, immediately greeted by all the aches and pains that often accompany a car wreck as bad as the one she'd just survived.

She winced, grunted, and squirmed, which caused her to notice just how little of movement she could muster, not just from the pain but from the binding ropes as well. She lay on her side, hands tied to her feet behind her back, which wasn't too comfortable of a state to be in as one could imagine. She still wore the duct tape across her mouth, which made her sick as the taste of the chemically enhanced adhesive was torture in and of itself.

At least the man was kind enough to remove the tape that was stretched across her eyes. Must've done that while she was out.

She tried to open her other eye, but it was sticky from the residue of the tape, so she had to give it a little force. It popped open and that's when she saw the dancing flame that licked skyward, along with the source of the whistle. The man in black. His shoulders wide, his hands larger than most. He sat on a log crumbling a dry leaf with his hands and tossing the remnants into the fire. His eyes were blacker than the night sky, his face covered with thick gray and black hair. He leered back at her with enough hate to steal her breath and take her soul into the darkest abyss known to man.

The eyes, just something about them wasn't right. They were like what one could imagine Satan himself to own.

Rebecca's heart sunk to the pit of her stomach, her breath caught in her chest, her heart pounded so hard it hurt. Gooseflesh rippled across her body as she began to tremble. Her mind raced back to the night of Connor's night terror. "He had lots of hair and a long gray beard. He was big and mean looking," Connor's voice echoed in her mind.

This is him. It has to be. This is Ethan.

The thought of running crossed her mind, followed by the reminder of her current binding. Not now. Maybe when he's not looking, but not now.

Those piercing black eyes just stared back at her, almost as if reading her mind by way of searching her soul.

"Well...long time no see, Rebecca. How in the world have you been?" the man said with a raspy voice.

It sounded familiar. This has to be Ethan.

Rebecca looked back at him with misty eyes as his voice and the thought of him knowing her name caused her to tremble even more.

"No worries...no need to answer. I'll do all the talking, you only need to nod or wag. Okay?"

Rebecca hesitated, frozen as fear washed over her like a wave from the deep.

"Okay?" the sternness in his voice demanded she answer.

She nodded with tears flowing down her cheeks.

"Oh, come on Rebecca, there's no need to cry. Honest. Mama said she didn't want *you*, only your company."

Rebecca's whimpered and wagged her head.

"Oh, there's nothing to fear. Ain't that right Mama?" He said as he twisted on the log and looked up behind him, high upon a tree.

The sight caused her to jump and scream through the tape as best she could. Rebecca wiggled in a vain attempt to break free, but the rope was just too strong.

Her heart raced, her body shook, every hair on her body stood fully erect. Just then a pain unlike anything she'd ever felt before, like two lightning bolts struck both of her hamstrings. She shrieked through the tape in agony. It felt as if each muscle had been ripped from the bone.

Along with that, the sight of a decomposed human skeleton, with long hair still attached, was just too much for her to handle.

The man rushed over and cupped his palm over her mouth and spoke softly in efforts to calm her.

"Ssshhh...calm down now. It's okay, I'm not going to kill you. You are a prized possession now, I have far more control with you alive than dead. Plus...Mother doesn't see any reason for your sacrifice...just as long as you behave like the good little girl that you are and don't do anything stupid," he said with an intense glare to be sure he got the point across.

His black eyes drilled into her like a hornet. He was looking right through her. He leaned in close, his tongue pressing against the back of his tight lips, his jowls began to quake. His eyes narrowed. his tongue protruded like a snake.

"Fear. It's puts off quite the odor doesn't it?" a smirk stretched the corner of his mouth, causing his beard to raise an inch.

The pain in her legs caused her to grow nauseous. She began to gag and heave, her cheeks filling with puffs of air.

Seeing this, the man waited until just the right moment, then ripped the tape from her mouth, allowing her to spew what could not be held back any longer.

"You really having it rough aren't ya?" he said with a grin.

Rebecca gasped for breath and coughed up what remained.

"Why? Why are you doing this? Who are you?" she managed to say in between breaths.

He tilted his head and grinned as if stunned to learn she didn't know who he was. He seemed to find it funny as he busied himself with retrieving something from his coat pocket. He pulled out a glass bottle of liquid and a cloth.

"Listen...about your legs. I removed the hamstrings...you know... in case you thought about making a run for it. They usually don't get too far without those. And as for why...I've done told you...to give Mother some company...as for who...well I have to say I'm surprised you don't remember me...I'm Franklin Ethan Thompson. Or as you might recall...Ethan."

It was him. Her heart stopped as the last thing she remembered seeing was his big hand approaching her face with the rag...then her head spun into darkness as she was dragged into an abyss of fear.

39

Lights flashed and flickered as they danced their way

across the trees. Fire trucks, ambulances, police officers, they were all here. The scene was an absolute mess and nothing less than chaotic.

It'd taken fifteen minutes for anyone to pass by and notice the carnage. This particular part of 179 wasn't a well-travelled route, especially late at night. But none the less, the Calvary was here.

Fireman busied themselves with the Jaws of Life on the passenger side, while paramedics and rescue workers were quick at work with James, checking for vitals and assessing the damage.

He still had a pulse, all be it was barely existent, but make no mistake it was there. The amount of blood oozing from the side of his head, revealed where the bullet had entered.

They remove James from the van and placed him onto a gurney before wheeling him to an ambulance. Something demanded a paramedics attention.

"Hey, hold up...did you see this?" the man said as he pointed to James's left ear.

The gurney stopped.

Two other paramedics stopped and looked, a younger man and older woman. Perhaps in their 30's and 60's.

They each leaned in for a closer look.

His left ear was missing. Cut clean off. Not only that, but there was something etched into his flesh just behind his missing ear... *GTK*.

40

Three hours had passed since Rebecca was last awake in this world. During those three hours, most of them were filled with her attempting to escape a thick dark shadow that relentlessly chased her through a dense black forest. That dream would pass, then right on its heels, she'd find herself inside a darkened home, where torn wall paper hung like ribbons, alongside black and white photos of missing people. Next to the missing people were photos of her and James in their home watching and episode of Dallas.

She knew where she was and the second she'd realize it, something would let out a deep roar, so strong it would rattle the entire home. Panic and terror would rush over her and she'd attempt to flee, only to be blocked by a large man in black with a long gray beard. Then she'd wake and start the process all over again. Chased through the forest and frightened from the home.

But this time after she'd been stopped by the man in black, which she now come to know was without a doubt Ethan Thompson, she began to wake in this world. The first thing she noticed was the sound of the crashing waves. She knew then, she was near the ocean, having lived in an ocean front home for quite some time now, she'd grew accustomed to the spilling of the breakers.

The next sound she noticed, was what seemed to be some type of wind chime, only with more depth than that of your standard high pitch chime. Like comparing the sixth string to the first string on a guitar. It still had the ting of the chime but was much deeper sounding. It was different and unique.

The place felt damp and sandy, she had to be near the ocean, didn't she?

Bam! The lightning bolts returned to both of her hamstrings, causing her to jolt and flash open her eyes.

There he sat not even ten feet away, just staring back at her, like the prized trophy she was.

All her jolting and squirming reminded her of her confinement. She was still bound with her hands tied to her feet behind her back.

Her mouth was duct taped once again.

"Well hey there...how you doing?" he asked quite bubbly, as if seeing a close friend after a good deal of separation.

Her breathing quickened, as did her heart. A sickening feeling arose in her gut.

Her instincts told her, this wasn't good, and her body had taken control of its own. This was her fight or flight instinct kicking in. But being bound as she was, she couldn't do either, so her mind and body were in a panic once again.

"You've been out for quite some time. Had me worried I may have overdosed you," he paused for a moment and glared at her with down cast brows.

He waved her off with a flash of his hand.

"Oh foot, I'm just kidding. I wouldn't do that to ya. C'mon Rebecca...you know me better than that. Right?" he glared once more, demanding a response.

She nodded.

He smiled, then turned his attention above her.

"Hey Mama...what'd you think? Think I should untie her?"

His monologue sent chills down Rebecca's spine. Though she didn't see her, she knew she was there, for she could feel her peering down on her. Almost felt like she was hovering over her shoulder and for all she knew, Mama might very well be. Maybe not physically, but perhaps spiritually. The thought caused even more fear. The trembling increased.

Slow down now...gather yourself. The body may be bound, but not the mind, he can't touch that unless he's allowed to.

He nodded and smiled as if having just received a delightful command from a high ranking official.

"Okay...Mama says I can untie you," he looked down with a smile.

ROAAAARRRRRRAAAAAHHH!!!!!!

It shook the ground it was so loud. Sand fell from the ceiling.

NOOOOO!

A deep raspy voice bit off as the sound bounced off every square inch of the place and sent a shiver throughout Rebecca's body. A dark shadow manifested in the corner before jolting upward and riding across the ceiling over Rebecca.

Quaking uncontrollably with tears soaking the sand she lay upon, the dark figure bolted behind her, still seeming to crawl across the ceiling until it was out of sight.

Glass jars rattled and crashed to the earth, sending Ethan into a rage.

"Kirkland stop it! You're going to get us caught!" he said with piercing eyes and a firm jaw directed behind Rebecca.

Everything in her said not to, but curiosity got the best of her. She forced herself into a roll and managed to flop to her opposite side, eyes off of Ethan, but locked onto the dark shadow which hovered over the decomposed woman known as Mama.

If that wasn't enough, the jars caused a greater storm within her as fear and dread tossed like a raging sea in her gut.

Laying on the sand among shattered glass and liquid, were fingers, both small and large, a thumb or two in the mix as well. Placed upon a wooden shelf and sealed in liquid, were at least a dozen mason jars which housed human body parts, such as fingers, two lips, a tongue, and an ear.

Numerous small canine like skulls surrounded the jars on both sides. Mama was stationed in the center stretched out upon a wooden cross. Candles gave light, as they formed a circle at her feet below.

YOU FOOL! YOU CAN'T KEEP HER ALIVE! YOU MUST KILL HER NOW! STOP PLAYING AND DO IT!

The voice growled like a rabid dog. The dark figure didn't need words just the tone of its voice was enough to cause terror and chaos within one's heart.

The tone must've struck Ethan as well, because there was a moment passed before he managed to respond.

"Yes Kirkland...but if I manage to keep her alive, I retain my power among the Randolph's. Besides Mother has done said she wanted company for when I am away. This I will do to please Mot-

DO YOU NOW TAKE ORDERS FROM A CORPSE?

The shadow cut in as the voice hissed and slithered throughout the room.

"Kirkland! Now that's enough! Sorry Mama...don't listen to him. How dare you speak of my Mother this way! I have done all you've asked of me, have I not? Now that Mother is finally getting her voice back, she has my priority."

The shadow huffed and swiped more jars from the shelf, sending them crashing to the ground. Shattered, they leaked their preservative, which by the smell of it was some sort of diluted vinegar. A lip and an ear now joined the fingers as they lay in shattered glass among the sand.

The darkness returned to its place above Mama. Multiple strains of hair lifted from her scalp before being ripped and tossed toward Ethan, but not having enough density to carry their weight they fell onto Rebecca just a few feet away from the candles, broken glass and body parts.

She screamed and moaned through the tape, squirmed as best she could before managing to roll back over to face Ethan, who stood frozen with an open jaw.

But not for long, as rage washed over him like a tsunami. He began to quake as he gritted his teeth, snarled his nose and lowered his face and glare.

"Kirkland...I've had enough. I will tell Lucinda of your actions, or better yet...shall I tell Ender?"

"YOU'RE GOING TO TELL LUCINDA AND ENDER OF MY ACTIONS? HUH...AND WHAT MAKES YOU THINK I WON'T TELL THEM OF YOURS?"

Just like that, the darkness was gone.

"Kirkland wait...don't do this! Come on...don't do this to me Kirkland! I'm sorry...I'm sorry. Please don't do this," Ethan begged as he dropped to his knees, palms covering his face. He sobbed so strong his shoulders jolted in rhythm.

It was a real sight to behold. Such a big and evil man brought to his knees in sobs at the words of something even more sinister than himself.

Rebecca swallowed hard and attempted to catch her breath as it escaped her at every grasped.

Her heart felt like it could leap from her chest any second. Every hair on her body was stiff as they sat upon tiny hills across her flesh.

Sweat trickled down her forehead only to be met by tears that ran sideways down her cheeks. The waves continued to crash in the distance and that odd windchime kept singing into the night.

Ethan continued his sobs, crying as if he'd just lost a dear loved one.

Rebecca squinted her eyes, bit her lip and forced her mind somewhere else. Anywhere but here in this seemingly homemade bunker crafted from sand.

She used her imagination and squinted a bit harder for greater effect. Suddenly, she was transported to her child hood in Southern Louisiana. Her grandpa's voice calmed her spirit, she turned and there he was toting a bag of fresh shrimp caught straight out of the bayou.

"Rest my little angel...it'll be all right. Just trust me. We've got our eyes on you up here, believe me. I love you more than you'll ever know, and I won't let nothing happen to you. Be strong and remember who you are. You're a Cajun through and through and us Cajun's don't go down without a fight. You're more powerful than you think and smarter than you know and loved beyond your comprehension...now how about giving your grandpa a hand with this here shrimp. Boy are we gonna eat good tonight," he said with a thick Cajun accent as he wore a grin so large it seemed to wrap Rebecca's heart in a warm embrace.

Her soul rejoiced and her spirit calmed as she spent the rest of the night in a deep sleep. In her dream, she sat beside her grandpa peeling shrimp.

41

Detectives were on the scene of the wreckage. James, Lily, Jason, Lauren, Kelly, and Connor had been rushed to Brunswick County hospital with James, Lily and Kelly in critical condition. Jason, Lauren, and Connor were banged up, but stable, including a broken ankle and arm for Lauren, a large gash and shattered wrist for Connor, and lacerations and bone bruising for Jason. They were expected to make a full recovery. As for the other three, only time would tell just how severe their injuries may be.

As detectives busied themselves searching the area and van for any clues, one of them found a neatly folded piece of paper on the floor mat of the driver's side.

The detective squatted his calves, placed the flashlight in his mouth and with latex gloves was careful to unfold it. It was a hand-written note.

"Hey, come take a look at this," he beckoned over his shoulder to two detectives.

They each were squatted beside the van with their lights shining along the side where the letters, GTK were scratched with a knife into the metal.

They rose and made their way over to Detective Davis Green who stood near the driver side door holding the note in hand. He waited for Detective Honeycutt and Detective Barnhill before he began reading aloud.

Dear Detective,

Hope you are well... I'm doing fine. Might you ask. It has taken me a long time to do what has just been done. Matter of fact, I first laid eyes upon the hardass some 25 years ago down in Georgetown. Tried to do it then, but just couldn't muster up enough courage. But tonight, I didn't lack any. I finally did it! Mama and Kirkland will be so proud. This will bring them great joy. Now, I am going to go ahead and warn you all... If you try and disrupt what I've done, it won't be me you'll have to worry about. I'd pay more attention to Mama, Kirkland, Ender, and Lucinda. They're the ones you'd be careful not to cross. I'm just simply the one who does their dirty work; but you see they are the ones who orchestrate everything and trust me when I say this... they're not someone you want as enemies. It would be in your best interest to drop this case and rule it as a drunken hit & run. Because if you decide to make this anything more... well... let's just say there will be hell to pay. Oh... and make sure you tell Walter I said hi. That is if he is still kicking, he may have done called it quits. And as for Rebecca... she'll give Mama some company while I'm gone, I'm sure they'll get along just fine. Will be one big happy family. So long Detective. Hope you use your head and don't do anything stupid.

Take care,
GTK

over →

Every breath you take

Every move you make

Every bond you break

Every step you take

I'LL BE WATCHING YOU

Every single day

Every word you say

Every game you play

Every night you stay

I'LL BE WATCHING YOU

Oh can't you see
you belong to me
How my poor heart aches
With every step you take

I'LL BE WATCHING YOU

— THE POLICE

Quite ironic isn't it?

GTK

42

Monday morning arrived, and Wilson Banther was pulling into the gravel parking lot at B&B Heavy Machinery and Equipment.

He exits his F-350 Ford pickup and finds the key for the front door on his key ring. But something in the back where all the backhoes, bobcats, bulldozers were stationed seemed off and begged for his attention. He peered through the chain linked fence and noticed what appeared to be someone sitting behind the controls of one of the company's prized backhoes. Wilson did a double take to be sure his aging eyes weren't fooling him.

The man was still there.

What in the world? Who the heck does this guy think he is?

Wilson marched through the front door, slammed it shut behind him and proceeded out the side which led to the yard with all their equipment.

Blood boiling and expletive words rushing through his mind faster than the speed of light, he stomped off toward the backhoe, ready to give this trespasser a piece of his raging mind. He had a good mind to yank the dude out of the seat.

Wilson bolted up the steps leading to the door of the driver's seat.

"Hey! Who the heck—" he yelled as he slung open the door.

The man slumped and fell out past Wilson, thumping to the earth.

Frozen, Wilson's rage subsided as the reality of the situation began transmitting in his mind like a code reader deciphering Morse.

He eased down the steps, eying the man lying on the ground. Dressed in a flannel shirt, blue jeans and boots, he could've passed for one of his workers if his face would have been more familiar.

He crossed to the body which lay on its belly, cheek pressed into the dirt. Wilson nudged the man's leg with his boot, giving him a good shake. Nothing. The body seemed stiff. No doubt it was a dead man.

Wilson swallowed the lump in his throat, retrieved his cell from his pocket and punched out 911.

As he was on the phone with dispatch, he noticed something out of place. He knelt down by the man's face.

"Sir, can you give me an address?"

Wilson stretched his sleeve over his hand and gently lifted the man's face enough to reveal the other half of it.

"Sir?"

Wilson jolted back and stumbled to the ground, dropping his phone in the process.

"Sir, is everything all right? I need an address, so I can send someone out for help. Can you do that for me?"

The dispatcher squawked in the dirt as Wilson was busy scrambling backwards on his haunches, eyes squeezed shut in an attempt to erase the image seared into his mind.

He took a deep breath and let it out with grace, then crawled forward and reached to gather his phone, the dispatcher still squawking.

He rose to his feet, dusted his pants and placed the phone to his ear.

"Ma'am, I believe this may be a murder. The man's eye ball has been completely cut out. You need to get someone out here as soon as possible," his voice loose and shaky.

"Okay sir, yes we will do that, but first I need an address to send them to."

"Right. It's 455 Smith Road in Supply."

"Okay thank you sir. Sit tight, I'll have officers and a detective out there shortly. In the meantime, don't touch anything and stay alert in case the perpetrator is still in the area. Help will be there soon. Stay calm and stay safe."

"Thank you, ma'am."

43

Jason was the first to wake at the hospital. It was *9:18.*

After opening his eyes and noticing his strange dwellings, his mind was sent into a panic, his screams grabbed the nurse's attention.

Two of them rushed into the room. Blue scrubs and name tag around their necks. One perhaps in her thirties with blonde hair and the other likely in her fifties with dark hair.

His breath was quick and labored, his eyes were the size of golf balls.

"Ssshhh...calm down now. Everything's okay. Take it easy," the blonde nurse said in a little more than a whisper. Her voice soothing as she rubbed his arm.

"Where am I? What happened? Where's my family?" Jason asked with quick tones.

"You're at Brunswick County Hospital. You and your family were in a bad wreck, but they're all here being treated. It's okay...you all are in good hands. We are going to take good care of you. Just relax and take it easy for me okay?"

Jason caught his breath and swallowed hard, then briefly shut his eyes and nodded.

"Have you told the McGaha's?"

The nurse tilted her head then looked to the other nurse standing over her shoulder.

"Are they family, or..." the dark-haired nurse questioned.

"Not quite, but they feel like it. You need to let Lee McGaha know. He is me and Lauren's History teacher at West Brunswick. We were actually just coming home from their Pau Wau. But he needs to know. Can you please make sure he finds out?"

"Yes of course, we will be sure that happens."

"Thank you. When can I see my family?"

The blonde nurse cleared her throat to buy her some time to find the right answer.

"Well, you see they are all resting too...so we think it would be best to wait until maybe tomorrow so you all can get rested up to quicken the healing process. Best thing you can do is relax and get some sleep and take it easy for the next few days. Maybe tomorrow we can arrange for you to see each other. Sound like a plan?"

Jason nodded with a gentle smile.

††††††††††††††††††††††

VOICES. The room was full of them. Coming from every direction and pitch. It sounded like passing through a high school hallway. One voice was louder than the rest and it was vaguely familiar.

"Stop it! Just stop it! I can't take this anymore! Haaaaaaaaa!"

Ethan's voice jolted her awake as her eyes opened quickly to the sight before her. Her vision still a bit fogged from her sleep, she caught glimpse of Ethan standing on a five-gallon bucket alongside his Mother still hanging from the cross.

Rebecca blinked twice to clear the fog. That's when she realized she wasn't on the floor anymore. Her arms were stretched above her head with her wrist restrained in chains. Her ankles just the same below her.

She wiggled, causing the chains to rattle which caught Ethan's ear.

He spun on his heels. "Oh...well...good morning! Sorry if I woke you. I was just having a little chat with Mother and the others."

Rebecca wiggled some more and tried to plead through the adhesive tape, but her voice was trapped as well. The tape had been wrapped multiple times around her mouth and head, so without the assistance of hands, there was no hope for ever getting her voice back.

Ethan gave his dead Mother a hug and whispered in her ear before stepping down from the bucket and making his way over to Rebecca.

"Rebecca...sweet little miss Rebecca. I hope you are enjoying your stay, I really do. Now...I have a few errands I need to run. I need to grab some things from the camp and check on some other things elsewhere. So, I shouldn't be gone long. And don't do anything stupid okay? Mama is watching, and she likes to run a tight ship and certainly won't mind dealing out a good spanking if need be. So, you best behave while I'm gone. The others are here too..." Ethan said as he gazed around the room and along the ceiling. "...They'll be watching, so you better be on your best behavior. You definitely don't want to cross them. Trust me on that one," he said with a twisted grin.

"Anyhow...there is something I need to do tonight, and I would like it if you came with me. There's something I have to get for Mama. I just have to talk it over with some folks first," Ethan said as he briefly locked eyes with Rebecca.

His eyes were just not right. They say the eyes are the window to one's soul, well these windows must lead straight to hell itself, because the blackness they emitted were enough to choke your soul and suffocate your heart.

Rebecca's pulse quickened as the tremble returned along with the gooseflesh.

"It's okay...don't worry. I don't plan on killing you, honest I don't. Mother and I just thought it'd be best to give her some company for a while. Now Kirkland doesn't agree, but I'm sure he will eventually. At least I sure hope so.

"Well...I guess I need to go so I can get back," he said as he crossed the room toward his Mother and stopped near all the candles which at the moment was their only source of light.

"Lights on or off?" he waited a moment then decided.

"Might be best to turn them off. Probably best if you didn't see what all lives down here. At least in the dark, you won't see them...you'll just hear them."

One by one, Ethan blew the candles out. Each one leaving the room darker than the last.

With the room now almost pitch black, Ethan leaned over the last candle and paused just above it.

"Remember now, if you get scared...Mama's here to hold your hand. I'll be back," he said before puffing out a short breath causing the room to be engulfed in darkness.

A darkness so thick, her eyes were useless as she couldn't tell the difference between having them open or shut.

The sound of shifting sand told her Ethan must've been climbing a ladder of sorts that had to be rested against the sand. The sound of keys jingling told her of his location. It sounded like he was high. The sound of a lock popping open, followed by the sound of what must have been a door of some type, scooted away which allowed the room to fill the room with a glimmer of light. Enough to reveal Mother was still in her place next to the smoking candles and jars of body parts.

But just as quickly as the light penetrated the room...it left as if being sucked out by a vacuum cleaner.

Darkness returned, and this time decided to stay.

44

Soon after Brunswick County detectives had finished investigating the murder off Smith Road which Wilson Banther had reported, they submitted it along with the Randolph's case to the FBI to see if there had been any similar recent reports. Within minutes Lieutenant Ray Mishoe received a call.

"Lieutenant Mishoe speaking." he said in his gravelly voice.

"Sir this is Federal Agent Ricki Vasquez I just received a report for the incidents there in Brunswick County. We are actually in the process of investigating two murders which give us reason to believe we may be dealing with the same guy. There were similar notes left with the bodies, each which were signed...GTK."

She paused to let her words settle.

Mishoe cleared a phlegm and asked, "Where did the murders occur?"

"Our first body was found in the parking lot of an abandoned gas station just on the outskirts of Houston. While the other body we believe was the first victim as according to the coroner they appear to have been deceased for at least a week. That body was found in the mountains of Big Bear, California. Now both bodies were missing facial features, with the lady in Big Bear, missing an eye and the gentleman in Houston missing his tongue along with two fingers. Each left with a note signed GTK."

"I see…I'm assuming you are well aware of what GTK may very well be referring to?"

"Georgetown Killer?"

"Yes."

"Yes…we are well aware. So, you have your suspicions also?"

"I do. As a matter of fact, the family that were involved in the wreck, well the husband and wife used to be acquainted with Ethan Thompson back in the late 80's just before he disappeared. They were even in the paper back when it took place. I have a gut feeling, this is the same guy."

The line got quiet.

"Agent Vasquez?"

"Yes…I'm here. Well, we need to meet in person. When do you think you could meet?"

"Depends on where it is. I mean I really don't want to leave my guys with everything that's going on."

"Understandable. Let me talk with a few people and see what I can work out. We will likely be bringing a team down your way shortly, perhaps within the next two days we can arrange a meeting?"

"Sounds good. Just let me know. Will this be broadcast?"

There was a brief pause in the conversation as Vasquez took a breath.

"Considering the connections…yes…it most likely will be. To be honest, I'd expect to see this on every news station by tonight or tomorrow."

"You sure that's such a good idea?"

"Well that part is out of my control. If it were up to me, I'd probably wait a little bit before spilling the beans, but something like this will be hard to keep a secret for long. Especially with all the rumors about this San Bernardino Phantom. They have over two dozen cold cases since 94. I don't know if this guys just a copycat or if he and the GTK are the same."

"Yeah. I've had those questions myself. Well...if you hear anything I should know, just give me or my department a ring and I'll do the same. Thanks for calling me back, see you soon."

"Thank you, we'll do and I'll let you know when we're in route. Stay safe."

††††††††††††††††††††††

LEE MCGAHA had just finished his first History lecture for the day at West Brunswick as the clock approached 10:30 and was washing down the white board in preparation for his next class. A few of the students began to trickle in.

He greeted each one with a bright smile which was custom.

With the board clean, he retrieved a black marker and began writing out the day's agenda along with a few reminders of upcoming quizzes and assignments.

"Mr. McGaha?" the teen girl asked.

Lee turned and gave her his attention.

"Yes, Sophie?"

"Where is Mrs. Randolph? Jason and Lauren weren't in lecture either. Just strange for her not to tell us anything and for Jason and Lauren not to be there. Just thought it was odd."

"I was just about to ask the same thing," said another student.

"Yeah, we waited for like 15 minutes, but they never showed up. I texted Jason, but he won't text me back," said Sophie.

"Really? That is odd. Well I haven't heard anything. Give me just a second, let me see if I reach them," Lee retrieved his phone from his desk drawer and walked out to the hall.

As he unlocks the passcode, his notifications showed he had 4 missed calls from the same number and one voicemail.

He checked the message.

"Mr. McGaha, this is Sandra from Brunswick County Hospital, we have a patient here by the name of Jason Randolph, he and his family were in a severe car accident late last night. They're here being treated. He just wanted us to be sure you knew. Feel free to give us a call back if you like. Thank you, bye bye."

The message was like taking a punch to the gut from Ali himself. It took his breath. His head swam with a million thoughts at once. He steadied himself with a hand against a locker.

"Oh Lord, have mercy on them."

He called his brother Clennon and told him to tell Uncle Wes and the others to start praying for the Randolph's.

Lee made his way back into the class room and dismissed them for the day. He grabbed a piece of white paper and scribbled with a pencil, the lead breaking once or twice, he taped his message to the door, cancelling the remaining classes for the day.

He snatched his coat from the back of the chair and rushed down the hall, one arm in, one arm out.

Within twenty minutes he was turning left off US-17 and pulling into the entrance of the hospital. He found a parking space and rushed inside. Once in, he speaks with a kind but heavy-set lady at the desk for directions. Moments later he found himself riding an elevator to the fourth floor.

Lord don't let this be bad.

It tings as the doors separate revealing white walls and another elevator. He exits and finds the hall which led to the desk where two ladies were stationed.

The dark-skinned lady appeared busy as she cradled a phone to her ear while flipping through files of paperwork, so he gave his attention to the light skinned lady, who may have been in a typing competition. Tap-tap-tap-tap.

"Excuse ma'am?"

"Hi there, how can I help you?" her fingers never lost their rhythm, her eyes glued to the screen.

"Yes, I am here to see the Randolph's. I received a message saying Jason Randolph informed you to tell me of their accident. I'm a close friend of the family and a co-worker of Rebecca's as well as Jason and Lauren's History teacher at West Brunswick."

"Oh okay...hang tight just a second let me find their folders," she said as she took a break from the computer, rose from her chair and crossed to a large file cabinet behind her.

"Randolph, correct?"

"Yes ma'am."

"Okay I have it here," she said as she came back to her desk and scanned through the paperwork.

"I believe Jason will be the only one available for a visit, the others are still in recovery. But you are welcome to visit Jason if you like."

"Okay and what room number would he be in?"

"Umm...let's see...uhh...room 427," she said as she found it with her finger.

"Okay...what exactly happened? I mean how are they doing?"

"Well...abiding by our policy there isn't much I can tell you since you're are not immediate family. You will have to speak with Jason and let him relay the messages. I'm sorry it's just the way the policies are. I do know it was a hit and run and I know there are three family members in the ICU with two others in recovery. Jason seems to have gotten the better end of the deal."

Lee played with the numbers in his head and even began mumbling names and counting fingers to be sure.

"You sure there were only six?"

"That's all that we have on file...why should there be another?"

"Yeah, it should be seven. Can you tell me the names of those here?"

The lady looked down and began flipping pages.

"Okay...we have James, Jason, Lily, Lauren, Connor, and Kelly." Lee felt his face drain of blood.

"Sir are you okay?"

Lee gripped the counter and wiped his face with his free hand.

"So, there's no Rebecca?"

"I'm sorry, I don't see that name."

Lee shut his eyes, took a deep breath and gently wagged his head.

"Okay...thank you ma'am," Lee said with misty eyes and a broken voice before heading for room 427.

45

Seated with his wife Annie at Red Lobster in an attempt to smooth things over for not being around much the past few weeks, David Hoffman busied himself with the cheddar biscuits.

A TV anchored in a corner behind Annie played the local news as they showed the highlights for the week. An attempted robbery at a McDonalds, a local lottery winner, a reminder to vote for upcoming mid-term elections, et cetra.

"Honey...what do you think?"

"Huh...bout what?"

She didn't say anything, she just gave him the look.

"You didn't hear anything I just said, did you?"

"I'm sorry...what were you asking?"

"Never mind," she said in a bitter tone as she crossed her arms and looked to the bar.

The scene of a terrible car wreck demanded David's attention. The newswoman's voice described the incident,

"Police are investigating a hit and run and possible kidnapping near Carolina Shores, which caused a family to be rushed to the emergency room overnight, three are in critical condition while three others are being treated with non-life threating injuries. The mother of the family is missing as police believe she was taken by the perpetrator at the scene. Oddly enough, the letters GTK were scratched into the side of the van, causing concern among the detectives..."

The scene cut to a newspaper article from the Georgetown Times in 1989 showing a rough sketch of the GTK.

"As you may recall from the late 80's, GTK or better known as the Georgetown Killer was the name police gave the man they believe was responsible for the murders of Stephen Rickles, Melissa Berkley and Father Louie Vendetti of Lady of our Ransom church in Georgetown. Upon further investigation, detectives learned there have been two murders that have recently taken place..."

The scene jumped to a map as it zooms in on Big Bear just northeast of Los Angeles, before moving over to Houston.

"...the first occurring in Big Bear, California where a 62-year-old woman's body was found wrapped in plastic and placed at the bottom of a ravine where she was discovered by two tourists. In Houston, the body of a 48-year-old man was found at an abandoned gas station just outside of the city. Both bodies were found with notes linking them to the Georgetown Killer."

The scene moves to flashing lights of police cruisers, yellow tape and detectives walking about outside of B&B Heavy Machinery and Equipment.

"Furthermore, at approximately 7:30 this morning, dispatch received a call from Wilson Banther, Co-Owner of B&B Heavy Equipment and Machinery who stated he'd found the body of a deceased man in the cab of one of his pieces of equipment. According to detectives the man appeared to have been deceased for at least 24-hours. Detectives are still investigating and there is no word yet if this may be related to the other crimes previously mentioned."

David eyes darted about the restaurant, sweat beads trickled down his forehead, his breathing was almost that of a pant. His anxiousness stole Annie's attention from the Television across the room.

"Honey...are you okay?"

He swallowed hard, placed a hand to his mouth, leaned over the table and spoke in hushed tones.

"There's something I need to tell you and there's something I need to tell police."

She looked at him with scrunched brows.

"I think I spoke to the GTK the other night."

Annie's face went pale as she swallowed hard.

"Remember the homeless guy I was telling you about? I think that was him."

46

Upon entering room 427, Lee was careful not to frighten the sleeping Jason Randolph. He eased himself into a chair next to the bed, took a deep breath and began a prayer. About half way through, Lee noticed Jason's hand twitch before moving up to his face and pawing just beneath his right eye.

"Jason? It's me Mr. McGaha. How are you feeling?" Lee asked softly.

Jason grunted before raising an eye lid. He wore a large gash just above his right eye brow and another down the bridge of his nose, both eyes were blackened.

He blinked twice, swallowed hard, then attempted to straighten himself, before finally reaching and finding a button alongside the bed.

As the bed was raising, a bright smile streaked across his face as he said, "Boy am I glad to see you."

The bed stopped, and Jason extended his hand toward Lee.

"It's good to see you too Jason. I've been so worried about you guys. I just found out about half an hour ago."

"Yeah...it's crazy, one minute we're all at the Pau Wau having a good time and the next minute we're in here with IV's and bandages," Jason said as he glanced to his arm decorated with IV's and wagged his head.

"Do you remember anything that happened?"

"Not really, I just remember seeing a flash of light just before the impact that sent us spinning and tumbling through the intersection. I was so out of it. I do remember hearing someone talking just before a loud pop went off like an explosion. I think something may have blown up, maybe in the other car or something, I don't know. Did they tell you anything?"

Lee tightened his lips and shook his head, "No...they can't tell me much since I'm not blood kin. It's because of the privacy laws. I can only know what you and your family tell me."

"Yeah, that figures. Well hey, if you can...think you can try and check on the others for me?"

"Of course. I'll see what I can do. Whatever I find out, I'll let you know. Guess I better get going so you can get some rest," Lee said as he stood from his chair and patted Jason's arm.

"It was good to see you kid and I'm glad you're okay," Lee said as he used a knuckle to catch a falling a tear.

"Thank you, it was good to see you too. Appreciate you coming. Hey, can you leave me your number so I can give you a call if I find out something or need someone to talk to?"

"You bet ya, good idea," Lee said in search of a pen, "Hang on a second, let me go grab a pen from the desk out here. I'll be right back."

"Okay."

Lee crossed the room and headed out the door into the hall toward the information desk. He found it strange all the nurses and workers were fixed upon the TV in the corner.

Must be another shooting or terrorist attack. Something sure had their attention, so he followed their glare. As he was a few paces from the desk, the sight in the corner stopped time. A sudden chill shot down his spine as his heart felt like it'd just leaped over a hurdle. Every hair stood erect.

The news was broadcasting the story of the GTK as they showed a sky view from the chopper of FBI and detectives investigating the scene on Smith Road and on the right-hand side of the screen was the sketch of the man believed to be behind such atrocious crimes.

The headline read:

COULD THIS BE THE REAL GTK?

September 22nd, 2014   Myrtle Beach, South Carolina

The Sun News

Spree of Murders, have Detectives and FBI concerned GTK may be back!

As some of you may recall, the term GTK or Georgetown Killer, was the name given to Ethan Thompson back in 1989 as he was heavily suspected of murdering Stephen Rickles and Melissa Berkley and attempting to murder Walter Avery. He of course alluded authorities shortly after Avery's accident at the Georgetown Papermill and hasn't been heard from since.

That is until perhaps now. With three murders occurring across the Country within a span of 7 days, each left with notes and clues claiming to be GTK himself, authorities have reason to believe this could very well be the real GTK.

David Hoffman, pastor at the Good Shepherd church of Shallotte, says to be

Could this be the real GTK?

childhood friends of Ethan Thompson and having not seen or heard from him since his youth, he claims Thompson paid him a visit on Friday night. Having completely changed his appearance, Hoffman says he figured the man to be homeless and never would have guessed it to have been Thompson.

-Continued on page C3

The Return of GTK

Hoffman says the man didn't fully reveal his identity until after ending their conversation.

"The whole time, I'm thinking to myself, 'where have I seen this guy? Why does he seem so familiar?' But I would have never in a million years thought it was Frankie until as he was walking off I asked him and he told me his name. I was just in complete shock and quite honestly too afraid to confront him. As I stood frozen just outside the church doors, with my mind going a hundred miles a minute, he just casually strode down the sidewalk whistling a soft tune before disappearing into the shadows."

Frankie, short for Franklin was the name Hoffman and others knew him by while growing up. According to Hoffman, Thompson's full name is Franklin Ethan Thompson.

Hoffman also mentioned how he's suspected Thompson of having been involved in the disappearance of 11-year-old Will Abercrombie in the summer of 1981.

"I always thought Frankie or his dad had something to do with Will going missing. Frankie's dad got into some kind of cult back then and he even became the leader at one point. Frankie used to tell me and Will all sorts of things back when we were kids.

Said his dad would preform animal sacrifices and blood rituals. Even said his dad had access to what he called 'the voice of God,' something about how he'd grab a pen a piece of paper before going into a trance as he began jotting down orders and prophecies directly from Heaven. I'm telling you the man was a nut case. He'd beat on Frankie and his mom all the time. It was bad, I always felt sorry for him having to deal with all of that. It wasn't long after he told us about his dad's cult, that Frankie started to change. He was just never the same. Stayed mean and angry all the time, something just got a hold of that kid and never let go."

After the disappearance of Will Abercrombie in the summer of 81, Hoffman and Thompson didn't speak again, until last Friday night.

When asked what Thompson spoke about, Hoffman said it was mostly just your normal small talk from someone off the streets, nothing out of the ordinary.

Detectives were led to Thompson's residence in 1989 after a freak accident at the Georgetown Papermill caused Walter Avery to lose both of his arms with Thompson being behind the controls...

At the time. After arriving at Thompson's residence, what detectives discovered inside was nothing short of a horror film.

Claw marks riddled the walls as the wall paper hung like ribbons next to spiked copies of newspaper articles of missing people from all across the Country dating back to the 1950's.

As if that wasn't enough there were photos of families inside their home's, which were clearly snapped from the cover of a wood line. A photo of James and Rebecca Randolph in the comfort of their home caused them to relocate to Holden Beach, North Carolina just a few years after the discovery. The Randolph's now seem to be the GTK's latest victims.

After a horrible hit and run accident left James and two of his children in critical condition with the other three still being treated for minor injuries at Brunswick County Hospital, his wife Rebecca has not been seen since. According to coworker Lee McGaha and the Randolph's son Jason, Rebecca was in the car at the time of the accident, but with her disappearance and the note left behind at the scene claiming to be GTK, authorities are in a desperate race against time.

Having already carried out what authorities are suspecting three murders in the span of 7 days, with the

attempted murder of James Randolph he and his wife's five children, along with the kidnapping of the wife Rebecca, FBI and local authorities are on high alert and asking you to be as well.

The body of the first victim to be discovered was that of 62-year-old Donna Shaw as a tourist noticed her body wrapped heavily in plastic in the bottom of a ravine in Big Bear, California.

Upon examination of the body, a note was discovered which linked the murder directly to the GTK. Two days later on the 17th, the body of 48-year-old Scott Key was discovered in the parking lot of an abandoned gas station just outside the city limits of Houston, Texas.

Again, with a note claiming to be from the GTK. Then two days later on the 19th, Hoffman is paid a short visit from Thompson himself. Then the Randolph's accident takes place last night on the 21st.

Just around 7 am this morning, dispatch received a call regarding a possible homicide on Smith Road in Supply, North Carolina just 16 miles from Holden Beach. As detectives arrive on scene they discover the body of 39-year-old...

Larry Conrad lying on the dirt just outside a backhoe belonging to B&B Heavy Equipment and Machinery. However, this time leaving behind no note or clue claiming responsibility.

Detectives and FBI agents are currently conducting a massive manhunt in Brunswick County in an effort to capture Frank Thompson before he has a chance to strike again.

Authorities are also asking for your help in finding Rebecca Randolph and ask if you know of any information that would aid in the search, to contact your local Police Station immediately.

Or if you have any info that may lead to the location of Frank Thompson contact the local authorities immediately.

Do not approach Thompson as he is considered armed and extremely dangerous. Avoid contact and conversation with the man at all cost.

If you do happen to encounter Thompson, remain calm and flee his presence as soon as you are able, then immediately call Police.

Page C5

At this time Police have not received permission to portray photos of Rebecca Randolph, as the husband and children are still in recovery at Brunswick County Hospital. Once Police have permission, there will be photos posted, to aid in identifying Mrs. Randolph.

Mrs. Randolph is a Science Teacher at West Brunswick High School. She is approximately 5'5 130lbs, long brown hair, brown eyes, and was last seen wearing blue jeans with a black long sleeve shirt with the words, Holden Beach, NC written across the front.

If you have information for police, but would like to remain anonymous, you may contact the Brunswick County tips hot line
at: 910-342-TIPS

By Senior Editor:
Randy Rice

47

The darkness was thick and choking like a cloud of

smoke. It was quiet for the most part, besides the crash of the waves against the slope and the chime in the distance. The pain in both of her legs had returned with a vengeance threating to make her vomit. Rebecca fought the urge with everything in her, knowing full well, if it came up, she'd choke on her own vomit as the tape gave it no place to go but back where it came from.

Death by asphyxiation. How terrible of a way to go.

It was inevitable though wasn't it? Everyone has their time, maybe this is hers. With the way things were at the moment, death might not be such a bad thing after all, at least she'd be out of her misery.

Rebecca...don't think like that, c'mon now...you're a fighter remember? Your family needs you...you can't give up. Not now.

The whisper in her soul gave her peace.

Grandpa's right. Her kids need her, James needs her. She's not a quitter, she's a fighter.

Her mind tumbled with images and sounds of the family. Lost in her memories, the shriek of a woman in distress caused her to drop her thoughts and almost the control of her bowels. Her skin must've leaped a foot off the bone. Her breath quickened as did her blood and heart.

All was silent within the sandy walls, except for the rattle of chains as Rebecca had disturbed them with her sudden movements.

Her eyes darted from side to side in a failing effort to pierce the darkness.

Black.

The air felt damp and chilled as if a cold fog had silently rolled in.

The moisture caused beads of water to develop upon her cheeks and forehead.

After failed attempts of seeing in the dark, she shut her eyes. She squeezed them tight as if to keep them from falling out. She gulped hard to keep the vomit down as it was fighting hard to introduce itself.

Ahhhhhhhh!

The woman shrieked again, causing Rebecca to jerk. She swung as the chains rattled and clunk against links.

He's got someone else down here! He has to. My word how many are down here? He said, "The others are here too." Didn't he? The thought caused Rebecca to groan through the tape as she attempted to cry out for help to whoever would listen. Her shoulders shook as did the chains, their rattle not far behind.

She screamed as loud as she could, but it was only muffled utters behind the tape. No one would hear her but those already within the walls. It was just a waste of energy and breath.

She hung her head and sobbed.

She felt someone or something approaching. She could feel its presence like a soft breeze on a fall day. She raised her head and blinked her eyes. Her heart knocked like a fist against an empty barrel.

A dirty and scaly hand with an out stretched finger was extended, edging closer to her face with every passing second. Hot breath wafted against her cheek, followed by the sound of a soft hiss. Rebecca screamed though the tape and shook violently as she hung from the chains, sending pain throughout her arms and wrist.

Rebeccaaaaa

A grotesque voice muttered through the darkness.

Rebecca slammed the windows to her soul and locked them like a vault as all she could see now was the dark red from the back of her eye lids.

The second she felt the finger touch her cheek, she felt a burst of energy and jolted as is having just been struck by lightning. A powerful force flowed from the crown of her head, throughout her entire body.

The presence shrieked and vanished like a leaf in the wind. A bright light filled the room causing Rebecca to open her eyes to see what was taking place.

Peace and courage had entered the room in the form of that pure light.

"SHE HAS AN ANOINTING FROM THE HOLY ONE! WHAT HAVE WE DONE? SHE DIDN'T KNOW OR ELSE WE WOULD'VE KNOWN," the voice hissed.

"Hands off! She is mine! She is my daughter she just doesn't know it yet. For when she learns of her royal lineage, her light will be blinding to all who oppose her. Leave her be!"

A gentle but powerful voice echoed throughout the room. The view of the place began to shift as did the energy. From darkness to light, from evil to good, from blindness to sight, from hate to love.

Rebecca blinked and scanned the room.

She caught glimpse of a silhouette beaming with light as pure gold shining from behind. Her chains were gone, the sand had turned into lush grass, the Sun beamed down its brilliance, the sound of a flowing River formed behind her, beautiful eagles flew overhead as they shouted their gratitude among the clouds.

"Rebecca?" a calm and gentle voice full of authority yet beaming with love called to her from the right. She turned to face it.

The silhouette of a glowing man was not more than ten feet away and approaching with a radiant smile.

His eyes seemed to pierce her heart, as if knowing everything about her, yet loving her unconditionally like his own child. She was fully known, yet fully loved.

He strode closer and wrapped her in his arms, as his power and light filled every square inch of her body, it took her breath. Her heart burst with joy and love. She locked her fingers around his back, overwhelmed with love and gratitude.

He squeezed her tight, his voice speaking without even having to be audible, "I love you my precious daughter. I am your Creator, you are the apple of my eye, you are beautiful, you are loved, you are strong, you are mine and you are of a royal dynasty, you are a Queen in my kingdom of light, you are the light of the world, I am in you and you are in me for we are one. I will never leave you nor forsake, I am yours and you are mine. You are safe in my arms. Trust me. I love you my child, never give up and fight for your family. I am with you and I am in you. Go in my strength."

Just like that as if being awakened from a dream, she was back in the darkened bunker. Though it was dark all around her, within she was full of light, for her eyes had seen the glory of the Father. Her heart was exuberant as fear seemed like nothing more than a weak bully searching for its next victim.

For what is to fear when you are the light of the world? Who could steal such joy and courage when it had been embedded deep within?

The sound of movement above was only a side note as she replayed her visit with the Creator. Light trickled in, first a small ray the size of her arm, then a full beam the size of a small hatch door. Ethan's shadow appeared as he lowered himself onto the ladder before lowering the door, it squeaked with rusted hinges, he secured the master lock.

He hurried down the ladder almost tumbling. He seemed excited about something.

"Rebecca! Rebecca...I'm back. Hang on let me get the candles going."

She could hear him fumbling in his pockets, before striking a match, illuminating his twisted grin behind the small flame.

The sight caught her off guard.

He'd shaved all his hair, beard and all. He now just wore a five o'clock shadow among dozens of warts and moles along with a shiny bald head.

"What you think huh?" he asked with a wide grin.

Rebecca nodded with kind eyes to appease him.

He hurried and lit the candles one by one, slowly revealing Mama still in place like she was when he'd left.

"Hello Mother...what cha think? You like it?" he asked as he rubbed his prickly face.

Eleven candles were lit as their flame danced beneath his Mama.

Ethan kissed her foot before turning his attention to Rebecca. He crossed the room still wearing that big grin. Warts and acne scars were scattered across his chin and jowls like a farmer tossing seed. Three warts along the bridge of his nose, while the rest found their place elsewhere.

He leaned close nose to nose with Rebecca. The invading of her space made her uncomfortable. His eyes locked on hers, he opened his mouth wide as it seemed to extend further than it should, similar to a small snake attempting to swallow an egg from the hen house. He held his mouth open as his black eyes stared right through her. He huffed out a breath. A stench arose like that of rotten eggs. The sulfurous odor awoke the sleeping feeling of vomit once again.

He closed his mouth and grinned.

"Sorry...I always like doing that. I don't know why, something just comes over me and I can't control it. Anyhow...guess what?"

He waited for her to respond. She shrugged her shoulders and raised her brows.

"Me and Kirkland have decided to take you for a ride tonight. We would like for you to tag along as we carry out the next assignment. That is of course if Mama is okay with it, which I'm sure she will be. I'm so excited, I can't wait. Trust me...it'll be something you'll never forget."

48

Wes McGaha sat in a makeshift circle in his living, along with his nephew Clennon and three of the tribe elders. Native American music played in the foreground with a melodic flute and chant of an elder as the lead, they each were deep in a sincere prayer as their stomachs were raging in hunger from the fast. They prayed, they worshiped, they gave thanks to the Mighty Creator and basked in His presence as He joined right alongside them.

Though they couldn't see Him, He was there. There's simply no mistaking His presence, for you know when you are among a King of such power.

††††††††††††††††††††††

KIRKLAND KNEW the instant Wes declared the fast among the tribe. He became weak as if coming down with the flu. The sincere prayer and fasting of a diligent one devoted to his King, always caused trouble for Kirkland.

Every time he seemed to have what he wanted, there always seemed to be someone who'd decide to fast and pray often not understanding what power and punishment they were releasing upon Kirkland and his fellow workers of darkness.

As he reclined in a chair made of snake skin, seated in a room full of red light from the dancing flames below his office, high in a loft, Kirkland held a hand to his forehead with the back of it resting against his scaly and rotten flesh.

People screamed in agony as the flames licked their flesh straight off the bone, while others ran full speed as large reptilian like creatures pursued them with outstretched razors for claws and protruding daggers for teeth. Others were locked in cages as they hung just above the flame before being lowered by a chuckling demon.

Maggots and flies filled the place like sand among a beach. The choking smell of rotten eggs was strong and vile from all the sulfurous gasses.

Scattered among the room where Kirkland reclined were battleplans and drawings for each assignment, the room was full. Every square inch of the four walls were covered in papers which were spiked to the rocky walls. Most were step by step action plans with a family or person's name and photo attached to the top of the stack. They were all labeled with numbers as some had the word, *'COMPLETE'* stamped across the front in red letters. The rest wore the stamped words, *'IN PROCESS.'*

Kirkland doubled over in the chair, clinching his stomach as if his bowels were being ripped from the inside out. It felt like lightning bolts striking his gut. His head reeled as if had been cracked with a hammer like the one he'd seen the Roman's use to nail Christ.

"It's the McGaha's...I know it is," his voice tight and strained, "I should've known they'd do something like this. Why didn't I see this coming!?" he yelled to the ceiling with clinched fists where large photos of Frank stared back at him. They progressed from the time he first received Kirkland at the Moreland's house. Each photo, he grew a year older. It could have easily passed for a mother's scrap book. The last photo was the most recent, just before Frank had shaved. There would be a new one going up in a few days. Each time Kirkland saw the photos, something inside his gut would leap. Frank had become like a son to him, he just hoped he could keep his strength and finish the assignment.

"Now their prayers have even become a guiding light for Rebecca and with her encounter with the Holy One, if she awakens to who she is, my plan will certainly fail! But I mustn't let them prevail! My plans have come too far to be hindered now. Ender! Lucinda!" he beckoned through clinched teeth with bulging black eyes.

Within minutes two large humanoid like creatures rushed in and stood at attention, neither saying a word before their master, their quick appearance said enough.

They stood with piercing eyes and snarled faces that shifted from that of a human to that of a feline, like the raging and flattening of a breaking wave.

"It's the McGaha's...their prayer and fasting have been heard and acted upon by the Holy One and His warriors. It's only a matter of time before our plans are turned to ruin. We must counter, and we must do so with speed or else we risk losing one of our greatest assets."

Kirkland raised a bony finger to his jaw and chomped among a nail until it was shortened to a quick.

"I need you to go with me tonight and do some convincing of Frank. He can't continue to disobey without punishment. He must know we mean business and are not going to be pushed around. Tonight, we shall counter this attack and have ample supply of warriors should things slip from our control. Because, I know our little ransom will have plenty of protection as ordered by the Holy One due to the prayers and fasting of His saints.

"This will be no easy task, I know. But the sooner we act the better our chances will be. As long as the Randolph's do not join the McGaha's or must I forbid it, the Hoffman's decide to join, we stand a chance. But you both know as well as I do, if the McGaha's gain more members with their rituals, our chances will diminish.

A moment passed.

"With that being said we must act, and we must act tonight!"

49

Packed tight within a conference room at the Brunswick County Sheriff office was several FBI agents, with Ricki Vasquez among them, along with Brunswick County Homicide Lieutenant Ray Mishoe and half a dozen others, including Houston Homicide Lieutenant Jeff Easley and Detective Sam Murphy from Big Bear who were there via Skype.

Agent Vasquez's boss, Agent Dan Turner led the meeting as he stood in front of a large cork board which showed a map of the US with tacks and strings at each murder location.

Next to the map was a large white board where he jotted down the names of the victims with their age, race, appearance, financial rank, et cetra.

"Going back to the murder of Rickles, Berkely and Father Vendetti in 89, along the attempted murder of Walter Avery at the papermill...the guy seems to go dark. Now that doesn't mean he never whet his appetite it just means that if did, he done a much better job of concealing evidence. Which makes me question, is he now trying to get caught?

"Or has he truly taken time off and is just picking up again? Either way the thing that confuses me the most...is there isn't much to go on as far as patterns. It's really just random people going about their lives. He doesn't seem to do a whole of planning. Almost, like he gets the urge from a passing wind or whisper, then uncontrollably acts out of pure passion. Another thing I have to question is, where the hell is his Mother that he talks so much about in the notes?"

A moment passed.

Turner rubs his neck.

"There's really only two possibilities: 1) She's still alive and maybe even a part of his plot, or 2) He murdered her way back when, which giving the circumstances with the family, would be simple to do. I mean none of the family had anything to do with them anyway, so they likely would've never missed her. The same can be said for the dad as well. It seems once he started his cult or whatever you'd like to call it, the family turned their backs and wrote him off."

Turner took a breath and cursed. He hated serial killers with a passion and if he had things his way, they'd all hang in the court yard like the old days with the gallows.

Mishoe cleared his throat, "Sir, what do we know about Frank's dad and this 'cult' of his?"

"Well, according to David Hoffman who claims to be a childhood friend of the guy before all of this took place, he says they were into some type of religious sacrifices and rituals, which he says may have ventured from animals to humans. And according to him, that is what likely happened to ten-year-old Will Abercrombie in the early eighties. Whether it was Frank or his dad who carried it out, Hoffman swears up and down, he believes Frank was ordered by his dad to murder Will for their ritual's. And since there has never been much clue or leads as to whatever happened to the kid, certainly makes for a reasonable theory.

A moment passed as Mishoe and a few others took sips of their coffees.

"Personally, I think it'd be wise if we sent another search crew out to Thompson's old residence and confiscate the grounds. I know they did that in 89, but I would like to see it done again. I think we need to have guys dig and search the entire property while we are busy hunting this sorry—" With that, Turner went on an expletive laced tangent.

"He has had to screw up somewhere along the way or is bound to sooner or later. My gut tells me there is something on that property that could very well lead us straight to him.

"So far, he hasn't left a murder scene without some sort of clue tying back to himself, so as for all the murders we've pulled from the database, what I've mapped out here, seems to be all he is involved in. That's not to say there aren't others that he never took credit for, it just seems that would rub against his ego. It tends to be hard for him to do what he does without taking pride in letting us know he's the one who decided the victim's fate.

"Which is why I honestly don't believe he's the San Bernardino Phantom. I think that's something he'd like to take credit for. I mean there's over two dozen cold homicide cases in their files. Just seems to me that he would have left a note or something.

"And I also wonder if he has taken up his Father's mantle so to speak in returning to the ritualistic sacrifices. He might just be using these body parts as trophies, but then again it could all be a part of his Father's old cult."

Turner sighed as he released his breath and scratched the back of his neck again to conjure up more thoughts.

Vasquez leaned to one side as she sat reclined in her chair while chewing on the butt of a ball point pen.

Lieutenant Mishoe sat with his forefinger lining his jaw, middle just under his lower lip and thumb supporting his chin.

Detective Honeycutt cleared his throat, glanced at those in the room, before settling his eyes on Agent Turner.

"What about Mrs. Randolph? Any leads I don't know about?"

Turner raised his eyes from the floor crossed his arms.

"Well...what you know is what I know. It certainly seems fitting to say that the GTK has come to finish what he started."

"Yeah...well any word on how Mr. Randolph and the kids are doing?"

"Mr. Randolph and two of the kids are in critical condition. I am supposed to be given an update today at noon. I do know the older son Jason is awake and seems to have fared the best compared to the others. I thought it'd be a good idea for one of you to head over there for questioning. Perhaps this evening? Just see how he's doing and if he can remember anything."

"Okay...yeah maybe me and Barnhill can plan to ride over before supper," Honeycutt said as he turned and looked to detective Steph Barnhill for approval. She gave him a quick nod.

"That'd be good. While you're doing that, I'm going to attempt to reach out to Randy Callahan, the homicide lieutenant from 89, see if he can offer any insight," said Lieutenant Mishoe.

"And we do have a search crew at the Randolph's place, correct?" asked Vasquez.

"That's correct. Yes, we have a crew at the place of residence and at their old home in Georgetown, in case he decides to take her to his old stomping grounds. We also have every highway going in and out of Brunswick County on high alert and on the lookout for what forensics believe must've been a dark green truck according to the paint and impressions left on the Randolph's van.

"Every police department in the Country is aware of what's going on and knows what to look for. We have to stay vigilant and use every resource we've got while leaving no stone unturned. We're going to catch this guy and put an end to his bull—" Turner said as he eyed each one for effect.

"All right, well...sounds like you guys have a plan there. If there is anything I can do to help, please do not hesitate to let me know. I mean that. And if I find out anything here, I'll let you know," said San Bernardino Detective Sam Murphy as his voice and picture crackled over the air waves via skype.

"Yeah same here, just let me know how I can help," added Detective Easley in Houston.

"Thanks fellas...we sure will. You guys be safe out there and be sure to let us know of anything you find."

Both men nodded with "Yes, sir," before waving and wishing everyone luck. The screen made a beep, then turned to black.

50

Monday night as the whole Country kept an eye out for the hairy bespectacled serial killer, Ethan and his clean shaven, contact wearing self was busy getting pumped up as he paced the sandy floors in front of the restrained Rebecca Randolph.

Her arms and legs sill wore the rusty chains as before and her mouth was still covered in duct tape. It'd only been removed twice since he'd stuck her in this awful dump. Once to feed her a mushy Kit-Kat bar, along with a swig of warm bottled water and again during the last hour, to give her a few bites from a days old chicken sandwich which seemed to be the rectangle kind you get from Burger King.

She needed to relieve herself, but was too afraid to ask, so she continued to hold it.

Ethan paced and mumbled, often times raising a finger or fist and blaspheming the heavens, then looking to his mother and offering his apologies.

He fussed with Kirkland as they seemed to go nose to nose at times as Ethan would bare his teeth and point a stubby finger like stabbing someone's chest.

This had gone on for at least the past two hours it seemed. It was as if something had overtaken him. Rebecca had noticed how much he'd change the later the day got. His countenance would even shift, as his eyes would widen and grow even blacker than before. His voice tuned down a full step like going from the standard E to a drop D on a six-string guitar.

The Ethan that had taken Rebecca captive was slowly fading, revealing a man, she had yet to become acquainted with.

Her heart picked up pace with every passing minute as the pain in her legs had returned with a vengeance. It'd come and go with sharp stabbing spasms, before finally ebbing away to numbness. She'd learned to hope and eagerly await that numbing sensation.

The pain was so severe, it caused her eyes to moisten the sand at her feet. She'd squirm and twist in effort to find a position that may alleviate the pain, but such a position was hard to find.

Ethan stopped on a dime. Shuffling dirt and sand as he did so. He stood silent with his back to Rebecca, hands and head hanging limp toward the floor.

He didn't move or say a word for at least five minutes, it was like he'd been tranquilized.

Sweat and tears fell from Rebecca's face like raindrops off a gutter. She could hear her own heart beat as the blood sped through her arteries.

A chill filled the room slowing the pace of her sweat glands. Her teeth began to chatter on their own accord. The candles under Mother, began to dim before being snuffed out by the cold darkness.

With the room now pitch black, the only sounds distinguishable was that of the waves and the occasional ting from that awkward distant chime.

The soft shuffling of feet in the sand demanded her attention. It came from her left which was opposite of the direction she'd last seen Ethan.

The shuffling edged closer as did the cold damp fog she'd felt before. She shut her eyes and did her best to calm her heart. As fast as it was pounding, she was afraid it'd tire out and quit.

The shuffling continued, accompanied now by a deep labored breath like someone struggling with an asthma attack.

Whoever this was, must've only stood a foot away from her face as their hot breath pressed against her cheek. The stench turned her stomach.

Shaking and panting behind the adhesive, she struggled to find her breath. Her lungs just wouldn't work. She went on like this for about the length of time it takes to sit at a red-light.

The hot, gut wrenching breath still pressed against her face. After minutes had passed, a raspy voice pierced the air in a low whisper, "I'm here!"

Rebecca jerked and screamed through the tape as best she could. Her heart and mind pounding harder with every passing second.

"Rebecca...its time," a voice said from her right that sounded like Ethan.

Footsteps thudded through the sand, before a large hand dressed in a damp cloth covered her face. She was out within two breaths.

51

The air was frigid as it swept past in a soft but steady breeze. Except for the moon giving its light from its fullness, the night seemed darker than usual. The sound of the howl garnered my attention, so I opened my eyes to take in my surroundings. Tall weeds brushed past me as I found myself walking through a thick field.

The howl grew louder and deeper, edging ever closer. I spun in a 360 to avoid any flank. A muffled cry called out from my left. The flicker of the flame against a pole was what my eyes rested upon.

The sight and sound caught me off guard, but the muffled cry came again, this time almost saying my name. I began to trot through the thickness of the field, getting stuck by briars with every other pass.

The pole and flame grew larger as the woman's cry became louder. That's when she said my name and I knew instantly it was Rebecca. I jolted into a dead sprint, tearing through the briars and tall weeds, swatting them away like bees.

Suddenly the weeds and briars were gone as I stood at the edge of a large circle. In the center, was a large upside-down cross which held my wife dressed in a white gown. A fire pit which incased a nice flame sat only a few yards away.

As I stood frozen for a split second at the sight before me, her tear stained eyes locked with mine. My heart ached and yearned for her embrace. I broke from my stillness and made a few steps before being met by the source of the howls.

A large black dog entered the circle from the field and stood in front of me, daring me to flinch. His nose snarling, his fangs begging me to become its next meal. This dog was massive and would have no problem taking me down.

I took an easy step back with my hands in front of me to calm him, but he wouldn't have it.

"Ssshhh...calm down now, calm down."

He barked and leaped a full step closer. Rebecca cried through the gag in her mouth as she squirmed upon the twisted cross.

"Why it's good to see you James. It's been a while wouldn't you say?" a deep raspy voice entered the air, but I struggled to find its source.

I turned every which way, all the while not allowing the dog to escape my peripheral.

That's when I caught glimpse of a large man, with long hair and beard stepping out of the field I just came from. He'd likely watched as I trotted past him. He entered the circle without ever glancing my way, his eyes were fixed on Rebecca. He strode towards way in short strides.

"I've always wondered how you two have held up since 89. Seems to me this side of the Country has been pretty dull without the GTK. Thought I'd give em something to talk about. Besides I need to finish what I started," I knew who he was.

He reached into the fire pit and picked up a torch. Held it high as its flame licked towards the heavens. He said something in what sounded like another language. He lowered his arm, glanced over his shoulder and locked eyes with mine.

It was him. It was Ethan from the mill. His eyes still had that way of penetrating your soul and stuffing your heart and lungs with acid.

The corner of his mouth raised in a smirk, his shoulders jerked as he gave a soft chuckle. He extended the torch toward Rebecca.

"Noooo! Stop it!" I screamed with all that was within me.

He stopped with the torch about two foot from her face. He twisted his head over his shoulder like an owl. His face contorted as it resembled that of a cat.

"What!?" he hissed as his tongue with a split at the end, rolled out of his mouth and hung past his chin.

"Don-

I didn't finish my words as something hit Ethan like a swinging wrecking ball, knocking the torch to the ground as he went flying through the air about 5 yards before thumping to the ground and skidding across the dirt.

A glowing light filled the right side of my vision. I looked and there stood a giant of a man, with long blond hair, thick burly chest, arms bigger than my legs and legs bigger than my body. He was clothed in armor from head to toe, toting a large bronze shield in his left hand with a large iron sward in his right.

It was then that I heard chanting and praying. I turned around and saw Lee with his Uncle Wes, brother Clennon and several others of the tribe knelt to the dirt in earnest gut-wrenching prayer. The glowing man seemed to grow stronger and brighter with every word they spoke. He stood with a clinched jaw and eyes fixed straight ahead at the recovering Ethan. The black dog by his side licking his bearded face. Ethan moaned as he squirmed in the dirt.

The big man, then looked to Rebecca as a wide smile broke across his face. He was by her side in two steps. He hurried and loosed her from the cross.

"Dear daughter of the most High, do not listen to his words, they are only poison that blinds you to who you are," he lifted and turned her up right, before cradling her in his arms.

"You are more precious in the eyes of your Father than you will ever know, and you are more powerful than you could ever fathom. All the power that the Father possesses is in you, because His spirit resides within you. You are the Light of the World and no darkness can ever overcome this Light. Hallelujah to the Lamb of God!" he said with a beaming smile, looking deep into her beautiful brown eyes. He brushed the hair from her face with gentle strokes, then raised his eyes to mine and marched toward me, still cradling my wife.

He stopped in front of me and said, "James...you are stronger than you know. Trust in the Father and He will give you the wisdom and strength to go on. In Him you can do all things, but apart from Him, you can do nothing. He resides within you, surrender to His will and still small voice, He will not lead you astray. Trust those He places in your path and never doubt His ways. And when you don't understand...trust. He is with you and He is in you. Lean on Him and He will guide you to your wife. Everything will be okay. Do not be afraid of the evil one, for the same power the Lord has given His angels, He has given you, but even more. Trust Him. Be not afraid. Fight and be strong, for the Lord is with you, you mighty man of valor," he ended with a gentle smile.

I looked at Rebecca as she looked back at me with those brown eyes that had melted my heart more times than I could count.

"I love you James."

"I love you Rebecca Randolph. You're my girl."

A bright white flash and loud crash followed by a resounding hum sent electric chills throughout my entire body. So much energy racing through my veins, I didn't know if my body could manage.

I awoke with a quick jolt.

Faint talking was accompanied with a constant beeping. I opened my eyes with an ounce of hesitation. Everything was blurry, like looking through binoculars before they've been adjusted. I twisted and turned, tried to rub my eyes, but my hands were restrained with skinny tubes that ran to something sharp stuck in my hands and arms.

Then it dawned on me. The crash. Him standing over me with that same smirk as from the field. I heard the hammer click, then a white flash and explosion.

I jerked, almost yanking an IV from my arm.

I'm in a hospital! Oh, dear Lord, where are my babies? Where's Rebecca?

"Rebecca!? Rebecca!?"

My cries caused movement to my right. Something or someone was causing a stir.

It sounded like a man cleared his throat.

My vision was still blurred. I blinked enough times to almost cause a cramp in my right eye lid, kind of started giving me a headache too.

"James! You're awake! Oh, thank God! Thank you, Lord!"

I knew the voice but couldn't place my finger on it.

"Who's there? Who are you? Where's the nurse? Nurse!?"

I screamed. Beginning to panic.

"Ssshhh, ssshhh…James, it's me…it's me…Lee. I'm here, calm down, you're okay."

Pitter patter slapped across the tile floor.

I heard someone enter the room.

"Everything okay? What's going on?" a feminine voice asked from a round blur.

I don't think she was asking me, at least it didn't seem like it.

I heard Lee stutter just a bit, and that's when I heard the round blur say, "Nancy! Get in here, he's awake!"

Seconds later, more pitter patter raced across the tile floors, before stopping at the door of my room. Still only a blur, it sounded like another two or three nurses had entered the room.

One of them sat at the foot of my bed. I knew not just from the movement of my bed, but by the covers raking across my feet.

Hey! My feet! How did I feel that?

"Touch my foot!" I blurted.

"What?" the lady asked.

"Just touch my foot!"

I felt her cold hand rest on the flesh of my foot. I could feel my foot!

"Touch the other one!"

She did, and I felt that one too! I haven't felt my feet in over two years! The flare up's gone!

Hey, wonder if I can wiggle my toes?

I squinted my eyes and strained. I heard them all gasp. Lee praised the Lord and clapped in excitement.

Then I bent and straightened my legs at the knee.

"Let me up. Get this stuff out of me, I want to stand."

"Uhh...I...I'm not so sure‑

"Help me to my feet, I just want to feel the floor beneath my feet, I want to feel the weight on my legs."

My bed began to rise as another nurse started pressing buttons and pulling IV's from my flesh.

Lee helped me as I twisted on the bed. I still couldn't see anything more than a blur, but I'd figure that out later, right now I just wanted to stand. Lee cupped my armpits and lifted me to my feet. I leaned on his shoulder as he gave me support. The round blur that first entered the room, hurried over and supported me on the other side. My feet hit the cold floor. A chill rushed up my spine.

I flexed my knees, twirled an ankle, bent at the waist, even started doing a little bit of the shag.

"Okay I think that's enough, let's not over do—"

Before round blur could finish, the pounding in my head sent everything into a tailspin. Felt like I'd just been hit over the head with a hammer.

I winced and reached to the side of my head as they eased me down into the bed. That's when I felt the bandage across my head and down the side. My ear was covered with a gauze.

As I settled beneath the covers, my exuberant joy of gaining feeling in my lower half was quickly erased by the throbbing pain in my melon. Then another throbbing pain smacked my heart.

"Where's Rebecca? How are the kids?"

They took a minute to answer. I'm sure waiting to see who'd step up and deliver the news.

"Uh ladies...do you mind giving us a minute?"

They excused themselves, shutting the door on the way out.

"Umm James...the children are doing fine. Lily and Kelly are recovering in the ICU. Lily suffered a collapsed lung and broken collarbone, but she is doing much better. They still have her sedated to help with the pain. Kelly has some head trauma and bleeding on the brain, but the doctors have taken care of it and she is doing just fine."

His words ripped at my heart like a vulture tearing through its new-found carcass.

"Lauren has a broken ankle and arm, but she's okay. Connor has a broken wrist and a large gash on his shoulder. Jason fared the best, he just has lacerations from the shattered glass and some bone bruising. But everyone is expected to a make a full recovery. James you are all lucky."

I nodded and swallowed the lump lodged in my throat as I caught the tears slipping down my cheeks with my knuckle. Lee reached behind him and grabbed a box of tissues.

I sniffled as I forced out my next question through a cracked voice.

"What about Rebecca?" my heart feared his reply.

It took him a moment to gather the words.

"James...she wasn't at the wreckage. Did you drop her off anywhere beforehand?"

"What!?"

He wouldn't say anything.

"Lee! What are you talking about? What do you mean she wasn't at the wreckage?"

"James...she just wasn't there. They searched the entire area, but never found her. Do you remember anything?"

I shut my eyes and went back to when it all happened. I could hear Lauren's voice as she recalled the native stories of Miss Suzy. That's when I mentioned Snake and dragging canoe...then the bright lights to my left...then...bam!

I remember the sound of the metal and plastic as it crumbled and cracked. Then the shatter of glass. My world spinning faster than I could think. The van came to a stop as it rocked upon the hood like a tipsy spun coin. I heard a car door open. Boots scuffed and thudded across the pavement. A soft whistle, I knew the tune. It was a song by The Police, I'd heard it a thousand times through the years.

The man approached us and went straight to Rebecca's window which had been shattered from the wreckage.

I could hear her moan in pain. The man squatted down next to her. He smacked his tongue against his teeth like calling a dog, that's when he let out a deep breath. He sliced her seat belt allowing gravity to do its work. She landed with a thump.

Something sloshed to one side of a bottle.

He forced a rag to Rebecca's mouth as she tried to scream and squirm, but she was out within a matter of two breaths.

I remember lying on my back, seeing the world upside-down through the glass window, the stars looked so bright against the night sky. I lay motionless as he drug my wife out of the car. His big boots pounding against the asphalt as he raced away from the van. A few moments passed, I tried to move, but couldn't, I tried to scream, but couldn't.

A car door slammed. His heavy feet returned. Shuffling across the pavement then thudding my way. Such an odd gait. Instantly my mind was taken back to the day I dropped Ethan off at his house after his first day at the mill.

He stops at my head. The window shatters, glass shards cover me. I open my eyes and see the eyes of Satan staring back at me from a face and head full of hair. A man dressed in all black

He grinned and chuckled at my mangled mess. He wagged his head and gave a whistle that trailed off at the end. His hand hung at his side, he raised and looked at a silver six shot. He checked the cylinder, gave it a spin, jerked the gun to snap it in place, cocked back the hammer, aimed and said, "Wow...you know James, we've waited a long time for this. Too bad it's just taken this long. At least you won't feel anything right?"

A bright flash. *BAM!*

I jolted in my bed as the shot rang out in my head.

That's when I remembered my dream of the field and the Angel and Lee and his family...and Ethan.

"Take it easy now James...just take a breath," Lee said as he squeezed my arm for assurance.

I gathered myself and looked to the right side of my bed, where I found his blur.

"Lee...I know who took her and you have to help me get her back."

52

As the nurses left the room to give me and Lee some time, they must've informed my doctor because it couldn't have been ten minutes before he was knocking on my door. I'd just finished telling Lee about my dream of Rebecca in the field.

He told me, "James...this is the Lord speaking to you. If you want to get Rebecca back, you have to trust Him."

I had never been much of a religious person, but this dream and visit from the Angel, really struck my heart. I knew Lee was right.

My thoughts of such an occasion were interrupted as another blur entered the room.

His voice sounded foreign.

"Mr. Rundolph? My nom dis Omar DaFini..."

He said as he extended his hand.

"I will be your primary doctur for de next few daze. So how are you feeling? My nurses tall me you have somzing to show me? Des?"

His voice beamed with curiosity through a thick accent.

"Lee...how about giving me a hand here would ya?" I asked as I grunted and twisted toward the side of the bed. He helped me to my feet again, where I displayed my knee and ankle bending talent. I swear I even done better than Tin Man.

Though I couldn't see my doctors face, his lack for words told me everything.

"Seen enough?" I asked with a wide grin.

He stuttered but forced out, "Uh...des. Dat tis...quite ama-sing."

Lee helped me back to my bed as doctor DaBlur took a seat in the recliner to my left.

He sat there mumbling to himself in what must have been his native language unless the whole experience had caused him to start speaking in tongues to try and explain. Either way I couldn't make out a word the man said. And it sure didn't help that I couldn't see his lips.

"Hey Doc?"

His mumbling ceased.

"Don't get me wrong here, I couldn't be happier to have my legs back, but I'm just curious...how long before I lose the blur?"

He didn't say anything.

"James, what are you talking about?" asked Lee.

"I'm talking about my sight. For all I can tell, you've packed on fifty pounds since the Pau Wau. You're just a fuzzy blob. Everything is fuzzy and foggy."

Dr. DaBlur scooted to the edge of the recliner, took a deep breath and said, "James...this is an absolut miracool. The angul of which the bullot entered your skull was in such a way that it travelled through three majur areas of your brain."

"The furst part being the Parietal Lobe. It controls basic movemants and sensation. The bullot then travelled through the Occipital Lobe which handles viszol recognition and basic viszon. The bullot being slowed, decided to rest at the border of the Occipital Lobe and Cerebellum which controls balance and muscle coordinazon.

"I thought it would have made your condition worse not butter. I will need to run test to be certain, but I believe the damage the bullot done, actually reversed the part of your bran which was damaged from your disease.

"Now...as for your viszon. I am hoping it will regain its strength and with time and I believe it will. But first I need to run further test to...verify my theory. Okay?" his words were just as hard to swallow as they were to interrupt, but I got the jist of what he said.

"So basically, I got a bullet still lodged in my head?"

"That is a true statement. Des."

"What about my ear? Why is it so bandaged up? Because going by what you said, I don't think the bullet did anything to it, did it?"

It took him a moment to answer.

"What happened to my ear?"

He cleared his throat to buy time to catch his words and frame them in English.

"Sir...the man who did this to you—"

"What? Tell me!"

And I'll never forget his words.

"He took it."

53

The sound of tire tread roaring against the asphalt became

constant as did the argument between Ethan and the raspy voice, she'd come to know as Kirkland.

A pot hole here and there would send the lightning bolts back to her hamstrings as Rebecca winced with each strike. Not wanting to, but knowing she needed to, she opened her eyes.

She was lying down in the back seat of a pick-up truck. Hands tied, feet bound, and mouth taped.

"Where do you want me to go!? What am I looking for?" Ethan asked with a raised voice and clinched teeth as he glanced to the empty passenger seat. He jerked his head back to the road in such a snap fashion, it caused a creak in Rebecca's neck.

"Just trust me! I know what I'm doing. Pull in this carwash," Ethan said in a deep grotesque voice, not his own.

"What!? A freaking car wash? Are you kidding me?" he asked toward the empty passenger seat. He snapped his head back around as he lifted his turn signal and eased on the breaks.

"Yeah...a car wash. Relax...I know what I'm doing," Ethan said in a voice deeper than James Earl Jones.

The truck roughed its way into the parking lot, squeaking and bouncing on bad shocks, jarring Rebecca's back in the process.

"Do you actually want me to get a car wash?"

"Yes."

"All right," Ethan grinded his jaw and eased to the meter to pay for the wash.

Rebecca was eying the passenger seat while also glancing at the side mirror. Little black fogs began to appear and swarm within the truck like bees. She jerked and grunted to keep one from landing on her cheek.

"Oh...well hi Miss Rebecca. I didn't know you were awake," Ethan said as he turned and gave her a crooked grin. His eyes the color and size of two billiards 8 balls. His voice even seemed off as it had a little rasp to it.

He turned his attention back to the meter and hung out the window just a bit to insert some paper money. Something flashed in the side mirror.

Rebecca blinked and steadied her gaze, but it was gone. Ethan saw it too and quickly retracted back into the cab like a shy turtle.

Head lights eased in behind his truck and took their place in line. Ethan froze, his eyes locked on the mirrors.

"Wait here. Don't move," the deep robotic voice commanded like a general.

Beep! Beep!

The car squawked two little honks to get his attention and let him know its presence. Ethan sat motionless, before being careful to slide his hand over to the passenger seat. Rebecca squinted through the darkness and tried to capture what he was reaching for. She kind of knew but attempted to fight off the thought.

The sound of the cylinder spinning made the thought too strong. It wasn't just a thought, it was a fact...he'd just grabbed his gun.

He sat calmly in his seat and stared straight ahead.

The car honked three more times, growing more impatient.

"Do not even think of doing anything...or else you all die! Capisce?" he said with a raspy contorting voice.

Rebecca mumbled through the tape. Her mind and heart flying like a jet about to break the sound barrier.

Ethan began whistling, Rebecca recognized, The Police.

He pulled on the handle, the door popped open with a slight whine, he lowered his boots to the black pavement, stuck the revolver in his pocket, shut the door, kept the tune and strode closer to the waiting car.

††††††††††††††††††††††

"HOW YOU FOLKS DOING?" Frank asked as he approached the driver side of the Ford Explorer, where a man around his fifty's sat opposite his wife of about the same age.

"Man...what you are doing up there...taking a nap?" The man asked in a sarcastic tone.

"No...but you're about to?" Frank said as he checked his surroundings, before returning his darkened glare.

"Huh?" the puzzled man said just before turning to his wife.

Frank scrambled and retrieved the revolver.

As the man was about to question his wife, her look of terror, told him something was about to go down.

She gasped for air as she attempted to scream but didn't have enough time.

POW! POW! POW!

The man slumped and landed on the center console. Two bullets entered the back of his head, one lodging and the other exiting his left eye socket.

The wife took a round to her left eyebrow, killing her instantly, as her brain lost all connection.

††††††††††††††††††††††

REBECCA FLINCHED with each shot that rang out. The back floorboard was now wet from her tears. Her heart ached for whoever had just received the brunt of Ethan's wrath.

Soon after the shots rang out, she could hear heavy footsteps pattering on the asphalt. Ethan threw open the door, reached over Rebecca and grabbed two boxes of saran wrap.

He hurried back to the explorer.

Within just a few minutes, Rebecca could hear his heavy feet pounding the pavement. He had to be flat footed.

He slung the door open, causing her to jump. As she craned her neck to look out the door, the sight froze her heart.

It was Ethan wearing a big grin, toting a body dressed in saran wrap over his shoulder.

"Welp...got us some meat to get us through the winter..." he dropped the body in the back seat, just inches from Rebecca still bound in the floorboard, "...I'm just kidding. I'm no cannibal, I promise. Now, for Mother and the others...well...that can be a different story," he said as he snickered and before entered a whistle as he returned to the SUV.

Moments later he came thudding back. His shadow blocked the light from a street pole that tried to beam in.

"And here's the last one. All right...time to get going," he tossed the body in the back, as it smacked against the other, before rolling off and landing awkwardly on Rebecca.

Ethan hopped into the driver's seat and must've heard Rebecca's cry and moan through the duct tape. She wiggled and squirmed with her heart about to bust a hole through the floor board.

"Aww...you'll be fine...they don't bite," he mocked, turned over the ignition and pulled out.

The body bounced on top of Rebecca with each bump and pot hole, her cries and pleads getting louder with each one.

††††††††††††††††††††††††

FRANK TURNED his attention to the stereo and switched stations, until he found one that fit his fancy.

After a few tries, he found it.

Aww...good ole head banging...grotesque voice from a demon...scream-a-thon.

Just what he needed.

Kirkland sat in the passenger seat, wearing a crooked grin, with that bony finger to his mouth.

Proud of what his prodigy had become.

54

The thought of Ethan or Frank or GTK, whoever the heck he is...having my ear, sent shivers down my spine. If he could do all of this to me and the others he'd murdered...what in the world was Rebecca going through?

My heart ached as my gut twisted, just yearning to see her beautiful face and hear her angelic voice. Gosh darn! I've got to get out of this dang hospital, my girl needs me, my kids need their mama.

Oh Rebecca...stay strong baby. Keep fighting. Don't give up. I folded my arms as I sat up in the bed, placed a hand to my face and wept. Sorrow had gripped me by the throat and was squeezing with all its might. My whole body quaked as my sobs were uncontrollable.

The doctor had just left the room, leaving me and Lee to ourselves. I felt his hand on my back as he tried to comfort me.

"It's going to be all right James...stay strong and keep believing."

"I'm just so afraid for Rebecca," I managed to force out through my broken voice, barely having enough air to say it from all the sobbing.

"I know...we all are. But the Creator is bigger than this. He hears our prayers and He will send His Angels to protect her. Just trust Him James. It's all going to be okay."

"You really believe so?"

"I know so."

His unwavering faith and confidence were quite appealing and reassuring.

"Lee...what do you think my dream was really all about?" I asked as I wiped my eyes, regaining myself.

He sighed, formed the words then said, "Well...to tell you the truth James, I believe the Creator is speaking to you. I think He wants to reveal Himself to you and show you just how much He truly loves you and to teach you who you really are."

"What do you mean?"

"I think the Great Spirit is calling you to awaken to see yourself as He sees you. He is longing to have a relationship with you. He yearns for you to learn how valuable you are in His eyes. He wants to teach you about your true identity in Him."

A warmth in my heart caused new tears to melt down my face. I'd never heard anyone talk like this before. To think God longed to have a relationship with me...I just couldn't wrap my mind around it.

A tingling sensation rode over my entire body as every hair stood erect. Such power and such love...like I'd never felt before. All I could do was cry. I suddenly felt so loved and so wanted...and...so valued. My word...no wonder they called Him the Messiah!

"That's it James...let Him wrap you in His arms and show you how much he loves you. Feel it...embrace it. He's here right now in this very room," Lee said as he began to utter a prayer mostly between him and the Creator.

There were never any lightning bolts or bright flashes, just a steady warm embrace. But that's when I heard a soft voice deep in my soul.

"You are loved more than you will ever know. I created you James...and I have never made a mistake. Everything I create is good. You are made in my image. I know the number of hairs upon your head, for I was the one who placed them there. I know the number of breath's you've ever taken, and I know how many you have left."

The words were as sweet as honey to my soul, I'd never experienced anything like it.

"Oh Lord...forgive me. I know I haven't always done right. I've tried to be a good person and live a good life, but I don't ever want to go another day without you. Lord, here's my heart. I want you more than anything. And Lord, please help us get Rebecca back. And please help our children recover. Please Lord...I want to live the life you died for."

Now Lee had tears streaking down his face as his hand trembled upon my back.

"I love you James...you are my beloved son in whom I am well pleased. You are the Light of the World. I am now in you and you are now in Me. For we are one. Love others as I love you. You are righteous, you are holy, you are redeemed, and you are Mine. Now therefore, go and rescue your wife whom you love dearly and who I love even more. Don't give up and don't quit. You will find her and you will bring her back home to your family. Have faith and fight for your family, your wife and your home. Be not afraid, for I am with you. Go in my strength and be courageous for I am with you."

I took a breath for what seemed like the first time in five minutes. My heart and gut were still warm with love. I felt different. I felt loved. I felt empowered. I felt wanted. I felt valued. I felt saved. I felt like a child of God.

55

A voice squawked over the radio as Brunswick County officer Dominick Farrell sat in his patrol car at the end of Red Bug Road facing Highway 17.

"Keep your eyes and ears open and try to move around every hour or so. This guy seems to be the most active late into the night. Agent Vasquez and I will stay near the Randolph's home for most of the night, while Lieutenant Mishoe and agent Wells will be at the south entrance to 17, with agent Harrelson and Detective Barnhill stationed near the Wal-Mart in Shallotte. If any of you hear or see anything out of the norm...tag it in and whatever you do...*do not* approach him alone. With as many as we have patrolled, shouldn't take long to have someone there to help. And if you need anything, just let us know. Good luck guys and be safe!" Agent Turner said over the air waves as his gravelly voice crackled even more with the static pause and pick up that accompanies a wideband radio system.

Going on ten o'clock and having not eaten anything since his wife's cooking at supper, Farrell decided to get into the goodie bag his wife packed him, just before he headed out. He took his eyes off the highway and leaned over to the floorboard on the passenger side to see what he had.

††††††††††††††††††††††

DRIVING ALONG US-17, toting two dead bodies packaged in saran wrap, one in which rode atop the squirming and crying Rebecca, Frank switched lanes in effort to pass a large Dodge Ram that was trudging along too slow for Frank's liking.

"Oh shoot!" Frank said as soon as he flipped his turn signal off. He sped up just a tad in effort to hide beside the Dodge as he passed what looked to be a police cruiser up the road on the right.

Staying beside the Dodge for cover, Frank waited until passing the cruiser to speed up and get back in the slow lane.

"Whew! Had me worried there Rebecca,"
he said as he stole glances in the side and rear-view mirrors. He hadn't seen any blue lights yet, so he must be good.

"How you doing back there anyway?" he questioned as he tossed a hand backwards and reached for her. His hand grasping the air, then finding and patting Rebecca's knee.

"Don't mind the misses, she doesn't mean to be such a pest. Just can't control herself sometimes," with that Frank busted into an obnoxious knee slapping laugh.

After enjoying his joke, he settled down, wiped the tears from his eyes, and sighed with a snicker.

He curved his spine and reached under the seat.

"Hey Rebecca...I almost forgot," he said as he grunted to find it. He straightened up and held it high and unashamed as he turned it just inches from his eyes to marvel at its beauty.

"Maybe this will cheer you up."

He tossed it in the back where it must've wedged between Rebecca and the center console.

He heard her flinch as it bounced off of her. He'd stored it in a sandwich baggy with some added vinegar. Funny how long you can keep things that way. He'd often drink the liquid once he'd transplant the goods from the bag to a jar.

She got awful quiet back there. Probably trying to figure what it is.

"It's your husband's ear. Thought you might like to see it."

She must've fainted, because she didn't make another sound after he said that.

†††††††††††††††††††††

THE BUMPY RIDE and the sound of gravel tinging against the metal under the truck was enough to wake her from her slumber.

She felt nauseous and weak. The air felt dry and dusty. Her head was foggy.

The misses bounced upon her with each pot hole that Ethan was sure to hit. James' ear rested at her waist.

Three distinct voices lingered from up front.

One was Ethan...one was who she'd come to know as Kirkland...but the other...sounded more feminine.

"You've done good Frankie...you've made us proud...but we still need more. And so does your Mother," said the mysterious voice.

Frankie?

Ethan responded, sounding as if he'd been crying, "Thank you Lou. That means a lot to me coming from you. I can't do it now but give me time and I will," he wiped his nose and sniffled.

"Just don't take too long, because by the feel of it, time may not be something we have much of," said Kirkland in his deep raspy voice coming from Ethan's inner most being.

Never opening her eyes in fear of what would be before them, Rebecca drifted back into a slumber, with the voices becoming farther and farther away before ebbing away.

Until the sudden jolt caused inertia to press her up against the center console. The squeal of the brakes hurt her ears. The misses rubbed back and forth on Rebecca's hip, until finally coming to a stop. James' ear was squished between her knee and center console.

She heard the lights flick off. What is he doing? He killed the engine and hopped out of the cab. He seemed exuberant, like a child arriving at a friend's birthday party.

The sound of water lapping against the shore, told Rebecca they had to be near some type of shoreline. It wasn't loud enough to be the Ocean, must be near the marsh.

The back door opened, causing Rebecca's head to give way and slip out, her hair dangling to the ground. Ethan had to catch her and the misses before they fell to the ground.

Catching glimpses of Spartina Alterniflora—marsh grass—just past Ethan's legs, she knew then they were near the marsh.

"Hey now...it ain't your turn...at least not yet."

Ethan chuckled as he grunted struggling to grip and gather the misses. He heaved her up on his shoulder, her body stiff and looking like a grasshopper caught and wrapped in a spider's web.

Ethan stood at the open door and looked to Rebecca with icy eyes.

"Don't even think of doing anything stupid. Now is not the time to try me. I'll dump you here with these two if you like. So, it'd be in your best interest to be smart."

He turned his back, kicked the door shut and marched away. Leaving her there with the man wrapped in saran wrap like his wife. He laid quietly in the back seat just above her.

A mosquito landed on her cheek. She could feel its little feet as it prepared its jack hammer of needle. She scrunched her nose and wrinkled her face, but it was no use, the little critter had done decided to steal her blood. She felt the sharp tip slither beneath her flesh, followed by the sting and burning itch. It sucked and sucked, pulling blood from her face. Her cheek tingled, the mosquito retrieved the needle and whined before buzzing over to her opposite cheek. It continued the routine once again. She felt the needle glide under her skin, the burning itch following. She kept wrinkling her face, but to no avail.

She breathed deep, shut her eyes and allowed her mind to settle. Doing her best to ignore the little pest. The sounds around her seemed louder. Cicadas, crickets, frogs, and a howling wind filled her ears. Then she heard heavy footsteps upon what sounded like gravel.

Ethan opened the driver door, which allowed a cool breeze to enter. He plopped down and turned to check on the Rebecca and man.

Satisfied, he fired up the engine, turned on his headlights and put the gear stick in reverse. Crunching gravel as the tires crawled over it. He rolled his window down and hung his left arm out for comfort. Without the radio blaring, Rebecca could hear the scream of the Cicada bugs as they wailed from the trees. If she listened closely enough, she thought she could hear the misses screams.

Oh...stop it. She was dead, already wasn't she? She had to be, she'd taken a bullet and had been wrapped in Saran wrap for at least half an hour.

"Rebecca?"

She froze.

"Hey Rebecca? Can you hear me?"

She mumbled through the tape, to keep him from getting upset.

"Okay...good. Hey there's some things I want to talk with you about."

He waited a moment, sighed, and began.

"If you remember right...I told you and James back in the day, that I went and stayed with my aunt and uncle after Mama died? And that I didn't have much to do with my dad?"

She mumbled again, to let him know she was listening.

"Well...that's not entirely true. You see...my Mama did die, but she didn't just die," he paused and gulped.

He sniffled and sighed once more.

"She was murdered. Better yet...sacrificed."

56

Ethan broke. He began to sob deeply. The whole driver seat shook.

He mumbled and fussed, beating upon the steering wheel. He gathered himself and continued.

"You see my dad started having visions of the times to come and god began showing him things that no one else could understand. He was giving the gift of discernment and could tell when someone had a hidden agenda against him. Not long after that...he received the voice of god.

Ethan wiped his face with the crevice of his arm.

"He'd get this feeling down in his gut and he'd have to grab a pen and piece of paper and sure enough...god would start talking. My dad would shut his eyes and look to the heavens, before scribbling wildly, but by the time he'd finished...god had spoken. As one would expect, this created quite the crowd. People started coming from all over to hear what the voice of god had to say. By that summer, dad had picked up a total of 23 followers. And they were devout. They'd do anything my dad said...or god said through my dad's chicken scratch.

"A lot of times it be about the end times and about how people just weren't living right anymore and how it was our job to punish them...and...in some cases...make an atonement.

"It started out with god needing an animal sacrifice to atone for the people's sins. So, every time Sister Judy Downs heard someone cuss or saw someone light up a smoke or swig a cold one, she'd come running to dad and spill the beans. Brother Fred Boster did the same thing. You couldn't sneak nothing by those two. Dad said it was their gifts...like his but only different. He'd say he was the voice of god, but they were the eyes and ears of god.

"So, each time they found out something about a follower, they'd come running and telling dad, then he'd call a special service the following night and the person caught in the sin would have to slay an animal and cover themselves in the blood to atone for what they'd done.

"It worked for while...as most people didn't like the taste and smell of blood, especially Mama, as it trickled down their face and body. But after a few months they'd just go right back to what they were doing. Get caught and then have to go through the whole process again. The whole group was in a constant cycle of sin, get caught by Downs or Boster, confess, kill, atone. It never ceased.

"Finally...we started running low on the supply of dogs, cats, chickens, and rabbits and what not, so dad had a vision from god followed by a message. It said it was time to up the ante as the blood of dogs and cats just wasn't cutting it anymore. It was time to offer human blood. Now, it started out as just a slice of the palm as they'd sprinkle it over the fire. That seemed to work, as most people didn't like the pain. But that didn't last long either. So, dad got another message. This time, blood wasn't enough...god wanted life.

"I remember when dad first showed mom what he'd wrote. She gasped and covered her mouth in shock. But dad was insistent that this was what god was requiring.

He said the people had gone too far and it was time to teach them all a lesson.

"I can still hear Sister Judy's voice as she came running up to dad as he busied himself tilling the garden. I was following behind him, helping Mama with the tomato plants. 'George! George! You're not gonna believe it! I saw Mr. and Mrs. Helms buying smokes and a twelve pack in the store just now!' she said with glee. Dad's face turned red as that vein on the side of his neck bulged. I knew he was mad, and I knew he'd do it. Mama tried talking him out of it, but it was no use, he'd done made up his mind...and so had god.

"So that night he called a meeting. Didn't tell anyone what it was about, just said he wanted everyone there because he had some exciting news to share. So that night we all met out in the barn.

"We were having a good time, even sang a few songs and hymns. After a while, dad got up and stood in the middle of us to give the exciting news that'd brought us all together. Me and Mama winced with each word...we knew he was up to something.

"'Behold fellow followers of the greater good. I have a new message from the throne of god!' The people cheered and clapped. 'Let him who has ears, hear what the voice of god says...' My dad then pulled out the piece of paper from his pocket and began to read in his preacher voice, 'For behold I know what manner of love you have showed to my cause and I know your inner most desires...but I also know your inner most sins. I have seen and heard enough...it is time to atone for what you have done. No more games...it is time you offer me life.'"

"He folded the paper, stuck it back in his pocket. Wiped a tear from his eye and let his words settle over the crowd, creating an uncomfortable silence. Finally, he spoke,

'People...I never wanted it to come to this, but here we are. I know if I don't obey what god has told me...then the ones within this group who have bad intentions, will ruin everything we've worked so hard at. And I can't let that happen. For if I let it slide, then I will be allowing the evil one to slither into our little garden and destroy our place of paradise. The new heaven and the new earth must start here with us, but I cannot allow heathens to hinder what god wants to do. For if we are not careful, the government will enter through those who aren't fully committed to the greater good, and they will rule over us day and night. That can't happen.' He lowered his eyes to the dirt for a moment, as he said a quick mumbled prayer. He raised them and looked to Mr. and Mrs. Helms to his right and gave a slight nod.

"'I'm sorry Bill and Cathy, but it must be done.' "That's when Ricky and Dave grabbed them both from behind. I never even saw them standing there. Before the Helm's could do anything, Ricky and Dave had done slapped them in hand cuffs and was pushing them towards dad in the middle.

"Dad and Ricky held them there as he instructed Dave to grab the crosses. Everyone just sat in shock, not knowing what to say or do. These people were devout followers for the most part except for the repeat offenders such as the Helms.

"Brother Wright spoke up and asked what he was going to do, but he was quickly quieted by the rest of the crowd. Dad told him to shut up or he'd be next. Brother Wright got up to storm out, but he was caught by Jack and Matthew. They were two brothers who'd grown up on a farm, so they had no problem restraining little ole Brother Wright.

"Dave came back dragging two wooden crosses. He dropped them at dad's feet. Dad shoved the Helms in the back as they stumbled forward. He dusted his hands to rid himself of such filth. Dave, Ricky and two others helped to tie Mr. Helms to one of the crosses and as soon as they finished, they tied Mrs. Helms to the other. They carried them over to two large holes that was covered with a sheet that dad had been praying on earlier as we sung.

"They dropped the crosses into the holes, giving the Helm's a good jolt. Mrs. Helms screamed as her elbow popped out of joint. Dave stuffed her mouth with his handkerchief. She bit him before he could retrieve his hand. He yanked it back and bounced around as blood dripped to the ground. He then pulled back and slapped her so hard with his other hand, it just about knocked her out.

"'Easy now...I know she's a feisty one, but no need for what isn't necessary.' Dad said as he began a short sermon about sin and punishment and about how the government was taking over and if we didn't deal with heathen's like the Helms, then we'd soon be forced to receive the mark of the beast.

"That's when he looked me in the eyes and said, 'Son...why don't you do the honors?' He removed a box cutter from his front pocket and held it out for all to see. I just sat there for a second, not knowing what to do. 'Son...come up here and do what the lord requires.' He said with that sternness that I knew couldn't be crossed without paying a price.

"So, I stood to my feet, Mama grabbed my arm, I turned back and saw tears flowing down her face. She gave me a soft nod, so I went. I got the box cutter and stood in front of dad, my head not even making it to his shoulders. I was still just a young boy. With hand on my shoulder, his fingers sinking into my flesh, he clinched his other hand around mine and nudged me closer to Mrs. Helms as she dangled from the cross. Her big blue eyes stared back at mine, begging me for her life, but dads' hand and voice guided me closer, with the blade fully extended.

"'Just a little slice...then we pass it off to the next in line...okay.'

"I thought it'd be quick. you know like putting a dear out of its misery after you missed the heart...but no...he wanted it to hurt and he wanted it to last.

"So, he guided my hand to her arm and made me dig the blade deep into the flesh before sliding about three inches down and doing an arc to finish it. Mrs. Helms screamed through the handkerchief with tears soaking the ground. Dad grabbed the raw bloody piece of flesh and held it out for everyone to see as it flapped with each wave he made.

"Sister Downs gagged and moved just enough to the right not to puke on Brother Boster, who was getting quite queasy himself by the looks of it.

"Dad patted me on the shoulder and said, 'Good job son...you've made me proud. God is well pleased.' He nudged me back to Mama who busied herself in quite tear-filled prayer. 'Next! C'mon up and carry out the wrath of god.' To my surprise people hurried and almost fought to be next in line. A few took their time and joined the back of the line.

"Soon after it started, Ricky had to shove something in Mr. Helms mouth too to get him to shut up. He fought and kicked to try and get to each person cutting away at his wife, but he couldn't do anything to get off that cross, no matter how hard he tried. This went on for hours. I made three cuts on Mrs. Helms, and I think five on Mr. Helms and so did everyone else. By the time we'd finish, the blade had grown dull. I think dad was surprised as to how long it took them to bleed out. I know I was."

57

At 10:27 pm, as Agent Turner and Agent Vasquez sat in a blacked-out Chevy Tahoe near the West end of Holden Beach, just past Sailfish drive and only three blocks from the Randolph's home, dispatch crackled over the radio.

"Agent Turner...we just received an anonymous call regarding a possible homicide at a car wash off Holden Beach road...the call came in from a pay phone at the Citgo just down the road."

Turner and Vasquez looked to each other for a second.

"Right on it! Thanks."

Within ten minutes, officer Will Humphry arrived on scene at the Citgo. He walked around the building, checked the pay phone, and went inside to question the clerk and customers, but no one saw anything.

Not even a mile down the road, Brunswick County Sheriff Richard Holloway, Detective Nick Honeycutt, and agent Mac Harrelson were pulling into the car wash.

Five to ten minutes later, Turner and Vasquez pulled in, followed by Lieutenant Mishoe and Detective Davis Green.

Leaving Detective Barnhill, Agent Wells, Agent Wright and officer Farrell still on patrol along with a few rookies.

"Whoever called this in...is our guy," said Lieutenant Mishoe.

"And Humphry didn't come up with anything at the store, said no one saw anything," said Vasquez.

"Well what about surveillance?"

"Yeah, we'll check into it. Hopefully they got something" said Turner as Mishoe had just stretched on some rubber gloves before ducking inside the Ford Explorer to examine the blood splatter.

††††††††††††††††††††

WITH MOST OF the attention being placed at the car wash, Frank drove two miles under the speed limit as he crossed over the Holden Beach bridge, singing along to *every little thing she does is magic* by The Police. Though not his favorite, it was still a great song. Frank crested the bridge and began the descent to the other side as his brakes squealed. He came to the stop sign, where Holden Beach Realty sat straight ahead of him, with a restaurant to his left and a church to his right.

He flipped his left blinker and turned.

††††††††††††††††††††

HAVING CROSSED the bridge a gazillion times since having moved to Holden, Rebecca knew exactly where they were by the feel of it and with the help of a few familiar billboards that passed by the glass window.

He didn't go far before making another left.

The landing, they had to be going to the boat landing.

He continued straight until the pavement turned to gravel as he made an arc to the left. He sat quiet for about five minutes likely scanning the area for any sign of life. With no lights, and not much of a Moon, it was darker than your average night.

"Don't make a sound...or else I might just have to get out my box cutter. You got it?"

Rebecca mumbled and nodded.

Ethan climbed out of the driver seat, planted his boots and opened the back door where he grappled with the man in Saran wrap. He slung him over his shoulder and marched toward the boat ramp.

Couldn't have been thirty seconds that passed, when Rebecca heard gravel crunching beneath a set of tires. Headlights beamed off the bridge columns.

A car door opened, a set of feet hit the gravel and took a few steps before being met by Ethan's heavy footsteps coming up from the boat ramp.

"How you doing tonight?" a masculine voice asked.

"Oh, not too bad...as long as the Foxes don't decide to dig up the dead."

"Pardon?"

58

It was ten after six on Tuesday morning when dispatch received the call from an old flounder fisherman reporting a body wrapped in Saran wrap lying in the grass next to a boat ramp in the Shallotte River. As Agent Turner, Agent Vasquez and Lieutenant Mishoe rushed to the scene and busied themselves with searching for anything that could point to the GTK, another call came in from a middle-aged woman who was enjoying a nice morning jog, until she noticed a car submerged in the water at the boat ramp under the bridge leading to Holden Beach.

The trio took the twenty-minute drive to Holden, where they discovered a white Toyota Camry parked half way down the concrete slab with water flowing freely through the windows and a body wrapped in Saran wrap, resting in the back seat.

††††††††††††††††††††††

IT WAS JUST after 7:30 am when I awoke from a deep and dreamless sleep. I was filled with so much peace, it's hard to put into words. I think I only woke once in a span of ten hours.

Lee went home just prior to me falling asleep last night. He said he'll be back around nine this morning. The nurse just left and said Dr. Dafini would be in to see me about a quarter after eight. The nurse told me I should be able to see the kids today before the Sun sets. I sure do miss em. Man...the pain of imagining them suffering is worse than my own. My heart aches as my mind attempts to wrap around all of this. Just to think what that scumbag has done to us...it sets a fire deep in my bones, as vengeance burns with a passion. I've got to see the kids, or the blur of them for that matter, then I've got to convince Lee to help get me out of here, so I can Rebecca and maybe put a slug this dude's eyes.

†††††††††††††††††††††††

REBECCA BLINKED to clear the blur from the night's sleep. She found herself once again chained to a cross opposite the sandy room from Mother, who still wore the rusty chains that kept her bound.

Lit candles rested on the table next to jars full of botched body parts. Their light gave just enough to show Ethan lying at the foot of his Mother's cross, curled into a ball on the sandy floor. He even snored as his rib cage rose and fell. It was like watching a sleeping Tiger, one wrong move or word could end it all.

Trying not make too much sound in fear of waking him, Rebecca craned her neck and glance to each. As she did so, the chains rattled and tinged. She glanced at Ethan, still in a fetal position, rib cage rising and falling.

Her wrists wore wide metal bracelets that were clamped tight with not even enough room to squeeze a tooth pick between them and her flesh. From the bracelets hung chains that were then fastened to eye bolts drilled into the wooden frame of the cross.

Her wrists were a lost cause, no way she could free them without help. She peered down to her feet and checked each one. They were bound the same as her wrist.

She sighed and hung her head as a tear dripped into the sand.

331

"Morning Rebecca!" Ethan's voice thundered.

She jolted back, sending the chains into a stir as the bracelets and anklets pinched her flesh.

How'd he get there so quick without making a sound?

"I see you've become acquainted with your confinements?" he asked as his big black eyes pierced her soul. He grinned, then waved her off, before placing his hands behind his back and pacing like a General about to give a scolding.

"I feel perhaps Mother would like it if I finished telling of what happened with the greater good congregation, following the sacrifice of the Helm's?" he locked eyes with his Mama for a moment before turning to Rebecca and giving it some thought.

She mumbled through the tape as she nodded.

"Oh, pardon me. I guess as good as you've been, it wouldn't hurt to maybe give your mouth a little freedom. Hey...whatdasay? Can you be a good girl and not scream? You wouldn't want to upset Mother, now would you?"

Rebecca wagged her head and said she'd be good with her pleading eyes.

"Okay...just for a little while, but I promise...if you make one peep louder than my voice...you'll regret it. Don't make me do it. Got it?"

Rebecca nodded once more, her eyes moist and harmless.

Ethan edged closer, eyeing her with suspicion

He reached behind her head and found the start of the tape, as he picked it with a dirty nail, it gave way creating a flap. It took a few laps around her head, but at last...it was off.

She let out a deep sigh. She could count on one hand how many times they'd went through this same routine. Except this time was different. He wasn't feeding her candy bars or potted meat and crackers or squeezing a bottle of water down her throat. To her count, she'd been captive for two days, and only eaten or drunk anything about four times. Her stomach and head were well aware.

This was the first time, he'd taken off the tape, simply just to talk.

"So...would you like to hear the rest?" Ethan questioned as he turned his back to her, wadded the gray tape in a ball and tossed it aside in the sand.

She didn't answer.

He turned and glared in her eyes.

She stammered just a bit as her mouth and throat were dry from the lack of proper hydration.

"Ye-yes...plea-ple-please. Tell m-me more."

"Good. So, I shall."

He folded his hands once more behind his back and returned to his pace as he recollected.

"After the Helm's sacrifice, it seemed to get the message across pretty clear. At least for the next few weeks. I can still hear Sister Downs voice as she yelled over the phone, she was so excited.

"'Pastor Thompson! You're not gonna believe this!'

Brother Phelps is messing around on Glenda!' Dad wanted to be sure before he did anything, so he pressed her for more information and she told him how she'd saw Brother Phelps stepping into a motel room the night before as she passed by after getting groceries at the Food Lion there next to Mick's Motel and Lodge.

"Dad got quiet and thought for a moment. I knew this would be tough one. He liked Brother Phelps, heck...they were practically Brothers any way. So, dad hung up with Sister Downs and ran to grab his pen and paper. Within minutes, the voice of god was rambling. Dad scratched and scribbled, this time with a little more force than usual. I think he tore through the paper a time or two. I knew it couldn't be good, god must've been pretty upset.

"Dad finished, then showed me and Mama what he wrote, 'This is what the great god says: Your people have defiled my name and now a sacrifice must be made to ever ease the pain. The life of the pure to purify the wicked. That is what I require. Their wickedness can only be blotted by the pure.'"

Ethan paused his pacing, crossed his arms and rubbed his chin as he forced out the words through a broken voice,

"So that's when dad said I had to get Will Abercrombie over to the house. I fussed and tried to persuade him, but it was no use. Because I wasn't just arguing with him...I was arguing with god. And whatever he said on that little ole piece of paper...well...was absolute. I mean it was god's voice.

"And so, after crying in my room most of the night, I finally managed to work up enough courage to do it. Mostly out of the fear that I'd spend the rest of eternity in a burning lake of fire if I didn't, so what choice did I have?"

Ethan stood before Rebecca with his palms facing the sandy ceiling.

Rebecca shut her eyes, drew a deep breath and wagged her head. As much as she didn't want to hear all of this, she knew she had to, so when she did escape, she'd have enough information to bring all of this to light.

Ethan sighed, then continued, "So...the next day at school, I talked to Will by himself and told him I was sorry for the little argument we'd gotten into the other day—you know how kids can be—and that I wanted to make it up to him. So, I invited him over to my house. I told him I'd made a new fort in the woods and told him how cool it was. After giving it some thought, he knew his mom would never allow him to come over, so he came with me straight from school that day and never told anyone. He was a calf being led to the slaughter.

"Dad had told me that morning before I left for school about what to do and where to do it at. So, I led Will down to the woods behind our house. We passed my old fort as Will thought that was what I was talking about, but I told him, I'd made another one further in the woods. So, as we marched on, having to block the branches from slapping across our faces, we started hearing voices. I knew it was them and as I peered through the dense forest, I could make out the forms standing in the field. They all wore white except for dad who stood in the center of the circle of about two dozen of his closest followers.

"Will started questioning who they were, but I told him it was my dad. Boy did that spook him, he tried to run, but I grabbed his arm and me having hit puberty a little earlier, had no trouble controlling the little runt. So, I dragged him out into the open. They all cheered as we broke through the forest. Dave and Ricky sprinted over and took Will by the arms. I can still see his face as he turned and looked at me as they drug him off, his feet stirring dust and old grass.

"I thought it was odd that there wasn't a cross in the center like last time. It was just dad all by himself, dressed in black. He turned his attention to his right, I followed his gaze to Mr. Phelps, since he was no longer considered a "brother", who stood next to a bubbly Sister Downs. All three-fifty of her. Boy was she a biggin.

"Dad lifted a finger and motioned for Phelps and Sister Downs to come near. That's when I saw the hammer by his side. Then dad looked to me and without saying a word, I knew I'd better come, if I didn't want a scolding.

Ethan shook his head at the sand and cleaned out an ear with a dirty finger nail. He huffed out a breath.

"So, there we were. Dad, me, Mr. Phelps, Will, Dave, Ricky, and the tattle tale. I scanned the crowd for Mama and found her at about ninety degrees to my left. She gave me a forced smile that came from a broken heart. I knew she didn't fully agree with all of this, but like me, what choice did she have?

"I faked back a grin. Then dad began. 'Hear me today my dearly beloved of the greater good. For yet again, sin has entered our flock through the open window created here by Mr. Phelps. If this sin is not dealt with, we will all see the wrath of God upon our families like never before. For behold, it is a fearful thing to fall into the hands of a wrathful god. As the ole Jonathan Edwards once said. That still rings true today. So, I submit to you what the voice of God has said in regard to Mr. Phelps grave sin. This is what the great god says: "Your people have defiled my name and now a sacrifice must be made to ever ease the pain. The life of the pure to purify the wicked. That is what I require. Their wickedness can only be blotted by the pure.'

"Dad folded the paper, giving it perfect even creases and placed it in his pocket before hanging his head with a deep sigh. He wiped away a tear that I'm sure took a lot out of him to make. He was never a natural crier.

"He lifted the hammer and turned it in the air in admiration. He pointed it to Mr. Phelps and said, 'Take the boy.' Mr. Phelps tried to recant by reminding him of the boy's innocence, but dad replied with, 'I know...that's the whole point. Didn't you hear the word of god? 'The life of the pure to purify the wicked.' Take the boy."

"So...Mr. Phelps reluctantly took hold of Will's arms and held them tight behind his back. That's when dad stepped to me and waved down the hammer like passing off a sacred warrior's sword and said, "All sin begins within and there is no cure without atonement. A sacrifice must now be made to ever ease the pain.'"

59

It wasn't long after Lee arrived that I spoke with Dr. Blur or more professionally speaking, Dr. Dafini. And after a quick chat with the doc, I was finally able to see the kids. Lee wheeled me to Jason's room first, I could've walked, but Lee and the Doc didn't want me over doing it. So, I at least got him to stop just outside Jason's door, so I could walk in and surprise him.

With Lee's help, I managed to walk through the door, a little wobbly and a tad light headed, but I did it.

I heard him gasp in amazement. If only I could've seen his face.

"Dad? What in the world? Your standing!" he gasped.

It was the first time he'd ever seen me on my own two feet in over two years, as this last flare up had been quite a doozy.

I smiled and made my way over to his bed where Lee helped me take a seat. I made a crash landing as his bed made some pops and cracks.

"What in the world happened? It's been two or three years since I've seen you walk," he said as we embraced.

"It's a miracle son. That's all I can say. It's a miracle," he pulled back and I patted him on the knee.

"What happened to your head?"

"That's where the dirtbag shot me."

"What? Oh, my gosh...so that was what I heard then. It wasn't an explosion. it was a gun. Who did it? Don't tell me it was the man from Connor's dream."

I took a deep breath and rubbed my beard and said through a reluctant sigh, "Yeah...that's our guy."

"Where's mom and the others? How are they doing?"

I took a second to gather the words, which made Jason uneasy.

"Dad?"

I cleared my throat and said, "Son...your Mama was kidnapped that night."

"What!? You mean to tell this sorry piece of crap took Mama?"

"I'm afraid so. But they're working hard and we're going to get her back."

He rubbed his face with both palms as tears begin to form in his eyes.

"You've got to be kidding me," he sighed then asked, "What about my brother and sisters?"

"They're doing good. If you want, you can come with me to go see them."

"Yeah of course. I want to see them. When are we getting out of here? I mean we have to help them find Mama."

"Well...I'm going to try and do some convincing with Dr. Dafini...hopefully soon."

††††††††††††††††††††††

WITH THE FOCUS split between the boat ramp with the body wrapped in Saran wrap tucked in the back of the submerged Camry and the scene of the other body found up in the Shallotte River by the old flounder fisherman, Mr. Brock Hodgkin wasn't expecting much out of the ordinary that morning as he made his way over to his homemade museum of sorts right off of Stone Chimney road only about ten miles from Holden Beach.

Mr. Hodgkin opened the place some twenty years ago after having received numerous props, old antique cars and busses from a buddy of his that worked for a film crew out in California. He had collected everything from realistic mannequins to 1940's antique cars and school busses.

One of the busses, he dressed up as what he'd called the Crackhead Express as it was full of mannequins dressed in white suits with all sorts of glass bottles filled with green liquid and tubes extending outward like that from a chemistry class. Large blocks of taped up flour to appear as the real thing sat in the windows next to suitcases full of fake cash. Apparently, the druggies were attempting to allude two police cruisers that trailed close behind. It'd become quite the attraction over the years and only if Mr. Hodgkin had a nickel for every photo taken with the thing, he'd be one rich ole fellow.

Mr. Hodgkin pulled into his normal parking space out front and jingled his keys around as he searched for the right one to open the front door. As he busied himself with the task, something seemed off, just didn't feel right.

He stopped searching for the key and raised his gaze as he twisted his head this way and that. It felt as if he was being watched. That old eerie feeling when it seems someone is standing right over your shoulder, breathing down your neck and taking pleasure in their invisibility.

Something just wasn't right.

Mr. Hodgkin backed away from the door and turned to face the road as he took his time scanning the yard full of dummies and antique cars and old gas station signs among a few other items that you didn't see on an everyday basis.

Like the sight of a man-made funeral where a handful of mannequins mourned their fallen friend as his casket was stopped mid-way into to the hole. Clutched tightly against his chest was a half empty whiskey bottle. A sign lay against the casket that read, "Mr. Daniels and Jack were good friends, Jack stayed by his side, even till the end."

Mr. Hodgkin continued to scan the yard, until his eyes landed on the Crackhead Express. A mannequin in the window had been displaced.

Must've fallen over. It happened from time to time and wasn't that unusual. They always seemed to have their way of calling out to their owner for help. So, Mr. Hodgkin waddled on over as he fumbled for the key to the old school bus he'd turned into the druggy's home.

He found the key and unlocked the door as he forced himself up and through the door with some grunts that could have come from a Gorilla.

"Now Hermie, what cha think you doing in here. You know better than to be moving around on me, I'm a getting too old to be climbing up in here like this. I'd apprec—"

The stench cut his words short as it seemed to slap him flush across the face.

"Whew wee! My goodness...what in the world have you fellas been doing in—"

His eyes locked on Hermie, but something wasn't right. Hermie had apparently gave up the crack and packed on the pounds. He'd never been him this big and round.

"Hermie?"

60

Tuesday just prior to noon, Agent Turner, Agent Vasquez, and Lieutenant Mishoe took a break from the crime scene under the bridge and made their way over to the Crackhead Express off Stone Chimney.

A lady dressed in a white suit with bold black letters that read, "CSI" across the back, busied herself with snapping photos of the body of 49-year-old Jensen Walker. A heavy-set real estate agent from Supply. Vasquez called out to Turner and Mishoe from the back of the bus.

They pass the CSI lady and stop next to Vasquez who had her eyes fixed on the back of a seat. She lifted her finger as Turner and Mishoe followed her leading. Three bold melting letters drew in blood returned their gaze.

GTK

Turner sighed, placed his hands to his hips and wagged his head toward the floor. As the three of them were left for a moment with no words.

The sound of tires over gravel begged for their attention. They each bent low to gaze out the windows where they witnessed a white Chevy Silverado pull in next to Turner's black Tahoe.

"Well I'd be," said Mishoe as he headed for the door of the bus.

Turner and Vasquez followed.

About the time their feet hit the gravel, a man perhaps in his mid-seventies and dressed in a golf sweater and khaki pants, stepped out of his truck stood next to the driver door.

Mishoe approached him with an empty palm.

"Mr. Randy Callahan...how you doing sir?"

"Aww...doing well, just thought I'd swing by and see what was going on," he said as he shut the door of his truck and shuffled toward the bus where Mishoe met him in the middle.

"You look good Lieutenant," said Mishoe.

"C'mon don't call me that, I'm retired remember?" he said with a wave of the hand.

Mishoe turned and introduced Callahan to Turner and Vasquez.

"I've heard a lot of good things about you Mr. Callahan. I guess you were the first to track this guy, weren't you?" asked Turner.

"Yeah, I guess so. Something I wish weren't true, but it is what it is. You know I spent ten years searching for him after what he did in Georgetown? Never as much as heard a peep from the fella. Although, I'd hoped he'd never do it again, I knew it was only a matter of time before he did. Someone with his psychological make-up are never satisfied with just a murder or two. Once they get the taste for blood and get that sick rush, it becomes an addiction they can't stop, unless someone like yourselves puts an end to it. Something just gets down inside of them and takes over and once those dopamine sensors are triggered...boy it's hard to rewire that stuff."

"So, you really think it's the GTK? You know...the real guy, instead of just a copy-cat?"

"Oh no doubt," Callahan said as he tightened his lips, pinched his eye brows and gently rocked his head.

"You see what gave it away for me, is when I heard about the song," said Callahan he removed his glasses and rubbed them with his sweater.

"Every breath you take?" asked Mishoe.

"As far as I know we never told anyone about that. So, the second I heard about him leaving notes with those song lyrics, I knew there were only three options. 1) It's the GTK, 2) Its somebody within the ranks that was a part of the investigation, which I don't even want to go there, or 3) Its somebody close to the GTK attempting to finish what he started. But I tell ya...deep down I really feel its him. It's just all too similar to everything I dealt with back in the day."

As he finished his words, the CSI lady exited the bus followed behind two Coroners who grunted and strained to haul the gurney down the steps of the bus. A plump body under a white sheet jiggled and bounced as it rode along.

"All sin begins within and there is no cure without atonement. A sacrifice must now be made to ever ease the pain," said Callahan as the four of them watched the gurney struggle toward the coroner van.

They turned their attention to Callahan and waited for his elaboration on the words that had so puzzled them ever since they read the letter.

"Look...I'm not saying I know what the creep meant by all of that...but, I do tend to think he might not just be working out of blood lust, but out of duty as well."

"How so?" asked Vasquez.

"Well...I think he's atoning for his sins. I know that's sort of an oxymoron, to kill someone to atone for your sins, but I think that's just how his twisted mind operates. I think somehow, all of these killings ease his guilt, because in his mind, his making an atonement. He's giving an offering to God, so it's not a sin...it's a sacrifice."

"Perhaps he's atoning for his Mother that he keeps mentioning in his letters," mentioned Turner.

"Perhaps so. That's something to consider."

†††††††††††††††††††††

IT WAS tough to see my kids in the kind of shape they were in. It was bad enough trying to see them through this irritating blur, but to know the extent of their injuries, especially Lilly and Kelly, it took all I had to keep it together.

I managed to convince Jason to stay at the hospital with his siblings at least for the next few days until me and Lee saw fit for him to join us on our search for his mama.

I talked to Dr. Dafini shortly after visiting with the children and was able to convince him to let me go tomorrow. He wanted to keep me until Thursday, but I haggled him down a day.

Now the clock was ticking. One more day and I'd be out there hunting the monster who'd done this to my family. Just one more day and I could actually do something about bringing Rebecca home, rather than lie here in a hospital bed and wait for someone from the Sheriff's office to give me an update.

After learning of the three recent murders, I've honestly wondered about the chances of finding Rebecca alive. The one thing that keeps me hoping though, is the fact that the GTK always leaves a body, so far, he'd yet to keep one for himself. So, that gave me hope that she was still alive, because if she wasn't, they'd probably found her by now.

Maybe, he can't do it, since having known her from the past. I keep telling myself, that maybe she'll be able to break through to him. Maybe, she'll remind him of our times in 89.

I sure hope so. That's really about all I can do at this point. Hope...and pray of course.

That's something I'm still learning to do, but with Lee's help, I'm catching on rather quick.

Two more days. Just two more days.

God...please protect her until then. Please God...two more days...two more days.

61

Just after 12:30 pm on Tuesday at The Good Shepherd

Church of Shallotte, Pastor David Hoffman, had taken a short break from studying for Wednesday night's service to enjoy a guilty pleasure of his since his youth.

Having spent the past hour surfing the web for the best images his lustful mind could find, he spent himself as his brain drove him onward. Afterwards, he became overwhelmed by guilt and shame. In a huff, he clicked the X in the top right corner, sending the lewd pictures and videos to the back of his mind where they'd take up residence for another time.

He loathed himself for having indulged in such perversion. Though, no matter how hard he fought the urge, he was powerless to overcome such an addiction. It was like being caught in a rip current, the harder he fought it, the further it took him out to the sea of hopelessness.

Ever since the day, him, Will, and Frankie stumbled upon that stash, it just had a way of pulling him back, time after time, rush after rush. His body felt numb from the electric charge having just disbursed throughout every vein and bodily member. His heart felt like a bowling ball, as shame weighed upon him like a loaded dump truck, crushing his spirit and hope for freedom.

"Lord...why do I do the things I do. I'm tired of living like this. I'm tired of going back and forth. I'm tired of being a hypocrite. Please Lord...set me free from this. Deliver me O'God from the pits of despair, create in me a clean heart and renew in me a right spirit. I'm not worthy of your forgiveness, but Lord, I ask for help. Please help me, Lord. Change me from the inside out. I want to be clean on the inside. I'm tired of putting on a shiny front and pretending to have it all together, while on the inside, I'm nothing but a rotten corpse of a man. Lord, help me get this right. Help me lead this church in truth...help me lead my wife. Help me be honest with her, don't let me take her for granted. You've given me an Angel and a Queen, help me treat her like one."

With that he broke. David buried his face in his palms as tears soaked the carpet. His chair squeaked with every jolt of his shoulders, as he sobbed from a place deep within. Freedom seemed so far away, as the shackles of his sin seemed to only tighten the harder he tried to resist the temptation.

Was there any hope? Could he ever be free from such an addiction? Could God ever deliver him from such a mess? Had he finally gone too far? Did God even care? Had he finally written him off as a reprobate mind?

David...my beloved son in whom I am well pleased.

The soft voice came from his spirit and seemed to wrap him in a warm embrace. The whole atmosphere of the room had changed. *What is this?*

Are your sins stronger than my Blood and Grace? Is your failure greater than My redemption?

A moment passed.

Never! My love for you and the power of My Cross, Death, Burial, and Resurrection are stronger than anything you have ever done or can ever do. Thinking you can somehow overpower my Grace with your sin, is no less foolish than thinking you can throw an ice cube at the Sun and expect it to freeze. Your sin is no match for My Blood and Grace. I love you with an ever-lasting love. You are my beloved son. I will never give up on you, no matter what. You are mine. I died that you may have life and life more abundantly. Let go of all your guilt and shame and awaken to who are. You are the Light of the World. You are the Salt of the Earth. You are of a Royal Priesthood. You are good. I created you in my own image and I do not make mistakes. Everything I create is good. Though you may do bad things and commit horrible sins as the tempter comes to destroy and blind you to who you are...you are not bad. You are my creation and I do not create anything that isn't good. You are better than the sin you struggle with, that's not who you are. You are not an addict, your struggle does not define you, unless you allow it to. Remember who you are and let go of all you think you know, to know the one who knows you. For it is in losing yourself, you find Me, and it is in finding Me, you find yourself. I am in you and you are in Me, for we are one. Nothing can separate you from my love, you were bought with a price. You are mine and you always will be. I love you David. Remember who you are.

With those words, he collapsed to the soaked carpet and wept without restraint. Something within him broke as the words penetrated his heart and mind with fresh revelation of who he was in Christ.

As he awakened to who he was, a cool ember from the remnants of a once burning flame, began to rekindle with a fresh passion.

He'd taken on a new identity, he was no longer David the porn addict, he was now David the Light of the World, a beloved son of the living God. His life had purpose, it had meaning, and now he must fight for his family and for the church God had bestowed upon him and he must fight against the darkness that had invaded the land through his child-hood friend. It was time to enter the battle of good and evil. It was time to fast and pray.

62

Back in the sandy bunker, Frank lay Rebecca down softly

to a blanket as she was still unconscious from the chloroform. Her limp body flopped to the sand, her chest rising and falling with each breath. Frank covered her with the rest of the blanket to keep her warm.

Once the chloroform wears off, he'd be sure to give her some food and water, after he'd allow her to take a quick break to relieve herself, as he was sure she'd probably appreciate.

He stood and crossed to the opposite end and retrieved a handful of baggies as he approached Mother and the mason jars full of offerings from those who'd been sacrificed for the greater good.

He grunted and curled over as if he'd just taken a ghostly sledge hammer to the gut. His innards twisted and churned as if being squeezed by a vice grip. He sank to his knees, clinched his abdomen and searched for his next breath. Nausea washed over him like a rogue wave in the ever-treacherous Artic Ocean. He tried to hold it down, but any effort to do so, only delayed the inevitable. He gagged and finally heaved up what had his gut in knots. Black stringy ooze emitted from his lips as a dozen large spiders scurried and scattered across the sand.

It felt as if his gut was being torn in two from the inside out. He moaned. It felt like he was trying to pass a stash of razor blades.

He curled into a fetal position as every muscle in his body entered into a spasm. With shaky hands, he managed to lift his shirt to reveal his hairy flesh. His eyes locked on his naval, where there was movement. As he winced and gritted his teeth with sweat and tears turning the sand into mush, a black bony finger protruded from his belly button digging its way out with a sharp and dirty nail.

Blood trickled down his side and landed in the sand. No sooner than he'd placed his hand to it to keep it from coming on out, it disappeared as a horde of flies. They swarmed about before vanishing like a puff of black smoke.

His head spun as it felt like it had taken on the weight of a wrecking ball. His body felt numb and weightless. everything went black. He joined Rebecca in a soft snore.

††††††††††††††††††††††††

IN A DISMAL dungeon, hot from the raging flames and filled with the screams of the multitudes, Kirkland was bent at the waist and screeched and clinched at the twisting in his gut. He hurled blasphemy and insults heavenward and beat against his abdomen in efforts to ease the pain.

There was loud chatter among the demons outside Kirkland's lair, something had them stirred. They screamed in their native language and coward from seven glowing men who'd entered their domain.

Kirkland knew by the sounds of it, they were being paid a visit from those sent by the Holy One.

The seven men were clothed in radiant gold armor that must've weighed more than three demons combined, all but one wielding large iron swords that stretched at least six-foot. The one who didn't carry a sword, carried a whip that was known in the Roman days as the Cat-O-Nine tails, it yielded nine leather straps each wearing shards of glass and bone that'd dig and shred through any flesh that crossed its path.

The seven men marched straight to Kirkland's lair. It wasn't the first time they'd done so. They punished a hand full of arrogant scaly demons that tried to stand in their way, those wielding the swords made quick work of them as each slice of the blade turned into nothing more than a vanishing black ball of sulfurous smoke.

Kirkland pushed himself from the floor and glared out into the pits of hell where his eyes met those of the man toting the whip. The blood drained from Kirkland's face as he stumbled backwards before tripping over his own two feet and landing flat on his rump.

Before he could even gather himself, a pair of burly arms yanked him to his feet. The one with the whip playfully slapped it across his palm, wearing a tight grin.

"No! No! Nooooo! You can't do this! Who do you think you are?!"

"Silence!!!" the taller of the bunch roared as his voice caused Kirkland to squint and grit his teeth. The demons below scurried in an attempt to find somewhere to hide.

"Mateo...scourge him!"

"Certainly!"

The two men drug Kirkland to the wall and stretched his arms, leaving his scaly back bare and defenseless against any punishment.

Long and crooked scars ran up and down his flesh like tidal creeks in the marsh. It was quite evident this wasn't the first of such scourging.

"How many Sir Nathaniel?"

"How about 40...one more than our Lord," the leader, Nathaniel said with a smirk.

The others agreed.

Mateo reared back and slung the whip into Kirkland's back, ripping flesh as he had to give it a good yank to break loose.

The Angels mocked Kirkland of his screams. Moments later, the once powerful and arrogant demon, who'd been the driver behind the murderous plots of the GTK, had become nothing more than a weak scaly, lizard looking collection of evil, whose back looked as if it'd just passed through a paper shredder.

"20...half way there my friend," said Nathaniel as he stood with his python sized arms crossed at the chest.

†††††††††††††††††††††

HOURS HAD PASSED as Tuesday afternoon entered the evening. Six o'clock, Ethan's grunts and groans, pulled Rebecca from her slumber. She blinked enough to clear the blur, then squinted her eyes and wagged her head to rid it of the dizziness, as it felt like a spinning top wobbling upon a table.

Her eyes adjusted to the darkness as her ears led her to Ethan. He lay beneath Mother, only about five yards away. The glow of the candles helped, but not much, as he'd only lit two of them, instead of the usual half a dozen.

Distant chatter seeped through the sand above.

Her breath caught in her throat. her heart didn't beat. She's hearing things, right?

Hoping for a rescue, it's her mind toying with her. Has to be.

There it was again. Laughter and chatter. It grew louder but was still muffled enough she couldn't make out the words. She laid still with her eyes and ears fixed on Ethan as he clinched at his gut and groaned in between snores.

She glanced down at her ankles, then to her wrists, she wasn't bound. For some reason, he'd failed to secure her in the chains. Was this a test? Was he playing possum and waiting for her to make a break for it, before pouncing on her like a cheetah on a baby gazelle?

More chatter. More laughter. Sounded like there were kids. Should she take a gamble and do it? What if she never got this chance again? But what if she put these people in danger?

He seemed to be in a deep sleep, but what if he was faking?

Only one way to find out.

Rebecca forced herself to sit on her haunches in the sand, but the stabbing knives in her hamstrings, told her otherwise. She winced and crashed back the sand. She stuck her hand down her jeans and felt the back of her leg, still tender from the botched operation, she glided her fingers over torn flesh, held together by make-shift stiches.

Her leg flinched as she touched a part of exposed skin, the sound of a little bell startled her. Ethan moaned and rolled to his side, his back now facing Rebecca.

She glanced down at her ankle and peered through the darkness to find a little bell that was attached to an ankle bracelet made from a small chain, held together by a tiny master lock.

Dear God...now what?

Her mangled legs and missing hamstrings were one thing to deal with, but now finding she wore an anklet with a rattling bell, was enough to steal her hope.

Giggles. Voices. Waves. The singing chime.

"God...how am I supposed to get out of here, with no legs all the while wearing a dang tracking system?" she mumbled under her breath, before lying in the sand and breathing out a soft sigh.

Ethan grunted and tucked his knees toward his chest, before whimpering like a lost puppy.

"I've got to make my move...I've got to take my chances. At least whisper to these people or something. Got to let them know I'm down here."

She glanced around the room for any sign of weapons. But all she saw were the candles, jars of body parts, Mama, and Ethan.

She was already facing an uphill battle with the shape her legs were in and the new jewelry he'd given her, but to add to all that, she was weak from having barely eaten anything over the past two days.

She opened her mouth and rolled her tongue around her lips to alleviate the dryness. That was another thing, she was dehydrated as well, she knew not just by the lack of water she'd received, but the color of her urine.

"All right...suck it up Rebecca. You can do this. God...please give me strength to make it out of here."

She rolled onto her stomach and began a slow army crawl toward the ladder. Having to pass within arm's length from Ethan in the process.

This still hurt but it was manageable and was quiet, so it'd have to do. Her next fear was the thought of climbing that ladder with two missing hamstrings. But...she'd cross that bridge when she got there...inch by inch...on her belly...through the sand.

Just a little more and she'd be able to reach out and take hold of the first rung.

"C'mon...you've got this...don't stop...don't give up. God help me."

Her heart pounded...her muscles quivered...she had to do this.

The voices began to fade.

No. Don't go. Wait.

The rung now within reach, she stretched her right arm straight as a tooth pick. The muscles and tendons tightened. Her fingers rubbed against the rung but were too far away to take grip.

"Just...a...little...more," she said each word accompanied with its own personal grunt.

She wiggled closer. Two fingers took hold, then a third, then a fourth...then she felt five fingers grip her ankles and yank her through the sand, scraping her belly.

"Ahhhh!"

"What do you think you're doing?!" Ethan hissed as he flipped her onto her back, by twisting her legs.

Her lips stammered as she managed to cultivate a decent answer.

"I-I-I had to pee. I wa-was trying to pull myself up. My legs hurt too bad to stand on my own."

He stood there with his big black pupils drilling into her.

"Hmm," he grunted before turning his back to face Mama.

He peered up at his Mother and stuck a fingernail to his mouth, while giving the matter some thought.

"Rebecca...I'm not stupid."

He turned to face her.

"And this isn't my first rodeo. You're not the first to try and climb that ladder while missing two hamstrings. Even if you did make it to the top, you wouldn't get far before I'd catch up. Trust me...it just be a waste of time and pain."

"Ethan...why are you doing this? You're a good person, this isn't you."

Her words seemed to catch him off guard, knocking him broad side like a round house jawbreaker.

He snarled back an answer, "Because I have to...okay...because I have to. For Mama's sake."

"But Ethan...I'm sure there's another way...right? I mean I'm sure your Mother would understand."

He sighed and hung his head, crossed his arms and picked at one of the multitude of warts resting upon his nose and cheek.

"Rebecca...now's not the time to talk like this. Not in front of Mother. I think it'd do her some good for me to tell the rest of the story about Will and what happened to Mother," he said as he glanced to the long-haired skeleton, before locking eyes with Rebecca.

That glare is enough to paralyze you. It's like stumbling upon a Grizzly in the forest. Sure, you can try and run, but your best bet would be to play dead...or in this case...play along with the man's warped view of reality.

"Okay...whatever will help you both feel better. I want to help and I'm sure it does some good to get this off your chest."

"Thank you, Rebecca. Well...as you probably remember, I stopped with daddy passing me the hammer as Mr. Phelps was forced to hold Will. I smashed him over the head with it three times. That was all it took to sacrifice one of my best-friends. The crowd of white-robed parishioners roared in celebration, some muttered toward the sky in their heavenly language. Sister Downs did her famous roll of the tongue as it sounded like an impending attack from one of those raged engine's.

"Dad patted me on the shoulder and said, 'Good job son...I'm proud of you.' He then wiped his hands in Will's blood and nodded for Dave and Ricky to grab Mr. Phelps who was already so distraught he could barely stand under those weak and trembling legs. They grabbed Mr. Phelps from behind, dad stood with bloody hands and approached Mr. Phelps. He stopped in front of him and said, 'The life of the pure to purify the wicked. All sin begins within and there is no cure without atonement.' He smeared the blood over Mr. Phelps face. Causing him to look like a ripened tomato."

Ethan paused, turned his back and wiped his face with both palms as he took a long, deep breath and sighed it out.

Rebecca wiped the tears that dripped down her cheeks and said, "Ethan...I'm so sorry."

"Please...call me Frank," he mumbled.

"Huh?"

"My names Frank. Ethan's my middle name. Just call me Frank."

A moment passed.

"Frank...you were only a kid at the time and you were just doing what your dad told you to do. Now—"

"Quiet! Let me finish."

"I'm sorry...yes, go ahead."

"So, after it was all done, dad made it my job to get rid of the body. There was a fishing pond not too far behind our house. Me, Will, and another buddy of ours would go there often to catch bream and catfish. It was loaded with them. So, dad made me take Will out to the barn, where I had to cut him into small enough pieces to fit into two five-gallon buckets. I had to wait until 3 o'clock in the morning before making the trek through the woods carrying the buckets of my friend. I had to keep stopping to catch my breath, as I was so scared of being out there that late of night, I kept thinking how a bear or coyote would get me. I finally made it to the pond and dumped Will off the small fishing pier. There were only two houses within view of the pond, and both of them were pitch dark, so no one ever knew but us."

Rebecca gulped and breathed through trembling lips as more tears rolled off her cheeks.

"Frank...I'm so sorry."

He ignored her sympathy and continued with, "The whole town began looking, but they never found anything.

The fish made sure of it. So, I guess it must've been a few weeks later when the last sacrifice was made. I came home from school early one day as I was still so shook up about Will, that my nerves got the best of me during one of my final exams, I puked right in the middle of it. Ms. Davis took me to the nurse where she wrote me a permission slip for the day.

"I remember entering the front door. Dad should've still been at work, as I imagined Mama would be busy knitting a scarf or getting an early start on preparing supper. I walked through the house calling out to her, but she never answered. The house was empty."

Frank took a deep breath and rubbed the back of his neck.

"It was obvious she wasn't there, so I headed out the back door to see if maybe she was in the barn praying, as she'd do from time to time. As I neared the big sliding door, the sound of a soft chant, caused my heart to drop. The thought of another atonement turned my stomach, but my curiosity put the vomit on hold. The chanting sounding like it was only coming from one mouth, it didn't sound like the usual crowd that'd gather for an atonement.

"So, as quiet as I could, I slid the door to my right and peeked inside...it was daddy...he was on his knees rocking back and forth in the dirt just below a wooden cross. I raised my eyes..." Frank sniffled and wiped his eyes and cheeks with the back of his hands "...it was Mama," he whimpered and puffed out air as his bottom lip folded and quivered. He finished through a broken voice, "He'd nailed her to the cross like Christ, feet and all. I rushed past daddy and wrapped my arms around Mama's legs and squeezed with everything I had, not wanting to let go. She was all I had and the thought of it just being me and daddy was too much.

"I looked up at her as I cried for her to wake up, but it was too late...she was gone."

He snorted a gasp of air through his nostrils, taking in snot with the process. He let it out with a huff.

"As if that wasn't enough, when I looked closer, I noticed she was missing her eyes, ears, nose, and lips, then I looked at her feet...her toes were gone. I looked to her hands, her fingers gone too. I knew he did it while she was alive, just like we'd skinned the Helms. I jerked around to daddy still rocking in the dirt, hands clasped tightly between his legs, uttering a prayer in that gibberish tongue.

"I glanced around the barn...I knew we kept a pitch fork nearby. My eyes found it over in a corner."

Frank stopped his pacing and placed his hands to his hips, then turned and faced Rebecca.

"He never knew what hit him. The rascal never came out of his trance.

"I dug a big hole under the house and that's where he is to this day. I kept Mama in the fridge for a few days until the stench was too much, so I placed her under there too. Then when I came back, I went and got her," he said as his eyes locked with Mother's.

"Rebecca..." he turned to her with watery black eyes, "Seeing Mama on that cross was the hardest thing I've ever been through. Will was bad enough, but Mama..."

He broke again and collapsed to his knees. face buried in his palms. His shoulders jerked like a jack hammer as he wept without restraint.

Rebecca's eyes flooded as well.

Frank dropped to his side and curled into a fetal position once more, weeping like a child.

Rebecca forced herself into an army crawl and drug herself over to him. Her heart ached for the man, despite all he'd done, something deep within her found compassion for him.

How could she have one ounce of sympathy for such a monster? But was he really a monster? Deep down...was he really a monster? Was he born the GTK? Or was he not molded into such a thing by his father? Would God create such an evil man?

With a light hand, she patted Frank's shoulder, like attempting to convince a stray dog she meant no harm.

He reached with his left and touched her wrist. Feeling his approval, she went in for a hug. She wrapped her arms around him the best she could. She felt him melt as she could tell a warm embrace was something he desperately longed for.

He sobbed as it took all Rebecca had, not to do the same.

"Why am I like this? Why do I do the things I do?" he asked through the tears and whimpers.

"I don't like hurting people...but if it means easing Mama's pain...then what choice do I have?" his breath became more labored as he wheezed and grasped for each one.

"Ssshhh...now calm down Frank...take it easy. Listen what your dad did was terrible, but do you really think your Mother would want you to go on hurting people the way he did? I mean surely there is another way...right?"

He sniffled and gathered his breath.

"I don't think so Rebecca...I wish there were...but there is only one way to ease her pain...sacrifice," he took a deep breath. gently patted Rebecca's hand and fell silent.

After a few minutes, he began to snore.

With Rebecca's arm still wrapped around him in a hug, she shut her eyes and prayed for rest.

63

It took about an hour to go through the discharge procedures. I hugged and kissed the kids goodbye. Jason, Lauren and Connor would be coming home on Monday, but Lily and Kelly would have to stay for at least another two weeks, maybe more. I made it home just after eight o'clock Wednesday night.

Lee stayed with me through the night and made sure I had everything I needed. Like the dozen different horse pills, they'd given me for pain. Boy those things are gigantic. Lee's been good to me though, even fixed me breakfast this morning.

After some convincing, I got him to find Lieutenant Mishoe's number. I dialed it out on my android and put it on speaker. It was just after nine o'clock, so I thought he might not be too busy. After the fourth ring, I was doubtful he'd answer, so I was already planning the message I'd leave him. As the fifth ring was about to end, static introduced his deep, gravelly voice.

"Lieutenant Mishoe speaking."

I could tell he wasn't too happy to answer.

I cleared my throat and fumbled with my words just a bit, "Uh...umm...ye-yeah...th...this is James Randolph. How you doing?"

Static breathing returned my words.

"Hello?"

"Yeah I'm here. I'm sorry...I just wasn't expecting to hear from you. I'm good...how you holding up?"

"Good. So...where's my wife? What's going on?"

A moment passed.

"WHERE'S MY WIFE?" I didn't mean to raise my voice, but I did.

"Calm down James..."

"Don't tell me to calm down! My wife has been taken captive by a monster and you're telling me to calm down?"

"I'm sorr-

"What are you guys doing anyhow? Do you even have any clues as to where she is?"

"James...listen we are doing all we ca—"

"How are you doing all you can, when there's been three bodies since she was taken? You call that doing all you can?! Bull..." I stopped myself before saying it. I was just so distraught over the whole situation and since I couldn't take it out on the GTK himself, Mishoe found himself at the end of my barrel of frustration.

"JAMES!" now he was upset, "I'm not going to listen to you tell me how to do my job! You got that! I am doing all I can do. We've got federal agents, bounty hunters, you name it, we've got it. This guy hasn't just taken Rebecca, pardon my bluntness...but he's murdered at least nine other people that we know of. The whole Nation is watching, and so is Washington. We're going to get this guy and we've got every resource we need to do that."

Static filled the gap.

Lee sat on our couch rubbing his eyes and face with his palms.

I took a deep breath and said, "Well...I'm sorry for taking it out on you, I've just got a lot of stuff building inside for this guy...do you think myself and a friend could help out in the search?"

He sighed. I could picture him shaking his head in disgust.

"Listen James...I can't imagine what you're feeling right now, but I really don't think it'd be a good idea for you to be a part of this. I think the best thing you could, is be there for your kids. They need you more than we do right now."

Lee nodded with his eyes distant but fixed on our ottoman.

I took a breath and rubbed my tear ducts with my right index and thumb.

"All right...but listen the kids won't be home until Monday, let me and my friend do our own searching. We won't get in the way. You won't even know we're doing anything. Once the kids get out of the hospital, I'll ease off and be with them. Whatdasay?"

He waited a moment passed before conceding with, "Yeah...I guess I can deal with that. Just don't make me regret this. My honest opinion though...I think you need to stay home and rest, but I know if I were in your shoes, I'd probably do the same thing. So, I understand. But like I said, don't make me regret it. Can you do that for me?"

"You got it. Well listen, I appreciate what you guys are doing and I'm sorry for jumping your back, it's just killing me, knowing she's with this sick nut bag and thinking of what she must be going through."

"James...listen, don't sweat it. Just relax the best you can and trust us to do our job. We've got every resource we need, his time's running out...we're going to get him and we're going to bring Rebecca home. Just trust me. Okay?"

"All right...well...good luck and be careful. Let me know what I can do and if you learn anything new, call me. I don't want anything getting on the news for my kids to see, without me having the chance to tell them. We clear on that?"

"I'll do my best. Take care James and get you some rest. Your kids need you. I'll be in touch."

"Sounds good...see ya."

The screen on my phone turned red, it gave a soft beep.

I looked to Lee, "Lee...we've got three days until the kids get here...let's hit it hard and see what we can find. Once they come home, I'll slack off to be here for them. Can you help me until Monday?"

He looked at me, with his sharp cheek bones, red skin, and black hair, I felt like the Lone Ranger awaiting an answer from Tonto.

"Absolutely. But listen...this situation is as much spiritual as it is physical. Now if you remember, I told you our tribe is fasting and praying over all of this. I think it'd be wise if you joined us. Now, that doesn't mean you have to do a full blown fast for the next three days, but if you can find a way to enter this fast with us, I truly believe that together we can push back the darkness invading our land. We must take this seriously and fight this battle in the Spirit, for if we attempt to conquer this evil in the flesh, we're only playing on the enemy's territory, but if we're vigilant to stay in the Spirit, then the darkness will be forced to play on our home turf," his words felt like trying to learn a new language, but what I could understand, made sense. He was the one more spiritually adept, and I knew that he believed what he said. So, now I find myself, with Lee's help, learning how to fast and pray.

††††††††††††††††††††††

AN HOUR HAD passed and Mishoe found himself in another briefing held by Agent Turner and Agent Vasquez. The three of them were piled into the conference room

366

once again at the Brunswick County Sheriff's Office along with another dozen or so detectives, agents, and officers.

"All right...listen up," aaid Turner as he clapped his hands twice after having just walked in behind Vasquez. He dropped a stack of paperwork to the long oval shaped cherry oak table and rolled up the sleeves of his neatly pressed white collared shirt. It was decorated with black suspenders, which toted his loaded 9mm.

He toyed with his thick graying mustache, before diving into the new information.

"Here's what we got. Agent Vasquez?" he said as he began passing photos for her to pin to the board.

"Our first victim...62-year-old white female...Donna Shaw. Discovered in the ravine up in Big Bear...wrapped in plastic, slit throat, her nose cut off and the letters GTK etched into her forehead. Our second victim...48-year-old black male...Adrian Key. Discovered just on the outskirts of Houston lying outside his vehicle...severed tongue...two .38 caliber rounds to the head...right index and thumb removed...and a note left in his mouth."

Vasquez pinned the crime scene photos of each body as Turner continued.

"Our third victim...found off Smith Road in the backhoe...39-year-old...Larry Conrad...his spinal cord severed by a ten-inch blade to the back of the neck. The letters GTK etched behind his right ear...left eye cut out."

He went on for another five minutes retelling the discoveries of the other three bodies, the woman found by the flounder fisherman, the man left at the boat ramp in the back of the Camry, and the man left in the crackhead express off Stone Chimney.

Turner paused and crossed his arms, bit one end of his reading glasses and glared at the gruesome photos pinned to the board. He scanned the room as most wore wrinkled foreheads with squinted eyes in attempt to decipher the crimes.

Turner cleared his throat.

"All right...now we've got the forensics back on all of the crime scenes. The prints match at each one. Even going back to the Berkley, Rickles, and Vendetti murders from 89...one note of interest though...the prints here in Brunswick County are not alone."

Confusion washed over the faces of everyone in the room. That was even news for Mishoe as he took a gulp, shut his eyes and breathed deep.

"There's another set of prints that's in play here. Now the troubling thing is, the new set of prints pull nothing from the database, so our new guy doesn't have much of a criminal history...at least nothing worth noting that is."

Mishoe tapped his pencil on his note pad as faces and suspects flashed through his mind.

Turner reached for his black coffee mug on the table, took a sip before adding,

"So now the question is...who's helping the GTK?"

64

The sound of rhythmic chanting had become secondary to Rebecca as she lay between her dreams and the harsh reality of the damp and cold sand bunker. Her vision placed her in a marsh surrounded by thick Spartina grass as it laid over with the hard-pressing wind, the chanting became louder, accompanied with the sound of crashing waves and a soft chime in the distance. She continued stepping through the marsh, her feet sticking in the deep, Sulphur riddled mud, filled with decomposition. The chanting, waves, and chime grew louder.

She raised her eyes to the water's edge about fifty yards ahead, a man rocked back and forth on his knees as an object wrapped in plastic rested in front of him.

Rebecca's breathing quickened, her heart raced as a clammy chill washed over her.

"Rebeccaaaaa," a soft, but tantalizing voice whispered from behind. A bony hand grabbed her shoulder and yanked her into a spin.

It was Mother!

Half decomposed with yellow teeth bared by missing lips, she hissed, then yelled, "Rebeccaaaaa!"

Rebecca jolted and sat on her haunches. The pain in her hamstrings reminding her of their absence. She fell back to the sand. Gasped for breath as the room felt heavy and neglected of oxygen. The darkness weighed upon her chest as the shadows seemed to move about like a cloud of turbidity left by a spooked fish.

She shut her eyes, rested the back of her right forearm against her head and breathed in quick gasps through her nose and out her mouth. She took a deep breath and let it out just after swallowing the gulp in her throat that felt as if it were attempting to block her air way.

Relax now, calm down. She kept telling herself.

The chanting returned.

She opened her eyes and darted them about the room without moving her head. The flicker from the candles cast a shadow on the wall to her left of a man on his knees rocking to and fro in rhythm with the chant.

Rebecca rolled to her right. It was Frank in earnest supplication to his Mother, as she glared down from the cross.

He uttered words that reminded her of something only a Catholic priest would understand. Had to be Latin. His voice hissed with a rasp as he finished each syllable.

He jolted to a halt as a hush filled the room. A soft chill meandered about like a Flounder taken by the current. It wafted by Rebecca before passing Frank, evidenced by the gentle ruffle of his hair, before finally landing atop Mother, flipping her hair to one side.

Frank was glued to the sand like a sculpture.

"Are you well Mother?" he asked as his voice pierced the silence.

No response, at least nothing Rebecca noticed.

"Good. I hope you find great comfort in these offerings. There are few more I think you will enjoy...I just have one request. I'll need you to keep an eye on Rebecca while I'm gone. I don't want her tagging along for this one. It's special, and I don't want any distraction. Apparently, I didn't do a very good job with my first attempt…so now I must finish what I started. I plan to leave tomorrow afternoon and will not return until Tuesday. Depends on how well everything goes."

Rebecca laid quietly in the sand, not moving a muscle in fear of interrupting the conversation between Frank and his Mother.

"Yes, Mama, I'll see to it. Rest well and take courage, your comfort is near."

The chill vanished like a passing breeze as each flame upon the candles danced in farewell.

Frank hung his head and let out a deep sigh before picking himself up off the sandy floor.

Rebecca slammed her eyes and entered a smooth breath as she forced her chest into a slow rise and fall. She even gave a few jerks and twitches for good measure. She felt him examining her. He just stood over her, quiet and still…watching her every breath.

"Rebecca. Rebecca?"

She grunted and stretched, rubbed her eyes and squinted as she pretended to gain focus of him standing at her feet.

"You must eat," he said before making his way over near the ladder to grab a yellow plastic bag with the words, "*DOLLAR GENERAL*", in big bold font and a tan bag with the words, *FOOD LION*, in blue letters.

He scrambled through the Dollar General bag and pulled out each item for show and tell.

"You like Beanie Weenies? How about Vienna Sausages? Sour cream and chive crackers? Tuna? Oh, and here is some water," he said while tossing her a bottle of Dasani.

She cracked the seal and took two long gulps. Spilling a splash in the sand.

"Slow down now, don't choke yourself."

She gasped before taking another gulp. The bottle now only a quarter of the way full.

Frank walked over to her, squatted and took the bottle and offered a can of Beanie Weenies along with a black plastic spoon.

In a normal setting, food like this would be the last thing on her mind, but with a growling stomach and no promise of another meal, Beanie Weenies never sounded so good.

She popped the lid and gulped down a few spoonsful.

Now be a lady...where's her manner's for crying out loud?

Frank eyed her with a faint grin as she busied herself with the can of pintos like a famished dog.

"Sorry...I don't mean to act like an animal. Thank you for the food Frank. Do you have something?"

"Oh yes, don't worry about me. I've got my favorite," he said looking down at the Food Lion bag and wrinkling the bag. He pulls out a pack of hamburger meat, pokes through the film with stubby finger and proceeds to tear away the plastic covering.

"Do you have a grill or something? You know you've got to cook that?"

"Psshhh...who are you kidding? I take it raw," Frank reached into the tray and pulled out a lump of red meat, packed it into a ball and tossed into his gullet. He chewed as if eating a soft bread roll.

Rebecca's eyes grew as did the knot of vomit creeping up her esophagus. She covered her mouth and gulped.

Frank paid her no mind and continued to eat the meat. Faster and faster, he chewed and shoveled. His hands and lips bloodied, he squatted on his calves and smacked like a feral child.

"You doing okay?" Rebecca's voice was shaky.

"Yeah-yeah, I'm good."

"Frank...can I ask you a question?"

He thought about it for a second, scratched the back of his head, then said, "Sure...shoot," before smiling at her with stained teeth. The odor of raw hamburger meat would forever make her nauseous.

"Well...why me? I mean...why us?"

He narrowed his gaze and furrowed his brows before bolting to his feet and spinning away toward his Mother.

"I've done told you...to give Mother company."

"But I mean...why my family? Why us?"

Her questions seemed to claw at his emotions like sand paper to a table leg.

He rubbed his face with his palms and made a loop with them over his forehead, across his scalp, down the nape of his neck and up his chin before spreading them across his cheeks.

"Look...I just do what I'm told all right?" he barked out as he spun and faced her, his teeth clinched, his breath in a huff.

"By who? Mother?"

"Everyone all right! Enough with the dang questions...just be glad I fed you...you ungrateful—!"

His choice of words caused her to gasp as she grabbed her heart and wrinkled her brows.

"Frank...I can't believe you'd call me such a thing."

He sighed and said, "I'm sorry...just no more questions ...okay?"

65

ee and I fastened our seatbelts in his Black Chevy Z71 truck, parked in my driveway. The air was brisk with a late September landward breeze. I could hear dead leaves and palm fronds skitter across the road. Whether because of my fuzzy vision or not, the gulls seemed chubbier than usual. The sky was overcast. I haven't seen the Sun much since I came home. Temperature must be in the low sixties, chill enough for the both of us to pack a light jacket or flannel.

Lee turned the ignition and put the truck in reverse as we crunched over the cream-colored pebble and shells. The sound of the waves crashing against the slope echoed in my ear until I rolled up my window.

Lee shifted in gear and we were on our way.

First stop, Smith Road, then the car wash, the marsh by the Shallotte River, the boat ramp in Holden, then finally, the crackhead express.

We wanted to drive to each location in the order the bodies were found and recreate the GTK's drive and scenery, hoping he'd left behind a clue, either on purpose or by accident and hoping Rebecca was able to leave something behind as well.

It was Thursday, September 24th, just after ten o'clock and the way we figured it, we'd spend most of the day here in Brunswick County, then tomorrow, ride down to Georgetown and check out Ethan's home from 89.

Granted, my eyesight was still subpar, Lee would have to take up the slack there, but hey, at least my legs were working.

We made our way to the boulevard and drove 4.2 miles before taking a left to cross the bridge to the mainland. The water tower on our left, along with a half sunken shrimp boat in the ICW. The tide was on its way out. The boat ramp where they'd found the Camry, was just below us.

"Bet you never thought they'd find what they did down there did ya?" asked Lee as he fixed his eyes on the road in front of him. The bridge feeling ever narrower as we climbed the sharp angle, before flattening out, prior to beginning our descent. Of course, the passing dump truck didn't help the matters.

"Yeah...man, I tell ya that was a shocker," I said with a wag of my head.

"The dude's got some guts, I'll give em that. The way he puts stuff out in the open and leaves behind the notes, that he does. It's almost like he wants to get caught," I added.

"Maybe he does," said Lee with just a little more than a whisper.

"Huh? What do you mean?"

"Well...maybe he really does want to get caught. Maybe he's tired of all the killing and ready to give it up, so this is his way of surrendering so to speak."

"Nah, I don't think so man. I think it's more of a taunt than anything."

"Like a cockroach, he only comes out when the lights are off and the darkness has set in, that's when crawls out and feast on the crumbs. I think it's time we cut the lights on?"

"You got a point there Lee. I just hope we're quick enough to squish him before he finds a crevice we can't reach."

"Yeah well, the Creator will help us with that. We must stay in the Spirit. I'm telling you, it's the only way. Along the lines of what MLK once said, 'Darkness can't drive out darkness, only light can do that. Hate can't drive out hate, only love can do that.'"

"But what do you mean? I'm supposed to love the guy that tried to kill me and my kids and now has my wife captive? How in the world am I supposed to do that?"

He didn't say a word, he just sat calm, hands gripping the wheel, his eyes trained to the road, wearing a gentle grin.

"Lee? You can't be serious man."

"Love your enemies, pray for those who spitefully use you. If your enemy thirst, give him a cup of water. If he steals your shirt, give him your jacket. And just as Jesus said to those nailing him to the Cross, 'Father forgive them, for they know not what they do.' For by this the world will know you are my disciples, the way in which you love one another."

I sat without words. I tried to take it all in, but it was just hard to swallow. Reminded me of my horse sized pain pills.

"Lee...listen man, I know you mean well, and I know Jesus meant well with his words, but you can't seriously expect me to love this guy? I mean the first thing I want to do tear his freaking head off!"

A moment passed.

"James...let me ask you something. If you buy a gift for someone, but they don't accept it, who owns the gift?"

I thought about it before blurting an answer. I didn't want to fall in a trap, but the only reasonable answer was...myself.

"I would assume, myself since I bought it."

"Precisely. Now much in the same way, if you waste your time on buying anger and try to give it to someone, but they don't except it or in a case like this, never even acknowledge it, guess who keeps the anger? You do. And it will build and build and build, until finally it changes you. Suddenly, you become the anger, and you lash out on anyone and everyone in effort to try and get rid of it, but it only returns with more strength than before."

The cab of the truck was quiet.

I cleared my throat, "Okay, so how do I lose the anger?"

"Give it to God and ask for an exchange of love. Release the anger, you're only hurting yourself. It's like jumping off a cliff in an attempt to reach a taunting bird. He can fly, you can't. Let it go, before it destroys you. It's not worth it. The Great Creator will see to it, that whatever injustice was done will be paid back equally, whether in this life or the next. Make no mistake God is not mocked, whatsoever a man soweth, that shall he also reap."

"You make it sound so easy. I just don't know if I can do it."

"You must James...it won't happen overnight, but in time, it'll get easier. I'm telling you now, you must leave vengeance to the Creator. It's His job to repay, not ours. Trust Him. Let it go."

I nodded and I glared at the sign of Holden Beach seafood on my right, *Fresh Crawfish*

Boy me and Rebecca have sure spent some money in that place over the years, between the crawfish, oysters, clams and fish. It was a small family owned market that'd been in business a lot longer than we'd been in Holden.

Their prices may have been a tad higher than what you'd pay at the Food Lion, but at least you knew it was fresh and plus you had the comfort of knowing you were helping out a locally owned business.

Anyhow, now that my mind was off the touchy subject, I decided to change it, "So, have you talked to Clennon or your Uncle Wes lately?"

"Yeah, I talked to my Uncle last night a little bit, but I haven't talked to Clennon in a few days."

"Has he had anymore dreams or anything? I'm assuming you told him about mine?"

"No, he hasn't had anymore, at least not that I know of. But yeah, I told him about what you said. He said pretty much the same thing I did. That it's the Lord's way of revealing himself to you and showing you who you are."

"Yeah...hey what about the preacher in town from the paper? You guys know anything about him?"

"You talking about Pastor Hoffman?"

"Yeah, you know the one in the paper, that claims he saw him last week and all that."

"Yeah, if I ain't mistaken he's come to a Pau Wau a time or two over the years. I think I may have met him one time. It's been a while. But yeah, I was thinking about him this morning. Figured it'd probably do some good to talk with him, if he'd be up to it."

"Yeah, let me see if I can find the number from Google. I'll give him a call and see if he'd be willing to meet."

† †

SITTING IN A fold up chair, among a wardrobe full of suits and ties, eyes shut, lips trembling, hands clasped tightly around a black Bible with the name *David Hoffman* etched at the bottom in gold. The buzzing of his phone gave him a jolt.

He rubbed his eyes, sniffed through his nose, cleared his throat and slid his thumb across the screen to answer the call.

"Hello...this is Pastor Hoffman speaking."

"Hi there, hope I didn't catch you at a bad time. My name is James Randolph, I have something I believe you may be able to help me with. Would it be possible to meet today?"

66

After spending the day going from scene to scene hunting for clues, I must admit I was a little disappointed we didn't find anything. But I'm hopeful that this meeting I was able to arrange with Pastor Hoffman can shed some light into who Ethan really is...or Frank...whatever his name is.

Hoffman was more than willing to meet with us, so we made plans to see him at his home off Seashore Road, only about an eight-minute drive from our place on Holden.

I rode shotgun beside Lee as he leaned on the wheel of his Z71, searching for Bellamy Drive. The preacher said it led to his house near the Intercoastal Waterway.

I couldn't offer much help in reading street signs as my eyes were still too blurry, but what the heck, I gave it a go anyhow.

"Ahh...there she is," said Lee as he knocked his turn signal down in time for it blink just a handful of times for the car behind us. They honked and yelled something about "It ain't it!"

At least that's what it sounded like, the guy had such a southern slang, it was hard to tell. But the bony finger sticking out the window as he sped off, told me otherwise. I think if you translated white trash crackhead to English it'd sound something like, "Idiot!"

But what do I know...right?

Anyhow, we turned onto Bellamy, Lee checking the mailboxes for 1102.

I scanned the houses as best I could, looking for a two-story on stilts with a center-console boat parked underneath. Pastor Hoffman said he was near the middle sandwiched between a white double wide and a yellow single story on stilts.

"Should be getting close...that one there was 1094," said Lee.

"Yeah...I think that might be it up there. Isn't that a yellow house on stilts?"

"Yeah."

"Okay...he should be right beside it."

We drove a little ways, Lee reading mailboxes as we passed, "1096...1098...1100...1102."

"Yep...this is it."

Lee pulled in behind a black Toyota Rav4 that was parked next to a white Tahoe.

I eased my legs to the ground. It felt unstable as it seemed to shift beneath me as if I were a ship upon a troubled sea. Which if I were honest, I kind of was.

Lee came over and helped me gain my balance, handing me my cane from the back seat.

"You good?"

"Yeah...that's better," I said as we edged to the front steps.

With Lee's help I managed to climb all thousand of them, feeling as if I'd just peaked Mount Kilimanjaro.

As I was busy catching my breath, Lee rang the doorbell. That sucker wasn't even winded.

After a few moments, footsteps thudded toward us. The deadbolt twisted away. The white door with a glass centered mural swung open. A man perhaps in his mid-forties, clean shaven, neat kept hair and prescription glasses stood before us with a gentle smile below kind eyes. He pushed the storm door open and greeted us as we each introduced ourselves. He invited us in where we stepped inside and waited for him to shut the door behind us.

"Hey Annie...the gentlemen are here."

A sweet voice beckoned back, "Okay honey...be right there."

"Wow...nice place you got here," offered Lee.

"Thank you, thank you. Well come on in grab you a seat," he said as he prodded us toward what appeared to be a den or study room to the right.

"You fellas want any coffee or tea?"

"Um...yeah sure, some coffee would be nice if it's not too much of a hassle," I said, "Would you like some Lee?"

"Yeah that'd be great. Thank you," he said as he busied himself with shedding his jacket.

"Listen...I truly appreciate you taking your time to meet with us tonight."

"Oh absolutely. Well listen, I know you have a lot of questions and are probably rearing to go. So, what I can I do to help?"

"Well...as I mentioned over the phone. My wife Rebecca has been kidnapped by this guy and according to the papers, you said you grew up with him. Now I worked with him back in the late 80's down at a paper mill in South Carolina, back when all this GTK stuff first started swirling around. You remember all that?"

He perked up at the mention of the paper mill.

"Yeah-yeah, I remember that. So, you worked with him back then?"

"Yeah. Remember the Rickles, Berkley, and Vendetti murders?"

He nodded with squinted eyes.

"Remember the cops going out to Ethan's house and finding all the pictures and notes?"

He nodded once more, this time leaning forward, hanging on every word.

"Yeah, well there was a picture of me and Rebecca hanging up in his house too. Apparently, this isn't the first time he's wanted to take us out."

He scooted back and looked about the room while rubbing his face.

Light footsteps pitter pattered against the hardwood floor as a pretty little woman with shoulder length black hair came prodding into the den with a tray of coffee and cookies.

"Why hello there!" she said as she placed the tray on a table in front of us.

"Gentlemen this is my wife Annie...Annie this is James Randolph and Lee McGaha."

We shook hands, before she stepped back and said, "Well I'll let you men get back to your conversation. If any of you need anything just let me know." She smiled and made her way back into the kitchen.

"Thank you, Mrs. Hoffman," Lee and I echoed one another before David said, "Thanks sweetie."

"So...with that being said, what can you tell me that I don't already know about this guy? You know, like his upbringing, his habits. I guess what I'm trying to ask is...who was he among just friends?"

He took a breath through his nostrils and let it out with puffed cheeks.

"Well...I don't know much, but I can tell you, a lot of this comes from his dad."

Lee and I both tilted our heads at his words.

"You see, his dad created a cult back when Frankie was—that's what we called him when we were kids—I guess he was around eleven, cause if I remember right, we were in Middle School at Forest Heights when he started talking about it. It was crazy stuff. Talked about how his dad would perform blood sacrifices with animals to atone for the follower's sins. But he said his dad did a lot of the same things as the group did that he atoned for. Like drink and sleep around, lie, cheat, and what have you.

"I remember he'd come to school with a black eye or bruises on his arm. He had it rough. He was just never the same after all that started. And once Will disappeared, I'd barely talk to him at school anymore. I've always thought his dad and him had something to do with it." He stopped and eyed the carpet.

"Will?" I asked in a soft, curious tone.

"Yeah...Will Abercrombie. The kid that disappeared in 81. Him and Frankie were my best friends. That was the gang back then," he said with side grin and glassy eyes.

"Yeah I remember when that happened. I remember his mom being on the news, begging for people to help find him. That was sad," said Lee.

"Wow...Will Abercrombie? I didn't know you were all friends like that. I'm sorry man," I said as I adjusted in my seat.

He swallowed hard, nodded, and continued.

"Yeah...its been tough. We were pretty close...but uh...yeah not long after that, Frankie moved off with his aunt and uncle after his parents died in their barn fire. They say his dad got drunk and drug Frankie's mom out there before dropping a lantern. That thing was full of hay, so it didn't take long to burn down."

"Dang...that's terrible. My goodness," Lee said as he winced and wagged his head.

"Now see that's totally different from what he told me and the guys at the mill. He said his mama died, but he lived with his dad for a few years before moving in with his aunt and uncle. Never mentioned anything about the fire. And if I remember right, he told one of the guys that his dad spent a short time in prison for murdering his brother-in-law out of self-defense. You ever hear anything like that?"

"No...now that's the first I've ever heard that."

"Well what do you think about all of this? I mean you just saw him last week...how'd he act?" asked Lee.

"He uh...um...just had a way about him that really made me uncomfortable and he took pleasure in knowing that. I first thought he was a homeless man off the street, but the more we talked, the more nervous I became, because he just seemed so...so...uh...sophisticated. I could tell something was really weighing on his heart. He kept asking if God would really forgive him of his sins, said he had a lot on him. Then he sort of got hostile and started questioning me about stuff that was rather personal. Like why I was here at the church so late, and not at home, just stuff that was out of order for him to ask.

"He also seemed like he was torn, you know like, half of him wanted to confess and start a new life, while the other half pulled him back from getting too emotional. That's when he started turning the spotlight on myself. He's a troubled man."

"Pastor Hoffman...what do you think we should do? Besides obviously praying...you believe much in fasting?" asked Lee.

"Oh of course..." he leaned closer as if concealing a secret, "...I'm actually on a fast right now."

Me and Lee looked at each other with wide grins.

"So are we."

"Get out...for real?"

"For real," I answered.

"Well...I guess that explains why there's still a pile of cookies on the platter."

"Yeah, I reckon so."

We continued to talk for another forty-five minutes or so. Between Lee and David exchanging beliefs, and us discussing the GTK, we felt we'd got what we came for.

David led us in prayer before our exit.

He called for his wife Annie. She came and sat beside him on the couch. We each inched to the edge our seats and held hands before bowing our heads.

"Lord...thank you for your goodness and mercy. Thank you for your love and grace. You are so good Lord and I thank you for it. I thank you for bringing James and Lee here today. I pray over this whole situation. I pray that you would send your angels to protect Rebecca and give her strength and courage to get through this. I pray Lord, you'd give her wisdom and that your presence would be there to comfort her.

"I pray for James Lord. I pray that you would encourage and comfort him and help him to trust you with all of this. I pray for a quick recovery. Lord, I also pray for the children, I pray healing and comfort over them. And Lord I pray for Lee and his family, that you'd continue to give them discernment and wisdom into all of this.

"We thank you Lord for your grace and mercy, your love endures forever. We are in you as you are in us, we are the light of the world and we ask that you help us to illuminate this darkness. We ask and pray all of this in Jesus Name, Amen."

67

The air was chilled as blackness settled in the bunker, off set only by the faint flicker of two candles. The air seemed heavy as the darkness was like a covering of black ink attempting to seep through the skin and penetrate the soul.

Frank stood in the corner ringing a bell in his right hand, next to mother. His head bent toward the sand, he'd been here for the past couple of hours. Not saying a word, just calmly keeping a rhythm with the bell.

Rebecca sat opposite the room with her back to the sandy wall and her arms crossed at the chest to keep warm. As she kept her eyes on Frank, she muttered prayers with quiet lips in effort in to not disturb Frank.

He'd been acting weird all day. His eyes were glassy and black, his face seemed redder than usual. The warts looked hot and scabby like.

Then...the bell stopped.

Silence.

The candle flames danced to the right and left as a swift breeze filled the room. It brushed Rebecca's hair into her eyes and did the same to mother.

Frank was slow to raise his head. He stuck a hand into his pocket and retrieved a pen and piece of paper, along with an envelope that wore a stamp in the top right corner.

He spun on his heels and marched to Rebecca. Black eyes bulging and warts growing larger with each passing second.

He bent at the knees and held out the pen and paper, "I want you to write a letter to James."

She looked at him, not breathing.

"Didn't you hear me?" he shoved the pen and paper to her face.

She reached and took them.

He jolted and squinted his eyes, grabbing his head.

"What do you want me to say?"

"Anythi—"

He turned and curled over as he hurled up black tar like liquid.

The stench of it burned Rebecca's nose. She covered it with her black sweater. The smell of rotten eggs made her want to puke. From all her time spent in the lab at Georgetown and Brunswick High, she knew immediately, it was Hydrogen Sulfide, or otherwise known as Sulphur.

She watched as Frank moaned and coughed.

The black liquid stained the tan floor. He had to grab it from his chin and sling it to the ground as it stuck to his flesh like rotten condensed milk.

The now blackened sand, began to crawl with life.

Rebecca's eyes glued to the black liquid as at least a dozen or more large maggots protruded and inched their way through the sand, before bursting and releasing a horde of black flies.

A few swarmed toward her and tried to land on her arm, but she swatted them away. Frank swatted in front of his face as the rest seemed to be drawn to his eyes as if being pulled by a magnet.

"Kirkland! Make it stop! Please!" he screamed. The flies vanished into a puff of black smoke.

Frank bent at the waist and placed his hands to his knees in effort to catch his breath. He took the back of his right hand and wiped the black slime from his lips.

Rebecca sat in place with the paper and pen trembling in her hands.

Frank straightened his spine then turned to face her, "Well...don't just sit there...write!" he barked as he placed his hands to his hips and gave her a death stare.

"What-what shou-should I write?"

"Anything you like. Just don't be stupid...because I will read it. But do be sure to tell James, his time is running out and he's got until Tuesday night to find you or else he may never see you again...alive at least."

Tears welled as her lips quaked at the thought of leaving James and the children behind.

She placed the pen to the paper and began to scribble the best she could as her trembling hand was against such an idea of writing. She filled the page, then handed it back to Frank who snatched it from her hand, wrinkling the paper.

"All right...I'm going to have to chain you up again as I drop this off at a post-office box," he said after giving the letter a quick glance over and folding it to fit in the envelope which was addressed to Brunswick County Sheriff's Office from THE WATCHER.

"I will leave here Saturday night and be gone for a few days. Your fate now remains in the hands of your husband."

He placed the envelope in his back pocket and bent down to take Rebecca by the arm.

He drug her over to the chains and shackled her around the wrist and ankles. The bell upon her ankle ringing.

"Now...don't worry, I'll be back tonight before midnight. Is there anything you'd like for me to pick up for you while I'm out? Food or anything?" he asked with a harmless grin and a pat of his hands upon Rebecca's shoulders. His eyes were still cloudy and glassed over, with an ink like blackness just beneath the white film.

She gave it some thought while scanning the sand.

"Um...uh...yeah a tuna sandwich from Subway would be nice. Oh, and a bottle of Smart water."

He tightened his lips and twisted them to one side with the tilt of his head and tapped a pointer finger to his chin.

"Hmm...I don't know. I can't promise anything, but I'll try. I'll see what I can do."

He leaned close and gave a soft kiss against her forehead. The stench of his breath and stubble of his days old growth turned her stomach as it took all she had not to puke in his face. She swallowed hard and forced back a smile.

He stepped away and strode toward Mother and the candles. His feet dragging through the sand, his slow and zombie like gait was enough to give her chills.

"Don't worry...you're not alone. I won't be gone long. Hope you're not afraid of the dark," he said with a soft chuckle as he patted mother's thigh before blowing out the two candles and proceeding to climb the ladder out of the bunker.

The hatch shut as the metal hinges squeaked and whined.

The cool air and darkness returned.

Her heart pounded against her chest, her breath quickened, her flesh crawled with tiny bumps.

She shut her eyes and prayed.

68

Emerging from shadow to shadow between the
streetlights along the sidewalk in downtown Shallotte,
Frank strutted towards the blue post office box a few
blocks over from where he'd parked.

Glancing about his surroundings, he grabbed the blue
metal handle and pulled it toward him before tossing the
envelope into the slit.

His thirteen-inch boots slapped the pavement as he
strutted back to his vehicle. Passing a few people along the
way, none in which knew the manner of man they'd almost
brushed shoulders with.

He rounded the last building and thudded to his wheels.
He sat down, took a breath and fired up the engine. He
proceeded to the stop sign that held him from entering
onto Main Street.

He took a right, passed under a few red lights, passed a
gas station in a corner next to a Walgreens and took
another right, before making his way to the parking lot of
an Office Depot and Subway.

He parked, locked his doors and strode for the Subway.
An elderly couple was just behind him. He holds the door
for them. They thanked him for the gesture and made their
way next in line. Frank just behind them.

After taking a minute to decide their order and being sure the workers got it just right, it was Frank's turn.

"Hey there...what can I get for you?" asked the teenaged boy, with a spotted face of acne from raging hormones.

Frank cleared his throat.

"Yeah...I'm going to get a twelve-inch Subway Club on white bread and a twelve-inch Tuna on wheat for the misses," he said with a grin in between taking a bite upon a dirty nail and glancing to through the glass at the parking lot.

††††††††††††††††††††††

IT WAS JUST after eleven o'clock that night when me and Lee made it back to the house. We were both exhausted from the day's search, so we wasted no time getting ready for bed. Lee took Jason's bed after seeing that I had everything I needed.

After about an hour of tossing and turning, with my mind racing and thinking about Rebecca and the kids, I finally switched on the lamp, crossed the room to a picture of Rebecca and myself from the day we got married, laid back in bed, clinched the picture to my chest and prayed.

"Lord...I'm not even sure how to really do this...but please help us find Rebecca. Lord...please bring her home."

My heart ached as tears landed on my shirt. I kissed her forehead and sobbed as I squeezed the picture, longing for her embrace. I pulled back and place my hand on the picture, "Lord...please watch over her and protect her. Give her courage to stand strong against this evil man. Send Your angels to guard her and surround her with your light. God, I pray, send light into this darkness. Please Lord...bring her home."

I laid the picture to the empty spot beside me and closed my eyes. Rebecca's sweet face the last thing I saw, before a peace gently washed over me and within minutes I was out.

††††††††††††††††††††††

SQUEALING TO A stop and crunching over gravel, Frank eased into a public beach access parking lot on Ocean Boulevard. He stepped out of the driver side and began walking along the side walk as he glared down at the screen on his phone. Thumbing his way to his music, he found his playlist, squished in some ear buds and entered a casual jog. No need for nothing too strenuous...he'd need his strength for later. This was just part of the planning.

About ten minutes into it, he skipped to his favorite song and hummed along as he passed by a large black mailbox which read, *1150 The Randolph Family*

He passed by peering out the corner of his eye. The place was dark except for the lights still on in the living room. The black truck in the driveway made him wrinkle his brow as the thought of who it belonged to, escaped him.

He continued his jog and passed a dozen houses or so before turning around and heading back toward the parking lot. The sight of a police cruiser heading his way, gave his heart the jitters.

He threw up a gentle wave and smile as the officer passed.

"Kirkland...you got to help me with this one. You got a plan I suppose?"

"OH, DON'T FRET MY FRIEND...I KNOW JUST THE TRICK. TRUST ME...THEY'LL NEVER SEE IT COMING," Kirkland said as he hovered alongside him, hiding in the shadows, picking the scabs on his back. He swallowed hard and said, "I'M PROUD OF YOU FRANK...YOU'VE DONE GOOD...BUT MORE IS STILL

REQUIRED OF YOU. YOU MUST FINISH WHAT YOU STARTED."

"I will Kirkland...I'll finish it and bring you all great joy. Just help me not to fall into any trap," he said as he sucked in air with desperate efforts to keep his lungs functioning.

"DON'T WORRY...WE'RE WITH YOU AND WE ARE IN YOU. WILL WE GIVE YOU THE POWER AND WISDOM TO ACCOMPLISH THE MISSION. YOU DO THIS, AND YOUR MOTHER WILL BE SET FREE ONCE AND FOR ALL. BUT YOU MUST STAY STRONG AND FINISH."

"I will Kirkland...I won't let you down."

††††††††††††††††††††

IT'D TAKEN HIM an hour and a half to reach Georgetown and another five minutes to find Oak Grove Cemetery. He cut his lights off and chose the gravel road that led through a tunnel of live oaks. Reminded him of something from Sleepy Hollow. His muscles were tense as he waited for the headless horseman to come charging at the windshield any second.

A fog had settled over the tombstones. The city was quiet and dark. Frank looked at his stereo, *1:23*.

He leaned over the wheel, looking for an entrance to visit the dead. The wheels crawling over dead leaves and twigs. There. He found a black iron gate and shifted the gear stick to park. He reached over to the passenger seat and grabbed a pointed shovel.

He eased the door open and stepped to the ground with light feet. He was careful with his steps as he approached the gate. Crouched low and dressed in black, his eyes darted about. The coast was clear. He opened the gate. It made a soft whine and creaked as he did so.

Eyes scanning the darkness. He was all alone. Except for those six feet under.

He took his time and angled to the back corner of the lot. A slate cross pierced through the fog and drew him closer. That was his marker. What he wanted was near. He edged closer, passing the cross, he crept another ten foot or so and found what he was after. A small head stone made from cheap limestone and corroded with age and weathering.

Frank grinned at the sight.

The name on the stone, read, **Turner.**

"Good to see you Jerry. Sorry about the smokes getting ya. Hope you don't mind a visit."

69

It was just after 5:30 am, when Frank checked his watch, about ten minutes ago. He busied himself with scanning the area for any sign of life before dusting the metal hatch with his foot, pulling on a handle and making his way down into the bunker.

The whine of the hinges gave Rebecca a start. She jolted awake, causing the chains to rattle in protest of her movement.

She trained her eyes to the ladder where two size thirteen boots rested upon a rung just below black denim pants.

He struck a match and lit three candles.

"Wake up sleepy head...I'm home," he said waving out the match. He plopped to the sand with a thump.

"You miss me?" he asked with a wide grin and a Subway bag dangling from his right hand as he waved out the flame of the match with his left.

Rebecca nodded and grunted through the cloth and duct tape.

"Hey...I got you what you asked for," he said as he reached in and pulled out a large bottle of Smart Water and held it at shoulder height along with the Subway bag.

Rebecca gave him kind eyes and nodded once more.

Frank sat the bag and water down on the table next to the candles, said hello to Mother and angled to Rebecca.

"Hang on just a second...let me get you down from here so you can have some supper."

He dug a key from his pocket and unlocked her from the chains, then removed the cloth from her mouth.

The pain in her legs were still there, but it was losing its power, as now they were sore rather than painful.

He eased her into the sand, where she scooted and propped her back against the wall.

He marched back to the table and grabbed the bag.

"I hope you like lettuce, tomato, mayo and salt and pepper?"

"Oh yeah, that's fine. Thank you for doing this."

"Your welcome," he said as he handed her the sandwich and Smart Water. He only took out half of his and placed the rest back in the bag.

Rebecca noticed, but didn't ask. She'd learned by now, not to ask questions if it wasn't necessary.

"So...you enjoy your end to the day?" he asked as he stole a bite from his sandwich and glared at her with those big black eyes still wearing a milky film.

"Uh huh."

Rebecca took a bite from the sub after giving it a quick glance and sniff while Frank wasn't looking. Nothing out of the ordinary. If he'd poisoned it, he done a good job getting it past the nose of a science teacher.

"Good...I'm glad. Well listen...there's one more thing I'd like to share before I leave tomorrow night."

Rebecca tilted her head and scrunched her brows.

"It's about how I met Kirkland."

That name sent shivers down her spine as by now she'd come to realize who he was.

"After me, Will and another friend of ours, David, messed around with a Ouija board at the Mooreland's old home, I started hearing and seeing him."

Rebecca swallowed hard and asked, "Wait...you mean old man Mooreland? Kirby Mooreland?"

"Mm hmm...yeah you know where Scott killed his mom and grandma and tried to kill Kirby."

"Yeah-yeah. Did you know them?"

"No...but Will's family did."

"Oh really? So why in the world did y'all go over there?"

"Oh, you know, just seeing who was the bravest. We kind of had a bet about who'd chicken out first. Anyhow, that's when I started hearing him. After that day, he'd whisper in my ear nonstop. The following week during recess...I saw him at the school playground. He kept whispering my name as he lured me over behind one of the slides. He was short, but stocky with pale, grayish skin, jet black hair and eyes. He wore plain clothes. You know jeans and a white shirt. Said he wanted to be my friend. He seemed cool," Frank took a bite of sandwich and continued while he chewed, "I glanced around to see if anyone noticed, but when I turned around, he was gone. He'll appear from time to time, but hardly ever like that anymore. Usually, he's just a passing shadow or sometimes a projected image of someone that's passed on. And when he's anxious, he'll be a ghostly figure with a droopy and melting face."

Frank said nonchalantly as if recalling a stray dog, he once befriended.

Rebecca's glare was frozen as every inch of her body crawled with gooseflesh.

"He'd visit me about every night it seemed. It started with him tugging at the covers, as each morning I'd get up with them piled in a corner across the room. Then it went to him running across my bed in the dead of night. He'd startle me awake as he jumped to the floor, giving it a good thud. Mama and Daddy got up a bunch of times, thinking I'd rolled out of bed or something. Then it went to him watching me as I slept. Sometimes he'd accidently touch my nose with his as he got too close, I'd wake up with that pale face only inches from mine, before he'd disappear with a giggle. Before long I could hardly sleep. He'd pester me all through the night, nudging me, pinching me, scratching me and finally...biting me."

He stopped to take another bite of his sub. Rebecca was too stiff to take one from hers. She felt paralyzed with his words.

He chewed through turkey, cheese, and bread and continued with, "I never told Mama or Daddy," he said looking to Mother.

"I hid the marks the best I could. Hardly ever wore shorts or short sleeve shirts. Which wasn't too bad, once Daddy started preaching how we'd go to hell if we did so. Something about us not being Holy in the sight of God if we wore sleeves that showed our arms or britches that showed our legs. I was fine with it, because it was easier to hide the marks that way. He drew blood a lot of times, I still got the scars to prove it. See...look here," Frank pulled the sleeve of his right arm up to his shoulder.

Rebecca gasped and covered her mouth with a quaking right hand.

Teeth marks as big around as a softball were embedded into his flesh as the scar looked like something a survivor of a shark attack might wear.

"Oh yeah...that's not the only one," he said as he dropped his sleeve and pulled up his shirt at the navel.

Rebecca gasped again, clinched her eyes and turned to avoid the sight.

Large claw marks and bite marks riddled his hairy abdomen like a picture of scattered lightning.

"Sorry. Didn't mean to ruin your supper. It just brings me comfort being able to share my past with someone who'll listen."

Rebecca took a deep breath and turned around to face him as he sat with his legs crossed over each other about two yards from her in the sand.

She shook her head and said, "Frank...there's no need to apologize. I'm sorry you had to go through that. That's...well...that's terrible," she rubbed her eyes and face to rid the images she just seen.

"Thank you. I remember not long after he started biting, this one night I woke at like three in the morning to the awe fullest jaw ache, I mean the corners of my mouth were even bleeding. I couldn't figure out why, so I went back to sleep the best I could.

"A little while later, I woke up to what felt like my gut being pulled though my throat and out my mouth. I opened my eyes and saw and felt two hands squirming and gripping along the outside of my mouth. I started gaging as I felt him crawl out of my throat. I squinted my eyes and tried to squirm, but I couldn't move. I was paralyzed from head to toe.

"This thing crawls out of my mouth, and all I could see was the silhouette of it, as my room was so dark anyway, but it's all hunched over on my bed. It hops to the side of the bed and thumps to the floor. It stands there for a second growling real low like. It turns around and walks to the edge of my bed, leans in real close. Boy you talk about stinking? This sucker was raunchy. As it gets closer, I cut my eyes to look at it, as I'm still paralyzed at this point.

"It was me. I was looking at myself, just if I was looking into a mirror. It smiled and started giggling just before it darted off to the other side of my room, where Kirkland stood waiting with open arms.

"They both turned and smiled as the embraced. By now I'm trying to scream to the top of my lungs when finally, my tongue let loose this blood curdling scream. Mama and Daddy thought that I was dying, they rushed into the room and flipped on all the lights, but everything was gone. They told me it was just a nightmare. So, they leave the room and tell me to get some sleep.

"I shut my eyes and tried to rest, but it couldn't have been ten minutes before the low cat like grow returned. I squeezed a pillow over my head and buried my face under the covers. Its presence growled and hovered over me the rest of the night and has done so off and on ever since."

He sat quiet for a few moments as he glared at the sand in front of him.

Rebecca fell silent as she tried to form the right words, but they never came.

"Hey, let's finish up and get some sleep. It's getting late, Mama needs her rest."

Blurted Frank before taking two quick bites from his sub, causing Rebecca to do the same.

He hurried and wrapped the sub back in its wrapper and placed it in the bag with the other half. He stood to his feet and carried the bag of left overs to the table. He turned to Rebecca and asked, "Are you finished?"

In mid chew she forced out, "Mm hmm. Yeah, I'm finished," she said as she wrapped the remnants of the sub and placed it beside her.

"Okay...get some rest now," he said with a soft grin as he blew out the candles, like a mother turning out the lights after tucking in her children.

Rebecca cradled into a ball and shut her eyes.

His feet shuffled across the sand where he plumped down a few feet from her.

All was quiet but the crashing waves, distant chime, Frank's heavy breathing and Rebecca's pounding heart.

She clinched her twitching eyes and breathed in her nose and gently out her quivering lips.

"Lord...where are you? Do you even care? Please...save me from this hell. Get me out of here. Lord please," she cried as hot tears streaked down her cheeks.

She swallowed hard.

"Lord please watch over James and the kids. Keep them safe and help someone find me. Please Lord...please save me."

70

The next morning just after ten o'clock, as Agent Turner was once again holding a meeting at the Brunswick County Sheriff's office, there came a knock on the door.

It was an office clerk with a white envelope in hand.

"What's this?" asked Turner as the rest of the roomful of agents and detectives wondered the same.

"Just got it in the mail. It's addressed to here from *The Watcher*. I thought you'd want to see it," said the petite blonde headed lady as she passed it off to Turner.

He took it and looked it over, then asked for some rubber gloves and an envelope cutter.

The blonde left the room and returned with his request in only about a minute's time.

He put on his reading glasses, stretched the gloves on and gently sliced the adhesive to peel open the back. He retrieved the three folded letter and read it aloud.

James,

So you know I'm okay. And please don't worry, I'm safe, for the moment. Never let them give up searching for me and I'll know you won't. Don't get discouraged. But keep your head up and have faith. Until I'm found, stay strong and be there for the kids, they need you. Nothing will be wasted. Know that all of this will only make us stronger. Everything will be okay. Right now we just need to stay positive and have faith. Wait until you and the kids are completely healed before you start searching on your own. And don't get in the way of the cops, let them do their job. Very soon, we'll all be together. Everything will be okay. Say hello to the kids and give them a big hug and kiss for me. Can't wait to see you all. Home never sounded so good. I love you James with all my heart. May you find strength in God. Even in the darkness, He is there.

                Love Rebecca

P.S. He says you have until Tuesday night to find me, or it won't be good.

Turner placed the letter on the table, removed his glasses, and said, "All right, so obviously "he" had a little dictation in the letter. He's challenging us," he turned to the blonde and said, "We need to get this over to forensics and do some testing for prints and handwriting analysis. Then once that's done, I want a copy given to James."

Mishoe cleared his throat and asked, "Sir, we need to find out where this letter originated from. I mean you know, where did the mailman pick it up at. A mailbox? Drop off box? If it's a drop off box, there could be cameras we could check."

"Good point. Sandra can you also be sure we reach out to the postal service and get that going?"

The blonde nodded as Turner places the letter back in its envelope and passes it off to her.

She exited the room and headed for forensics.

††††††††††††††††††††††††

LEE AND I SPENT most of the day searching for Rebecca and for any clues he may have left behind. When we weren't doing that, we found ourselves praying for help and guidance. Lee said his family were still earnestly fasting and praying. Pastor Hoffman and his wife were doing the same, and now even a handful from his church were as well. Surely God would hear our prayers and if He is half of what I am beginning to believe He is, then it's just a matter of time before this thing comes to a head.

We hadn't been home long. it was about ten thirty. I crashed on the couch as Lee was kind enough to prepare something in the kitchen for us. Honestly don't know what I'd do without that man. There was a package leaned against the door when we came in. I didn't give it much thought at first, as I figured it must've been something Rebecca or one the kids ordered from Amazon. But my curiosity got the best of me, so I stood from the couch and angled to an end table where it sat nestled along with a collection of junk mail.

I put my glasses on and pick it up.

I checked the label on the front, though it was a bit blurry, I could make out that it was addressed to myself, but from a Lucinda Kirkland. I don't know a Lucinda Kirkland and I don't remember ordering anything online.

I tore into it.

Protected with bubble wrap was a VHS tape with a white label stuck to the front that said, "For the Greater Good."

I held the small package upside down and gave it a good shaking. A white piece of paper settled to the carpet like fresh snow.

I bent at the knee and picked it from the floor with a flick of my nail. My head spun as a rush of blood knocked me off balance. I gathered myself and rested a hand atop the wooden fire place.

In black writing were the words,

FOR YOUR EYES ONLY. NO COPS OR REBECCA WILL PAY. I'LL TALK WITH YOU TONIGHT AT 1:30. BE SURE TO WATCH UNTIL THE END.

As I stood there with a wrinkled face, eyes scanning side to side, heart thumping, lungs laboring, the buzz of my cell caused me to jolt. I wrestled it from my pocket. Lieutenant Mishoe.

"Hello?"

"Hey James...this is Lieutenant Mishoe."

I made my way into the kitchen and showed Lee the package and tape. He scrunched his brows. I took a deep breath and shrugged my shoulders.

"Yeah...I know. You find anything?"

"Well...we received a letter today at the Sheriff's office. It's from your wife."

My breathe and words escaped me.

"James...she says she is okay and not to worry. I think you will find it quite comforting. Can I email it to you?"

I fumbled for my words.

"Uh...yeah-yeah, that'd be great. So, I mean, did she say where she was or who she was with?"

"No, she didn't give much detail, it's obvious the guy had some dictation with it. She did say that we have until Tuesday night to find her."

"Oh God," my heart sank at his words. I wagged my head and braced it with the palm of my left hand.

"But text me your email and I'll send a copy. If it'd be possible, we'd like to speak with you in the morning. Could you be here, oh say...nine o'clock?"

"I'll be there."

"All right. Well...look over the letter and get you some rest. We'll talk in the morning. Take care James."

"Thanks. You too."

I ended the call and texted him my email as I also attempted to fill Lee in on the situation.

"Hey, can you plug up that laptop over on the desk next to the printer? I'll print it, instead of reading it from my phone."

"Yeah-yeah. What's with the tape?" Lee said as he made his way to the desk in the corner.

Couldn't have been thirty seconds, when I received the notification for the email. I forced myself to my feet and hobbled with my cane over to Lee.

"I don't know, but as soon as I print this letter, we'll have to go in Kelly's room to watch it. She's the only one with a VHS player."

I signed into my Gmail account and clicked on the attachment in the message from Mishoe.

I snatched the paper the second it finished printing and hurried to read over it. Tears filled my eyes as my heart didn't know what to feel. Part of me was happy, while another part was angry, fearful, and confused. I was torn.

The writing just didn't seem right. It was off. It was definitely her handwriting, but her choice of words and the way she structured her sentences, just didn't feel right.

Lee and I took turns reading it over word for word for about half an hour as we took bites from our plates of rice and beans, which were now cold.

"All right...let's see what this tape is all about," I said as I folded the letter and placed it into my pocket.

I headed for Kelly's bedroom with Lee just behind me.

I twisted the knob to her pink riddled room full of fairy's and Elsa. I shut my eyes and took a deep breath. Forced down the lump catching in my throat. Lee's hand patted my shoulder.

I pushed through and stood in front of her TV, tape in hand, eyes glued to the VCR. I glanced at the black rectangle in my hand, white label with black writing begging me to watch it.

I stuck it in, the VCR engulfing it with mechanical sounds, fearful it'd eat it and erase whatever this Lucinda Kirkland wanted me to see.

71

After a quick search for the remote, I found it tucked under Kelly's pillow. I switched the input to av/tv. Blackness filled the screen as a staticky hiss filled the room. A fuzzy gray line streaked across the width of the television and slowly rolled south before repeating its motion.

The screen shifted to a jumbled view of someone walking through a darkened home with a voice chanting in another language. The voice grew louder with each step the person behind the camera took. They passed through the kitchen where plates were almost piled to the ceiling near the sink and chairs weren't tucked back into the spot at the table.

The camera makes it to the hall, where a silhouette swayed upon torn wallpaper as it appeared to rock back and forth like they do at the praying wall in Jerusalem.

The voice grew louder. The rocking quickened. The camera edged closer.

The camera stopped at the open doorway and peered into the living area. A man sat in a chair at a desk, pen in hand as a piece of paper lay in front of him. A woman stood at his side.

In an instant, the chanting stopped. The man sat motionless. An eerie hush followed.

A cold draft swept through Kelly's room and fluttered her curtains.

The man on the tv jerked his face to the ceiling, twitching and moaning, his chair screeching against the hardwood floor as it shifted under him.

My blood chilled. I crossed my arms and rubbed my shoulders before turning and looking to Lee who stood to my right, eyes wide and fixed to the television.

The man on tv jerked to a halt, eyes trained to the wall less than two feet from his face. The woman rubbed his shoulders and whispered in his ear. He snapped his head to the right and glared straight into the camera, eyes like glazed cotton balls. The camera fumbled, footsteps pattered just before the screen turned to an irritating gray static.

I took a deep breath and rubbed my face, resting my fingers under my chin, with my left hand nestled under my arm pit. Just as I was reaching to press stop, the video started again.

I backed away and gave the screen my attention. The sound of toenails digging into wood along with a deep growl and bark filled the room. The screen was dark all but a faint yellow line in the top right of the screen that wore black splotches like a domino. The black spots paced side to side.

The more you stared, you could begin to make out the silhouette of a door frame. The video seemed to be shot from a bed as you could just about make out a set of knees tucked under the covers. The door shook upon its hinges as the sound of heavy fists pounded upon its frame. A loud wail from what sounded like a dying woman shot a dose of ice water up my spine.

The beating, scratching, growling, and wailing only grew. With one last pound, the door gave way as light burst in and lit up the room. A large black dog stood in the doorway, crouched and only seconds from pouncing. A shadowy figure ran atop the door frame and across the ceiling. Hissing and cursing as its feet pounded against the sheet rock. The dog jolted toward the bed...the camera went black, the shadow screeched as it thumped onto the bed. The springs begged for mercy. The film crackled and hissed.

Blackness filled the screen followed by static.

The static ceased.

"Why hello James. Long time no see?"

Gooseflesh plagued my entire body. My throat seemed to have swollen, as I found it hard to breath let alone swallow. A tingling sensation crawled over me, numbing my flesh.

The screen was black, but the crickets, cicadas, frogs and crunching leaves told me he was outside.

"Well...listen I'll just cut to the chase. By now, I figured you'd be dead, especially after taking a bullet to the head, but I guess you're stronger than I thought. Well, since you got your legs back...there's something I need you to do for me. Think you're up to the challenge?"

He paused and allowed the sounds of night to answer.

"Good. Now as you are aware...I have Rebecca. Don't worry, she's being taken care of. Mother always made a good baby sitter. She really likes Rebecca. Anyhow..." the camera shifted vertically, revealing the outline of a house, "...I need you to come by my place. You know where it is. The one you dropped me off at back in 89, the one over near crow creek. Yep. That's right. I need you to come by and get something for me. I have all the instructions here waiting for you. Along with an old friend of yours as well. All you need to do...is...come. And don't for one second, thank about calling Mishoe or Agent Turner or any of the others, because if word gets out to anyone about this...huh...well it won't be good. Okay? You want to stay on my good side and give Rebecca a chance, right? Then you'd best be careful to follow instructions. I'll call at one thirty, you will be at my house when I call. Talk to you later James. Bye now."

The screen turned to fuzzy salt and pepper as a loud static raked against my ear drums.

72

Mind racing, my heart pounding, we managed to make it into Georgetown about a quarter after 1. It was 1:23 when we pulled into Ethan's drive. That old, ran down, paint peeling and termite infested home glared back at me, bidding me to enter.

"You sure you want to do this James," Lee asked as he leaned on the wheel and craned his neck my way.

Eyes trained in a stare down with the GTK's homestead, mind filled with memories of what was found in there 25 years ago, I nodded.

"I have to. I don't have a choice."

Lee took a breath.

"James...I can't let you go in there by yourself."

I turned and faced him.

"You have to."

He tightened his lips and sighed out his nostrils. Knowing my mind was made, he didn't waste another breath trying to convince me otherwise.

"You stay here and keep a watch out. If I need you, you'll hear me."

"Same here."

We waited for what seemed like a lifetime for the call. The stereo showed *1:30.*

I wiped my thumb on my pants leg as it was too damp to unlock my phone. It showed *1:29*.

It's a trap.

My heart quickened. I scanned the yard and porch for any silhouette. Anticipating an ambush any second, the buzz vibrated my heart, I fumbled to answer. Restricted.

"Hel—"

"Glad you could make it James," his voice crackled as it resonated down my spine.

"I'm here. Now what."

"No time for small talk huh? I like it. I assume you watched the tape?"

"I did."

"Good."

"Now what?"

"Come inside and you'll see. I have it all mapped out for you. All you have to do is follow instructions. Think you can do that for me?"

I took a breath before answering. My gut burned with sharp enough words to slice through a concrete building.

Not now. Vengeance isn't mine.

"James?"

"I'm here."

"You follow me?"

"Yeah."

"All right then. I'll call back at 1:50, after you've found the treasure. Ciao."

"You..."

The phone clicked before I could finish. That last word turned my blood into a boil. He was rubbing it in my face. That was Rebecca's word for bye. Serving as a connection to her Cajun roots. It was pronounced as *Chow*.

"You sure you're up to this?" Lee asked as he grabbed my hand on my way out of the truck.

I nodded, clicked on a flashlight and said,

"Just keep your eyes and ears open. I should be back in twenty minutes, if not, I'll flick the light three times through the window. Honk if you see anything."

"Be careful James."

I nodded, checked the clip of my *9mm* and shut the door.

Fifteen paces later, I conquered the first step. After three, I was on the porch.

I shined my light to the door knob, breathed deeply and gave it a turn.

The door gave way with a creak. A thin white string stretched across the living area and into the hall. A small note attached to the line flapped in the draft.

I peered at it through my glasses,

FOLLOW ME

I rested my hand around the line and crossed toward the hallway. Scanning the home with my light, being sure to check every darkened corner. The floor barked its displeasure of my presence with each step I took. A few soft spots made me feel like I could end up on the ground any second.

Dust, mold and rotten eggs filled my breath and lungs. I covered my face with the crevice of my arm, but it didn't keep my sinuses from their natural reflexes.

Two short blast back to back. A stale irony taste lighted upon my tongue. I must've sucked in a gulp of dust in the process.

I sniffled, blinked and continued to follow the line into the hall. Its soft fibers tickled the tip of my fingers. I shifted it to my palm.

A cricket had made this place his home and screeched his disapproval of my arrival.

I shone my light down the hall, the thread led into a bed room. I continued onward.

I reached the open door and filled the room with my light. I followed the string, it led to a rocking chair stationed in a darkened corner. The outline of a small child gave my heart a jolt.

My light flickered, then winked out. I smacked it. Its halo enlightened the child.

It was an early 19th century style doll dressed in British royalty, rosy cheeks and a feathered top hat. A thread tied around its soft little hand as it rested in the chair. Its feet dangled off the edge, dressed in polished black slippers.

I steadied my breath and edged closer, string in hand. Another note. This time a piece of paper folded neatly and pinned to the doll's chest. I unsnapped the pin, careful not to disturb its owner.

UNDER THE FLOOR I LAY

IT'S A SHAME I COULDN'T STAY.

MY BONES YOU'LL FIND

LEAST YOU RUN OUT OF TIME.

YOU BEST GET BUSY

FOR IT WON'T BE EASY

I WAIT TO BE UNCOVERED

SURELY YOU WON'T MIND TO SHUTTER

AS THE LIFE OF THE FLESH IS IN THE BLOOD,

SO DOES LIFE AND DEATH ABIDE IN THE TONGUE.

I LONG TO BE AWAKENED

IT'S UP TO YOU, YOU MUST'NT BE SHAKEN.

I straightened my spine, tucked the note in my shirt pocket and stole a glance at my phone.

1:39

Eleven minutes before he'd call. I angled to the window and looked to Lee's truck. He sat with an arm dangling out the driver window, his right thumb and index supporting his chin.

What is he talking about?

As my mind fumbled with questions, I turned and scanned my light across the floor. I searched for any sign of a doorway or hatch leading beneath the house.

A rug stretched itself under the rocker. I tapped it with my foot. I moved the rocker aside and pulled back the rug, going to my knees in the process.

It was a hatch of sorts with a metal black hinge. No lock. I stilled the storm within and lifted the doorway leading to a cramped crawlspace.

A horrible stench welcomed me. The bidding blackness reeked of mold and death.

I laid on my belly and tucked my face beneath my shirt. I ducked my head and light into the opening and scanned my soon to be tomb.

Stale, damp dirt, and mold were in abundance.

A string drooped from a wooden plank, dangling a small garden shovel, less than a foot from the opening. I shifted to my haunches and lowered my right foot through the hatch. The thought of being yanked through, crossed my mind more than once, I must admit.

I lowered my left and scooted to the edge, planted my feet in the dirt. Crunched to my knees, light clinched between my teeth, palms planted in the soft dirt.

I took the light with a balmy left hand and shone it to the shovel. I yanked it free, then followed the line for about ten feet before it disappeared behind a cinder block column.

I adjusted my glasses and began my trek on all fours, light cinched with my teeth. The taste of metal and the horrid odor turned my stomach.

I crawled on.

The line made a sharp angle to the right and stopped where it tied to a wooden stake planted in the earth just behind the column. A tag like you'd see draped around a toe of the dead in a cold morgue, wore my name in bold black letters.

I snatched it loose and flipped it over.

YOU'VE COME THUS FAR

YOU 'LL SOON FIND THE SCAR

A HAMMER AND NAILS, TO MAKE ONE FRAIL

DOESN'T TAKE MUCH TO FALL FROM THE RAIL.

MY DEATH A SACRIFICE

MY BONES, THE GIVER OF LIFE.

I tucked it next to other note in my pocket and switched the light from my right to my left. I gripped the shovel in a balmy palm and jabbed it in the loose earth.

I felt the glare and presence of a million beady eyes as they mocked me beyond their veil of darkness.

I had to glance over my shoulder more than once to be sure I hadn't taken on any spectators. I couldn't see anyone, but I sure as heck felt them.

The nots in my gut screamed to get the heck out of here. My initial instinct told me I'd made a mistake by following his instructions, but my intellect said if I ever wanted to see Rebecca alive, I had to obey his orders, regardless of how daunting they were.

Couldn't have been more than seven or eight tosses of dirt, before the tip of my shovel clanked against something metal or tin like.

I hurried and dusted the top of it off, shining the light with my mouth. It was an old red Folgers coffee can, resting on its side. Duct tape sealed the plastic lid. Another note was stuck to the side, protected from the elements with clear plastic tape.

TAKE ME WITH YOU, BUT DO NOT OPEN!

LEAVE ME BY THE WATER TOWER, NEXT TO THE ICW

Curiosity getting the best of me, I gave it a good shake. Something rattled and clanked. Could be bones. Human? Dog? Maybe it contained the remnants of my ear? Or maybe it was nothing more than a few sticks and rocks?

I checked my phone.

1:46

I cradled the can under my armpit, gripped the light with my right fingers and waddled like a duck towards the opening. All the while praying it'd remain open.

✝✝✝✝✝✝✝✝✝✝✝✝✝✝✝✝✝✝✝✝

OUTSIDE, Lee sat with darting eyes and chattering lips as he searched for the faintest sight or sound and mouthed an earnest prayer to the Creator.

A crackle in the brush to his left demanded his attention. He snapped his head around just in time to hear its howl. A long drawn out O to U guttural tone emitted from the dense patch of woods.

Lee slammed his palm against the center of the wheel.

✝✝✝✝✝✝✝✝✝✝✝✝✝✝✝✝✝✝✝✝

I WAS HALF WAY to the opening when that howl stopped me in my tracks. My skin tingled as the sound seemed to crawl over my whole body, even seeping into my flesh and disturbing my organs.

Three quick honks followed shortly after.

I quickened my pace and shifted through the dirt, longing for the feel of the wooden planks beneath my feet.

The faint square light emitted ahead. I edged closer.

Reaching the opening, I gripped the edge with the meaty part of my right hand, still squeezing the light with my fingers.

I knelt in the dim light of the opening, took the can beneath my arm and sat it on the floor, then pulled myself from the hole and sat my haunches upon the dust covered floor.

My head spinning faster than a spun coin.

I forced myself to my feet. Another long howl drummed into the night.

I rushed to the door, coffee can next to my breast.

I fumbled for my phone and did a quick glance.

1:48

I yanked the front door open and stumbled onto the porch. My eyes found Lee leaning against an opened driver door, flagging me to quicken my pace.

He plopped in and turned over the ignition.

The engine roared, silencing the fading howl. The headlights almost blinded me as they flashed just a few paces before I reached the passenger door.

I squished my rump into the seat. Panting for breath. I looked to the stereo clock.

1:50

"You all right?" asked Lee as he gave me a quick glance before returning his eyes to the wood line.

Through huffed breaths, I forced out,

"Yeah...yeah. I'm good."

I sat the can between us, the rattle catching his attention.

He turned and eyed it.

"What's this?"

"I don't kn—"

I retrieved my cell. Restricted.

I answered but didn't say anything.

A breathy static filled the line.

A moment passed.

"So…you got the treasure I suppose?"

"Yeah."

"Good. That wasn't so bad was it?"

I didn't answer.

"C'mon Jimmy boy…don't turn sour on me now."

"Listen…Ethan…I did what you asked didn't I? Let me talk to Rebecca."

"It's Frank, but anyhow, I'm afraid that's not possible."

His words crushed me like getting splattered by a semi. They're vice grip squeezed the breath right out of me.

I looked at the coffee can. Does it contain my wife's remains? Did I just disturb her grave? Oh God. What has he done?

"You see, she's not with me at the moment. She stayed behind to give Mother and the others company. Don't worry…she's a champ. She's doing great."

I delayed my response long enough to carefully form my words, straining out the one's I really wanted to use. I gathered myself and spoke in a calm, steady tone.

"You listen here. Vengeance is not mine to give. God will see to it that you get what's coming to you. Be careful what you do, because your day of reckoning is coming. Make no mistake about it, you won't get by without paying for what you've done."

He breathed out a sigh as his breath wafted over the receiver, clawing at my eardrums.

"I'm petrified," he mocked.

I gave no reply.

"Listen James...you've done good tonight, but don't ruin it all trying to be a hero. Leave the can at the water tower and don't for a second, think of taking a peak. I'll know if you did, so don't try me."

Click

I sighed to let out the steam building within. I rubbed the back of my neck.

"Everything all right?"

His words were like gasoline.

"No! It's not Lee! Nothing's all right!" I whipped my head around so fast, I got a cramp in my neck.

I barked out the words before I even realized it.

A wave of guilt washed over me, briefly extinguishing the flame of anger I felt for Ethan.

I shook my head, my vision blurred, my eyes stung with tears. I looked over at him as he sat there looking out the windshield.

"I'm sorry."

He turned and said,

"I know those words weren't really meant for me. I understand James. I do."

He said as he nodded and shifted the truck into reverse.

"Thank you. Let's go home."

††††††††††††††††††††††

6 AM, and Frank found himself across the road from the Randolph's home, crouching through the marsh like a cat. He came to the edge of the marsh, with the cover of sea oaks, he waited a few moments before crossing the street. Checking for any sign of traffic.

It was mostly silent, except for the screeching of the night bugs in the trees, the buzz of gnats and mosquitoes and of course the crashing waves.

The moon was only a faint rounded line, as it was just a day from becoming a new one.

It was dark. Just the way Frank liked it.

A gentle breeze rushed against his cheek, rattling the tall marsh grass next to him.

Above him a horde of blackness hovered and swarmed as Kirkland had brought along a few of his friends.

Voices hissed and shrieked in Frank's ear as he patiently sat and waited for Kirkland to give the orders.

An hour would pass before the order ever came and with the help of Kirkland, Ender, and Lucinda, Frank found himself easing through the Randolph's home, before making his way to the attic.

"Kirkland, something didn't feel right when I stood in the doorway of James' room. Did you feel that?" Frank asked in a faint whisper as he sat on his haunches in a darkened corner next to a pile of insulation.

"Oh, don't worry about it. It was just your nerves," said Kirkland as he gave a side glance to Ender and Lucinda while chewing on a nail.

Frank did the same as he relaxed and fell asleep just above James who'd already succumbed to his weariness.

73

The morning came hard as it was just after seven, when my alarm began its irritating screech. I twisted and turned, wishing the darn thing would die. Finally conceding victory, I rolled over and gave the snooze button a nice smack with my palm.

I grabbed my cane next to the bed as early mornings were quite dizzy to start. I managed to make my way into the bathroom to relieve myself before undressing and starting the shower, so I could freshen up for our meeting with Mishoe.

Just the thought of facing that man after what I had to do last night was enough to cause my gut to twist in a knot. What if he caught on? What if he disregarded Ethan's warning and did something to jeopardize Rebecca?

I secured the bandage around where my ear should've been, as doctor blur said the area still couldn't get wet in fear of it setting up infection.

Just as I was stepping into the shower, a loud pop sounded off in the ceiling. Which wasn't that all unusual, I mean it does it from time to time. I just haven't heard it quite that loud before.

Anyhow, I took a well needed steam shower, put on some nice clothes, then went into my closet to pray.

I'm still new at this, so it can be hard to get started, but once I begin, I find it comes more and more natural for me.

I just try to be as honest as possible with God, I'm not in there uttering some hour long four-word prayer, but I'm just simply talking to God from my heart. I tell him everything, because hey, it's not like He doesn't already know, right? No sense in keeping secrets.

But I find that the more honest I am with God, the more honest He is with me, in the sense that He doesn't keep secrets either. If I'll open up to Him, He'll open up to me.

I know it sounds strange, but if I'll just talk to God, like I'm talking with Rebecca or Lee or one of the kids, man...it'll be like He's literally sitting right there next to me. It's hard to explain, but it's like He's really in the room with me, listening to everything I have to say. And not just listening, but actually caring.

That's been the key for me in learning how to pray. Just be honest. No hidden agenda. I'm just simply talking to God like He's my best friend. But more than that, I'm starting to feel like He's my dad. I guess after having not talked to my real dad all this time, it feels good to have someone fill that void.

I don't know, I just feel such a connection to Him, I just feel like a little kid again. In a good way.

It just feels like it's meant to be. Like as if all my life, I've been longing to speak with biological Father again, so much that I've missed and ignored the presence of my Heavenly Father, my very Creator.

Well...anyway we got a meeting with Mishoe at nine to talk about this letter. I sure hope we can piece things together and I hope Lee and I can keep last night to ourselves.

Buzz-Buzz-Buzz.

It's David Hoffman. Wonder what he's up to this early in the morning?

"Hello?" I answered as I was busy buttoning up my shirt.

"James...I didn't wake you, did I?"

"No-no...I was just getting dressed."

"Oh good...hey listen. Me and Annie were talking last night, what do you think about having a get together here at our place? And invite Lee's family as well, so we can all gather in one place while we're fasting and praying about everything."

"Perfect! Sounds good to me. When do you want to start?"

"Well...how about Monday night? Say six-thirty?"

"Sounds great. I'll tell Lee, so he can let his Brother and Uncle know."

A moment passed.

"I haven't had the chance to tell you, but last night I got a call from Mishoe."

Static.

"Yeah...what'd he say?"

"They got a letter yesterday at the police station addressed from *The Watcher*. But it's from Rebecca. It's her handwriting. She says she's okay and everything, but said we have until Tuesday night to find her or else it won't be good."

David sighed on the other end.

"Something about the letter just doesn't seem right though. The way she worded things is kind of off. Just not like her to have such poor grammar and sentence structure. I don't know, I'm sure he probably stood over her shoulder as she wrote it, so that might be why."

"Huh. Yeah, maybe that's what it is. Well…give me a call once you leave the meeting and let me know what they say."

"I will, David. And I'll talk to Lee about Monday. Appreciate your help and prayers. I'll talk to you later."

"You bet. Sounds good. Take care."

Creak!

I glanced toward the ceiling and scrunched my brows. I guess with the air cooling a bit, it's got the house creaking and cracking to adjust.

I'm glad David called. I think that prayer meeting could really do us some good.

I glanced at my watch.

7:42

Best go check on Lee and make sure he'll be ready to leave by a quarter after eight.

† †

JUST ABOVE James, Frank busied himself gently rocking to and fro on his knees as he spoke in a unique tongue, attempting to garnish enough courage to carry out the plan. An empty hamburger container sat to his left.

The Voice, now joined by two others, hissed and clawed in his mind, replaying forward and backward. All the while repeating every wicked thing Frank had done since the moment he was old enough to walk.

"All sin begins within and there is no cure without atonement. A sacrifice must now be made to ever ease the pain."

The voices hissed over and over, reminding Frank of his mother. Frank gritted his teeth, tightened his jaw and clinched his fist as he beat the two of them against his chest. Tears dripping to the plywood he sat upon.

"When Kirkland? When?"

"THREE O'CLOCK, MONDAY NIGHT. THEY'LL ALL BE HERE, BUT REBECCA. WE'LL HAVE YOUR BUDDY TAKE CARE OF HER, UNLESS YOU THINK YOU CAN MAKE IT BACK IN TIME? THIS WAY HIS KIDS WILL SEEM HIM SUFFER."

"I'll do it. I got to finish what I started."

"GOOD. THAT'S THE FRANKIE I KNOW."

"Don't call me that."

"SORRY. I FORGOT. WELL...KEEP IT UP, DON'T BACK OUT ON ME NOW. YOU DO THIS AND YOUR MOTHER WILL BE FREE FROM THE PAIN AND SUFFERING ONCE AND FOR ALL."

A moment passed.

"Oh Frankie," a soft, but troubled voice traveled from a darkened corner opposite from Frank.

He raised his vision and there she was.

It was Mama. Still wearing the same dress, she wore the day she was sacrificed in the barn. Her eyes, ears, nose and fingers still missing. She stood in the corner, black holes for eyes, fixed on Frank. A faint smile twisted her lips as they curled upward. She tilted her head at him, then hung it low toward the insulation.

Frank gasped as he placed a hand over his mouth and scooted across the plywood on his haunches.

"Mama?"

She didn't say a word. She vanished like a passing fog.

"SEE? YOU DON'T WANT HER TO CONTINUE IN HER PAIN AND SADNESS, DO YOU?"

Frank shut his eyes and wagged his head.

"GOOD. THEN YOU'LL SEE TO IT AND CARRY OUT THE PLAN."

Frank sniffled and bobbed his head. Worms of raw hamburger meat stuck to his teeth and scattered across his lap.

74

The croaks from a horde of Pelicans played in her ear like classical music at a fine restaurant. There, but not begging much attention. Her eyes stung from the lack of a decent sleep. She felt the sand beneath her back. The stale taste of a dry mouth caused her to give it relief with her tongue. Rebecca raised an eye lid, a black jagged line opened like a window blind, revealing the dismal bunker.

She lay in the sand on her back. She scanned the room for Frank. He wasn't here.

It was just her and Mother.

Wait. The chains? Had he forgotten to bind her? Had God set her free? Was this a trap?

Her heart palpitated at the thoughts.

She raised up, supporting herself with her palms.

"Frank?" her voice a slight echo.

Silence.

She glanced around and peered into each shadow that surrounded her.

If Frank was here, he was doing a good job of staying hid. She locked eyes with the ladder's rungs.

Her adrenaline serving as a pain reliever as she used it to her advantage to force herself to those horizontal lines upon the sand. At the moment they felt like an orange life saver tossed into her sea of fear.

She had to at least reach for it.

And that she did.

Blocking her barking hamstrings with the thought of her family, she pulled herself up one rung at a time. The metal hatch above mocked her as it seemed to distant itself like a cruel master taunting a tiger with a piece of meat.

Teeth clinched, sandy hands gripping the rungs, she inched skyward. For what seemed like an eternity later, she did it. She glanced back down, to be sure Frank wasn't on her heels.

Nothing.

Her heart leaped with thoughts of escaping such a formidable nightmare she'd been forced to endure.

She pressed a hand to the hatch, it gave away, lifting only a few inches, a stream of light flooded the darkness.

Her eyes numbed, she squinted. The wave's roar grew louder. Pelican's hopped and flapped away startled by her sudden arrival. The sky was beautiful, hardly a cloud in sight. A gentle salty breeze laid the grass low.

She took a deep breath as it was like a cold glass of water in a hot desert. Hope.

Her heart soared like the gulls above.

That's when a pair of calloused fingers squeezed her ankles and jerked her southward. Her gut remained at the opening. Within seconds she thumped to the sand, knocking her out of breath and hope.

Darkness returned.

75

"C'mon Rebecca...let's quit wasting daylight and get on out there. The shrimp ain't gonna catch em selves." The old man said with a chuckle.

"I'm coming, I'm coming," she said as she tossed on a jacket, her little feet thudding against aluminum in a race down the dock. Grandpa sat waiting on the boat, steering wheel in hand.

One foot on the dock, another in the boat.

"Hey, untie us before you hop in, will ya?"

"Oh yeah, almost forgot."

Rebecca turned and made her way to the cleat where the rope was wrapped in a tight knot. She undid it, carrying the rope in hand, placing a foot in the boat and pushed off with the other against the dock.

Sending them into the swift current.

Grandpa fired up the engine and placed it in gear as they began another slow trek out into the open ocean, in search of every Cajun's prized possession...shrimp.

Grandpa gave a toothy grin as they glided over a large wave. Causing her stomach to drop on the decent.

She jolted awake. The bell upon her ankle rattled. She blinked her eyes as they attempted to adjust to the darkness. The damp chill, crashing waves and sound of the distant chime told her she was back in the bunker.

She bit her bottom lip to keep it from quivering. The emptiness in her gut and longing in her heart was too much as she could no longer restrain her heart.

"Ahhhhhh!"

She screamed through the cloth and tape with everything in her as the pain was just too much. She yanked against the chains and screamed again, this time even louder.

"Ahhhhhhhhh!"

She broke. She groaned in agony as the pain in her heart was overwhelming. Oh, how she longed for her family and oh how she missed those days with Grandpa. She'd do anything to have them back.

Her shoulders shook up and down as the chains gave their irritating rattle.

She yanked and squirmed, the pain in her legs telling of their displeasure in such movement, but she ignored it and continued on.

She screamed and wept through the gag. Something she longed to do as he'd even taking her freedom to express her sorrow.

"Oh God...where are you? Have you forgotten about me? What are you doing? Please! Please!" She mumbled with tears drenching her dirty sweater and jeans.

"God...please rescue me, get me out of here. If you're real and so loving how could you allow me to suffer down here like this? Why?" she said with choked syllables as they attempted to force themselves through her gagged weeping.

Dear daughter, you are more precious than all the things the finest rubies or gold could ever buy. You are mine! Do not let the fear of the unknown choke the power of knowing who you are. You are my daughter and I have laid down my life for you. I will never leave you or forsake. Even in the darkest of hours, I am here. I am never further than a breath away. Whether you realize it or not, I am here. No darkness can overcome my Light. No fear can overcome my Peace. No sorrow can overcome my Joy. I am the Creator of all you see and you are mine. If only you could glimpse how valuable and precious you are in my sight. Trust Me. The chains that bind you can only bind your flesh, they cannot bind your spirit. All fear is only a binding of the flesh. Release such fear and walk freely in the liberty of the Spirit. As long as you allow yourself to be chained by your old way of thinking, you will stay grounded and bound by earth's cruel law of judgement. But awaken and abide in Me, where My Spirit will guide you into all truth. In this you will soar above and beyond anything that would try and bind you here on earth. You were not put here to walk in fear and sorrow, that's only the chains the world uses to bind you, as it fears the power within you. You were put here to soar freely in My love and grace and be in awe of my splendor as you gaze in reverent wonder of who I am. The Creator and lover of your soul. Rebecca you are loved more than you can ever fathom. Release the chains of your old mind and step into my rivers of grace as you remember who you are. You are my daughter and I am King above all kings. You are mine!

The voice soothed her soul, allowing her shoulders to relax. Her heart was held in the hands of its Creator.

"God, forgive me for questioning you."

She shut her eyes, took a deep breath, and sighed it out. In mid sniffle, the sound of shuffling sand startled her.

The bunker was dark as night due to the lack of candles. But the sound of footsteps sent a shiver down her spine.

"Remember...there's nothing to fear. I am safe in the arms of my Father."

The popping of a joint told Rebecca she wasn't alone. She first thought it was Mama or that fellow Frank seemed to call Kirkland, but she didn't feel their presence like she had in the past.

There was no sudden chill or gentle breeze or the thick enveloping darkness she'd felt before. She felt uneasy, but not like the other times.

"Rebecca?" a deep guttural voice pierced the air.

She froze. Tiny bumps spread across her arms and legs as every hair on her neck stood at attention. This voice was different.

Her eyes darted side to side, scanning for the source of the voice. Though it did no good, as she could only see about five feet in front of her. The darkness had multiplied so much she could feel it.

"Rebecca?"

She snapped her head to the right.

"Calm down. I don't bite, at least not on the first date," the voice chuckled in the darkness and edged closer.

A face emerged like a ship through thick fog. He was a short man with a graying hair, glasses, a thick mustache and a fat head that rested upon narrow and weak shoulders.

He took another step.

He wore blue jeans with an old AC/DC shirt he'd likely picked up at a concert back in the day.

He stood only about two foot's length from her as he toyed with his mustache and grinned.

"Rebecca...I'm not who you think I am. At least I don't think so. Having been down here during most of the time you and Frank have shared, I'd imagine you're probably thinking I must be Kirkland. Am I right?"

She nodded with wide eyes.

"Well...I'm not. My name is Robert," he glared at her, given his words time to resonate.

She swallowed hard and blinked.

"Still not ringing a bell?"

She wagged her head.

"Well...don't worry it's not like your life depends on it or anything."

He said as he inched closer and ripped the tape from her mouth.

She squinted and winced.

"Oh sorry, didn't mean to hurt you," he said as he tossed the tape and gag to the sand.

"Anyhow...you see it's my job to be sure the mouse doesn't play while the cat's away. Not that Miss Thompson couldn't handle you, because believe me, she could. It's just that Frank feels a little more comfortable knowing I'm here to keep an eye on you."

Through breaths, Rebecca asked, "Where's Frank?"

"Oh, he's out doing some work for Kirkland. He should be back in a few days. Usually doesn't take longer than two or three."

A long beat as he fixed his eyes to hers.

"Anyhow...hey you getting hungry? I know I sure am," he said as he clacked his teeth before disappearing into the darkness.

He struck a match and lit some candles, allowing Mama and the jars of offerings to appear.

He rattled around in the Dollar General and Subway bags and retrieved the half of sub Frank had left for him.

"Want some?" he offered as he held it toward Rebecca.

She shook her head and told him no thanks.

"You know...you're a pretty one. I'm surprised. Frank usually don't have much of a taste for women, but he done pretty good with you. I'm impressed."

"Well thank you," she said with a smirk.

"Hey, I didn't mean it like that. I'm just saying, I'm glad Frank's eyes are getting better," he said with a big grin as he took a bite from his leftover sub.

"But uh, on a serious note, how about we get to know each other a little better."

He placed the sub on the table and stood to his feet. Eying her up and down like a steak.

††††††††††††††††††††

"IF HE SO much as lays one finger on her...I'll drop him dead where he stands," Mateo said with a tight jaw and clinched fist locked on the sword by his side.

Nathaniel stuck out an arm and placed his hand to Mateo's gut, "Easy Mateo. Patience dear warrior, patience."

76

The room seemed smaller as the air was scarce. Rebecca dangled hopelessly in her chains and shackles, while Robert wore a smile that sent a shiver down her spine. He marched to her with a faint giggle.

Now within a few feet's distance, he outstretched his arms toward her face.

Rebecca recoiled in disgust and twisted her face away.

Robert started to touch and rub her cheek, but he stopped for some reason. He smiled. She could see his eyes widen as he licked his lips. She watched him close his eyes, breathe deep, and shudder.

"You should be so glad Frank is in charge of this. You have no idea how lucky you are."

She narrowed her brows at him and huffed.

Rebecca watched as he slithered back into the shadows.

†††††††††††††††††††††††

WE MADE IT to the police station about ten minutes before nine. Mishoe greeted us and directed us into a conference room.

"Well what do you think of the letter?" Mishoe asked while closing the door behind us.

"I know it's her handwriting, but the way she wrote it, just doesn't seem right," I said as me and Lee took a seat.

"Yeah, that's what forensics have told me. James...how are you holding up with all this? You seem a little pale."

Time froze as I'm sure my stare didn't help my cause. My voice caught in my throat.

For the life of me, words just wouldn't form.

My pulse soared.

"James...is there something you'd like to tell me?"

I wagged and rubbed my forehead.

"These past few days have been rough on him," said Lee.

I raised my head in time to catch Ray glaring at Lee out the corner of his eye.

"Is that so?"

I cleared my throat. Face feeling hot, I managed to form the words, "It's just hard knowing what she must be going through."

I pulled out the letter and sat it on the table in effort to the change the subject.

"Are you guys getting any closer? I mean what's the plan between now and Tuesday?"

"Well...we did get a phone call around midnight last night. It from was from a woman by the name of Leslie Luender in California. She's claiming to be this guy's wife."

The room went silent. Mishoe tightened his lips and nodded.

"What...what...what did she say?" I asked as Lee scooted closer to the table.

"Well she said they'd been together for about twenty-years, even have a kid together. He's seventeen. They live in Southern California near the Palm Springs area. Said he left them high and dry a few weeks ago and hasn't been heard from since," Mishoe scratched the back of his neck, "Their within an hour or so drive of the Phantom murders."

"What? Are you serious?"

Mishoe nodded, "Yeah. We think he's also the San Bernardino Phantom."

I lowered my face to my chest and rubbed my forehead with my index and thumb.

"She said he had been living on the streets out there before they met. Then said he got a job as a handy man a few months after they meet up at a local bar. Said he was the nicest and kindest person she'd ever met. It wasn't until after their son was born that he started changing into a monster. Said that's when he developed a violent temper and extreme jealousy and control issue."

"Wait wait wait...so you're saying this guy has a family out in California that he just up and dumped?" Lee asked with bewildered eyes.

"That's right."

I rested my elbows on the table, covered my face with my palms and sighed, "God help us."

"James...maybe this woman can help us, maybe she can give insight into his tendencies and habits. I mean I would think if anyone knows where he's likely to be, it'd be someone who has spent the past twenty years with him," Lee said as he gave me a reassuring pat on the back.

"He's right James...I think Leslie could be a big break for us. She said she'd be more than willing to speak with you. And I have another call with her today at three, so I'll let you know what she says."

I uncovered my face, gave him my attention and nodded once more.

Though his face was a bit blurry, I could make out that he had a lot on his mind and was doing his best with what he had. My stomach growled with hunger pains. I'm sure Lee's was probably doing the same.

"Look Ray...I know you're doing all you can and I appreciate it. But please...bring Rebecca home," I wanted to say more, but couldn't, my voice stopped in my throat as tears flooded my eyes.

I broke. I wept.

I released the flood of emotion as it's build up was just too much to hold back.

"James...we're going to find her and we're going to bring this scumbag to justice."

††††††††††††††††††††††

PACING TO AND FRO in the attic next to Frank, Kirkland chewed on a nail and mumbled his plan as it tossed around in his mind like a drunken sailor.

OOMPH

He doubled over and was forced to a knee. He grabbed at his gut and winced.

"AAAAHHHH!" he roared as he slapped the plywood giving Frank a jolt.

"What!? What is it?" Frank asked as he scanned the darkened attic in search of Kirkland's whereabouts.

"THEY'RE STILL FASTING AND PRAYING," he answered with a strained grunt.

"Are you all right?"

"YEAH-YEAH I'M FINE. LISTEN THEY'RE GOING TO BE GONE UNTIL LATE TONIGHT, SO IF YOU WANT TO GET OUT OF THE ATTIC, YOU'D HAVE NOTHING TO WORRY ABOUT."

"You sure?"

"WHAT DO YOU THINK I'D SET YOU UP!? OF COURSE I'M SURE!" Kirkland roared.

"All right...well if you say so," Frank rose to his feet and dusted off his pants then made his way to the door, twisted the knob and began his decent down the stairs before making his way into the kitchen.

He opened the refrigerator and after some thorough searching, found a plate of leftovers.

"Dang James...what do you eat? Guess you living on fast food right now aren't ya? Ain't got nobody here to cook for ya," Frank said with a chuckle as he placed the leftovers in the microwave.

As he waited, he exchanged glances with all the pictures stuck to the refrigerator.

"Man, I didn't realize you had this big of a family. Hmm," he said sipping a glass of wine.

Smacking his tongue against the back of his teeth and wagging his head, he said, "Well...it's a shame. They gonna be left all alone. Sure hope you got some good insurance."

Beep...Beep...Beep

The microwave finished.

He retrieved the plate and sat at the table. In the same chair James used to sit in before he became confined to the wheel chair.

"Appreciate the hospitality James," Frank said in mid chew as he sniffed the wine and gave a toast toward a photo of James and the family on the fridge.

77

Saturday around noon, I made the call to Leslie.

Ring
I swallowed hard.
Ring
What would I say?
Ring
I take a deep breath and scratch the back of my neck.
Ring
I don't think she'll answer.
Ri— "Hello?"
Caught off guard as I was busy rehearsing the message I would leave her, I cleared my throat and said, "Um...hi is this Leslie?"

"Yes it is...and who is this?"

"My name's James Randolph...I was given your number by Brunswick County detective Ray Mishoe."

"Oh-oh...I'm...so sorry to hear what you are going through."

"Thank you...it's been rough...uh...just taking it one day at time."

"I see. I can't imagine what it must be like. I'm truly sorry this has happened."

Her sympathy was returned with a brief staticky pause.

"Thank you. Uh, listen, I was wondering what you could tell me about your husband?"

A moment passed.

"You see, I knew him for a short time when he was nineteen and working at the papermill, but Mishoe was saying you were with him for what...twenty years?"

She took a breath and said, "Yes, and those were some of the most difficult years of my life. Especially after Allan was born."

"He's seventeen, correct?"

"Yes. He'll be eighteen next month."

"Our son Jason just turned seventeen this past summer. So, what kind of clues can you give me? You know like habits, preferences, tastes...I mean anything that would give us an inside look as to who and what we're dealing with."

"Oh certainly...well first...he's a night owl. Always had trouble sleeping. He'll go days at a time without getting any sleep. Some nights he'd be up till four in the morning, pacing the house ringing a bell to help calm him. Always said there was too much noise...it was like he was always paranoid about something. Doctors diagnosed him with insomnia, bipolar, and schizophrenia about three years ago. Put him on some medication, but he rarely ever took it and when he did, he always double up on it."

She paused and sighed.

"The last few years have been horrible. he's become so short tempered and unpredictable it's scary. I mean the least little bity thing would send him into a rage. There have been a handful of times me and Allan had to hide in the woods as we were in fear, that he'd kill us. Then he'd come crying back, begging us for forgiveness, promising he'd never do it again and going on and on about how much he loved us."

Muffled cries and sniffles filled the line.

"My goodness...Leslie I am so sorry you and your son have had to go through that. That's horrible. No wife and son should ever have to deal with something like that. That's not love...that's abuse. It takes a sick and evil individual to do what he done to you and your son. I don't care what the doctors say, if he had any ounce of love for you two, that'd never of happened."

"I know...I know. I don't understand it. We were always on edge with him, just waiting for something to trigger his rage. I'd lay in bed at night, eyes wide open, just waiting for him to force a pillow over my face."

Her voice shook as she recalled the painful memories.

"Another thing...he always kept a loaded pistol in the night stand. I begged him not to get the thing, but he wouldn't listen. He finally told me, *'I'm getting a gun.'* I barely slept for the three years since. I was always afraid he'd pull it out in the middle of the night and do a murder suicide with all of us. That's when I started moving stuff around in the drawer, so that a grocery bag he kept the bullets in would crinkle and rattle if he ever tried it. I tell you, I can hear the rattle of a grocery bag from a mile away and get the shakes as my heart will start pounding."

I was speechless. I just couldn't form my words.

"And he always talked about wanting to live out in the wild. You know, like the tv shows where those people live in the mountains and off the grid?"

"Yeah-yeah."

"Yeah, he always talked a lot about living in the woods. And said he wanted to go back to North Carolina to see his mom. She's dead of course, but he talked a lot about wanting to go back and visit her at the cemetery."

My eyes widened as my ears grew attentive.

"Did he ever say how she died?"

"Yeah, said she and his dad died in a house fire when he was a kid."

"I see. Did he ever mention having friends back this way?"

"Yeah, he talked a lot about Will and David. Two buddies he grew up with, but other than that, I don't think he really had many friends."

"I see...well what did he do for work?"

"He found a job at a tire manufacturing place, working third shift. He done that for about ten years or so before quitting and working for a cable company helping people fix problems with their tv's or internet. Then he did handy man work on the side."

Lee eased into the left turning lane, about to cross the south side of US-501 as a large green sign read,

Waccamaw Tribal Grounds

We talked for a few more minutes, then I said, "Well Leslie, listen I have to go. I truly appreciate you taking your time to speak with me. You've been a tremendous help. I will keep in touch and give you a ring if I have any more questions."

"My pleasure. Anything I can do to help. Yeah, if you think of anymore questions, just give me a call."

"I sure will. Thank you, Leslie."

"Oh, you're welcome. And hey one last thing before we hang up."

"Yeah, what's that?"

"Don't be deceived by his charm and lies and don't let him intimidate you. When he's in a rage, there's just something about those eyes...they'll paralyze you. It's like satan himself staring you down. Don't let such fear creep into your soul, because if you do, it'll haunt you for the rest of your life. I'm a prime example."

Silence.

The cab of Lee's truck felt cold. The hair on my arm prickled.

"I'll do my best. Thank you, Leslie...I'll be in touch."

"Stay safe. Bye bye."

"Bye."

I ended the call as me and Lee pulled into the gravel drive of a small home next to a large field with hay bales and carved wooden images depicting Hawks and Eagles dressed in Indian regalia.

"So, what'd she say?" asked Lee as he shifted the gear stick to park and interlocked his fingers before resting them on top of the steering wheel.

I took a deep breath, raised my eye brows and said, "I'm sure glad we've been fasting and praying, because we're going to need all the help we can get. This guy is something else."

"So, this kind comes out only through fasting huh?"

I turned with curious brows, "That in the Bible?"

"Written in red."

I nodded.

"That's good to hear," I answered before taking the next few minutes to give him the run-down of what Leslie had just told me.

"Wow," Lee said rubbing his face.

"I know. All these dreams are starting to make sense."

"For sure. Well...let's go talk to my Uncle, he'll want to hear this," said Lee.

His eyes went to the porch of the home where I could make out the old Native rocking in what appeared to be a hand-crafted chair.

We exited Lee's truck and with the help of my cane, we approached his Uncle Wes.

"Why hello there strangers...how we holding up?" he asked with an exuberant smile.

"Uncle Wes...you remember James right?"

"Of course. How you doing son?" he asked, extending a hand.

"Hey Mr. McGaha, I'm doing good, how about you?"

"Listen, now I know the white man doesn't like to talk much about his feelings, but how are you really holding up?"

He had me there. I gave a reluctant nod and said, "Well to tell you the truth, I'm scared and worried out of my wits. But I'm beginning to feel the Lord's hand as it rests upon my shoulder to keep me steady and free from falling. Kind of like this here cane I reckon."

"Just like he promised in Jude, right?" he asked with a wide smile.

"I guess," I answered with a nod and smile as I noticed a plaque like frame next to the door as you enter the home. The words were blurry from where I was standing, so I hobbled closer, put on my reading glasses and had to get nose to nose in order to read it.

It read,

The Ten Indian Commandments

'1) Treat the Earth and all that dwell thereon with respect.

2) Remain close to the Great Spirit.

3) Show great respect for your fellow beings.

4) Work together for the benefit of all mankind.

5) Give assistance and kindness wherever needed.

6) Do what you know to be right.

7) Look after the well-being of mind and body.

8) Dedicate a share of your efforts to the greater good.

9) Be truthful and honest at all times.

10) Take full responsibility for your actions.'

"Wow. I like that. That's good," I said as I backed away and nodded to Lee and Wes.

"Yeah that's our mission statement I guess you could say," said Lee.

"My great grandfather wrote that in his journal just weeks before he passed. You obey those and it'll serve you well in life. Keep you out of trouble and put you on the straight and narrow," said Uncle Wes.

"For sure," I replied.

"Well, I'm guessing Lee has told you what we're doing this evening?"

"Yeah, he told me about the smudging ceremony."

"Good, yeah soon as the Sun sets, we'll get started. Should have a decent crowd. Seems our prayer circle keeps getting bigger and bigger each night."

"Well...I can't think you enough for doing what you're doing. I appreciate all of your prayers. I really do."

"Happy to help my fellow man. That's what the Great Creator requires of us and to do it with a cheerful heart. We're in this together and with our unity and the Creator's wisdom and power, can't nothing stand against us,"

He said with a peaceful and confident smile.

††††††††††††††††††††††

AFTER FILLING A grocery bag with can goods from the far back of the Randolph's pantry, Frank toted it with him up the stairs and back to his corner in the dismal attic.

It was here he'd spend the rest of his day plotting and planning with Kirkland, Ender, and Lucinda.

While every so often popping a small can of Vienna sausages to curb his hunger and being sure to build his strength.

He held a family photo of the Randolph's between his left thumb and pointer as he rubbed it with the back of his right knuckles which held a sausage.

He wagged his head and said in a guttural tone, "I've waited a long time for this, and it'll be the happiest day of my life hearing you scream. It didn't have to be like this James, if you'd only stood up for me when I needed you most. But now you have to pay...you have to atone for your sins...and you must ease mother's pain. She needs a feeding...and I hear her calling."

78

Twenty minutes past six, I found myself walking out to the field along with about a dozen others including Lee, Wes, and Clennon. The three of them dressed head to toe in their native dress. Me and a few others stopped at the circle of hay bales as the three continued into the circle.

Wes and Clennon stood side by side in the center as Lee placed some herbs and spices into half a seashell which was being used for a bowl. He used a small bundle of burning tobacco to light the herbs. Smoke began to billow skyward as he gently fanned it with Eagle feathers which were bound together and used as a wand.

The sweet savory smell of tobacco and other spices filled the air as Lee began a slow march around the circle in a clockwise fashion. Waving the wand and spreading the bowl's aroma and smoke.

"Please join me in prayer," said Wes as he and Clennon bowed their heads.

"May your hands be cleansed, that they create beautiful things. May your feet be cleansed, that they might take you where you most need to be. May your heart be cleansed that you might hear its message clearly. May your throat be cleansed, that you might speak rightly when words are needed. May your eyes be cleansed, that you might see the signs and wonders of this world. May these people and this space be washed clean by the smoke of these fragrant herbs. And may that same smoke carry our prayers to the heavens.

"Now Father and Great Creator we ask in humble petition that You would bind the efforts and desires of the wicked one. We claim power and authority over all evil spirits and negative energy. Grant us strength where it is needed and give us wisdom and discernment to recognize all evil among us.

"I pray against the plans of the evil one and I ask and pray for protection with a legion of Your strongest and most valuable Angels to watch over Rebecca and guard her with all diligence. I pray for James and the children and I ask that You comfort them during this time and help them to trust You to do what only You can do. Great Creator... may this time of prayer and cleansing be pleasing in your sight and may our prayers and petitions rise heavenward to Your throne as a sweet-smelling aroma.

"We thank You Father for Your goodness and blessing. We are in You just as You are in us and we are one. Thank You Father. In Jesus name, amen."

I took a deep breath being sure to take in all Wes had spoken, letting it settle deep into my spirit. Lee still busied himself fanning the herbs and spices with the feathers as he was now walking past me. I took a big whiff of the fragrances. They were sweet to the soul, full of a sweet savory, smoky flavor.

"Boys, would you come and lead us with a song?" Wes asked as he looked to three men who I'd met just prior to walking to the circle. Their names were John, Bobby, and Dalton.

John toted a small handmade drum that wore tight rawhide, and Dalton carried a wooden flute.

Wes and Clennon came and sat next to me as Lee finished his trip around the circle. He came around to me and stopped to fan the smoke over me, drenching me head to toe. They instructed me to take and waft it over my face and body. I did.

Lee sat next to me and the men began the song.

It started out soft and mellow with a small steady beat from the drum and a faint hypnotizing tune on the flute. The pace picked up a bit as Bobby began to sing in his native language. The sounds those men could make together were so beautiful...it's just hard to explain. I mean I could literally feel my soul dancing to the rhythm.

The drum kept a steady beat with the pace of my heart as it resonated deep within me. I closed my eyes and breathed deeply as a warm feeling washed over me like a tidal wave. It was like I was a kid again, being held in my Mother's arms, resting in her goodness and love. Like as if a warm blanket had been draped over my shoulders after a long journey through a harsh blizzard. The storm of worry and anger and bitterness was being calmed with every beat of that drum.

Trust me James, I love you with an everlasting love. You are mine, I will never let go, I will never leave you nor forsake you. You are my beloved son in whom I am well pleased. I delight in you and smile at the very thought of your name. You are the Light of the World, My spirit is within you and nothing can stand against you. It is only when you become blinded by the world's lies do you fall into anger, bitterness, shame, and every other work of the flesh in which you were not created for. Rest and abide in Me and I will show you a better way. Let my peace wash over you and still your heart. Trust Me to take care of you in the same way you trusted your Mother when you were only a child. I only want what's best for you and I will never allow anything to happen to you or your family that I cannot use for your good. It may seem hard and unfair at the moment, but I promise you, good will come from it. Trust me. I am your Creator and I am your loving Father. I love you James.

My lips trembled as a lump formed in my throat. Tears flooded my eyes. I covered my mouth and began a gentle sway side to side with the rhythm of the music. My soul was at rest in the arms of my Father as he embraced me in His arms right there out in the middle of that field, sitting upon nothing but a bale of hay.

79

After the incident in the bunker with Robert, he left to grab a breath of air, leaving Rebecca in the dark with Mother. That was hours ago and he'd yet to make it back.

Maybe the sudden flash had driven him off. Or maybe he was just setting her up to see if she'd try and make another escape. Which as long as she wore these shackles, she wasn't going anywhere. She'd done figured that out days ago. So, instead of wasting her energy, she closed her eyes, thought of James and the kids and prayed.

††††††††††††††††††††††

ON THE RIDE home from the meeting, Lee and I talked about the ceremony and its meaning.

"I tell ya though, that music and your Uncle's prayer...whew...that was touching."

I said as Lee bumped his turn signal up to turn onto US-179. We are only away minutes from where Rebecca was taken at the crash site. Lee didn't think it was a good idea to go that way, in fear I wasn't yet ready for such an encounter, but my persistence paid off.

"You know Lee...I've never in my life felt so alive, so full of...of...of hope and love. I just can't really put into words what I'm feeling. You know what I'm talking about?"

"I do. That's the Great Spirit within you. That's the same Spirit and the same power that rose Jesus from the dead. And with His Spirit within you, can't nothing stop you," Lee said with a confident smile, "You sure you want to do this?" He turned and asked one last time before we neared the intersection.

I shut my eyes, swallowed and nodded.

"Okay," Lee glanced in the rearview mirror. There weren't any cars behind us, so he slowed down just a bit as we went through the red light.

My heart quickened as a bead of sweat trickled down the bridge of my nose. I dried my palms on my pants leg. I looked out the window past Lee and could see in my mind's eye, the headlights from that night. The sounds of screeching tires against the asphalt echoed in my ear.

I twisted my head around and angled it toward my knees as I rubbed my eye lids with my right fingers.

"You okay?"

"Yeah...I'm good."

We continued on US-179 and made it to Holden Beach in little over half an hour.

It was just past ten-thirty when we walked through the front door. My plan was to shower, say a little prayer and read a scripture to maybe ease the hunger pains, then look over Rebecca's letter before getting some shut eye. I'm sure Lee was thinking the same.

†††††††††††††††††††††††††

THE SOUND OF shower water penetrated the ceiling as it reverberated into the attic space where Frank sat on his haunches, only feet above James. Knees tucked to his chest with fingers interlaced around them. Eyes shut, lips sealed tight and stretched into a grin as he gently bobbed his head.

"All sin begins within and there is no cure without atonement. A sacrifice must now be made to ever ease the pain," The voices whispered in his ear over and over...and

455

over again. Kirkland, Ender, and Lucinda rested in the shadows as they peered from the darkness with their piercing red eyes and sulfurous breath.

Their faces were drooped, looking as if they just ran a 10k race. Their eyes darted franticly side to side, much like the thoughts of what they were likely about to endure.

"WE HAVE TO STAY STRONG. WE CAN DO THIS. WE CAN'T GIVE UP NOW. WE'RE TOO CLOSE. WE GOT TO KEEP IT TOGETHER. I'VE TALKED TO LUCIFER, HE'S SENDING HELP. WE CAN'T LET THESE PEOPLE CONTINUE TO SEE WHO THEY REALLY ARE. WE HAVE TO KEEP THEM IN THE FLESH. WE HAVE TO TEMPT THEIR FLESH WITH EVERYTHING WE HAVE. THEIR FLESH IS THE KINK IN THE ARMOR. THAT'S HOW WE'LL WIN THIS BATTLE, IN THE FLESH," Kirkland said with a whimsical eye as he tapped a bony finger against his chin and glared skyward towards the rafters.

80

Exhausted. Hungry. Worried. Hopeful. My emotions were all over the place. My head throbbed much the way my thumb had done all those times I smashed it with a hammer. My gut was twisted in knots, as a nice juicy steak screamed my name.

After falling asleep with a spirit full of peace and hope, I now found myself bent under a burden of doubt as a crouching lion of fear crept through my mind. I struggled to steady my breath and glanced at the alarm clock which rested on the dresser at the foot of the bed.

In bold digital red numbers, it read, 3:27

I sat in bed with a straight spine. I glanced around the darkened room. The air was scarce as it felt like I just couldn't suck in enough for my lungs liken. I felt smothered by a thick cloud of blackness. Like I'd been covered in a blanket of darkness. Leering eyes seemed to penetrate my soul from the cover of shadows, as if I were a baby fawn crying for its mother in the lonely night.

I felt vulnerable and exposed. The room just didn't feel right. My eyes began to make out all sorts of faces and monsters with the shadows on the ceiling and walls.

All right...enough with the child's play.

I flicked on the lamp. The price of air returned to a reasonable price, as I didn't seem to struggle for it as much.

The lamp's light licked up the darkness as the monsters vanished like a roach caught in the act.

The room felt lighter and the weight of the ceiling lifted off my shoulders, giving my lungs a chance to expand.

That's when those words hit me like a line drive back to the pitcher.

You are the Light of the World.

The roomed filled with that gentle warm embrace I felt at the tribal grounds. Love and peace were so real and present, I literally felt I could reach out and touch them.

I was in the presence of my Creator. His light had entered my room and driven out the darkness. But it was there the whole time, just like my lamp. I just simply had to turn it on to see and feel it.

The light shines in the darkness, and the darkness can never extinguish it. You can't fight darkness in the dark, much like you can't fight flesh in the flesh. You must fight darkness with light, and you must fight flesh with Spirit. My Light is in you. My Spirit is in you. I am in you as you are in Me and we are one. No evil can stand against My light. No hate can stand against My love. Never fight darkness in the dark, fight it in the light.

Tears filled my eyes as my heart was washed and wrapped in that warm embrace once more. I rested my head onto the pillow, thanked the Creator for His love and goodness, then drifted out to the sea of slumber.

†††††††††††††††††††††

IN THE GLOOMY attic above, Frank lay on the plywood, curled into a fetal position, gripping his ears as he squirmed and shuddered.

Kirkland chewed a nail down to the quick, huffing his hot, sticky breath, filling the attic with that sulfurous stench. Ender, and Lucinda paced to and fro as they rubbed the scaly nape of their necks with bony fingers.

The smell of rotten eggs filled the air as a horde of black flies emerged from a darkened corner and lighted upon Frank like a blanket.

He was too distraught to shew them off.

"STAY STRONG. WE MUST CONTINUE TO FIGHT. HELP IS ON THE WAY. OUR BEST FLANK IS TEMPTATION. ANYTHING TO PULL THEM BACK TO THE FLESH. WE HAVE TO PRESENT OUR SHINIEST OBJECTS. KNOWING HUMAN WEAKNESSES LIKE I KNOW MY WAY BACK TO HELL, I THINK I HAVE JUST THE TRICK," Kirkland snickered.

Ender and Lucinda nodded in joyful agreement. They knew what they had to do, and they always enjoyed bringing out the best bait to catch the biggest fish.

81

It was just after ten Sunday morning when Rebecca was awoken to the creaking of the rusty hinges. Light scattered the darkness, causing her to squint as her pupils adjusted.

A pair of white Sketchers stepped down onto the rung of the ladder, then lowered closer to the bottom, revealing a pair of light denim blue jeans, and white AC/DC shirt neatly tucked and secured with a black belt. The door shut before the man's face was visible in the light.

The man toted a red Folger's coffee can.

He leapt from the last few rungs and crashed in the sand.

"Honey...I'm home!"

He struck a match. His face illuminated as he glared at her with a wrinkled grin.

He lit three candles and fanned the flame away.

"So...you miss me?"

Rebecca hung hopelessly from the shackles.

"Oh...are you sad?" He mocked with a tilt of his head and pucker of his bottom lip. He trudged closer but stopped before invading too much of her space. He drummed the coffee can, just before ripping the tape off and popping the lid. He reached in his fingers like drawing numbers from a hat.

"Ah hah," he retrieved his hand. In it? Another hand. Much smaller and decayed to the bone. He placed the hand in his pocket and reach in again. This time he pulled out a bigger hand that wore a silver watch on around the wrist. He held it at eye level and turned it over this way and that to get a good view.

"Nice. You getting hungry?"

Rebecca didn't answer, her eyes were glued to the hand.

"I ain't gonna get struck by lightning again if I get too close am I?"

Rebecca wagged her head.

"All right. Well...reckon you need to eat something anyhow," he said with a quiver in his voice and hand as reached and ripped the tape from her mouth before jolting backwards. Can tucked under his arm and hand gripped in his fingers.

She flinched.

"All right. That wasn't so bad," he said as he turned and angled toward the table where a small yellow bag rested. He sat the can and hand on the table, then managed to slide the watch off the hand and made haste to slip it on his own.

"Now...what cha want? I got beanie weanies...Vienna sausages...uh...oh, you still got the rest of your sub."

Rebecca took a second to gather herself before answering, "The sub's fine. And can I have my water, please?"

"You certainly may."

He scrambled through the bag as it crinkled with each stroke of his short stubby fingers.

"When's Frank coming back?"

"Eh...he should be back late tomorrow night I'd imagine. He's got a big job to take care of. You got a big family," he smirked.

Her heart sank, as a burning sensation started in her gut before crawling toward her face, flushing it hot and red.

"If he lays one finger upon my family," she said with a firm jaw, eyes trained to the back of Robert's head.

Feeling her glare, he turned and faced her.

Their eyes locked.

She didn't back down but kept the glare steady.

"Hmm..." he said as he bit the inside of his lip and narrowed his gaze, before turning his back to her.

It felt as if a tornado had just touched down within her as she began to tremble, her hands balling into fists, her fingers digging into her palms. He better be glad she was chained up.

Do you trust Me?

The soft voice permeating from deep within.

"Yes."

She answered after a deep breath.

Then release your anger and need for vengeance. It'll only cloud your vision of who are you and who I am. It'll do more harm than good for you to waste your energy on such thoughts. Remember who you are. You are my daughter. You are safe in my arms, just as nothing can harm me, neither can it harm you.

Robert stood from a safe distance and stretched the sub toward her mouth.

"Hey...you gonna take a bite or what?"

In a daze, she didn't respond.

He snapped his fingers in her face. She jolted and looked past the sub in her face to find his.

"Well..." he said in a sarcastic tone.

Rebecca cleared her throat and asked, "May I have some of my water first, please? My throats kind of dry."

He lowered the sub in a huff, twisted the cap on the bottle, then raised it to her lips, as if feeding a nursing kitten.

Three gulps later, she nodded.

He lowered the bottle and took swig for himself. The sight turned her gut. That'd be the last time she asked for water. At least from that bottle.

"Thank you, Robert."

He nodded, then raised the sub for a second try. Eyeing her with squinted brows.

82

Needless to say, the lamp still burned when I awoke Sunday morning. I had no desire of flicking that switch. I rested well in the warmth of its light.

I'd been up since eight, reading over Rebecca's letter. I scanned it over like a printer making a copy. It was burned in my minds eyes as I could see it without even looking at it.

I searched for every clue I could think of. I knew there had to be something. But what was it? Rebecca's as witty as they come, I knew she'd had to of given me something. But would I be smart enough to notice, even with it right under my nose and only inches from my degraded vision?

I breathed out a deep sigh and tossed the note on the bed. I took off my glasses to rub my eyes. I rested my free hand on my hip.

"Lord...if there's something here I'm overlooking, please help me see it."

After a few minutes of volleying ideas back and forth, a gentle knock sounded on the bedroom door.

"You up James?"

I cleared my throat.

"Yeah man, I'm up."

"Okay, just wanted to let you know I got some fruits and vegetables prepared when you're ready."

"Okay...thank you Lee. I'll be down in a sec."

"No problem. Take your time bud."

Having completed a full fast for the past two days, Lee and I agreed to continue with what's known as a Daniel fast. Its where you only eat fruits, vegetables, nuts, seeds, and the like. Avoiding all meat, bread, sugar and dairy. It's what they did in the book of Daniel, hence, the term Daniel fast.

My gut growled at the thought of any food source. For some reason I'd been craving pizza and tacos over the past two days, even though I rarely ever eat such food.

Anyhow, I headed for my closet to find something to wear downstairs other than my sleep clothes.

I slid open the glass mirror which concealed mine and Rebecca's walk-in closet. It squeaked as it glided along the track.

My phone vibrated in my pocket.

I snaked my thumb along the screen to unlock it.

As soon as the screen saver of my family faded away, a lewd pop up of some random porn site filled my screen. I pulled my head away. What the heck? I squinted my brows and hurried to exit out of it. Sounds began to moan out of the speakers. What in the world? Just as I was able to click it away, I could have sworn I heard a women's voice call my name. Phone's got have a dang virus or something. I wagged my head and sighed.

Pop! Creeeaakkk!

I jerked my head skyward. There's that pop again. It came from the attic. I scrunched my eyes and rubbed my chin. I snatched a shirt off its hanger, hurried and threw it on along with a pair of khaki pants. Curiosity got the best of me, before I knew it, I found myself half way up the stairs leading to the attic. Flashlight and key in hand.

††††††††††††††††††††††††

HEARING THE CREAKS and squeaks of the stairs, Frank's heart pummeled to the plywood. His mind raced like a computer's hard drive as a trojan horse attempts introduce itself. Jittery and annoyed, the sound of jingling keys only made things worse. He retrieved his revolver and rushed to gather the empty Vienna sausage cans along with the grocery bag and empty meat package. The keys helped block the sound. Frank faded into a gloomy corner, like a Gecko in the jungle. The darkness welcomed him.

††††††††††††††††††††††

I FUMBLED THROUGH the keys. Having not come up here much over the last few years, it took me a second to find the right one. But I did. I twisted the knob and pressed on through. The room was dark and musty smelling, even had a faint whiff of rotten eggs. Probably a dang rat or squirrel done got up here and died.

I felt along the wall for the switch. Found it and flicked it, but nothing happened. After giving it a few tries, I concluded the bulb must've burnt out. I sighed then crossed my arms and kept them tight to my chest, wishing now I'd brought a jacket or something. Light trickled in from the window across the room giving off a small fraction of heat. But it sure wasn't enough.

I clicked on my pocket-sized light and shone it around, doing a quick sweep of the room, licking up each shadow like a shop vac. If only it'd lick up the stench and chill.

I paced around, searching for anything out of the ordinary. Which to tell you the truth, it'd have to be obvious, because it's been a few years since I was last up here. Never did like climbing stairs in a wheelchair.

††††††††††††††††††††††

ONLY A FEW feet away, Frank crouched in the cover of darkness, surrounded by boxes. Mostly full of Christmas decorations. This was the closest they'd been from each other since Frank pulled the trigger, sending the bullet into James' skull. Which turned out to be both a blessing and a curse.

Frank aimed the barrel around a box and leered with one eye, locking on the back James' head.

James swept his light to and fro about the attic.

Frank tightened his grip, his palm greased with sweat.

He could take him now and be done with it or he could wait till they were all together and take them out like shooting fish in a barrel. Either way, it'd be nothing but pure enjoyment. A dose of ecstasy. A rush of euphoria. He eaten his meat. He was strong. He was ready...and so was Mother.

Stick with the plan or deviate and take advantage of the opportunity in front of him?

Kirkland looked on with wonder as he gazed upon Frank with a wide grin. Ender glared with his piercing red eyes as large as baseball's, rubbing and rolling his hands together. Lucinda growled and mumbled like a rabid wild animal, teeth bared, lips raised tight against the gums. She whispered in her native language.

††††††††††††††††††††††

IT FELT AS if the room had grown blacker. Like my light was being smothered by a thick shadow or something. The air felt heavy. I could feel the darkness weighing on my shoulders, those invisible eyes were watching me again, peering behind every shadow. My heart felt like someone had it in a vice grip and with each passing second, it seemed to cinch tighter...and tighter...tighter...and tighter.

I slammed my eye lids, my breath now a pant.

"Father...fill this room with your presence. Remind me who I am. You are the Light of the World and you live within me. I am of that same Light and no darkness can overcome it. You are in me just as I am in you. We are one. Father...fill this room with Your Light."

††††††††††††††††††††

FRANK GRIMACED as did the trio next to him. Kirkland gritted his canine like teeth, mouthing curses as he covered his ears. His skin crawled with each word from James' lips, causing a severe burning sensation to explore every inch of his scaly flesh. He twisted and squirmed in effort to find comfort for his burning skin, but there was none.

Lucinda wailed like a banshee as her skin seemed to melt from the bone. She scratched and clawed her shoulders as she now sat in the floor, arms crossed, rocking while uttering blasphemy in between each screech and wail.

Ender protruded his large set of wings, as the pain had become too much, he hurried and leaped through the window, vanishing higher into the clouds with each thunderous flap.

Frank squinted his eyes and bit his bottom lip. Nose and brows snarled, he placed his finger on the trigger and steadied his aim once more.

††††††††††††††††††††

AS MY EYES were shut in earnest prayer, I could feel the atmosphere changing. That warm embrace, I'd felt the night before was back. Suddenly the red from the back of my eye lids, turned to a faint yellow.

"James? What are you doing up here?"

I opened my eyes, the room was full of radiant light. It was Lee. So, the bulb did work.

I could breathe again. The Light had entered, God was here.

83

Sunday morning and afternoon came and went without any new leads or insight. I talked to Mishoe and Leslie, but neither could tell me anymore than I already knew. With Jason, Lauren, and Connor coming home tomorrow, I spent a good portion of the day tidying things up. Funny how messy things can get when Rebecca isn't here. I didn't want the kids seeing the place like that, so along with Lee's help, we had it looking like it did the day of the Pau Wau.

We made it up to the hospital afterwards. We've been here visiting since about five. Jason and Lauren were doing good considering how bad the accident was. After having spent a little over an hour and a half with Lauren, just as we did with Jason. I needed to go see Connor, Kelly, and Lilly. I hugged and kissed Lauren, wrapping her in my arms, not wanting to let go.

"You'll be home in the morning. You'll get to sleep in your own bed," I told her with a smile and misty eyes as I leaned and kissed her forehead.

"Love you daddy."

"Love you too baby girl."

We left the room to find Lily. She was on the floor above us as was Connor and Kelly.

We spoke to Lily's doctor, who told us she was resting and to be sure not to wake her. He kept stressing how vital her rest was for a speedy recovery. Lee, stayed in the hallway, as I made my way into her room, tiptoeing across the tile.

The sight of her hooked up to all the machines and IV's broke my heart. I'd do anything to trade places with her. She lied peacefully on her back, her beautiful brown hair with a tint of blonde resting along her shoulders. She was a spitting image of her mother, beauty, heart, smarts and all.

I rested my hand atop hers and wept.

No matter how many times we come in here, I will never get used to seeing my kids like this. And for the third time this week, here I was in a hospital room with one of my babies...broken.

I gathered myself and managed to say a prayer over her before giving her a soft kiss.

I walked out and shut the door behind me, wiping my eyes as I did so.

Lee comforted me as we made our way to Kelly's room where I went through a similar routine. She was sleeping as well, so I didn't stay long, just enough to pray over her and tell her I loved her.

Now it was Connor's turn.

We paced down the long corridor of white wall's with blue trim, white tiles with blue and black specks. Passing a few nurses in their scrubs rolling around machines and metal IV racks as they toted them from one room to another. Voices echoing over the intercom. The black window at the end of the hall, reminding you of the darkness outside.

"Here it is." Said Lee.

Room 342 C. Randolph

"I'll just stay out here like I've been doing."

"You can come in if you like."

"You sure?"

"Of course."

I gave a soft knock before opening the door.

He sat straight up, arms stretched tight and shouted, "Daddy! Daddy! Daddy!"

If he wasn't constrained to his bed, he would've run and leapt into my arms.

"Hey boy. What you doing?" I said with a chuckle as I rushed over and gathered him in my arms.

"Look-look...look what I did," he said as he pointed to the wall at the foot of his bed. I followed his gaze to a bunch of drawings he'd made of our family. Just like he'd done countless times at home, but these all included Indians wearing their head dress with painted faces.

"Wow, those are good, buddy."

"This one me?" Lee asked with a grin as he tapped the paper with the back of a knuckle.

Connor smiled and bobbed his head up and down more times than I could've counted.

"Oh...and look at this one," he said as he hurried and reached under his pillow.

He pulled out a piece of paper he'd folded over. Snapped it open and held it out, hands on each end. Right hand still wrapped in a cast to aid the broken wrist.

It was two wolves, one black, the other a light tan, with a large man dressed in black standing between them.

You could've heard a pen drop. Neither Lee nor I said anything for what seemed like the same amount of time my gut last remembered digesting a nice juicy steak.

We were speechless.

"I dreamed it last night. So, I thought I'd draw it."

"What do you mean? What did you dream?"

"I dreamed I woke up in a huge field," Connor said as he demonstrated with outstretched arms.

"And there were these two wolves, one black, one white standing on each side of the field. Then there were hundreds of people walking out towards the center in between the two wolves. They each had some type of food, some carried what looked like steaks, but others had some kind of apple or fruit looking thing. They'd walk up and stand between the wolves, look to each one then toss the food to either the black or white wolf. The meat went to the black wolf and he gobbled it up like he was starving, and the fruit went to the white wolf. But he didn't just gobble it up like the other wolf, he'd eat a little bit and then save some too. He was different. I liked him. The wolves got bigger after eating what the people threw them. Oh, and after each person fed the wolf, they'd go and stand next to it. All those that stood with the black wolf, just weren't happy, it was like they knew something bad was about to happen. But those that fed the white wolf, they were happy and smiling, hugging each other, laughing. And they seemed stronger and bigger than those people with the black wolf. That's all I really remember though."

I turned to Lee who stood with his left hand tucked under his right elbow, with his chin resting in his right hand.

"What do you make of that?" I asked.

"Sounds like the tale of two wolves to me. The black wolf is the flesh and the white wolf is the Spirit. If you sow to flesh, you'll reap corruption, pain, regret and sorrow, but if you sow to the Spirit...love, joy, peace, strength and life everlasting. Seems to me, that's the Creator's way of telling us were doing the right thing."

"Hey, can we get a big white dog like that?" Connor asked as he pointed to the paper, which I now held in my hands. Blurry, but not too much so that I couldn't make it out.

"Sure kid, when the time's right, we'll get you one just like it. I think it'd be good for all of us."

††††††††††††††††††††††

THE FOLLOWING DAY around noon, as myself and Lee munched on some apples, I got a call from David.

"Hey David."

"Hey James, how you doing?"

"I'm doing good, just heading over to get the kids from the hospital."

"Awesome...I hear ya. I bet you're all excited."

"Oh yeah...we can't wait."

"Are the kids going to be able to come with you tonight?"

"No, they want be able to. Lee's sister-in-law is going to stay with them, and we have an officer that'll keep an eye on the place while we're gone. Shouldn't be too long of a meeting should it?"

"Nah-nah, we should be done by eight. We'll keep it short, so you can get home to your kids. Is Lee's folks still coming?"

"Okay great. Oh yeah, as far as I know."

"Sounds great. Well...I guess I'll see you all around six-thirty."

"Great. Thanks David. See you tonight."

I hung up. The light vanished as Lee entered the parking deck in search of a spot.

After making two complete circles, he found an empty space. About an hour later, we found ourselves back at his truck, only this time with a few guests. Lauren rode shotgun, as me, Jason and Connor rode in the back.

Lee turned the ignition key, the engine roared. Within minutes we were headed home, needing only to stop and fill what seemed like a dozen prescriptions for their pain meds at the Walgreens in Shallotte.

"I bet y'all are ready for some good tasting food aren't ya?"

Connor perked up and barked out Mickey D's.

"Yeah...if you only knew," Jason said with raised eye lids and a smile, wagging his head.

Oh, I knew all right.

††††††††††††††††††††

NO SOONER THAN we'd made it through the front door, Jason, Lauren, and Connor all crashed to the couch as gravity sucked them to it like a vacuum. Lauren still wore a boot for her recovering ankle and a cast for her arm.

"Wake me up when September ends," Lauren said as she covered her forehead with her good arm.

"Yeah same here," I said as I sat on the ottoman in front of them.

"So, where's mom? Have they heard anything?" asked Jason, his question changing the mood quicker than a snapped finger.

I hesitated before answering.

"Yeah, where's mom?" asked Connor.

Lauren moved her arm and fixed her eyes on me, accompanying Jason's and Connor's and Lee's as well as he stood next to me.

"Well...we're getting closer. I do have a letter she sent us," I said as I dug it out my wallet and unfolded it to show the kids. Jason read it aloud for Connor, having not yet learned to read or write in cursive.

Their brows furrowed as their faces grew pale.

"Dad, how are they going to find her before tomorrow night?" Jason asked with a cracked voice and part whisper as tears leaked from his eyes. Lauren fell into her brother's side to hide her face of tears. He placed his arm around her. Connor stricken with emotion leaned on Lauren and sniffled.

I moved in to give a group hug. Squeezing tight and not wanting to let go.

"We are going to find your Mother. God is with us and with His help, we're going to bring her home."

I heard a sniffle behind me, I looked over my shoulder, it was Lee wiping tears.

"Get over here Lee," I said with a quick wave as I threw my arm around him.

Lord, help us find Rebecca. These kids need their mama and I need my wife. Father, please bring her home.

††††††††††††††††††††††

THE AFTERNOON PASSED quicker than I'd hoped. I spent from the time we got home until now, about a quarter till five, watching movies and shows with the kids. Lee spent a lot of that time talking on the phone with his Uncle and Brother.

Right in the middle of the part where the kids are working all their contraptions in efforts to get the ball back from the beast in the movie *The Sandlot*, the doorbell rang.

"Must be her," I said as I forced myself off the couch.

Just as I was heading for the door, Lee came from the den.

"I guess that's Starla?" said Lee.

I nodded and opened the door to reveal a small middle-aged Indian lady with beautiful jet-black hair, sharp cheek bones along with that signature reddish brown complexion.

"Hi I'm Starla. You must be James," she said with kind eyes and a gentle smile.

"Why yes, I am, nice to meet you. Come on in."

"Hey Starla. Thanks for doing this," said Lee as he gave her a quick hug once she stepped in.

"Of course, Lee, glad I can help."

"Well kids this is Starla...she's going to stay here with you for the evening like we talked about on the way home."

They each shook her hand and introduced themselves, as Starla did the same.

"Well make yourself at home. Can I get you something to drink or anything?"

"Oh no-no, I'm fine thank you."

"Okay, well if you need anything just ask them or Lee. I'm going to go shower and get dressed right quick. Thank you again for helping out."

"Oh, you're welcome," she said as she took a seat on the end of the couch.

"Oh, and officer Humphry will be on patrol outside should you need anything."

"Okay. Great, that's good to know."

"All right, well like I said just make yourself at home." I said as I turned and headed for the bedroom.

††††††††††††††††††††††

ALL THE LAUGHTER and commotion below had Frank rocking once again. He sat on his haunches, arms crossed above his knees, rubbing his shoulders as he hissed and mumbled through clinched teeth. Top lip and nose met in snarls as if they were tapping in Morse code. His bottom lip twitched in all directions. his head jerked from side to side like a dog ripping into his opponents' neck.

Sweat melted off his forehead as it trickled down his flushed face.

"All sin begins within and there is no cure without atonement. A sacrifice must now be made to ever ease the pain," those words repeated in his mind like a malfunctioned Ferris wheel that just wouldn't end its revolutions.

His eyes shook beneath their lids, pressing against the flesh. His head jerked skyward, his mouth hung wide, his arms outstretched. A horde of locusts emitted from within, filling the room like floating dust.

His eye lids flashed open exposing two black pupils like magic eight balls, except without the white circle. These were solid black, stripped of color, just a deep void and full of darkness.

He lowered his gaze, the corners of his mouth rising like a growing wave in the Pacific.

He scanned the attic and rocked his head at the room full of black, winged, lizard like creatures. They seemed to take the place of air itself. He'd never seen this many at one time. It was a legion of darkness and they were many.

84

After taking a relaxing shower, I put on some appealing clothes, then knelt at our bedside and prayed.

I finished and rose to my feet before heading to the living room. I stole a glance at my watch as I did so. It was now a quarter to six. It was time to get going.

I hugged and kissed the kid's goodbye and thanked Starla once more. Just as me and Lee were stepping onto the porch and taking the first few steps down, Connor stuck his head out the door and called for me.

"Hey. Remember . . . those that fed the white wolf were bigger and stronger than those that didn't," he grinned then tucked back inside.

"Love you dad," his voice coming from within.

I stood along the railing leading to our driveway, eyes wondering, brows scrunched. I looked at Lee, he wore a similar expression.

"Thanks. Love you too, son."

We waved at Starla and headed for Lee's truck.

†††††††††††††††††††††††

CROSSING THE BRIDGE over the ICW the sky was cloudless as it wore a breathtaking purple, pink, and orange glow above the setting Sun. The water barely had a ripple as it reflected the sky's glory like a mirror.

A pearl white Sail boat drifted aimlessly down the channel, as a well-fed Pelican bounded heavenward with each gentle flap. It would have made for a nice postcard.

We descended to land and made it to the red light, where we took a left turn beside the gas station. An abandoned Wings beach store to our right and a Walgreens and Food Lion at our 2 o'clock. Less than a mile down the road, we passed the carwash where they found the Idyllwild's explorer.

Just down the road a little way, we made a left turn onto Seashore, before finally turning onto Bellamy. We pulled into David and Annie's driveway. We were the only vehicle there besides the Hoffman's.

We climbed the wooden stairs and gave the door a soft knock. Feet thudded through the house, edging closer. Tires rolled over pebble and crushed shells behind us. We both gave it our attention. The tires belonged to a Black Jeep Grand Cherokee, one of the newer ones, must've been about a 09 or 10.

"That's Clennon and Uncle Wes there," said Lee just before the front door opened where David stood with an inviting smile next to his wife Annie.

They welcomed us all in, offering tea and coffee. We kindly accepted and settled into their comfy living room. Tan, cloth couches that felt like you were sitting on clouds. An elegant fireplace with a cozy fire licking skyward behind the pane glass. Book shelves overflowing with both hard copies and paperbacks on either side of the television set mounted to the wall.

Lee introduced his Uncle and Brother to David and Annie. We chatted for a good twenty minutes or so, just carrying on small talk.

"Well...you want to get started with the reason we're all here?" David asked as he glanced at each of us with kind eyes.

"Sure. Let's get started," I answered.

We formed a circle, reached for the hand of the person next to us and began to pray.

†††††††††††††††††††††††

NATHANIEL AND MATEO along with over two dozen others, clothed in glowing white, arms the size of pythons, wearing iron swords taller than the average man, stood in the living room, looking on at James, the McGaha's and Hoffman's as they prayed.

The glowing men grew stronger with each syllable uttered. It was like finding a fresh source of water in a dry and weary land. They breathed deep, soaking in strength for the battle that lied ahead.

†††††††††††††††††††††††

IT WASN'T LONG after we began praying, that the same feeling I got during the smudging ceremony, and the other night when I awoke in the thick darkness and flicked the lamp on, had returned. The warm embrace, like that of a loving mother or father, was here. I'm safe, I'm cared for, I'm loved, and I can rest knowing that just as a child can rest in the arms of their mother and father, I can rest and trust that my Father will take care of what concerns me.

As this presence grew thicker and more tangible, it was as if the Great Creator Himself had entered through that front door and plopped onto the couch next to us. We continued in earnest prayer as neither of us wanted to hinder what was taking place. We could sense that something was happening in the unseen world.

After a few minutes, Uncle Wes spoke up and led us in prayer much like he did at the ceremony. His words carry so much weight and truth with them, you can literally feel them resonate within your heart.

We must've continued like this for half an hour. It was refreshing and something we all needed.

We spent the rest of our time talking about Rebecca and the kids, as I showed them the letter she'd written. We all looked it over, feeling as if there was an underlying message she tried to convey. They passed it around as they offered me encouragement and hope.

When I finally got it back and folded it in neat creases, I tucked it into my coat pocket and I stole a glance to my watch, it was a quarter to eight.

"James...if there's something there she wants you to know...you will find it. Just trust the Great Spirit to reveal it to you," said Wes as he gave me a reassuring pat on the knee.

"Thank you," I said with a nod.

I dried my eyes and sniffled.

"Well...I hate it, but I guess we better get going, so I can get back to the kids," I said after a puffed cheek sigh. I rose to my feet and hugged and thank them all for the support.

"Stay strong James...you're doing the right thing and good things will happen," David said as he gave me a slap on the back with his left as I shook his right.

We said our goodbyes as me, Lee, Wes, and Clennon headed for the door.

My mind's eye scanning the letter. What am I missing? There has to be something she's trying to tell me.

We hugged and told Wes and Clennon bye before they left in the Cherokee as Lee and I climbed into his black Z71.

I fastened my seat belt as Lee turned the engine over. Still scanning the letter word for word, imagining Rebecca herself reading it to me.

We backed out and made our way to Seashore Road.

"Lee...there has to be something we're missing with this letter. I just can't get it off my mind."

His turn signal clicked as he focused his attention out the driver side window, before making a right turn.

He cleared his throat and said, "So, you think it's odd the way she wrote it?"

"Yeah, I mean she's a science teacher, she doesn't write like that. I don't know, just the way she structured her sentences and stuff, just doesn't feel right."

As we were passing the Citgo gas station on our left, approaching the stop sign, it hit me.

Look at the first letter of each sentence.

My heart quickened as my breath shortened.

I grabbed the letter from my pocket and scrambled to turn the interior light on.

"You have a pen and piece of paper? Something to write with?"

Sensing my eagerness, Lee looked on with curious eyes and said, "Yeah-yeah, check the glove box. I have the manual book in there and there's a pen and piece of paper I keep track of oil changes and stuff with. What you thinking?"

"Hold on, I don't want to lose my train of thought."

I unzipped the black book and snatched the pen and tore out a piece of blank paper. I bit off the end cap, dug my glasses out and prepared myself to decipher the message as if I was cracking a bank vault. At least my heart felt that way.

So...S. I jotted down S.

And...A.

Never...N

Don't...D

But...B

Until...U

Nothing...N
Know...K
Everything...E
Right...R
A tornado of emotion ripped through my gut. I continued scribbling. My hand now trembling as I could barely read my own writing.
Wait...W
And...A
Very...V
Everything...E
Say...S
Can't...C
Home...H
I...I
May...M
Even...E
S.A.N.D B.U.N.K.E.R W.A.V.E.S C.H.I.M.E
"What? What is it?"
Having to catch my breath, I had Lee pull over so he could read what I'd just wrote.
He bumped his turn signal up, we eased into the Dollar General parking lot.
I passed him my decoded message.
His eyes widened.
"But where?"
"Let's start here."
"Tonight?"
I nodded.
"Tonight."

85

We started the search on the West end not too far from our house. It was about ten after eight, I called Starla and told her we'd be home in an hour or so and I thanked her once again.

Lee and I conquered the steps of the last public beach access on this end. The waves roared as they crashed against the slope. The wind ripped at our face. our feet shifted in the loose sand.

Flashlights in hand, we angled south towards the inlet, while walking just on the ocean side of the dunes. Ears trained for any hint of chime from a place that looked to hold a bunker of some sorts.

A flip flop here, a pair of sunglasses there, a ghost crab scurrying to its hole and the remnants of a sand castle.

The sand pulled at my feet and legs like a corpse from the grave. My muscles were burning and on the verge of cramping. We had to stop a few times so I could catch my breath and allow my head to clear. I lost my balance a few times and if it hadn't of been for Lee's help, I'd probably have done a face plant. He grabbed my arm and steadied me as we continued to scroll down the beach, listening and searching for Rebecca's confines.

It was eerie, being out here in the dark, thinking there could be a bunker hidden beneath the sand, among so many houses and beach goers. It felt like those hidden eyes from my bedroom and attic were strategically disguised behind the mask of shadows and cover of darkness.

After another ten-minutes of trudging through the soft sand, we passed the last house and made it to the inlet. We shined our lights to the right where the dunes flattened out a bit, wearing sea oats, seashore elder, and Indian blankets with pride. All of which I'd learned from Rebecca.

I crossed over a small dune and scanned the area for anything peculiar. Nothing.

Feeling a bit disappointed, I still had hope, because we still had the East end to check.

†††††††††††††††††††††††

ABOUT HALFWAY through Harry and the Henderson's, Starla turned to ask Jason and Lauren about finding their restroom. But they were out cold. Connor as well.

She smiled with a brief giggle and rose from the couch to find the bathroom. After searching down the hall for a bit, she found it and entered.

Moments later she was making her way back to the living room. She stopped in her tracks, adjacent to one of the darkened bedrooms. Connor was missing. As she went take a step forward, her foot never landed as a large hand dressed in a white cloth, pressed firm against her face.

Within seconds she was out.

†††††††††††††††††††††††

AFTER MAKING THE drive from one side of the Island to the other in a little less than ten minutes, we exited the truck and headed for the opening leading out to the beach.

To our right stood a big yellow house with the words *Amazing Grace* painted on the front.

We came to the trail leading to the ocean and a wooden board with plastic signs, warned of the rip currents and gave instructions as to what to do if caught in one. Relax and don't fight against but rather swim parallel to shore. Neither against it nor with it, but in a direction you'd likely not think of in the heat of the moment.

We swept our lights side to side, our feet wobbled into the loose sand once again. This time we made a left and began the trek to the far East end.

Eyes and ears attentive with every passing breeze, listening for that chime. Waves crashed once more, spreading their foam landward as they played tag with the tide line.

I noticed foot prints here and there, some big, some small. I couldn't help but wonder if some of the smaller ones where Rebecca's. And I also couldn't erase the thought that maybe a few of the big ones belonged to Ethan. Then I caught sight of deer tracks...but then I had a strange and daunting thought cross my mind...was it the devil's hooves?

Then I noticed a cluster of Lightning Welk eggs—I only knew because of Rebecca's science background—they could easily pass for the skeleton of a snake...or the spine of a human. Stop it James.

I stopped and took a deep breath.

"You all right?"

I nodded.

We had a lot more ground to cover on this end, because the big yellow house was the last one for the next half mile or so. So, we made our way over the small set of dunes and focused our attention at the end of our lights halo. Ears picking up the whistling of a passing breeze as it came and went like the different verses of a song between the chorus. Each verse the breeze presented had a different howl and tone.

The Sun was fading and only offered a slight glimmer as it peaked just above the horizon like a child looking over a table. A few gulls stood by the water's edge, waiting for feeding time. They knew just as any fisherman, when the tide goes out it leaves behind small pools of baitfish, which make for an easy meal for a waiting gull. They called to one another to announce the nearing of supper.

In about fifteen minutes, we'd covered half of the area. Sand had wedged itself in my shoe, rubbing against my flesh with pleasure. I stopped, leaned upon Lee as I had to empty the sole of my irritating guest.

"You think he went back to Georgetown?" Lee asked.

I sighed and grunted as I busied myself with squishing my shoe back on.

"I don't know man...he might have, but it'd sure be a heck of a drive back and forth. I mean you saw last night, that's at least a two-hour drive. Let's finish this end and if we don't find anything, I'll call Ray and see what he says about the code."

As I was crouched down tying my laces, a quick rustle in the brush and sand sounded off to the left of us.

Lee jerked his light.

I stood, a bit wobbly, but gathered myself enough to stand on my own. I shined my light as well.

There it was again, this time more so in front of us. It thrashed about as we both snapped our lights straight ahead.

Waaaahhhh—Waaaaahhhhhhh—Waaahhhhhh

The hair on my neck straightened at what sounded like a baby crying for its mother. I was speechless, my feet seemingly cemented in the sand.

It sounded like it moving to our right, attempting to flank us.

"What the heck is that?" I forced out through a tight throat.

"It's a fox. He won't bother us, he's just curious," Lee said with a firm, unwavering assurance.

"C'mon...just ignore it, he'll leave us alone."

Lee began the trek toward the East end, scanning his light, as I did the same.

Waaahhhhh—Waaaaahhhhhhh—Waaaaahhhhhhh

There it was again. That spine-tingling wail of a baby from the cover of darkness. I guess this was the chorus to the wind song. This time it was a good distance behind us and ebbing. He was moving on just like Lee said.

As we approached a sharp bend, I could make out the dark silhouette of the Kindred Spirits mailbox. It'd been here ever since me and Rebecca bought our house. We've even left a few notes in it a time or two over the years, like so many others.

Just beyond the mailbox, the topography went from sandy dunes and shrubbery to a more wooded vegetation, with sea oaks and salt pines.

The wind was dead and so was the fox's chorus.

The crash of the waves was now behind me as the sound of rushing water emitted to my right as the ocean made haste to drain the inlet of its tide.

We passed the mailbox and continued around the bend, the halo of our lights beaming in the sand in search of any prints. Disturbed Ghost Crabs scurried about as the light stumbled upon them. Much to the liking of a horde of roaches scattering at the flick of a kitchen light.

I switched the light to my left hand and dried the palm of my right onto my pants leg. I felt swallowed by a cloak of darkness. It was as if a canopy of black had fell from the moonless night and stopped just above my shoulders. I felt smothered. My breathing became labored as my wind pipes seemed to tighten.

"Lee...stop...do you feel that?"

He stood at my 10 o'clock maybe three yards away. His back to me, he angled his chin toward me, peeking over his shoulder and said, "Yeah...the air got heavy didn't it?"

"Yeah"

I could feel those invisible eyes leering at me once again, as they crouched beyond the shadows, waiting to pounce upon a helpless gazelle.

"C'mon...let's check this bend then get out of here," I said as I strode next to Lee.

"Yeah...all right."

As the bend straightened, our lights landed upon a small Jon boat beached on shore. Rocking gently with the ripple and rhythm of the water.

Puzzled. We edger closer.

A tight white rope was tied to a cleat on the front. We followed it with our lights, it led to a tree in the thicket. Just under the rope was a pair of tracks leading to the tree.

Lee and I stood motionless as we pondered the enigma.

Lee rubbed the back of his neck and took turns looking to the wood line and Jon boat.

"Think we ought to call Mishoe?" he asked.

"I don't kn—"

Before I could finish my sentence, the wind decided to play us another song. This one included a chime. Our lights jolted toward its origin. It clanked and rattled just beyond the first layer of woods. We scanned our lights from the safe distance of shore.

"There...look!" said Lee with a raised voice as if he'd just struck oil.

I added my light to his. A small trail cut into the thick brush, like a hole hollowed out of rock leading to a den. But it was the dancing sea shells that caught Lee's eye. They appeared to be hundreds of shells tied to bony branches, hanging freely and singing in harmony as each breeze strummed the strings.

We now had three out of four checked off the list. The only question now, where's the bunker and where's Rebecca?

I took a step forward, my blood neutral, yet to decide to burn or chill. Half of me wanted to tear this guy's head off, while the other half was afraid that's what he'd do to mine.

I felt Lee grasp my arm in protest.

I turned,

"Lee...I've got to—"

"Why hello James," a deep guttural voice pierced the air. Emitting behind me from the wood line.

I didn't have to turn. I knew it was him by the expression on Lee's face.

"Welcome to the Devil's Den."

86

His voice stung my heart like a hornet. My gut quaked as my heart rushed to pump blood through my veins fast enough to keep my brain functioning. Gooseflesh rifled over my entire body.

I looked into Lee's eyes, at first, I sensed fear, but now they were steadying with courage as he furrowed his brows and angled his gaze. He swallowed hard and glared ahead.

I swiveled in the sand. My heart sank at the sight before me.

There he stood, looking nothing like the sketch in the papers, cradling Connor like a baby.

My throat tight, through a firm jaw, I forced out the words, "Ethan...you put my son down right now! Or I'm gonna—"

"Gonna what? Huh...what're you gonna do?" he barked back through clinched teeth. His eyes piercing through my soul.

He snickered and adjusted Connor, shifting him upward.

"Connor! Connor!" I yelled.

No response.

"Oh, he won't wake for a few hours. Chloroform's pretty strong," he chuckled as he whispered and smooth-talked Connor, rubbing the back of his hand down his forehead and bridge of the nose.

"Where's Rebecca!?" I demanded.

In a slow sweeping motion, he raised his eyes to meet mine.

"Oh, she's in the den. Would you like to see?" he said as pointed toward to hollow black trail beyond the dancing shells.

"And I have a gift for you. Payment for what you did the other night."

He dug in his pocket.

Me and Lee braced ourselves.

"Ahh...lookey here," he said as he held what looked like a small cross up to his eyes. He twisted and twirled between his fingers, then swung his arm back and tossed to the sand in front of me.

I squinted, doing my best to keep Ethan in the top of my vision.

I squatted on my calves, one hand gripping my cane, the reaching out for the cross.

Just as I was about to grasp it...my heart knocked against my ribs. It was two fingers lapped over one another. I bolted to my feet and stumbled backwards.

"Why it's just an old friend of yours."

I swallowed hard and steadies myself. My breath coming in huffs, my blood boiling.

"You remember Jerry, don't you?" he said in such a careless tone, if I had brought my *9mm* I would shot him right him then.

"I figured you'd appreciate it...I mean the least you could say is...thank you," he smirked. His face the face of satan.

The second I flinched my knee toward him, he bolted through the thicket, toting Connor under his armpit. He laughed as he fled, his voice emitting from the woods like an archeologist in a dark cave. I knew I would be entering my tomb if I pursued him, but if it meant saving my family, I didn't have to give it a second thought.

I took two quick steps and forgetting my cane and predicament, I fell flat on my face. Lee grabbed my arm and pulled me to my feet. With Lee's help we hobbled into the dark, passing through the string of shells like entering a gypsy's lair.

Branches and twigs crunched just ahead, he still mocked us with his laughter. But it began to fade. About twenty feet into the woods we stopped to listen for him as it got eerily quiet.

We scanned our surroundings. But there was nothing.

"James..." his voice crackled behind us.

We both yanked around.

"...why didn't you stand up for me? How could you have let him take me?" he said with a tight jaw and sniffle.

I shined my light at his chest. He stood holding Connor in his right arm while wiping his forehead with the back of his left hand which gripped a small revolver.

"Ethan...what are you talking about?"

He whimpered, "Don't call me that...my name's Frank!"

He wiped his nose and said, "You failed me James. You allowed him to take me, you allowed him to make me what I am. It's all your fault. All of this blood is on your hands James. Your hands!"

"Frank...relax. Let's talk this out," said Lee.

"I'm not talking to you Mr. Redman!"

Lee narrowed his gaze, his fist balling at his sides.

"Frank...listen, I honestly don't know what you're talking about."

He thrust his gun towards me and shook it like the accusing finger of a fire and brimstone preacher.

"Yes, you do...you remember. You've just denied it all these years and tucked it away somewhere deep in that worthless brain of yours. Think about it, James...you think I just showed up at the mill for no reason? I'd been following you. I knew everything about you and Rebecca."

I squinted my eyes, attempting to follow where he was leading.

"I've kept a watch on you ever since that day on the trail to the playground. When George Thompson stepped out of the woods and took me. I was five years old James...you were fourteen and you did nothing!"

I blinked. It was like everything had entered slow motion. My mind fogged, my gut knotted.

His words were like stirring up a hornet's nest as suddenly flashes of scenes and words that I'd never heard before buzz about my mind as if I were watching a movie.

Lee turned and asked me something, but his words were only white noise compared to the voice of that man dressed in black.

Lee grabbed my arm and gave me a good shake.

"James...James...hey!"

I blinked and swallowed a lump in my throat to loosen my airway.

"He's right. I did nothing. I froze."

My brother's screams echoed through my mind as I could see him being carried away through the woods.

"Yeah...you did nothing! Nothing! It's because of you I've become what I am. It's because of you I've murdered all these people to ease Mother's pain. You're just as guilty as I am. Now it's time for your atonement."

Frank steadied the barrel at my face.

I froze.

Heyyyyyyy...heyyyyyyyyyyyy...help!
Came a faint voice below me. Rebecca!

Before I could turn, the sound of a squeaky door hinge cut through the stillness. I caught glimpse of Lee being cut to the ground, as two hands wrapped around his ankles, and yanked him in what looked like a trap door spiders lair.

Before I could reach for him, the metal door, which was covered in sand and branches, slammed shut.

Pow!

I heard the chunk of lead whizz by my head.

I made a quick bolt for the thick woods only feet away.

Pow!

Pain ripped through my shoulder just as I entered the canopy of woods, stumbling my way through. A hard thump in the sand followed pounding foot falls. I knew what the thump was. He'd just threw Connor in the sand and now he was after me like a crazed grizzly. Grunts and growls emitted beneath me. Lee sounded as if he was fighting for his life. Rebecca screamed.

Pow! Pow! Pow!

The three quick shots rang out from under me, followed by silence. My heart was heavy as it felt it was riding in my intestines, bobbing up and down as I forced myself deeper into the thicket.

My shoulder begged for attention as it felt like fire should've been emitting from it. I checked it with my fingers and they instantly stained red.

A soft whistle resonated behind me as it sounded like he'd slowed his pace. No doubt knowing these woods and dunes like he knows the taste of his favorite meal. He had me right where he wanted me. Right in the Devil's Den.

"Oh, Jimmy bouy, come out, come out where ever you are," he called with a mocking British accent.

I crouched and hid behind a bush. I grabbed one of the many empty beer bottles sprawled about the land...and waited.

He continued his whistle, soft and hypnotizing.

The tune reminded me of the early 80's, I recognized it as a song by The Police. It was what he left in the notes. Every breath you take. Dear God...help me!

Twigs crunched as he edged closer. I tightened the grip on the bottle and waited for my chance.

His silhouette broke the darkness. A dark shadow on a black canvas. He stood there whistling as if knowing he was close.

I knelt motionless. My head swimming with thoughts, voices, and long forgotten memories. I could feel my heart beat in my shoulder as it pumped out blood faster than I could think. Plotting my attack and preparing myself for a million different scenarios. the sound of my heart and breath seemed too loud. Time seemed to crawl, as he continued to stand there, now in mid chorus of the song, scanning the darkness. Feeling like those eyes I'd felt in my room and attic were scanning the terrain with night vision glasses. Surely, I stood out like a white duck floating upon a blackened pond.

He glared side to side...then stopped about a yard to my right. He took a few steps closer and paused. He raised his head and sniffed the passing breeze. I heard a soft hiss and that's when I saw it...his tongue hung past his chin, flicking like a snake.

The shells rattling upon their strings, the waves roaring in the distance. The sound of a deep, guttural howl rising in pitch toward the black sky, sent my hair rising with it. Somewhere beyond the miniature desert of rolling dunes, I could picture perfectly that black wolf I'd seen in my vision. The same one, Wes and Connor had talked about.

The same one I heard only nights before in Georgetown.

Frank ended his whistle. He snickered and glared toward the stars.

He lowered his head and continued past me.

I waited till he was in just the right spot.

I bolted out of the brush and slung the empty glass bottle that used to house forty ounces of booze.

It cracked against the back of his skull, sending him and me both to the sand as I lost my balance in the effort.

He lay spread eagle on the ground, arms extended in 45-degree angles along his side.

He groaned and shuffled his hand in the dirt feeling for the revolver that lay less than a foot from his reach.

Still clinching the bottle with its jagged remains, I rolled and slammed it down onto his left forearm. It dug deep into his flesh as blood splattered on my face, as if I'd squished a tomato.

"Aaaaahhhh!" he grasped at his arm.

I forced myself to my feet, he did the same.

We stood perhaps ten feet from each other. eyes locked in a stare down.

Leslie was right, his eyes could paralyze. It seemed like my entire body had been turned into a pillar of salt. My heart even felt like it'd quit beating. His brows were sharp angles above big black eyes.

"You never should've forgot about me James...you were my big brother. You were supposed to take care of me," he said in a raspy hiss, as his tongue dangled lazily past his chin in a peculiar long slender frame.

Tucking his bleeding arm tight to his gut, he bent at the knee, looking like a linebacker he entered a dead sprint. All

I could do was brace for the impending Mack truck of a man.

The blow felt like it crushed my ribcage. I slammed into the sand, Frank mounted me and grabbed my throat, squeezing with all he had.

Seconds felt like hours. His teeth bare and cinched tight, his eyes and veins bulging. This man was going to kill me.

"I want to feel you die. I want to taste your last breath," he said with locked teeth, quivering jowls and bulging eyes. Saliva formed on his lips and dripped onto my face. His hands felt like a python around my neck. I'm dead.

I reached for his eyes and face, but he jerked back each time I tried. I thrusted my knees into his rump, trying to find the soft spot. It was like kneeing a brick wall. My blurred vision worsened. I gasped for each escaping breath.

He leaned closer, sniffing, he shut his eyes and quivered in a euphoric rush. He swallowed. I watched the lump swim down his throat. He made a clacking noise with his teeth, then his mouth popped open like a snake...his tongue fell out as he began to hiss.

I thought I felt something pop in my throat. Did he crush my windpipe? Had he squished my Adam's apple?

That's when I heard the rustle and saw the dark figure emit from the woods behind Frank.

A gut-wrenching crack cut the air, as Frank grunted and slumped in the sand.

It was Lee standing with a log the size of a keyboard. Then I saw Rebecca for the first time as she rushed over and snatched up the revolver.

Frank squirmed in the sand, recovering from the blow to the back, I forced myself to Rebecca and Lee.

"Rebecca..."

That's all I could say as my voice was barely a whisper. I wrapped my arms around her, squeezing her tight. We kissed as if it were the first time. For that mere second, I was in paradise. I left the darkness and entered the light.

"Oh, James...I love you," she said pulling back as she must've felt the blood on my shoulder.

Her attention fixed on the wound, "My goodness you've been shot."

"Hey..." said Lee with a quake in his voice.

Before we could turn our attention, the sound of a growing growl sent a chill throughout my body.

Frank was rising to his feet, his back toward us, slumped at the shoulders.

I snatched the gun from Rebecca and steadied it right at the back of the devil's head. Hammer cocked, finger wrapped around the trigger. Every instinct screaming to pull the trigger and end it.

Frank glared back at me over his shoulder with a crescent mouth, daring me to do it.

"You sick good-for-nothing pig!" My voice raspy from what my throat had just endured. The tremble in my hand coming from the tornado of emotions within.

"Go ahead...do it. Like I said you're just as guilty as I am. What's another murder gonna hurt? Do it?"

"James...don't listen to him," Rebecca's hand rested on my other shoulder.

My eyes crazed, my breath steaming, pulse pounding, heart knocking harder and harder.

"She's right James. We've got to pray," said Lee.

Against every instinct, I couldn't believe I was doing it. I lowered the revolvers aim.

"Hahaha...you think your hopeless little prayers can save you from me," Frank said in a deep robotic like voice as he spun on his heels to face us.

His face had contorted as his jaw was elongated, his ears sharper, his fingers longer and slimmer. He looked like the black dog in Connor's drawing. The same one I saw in my dream. The one Uncle Wes talked so much about. Here it was.

You could feel the darkness as it wafted through the air, seeking any that'd welcome it.

"Great Spirit...we call upon You now to protect us from this darkness and deliver us from this evil. You are stronger and far greater than anything hell has to offer. Father we ask for the protection of Your Angels, Lord send them to fight on our behalf and drive out the darkness in this man..."

"Noooo!!" Frank barked with a short breath and hiss, his tongue seeming to tag his chest as it popped out of his mouth.

"Your words are useless!! There is no god! You are all alone! And you are all going to die and burn in hell!"

"Pray with me...c'mon let's pray."

Rebecca and I joined hands with Lee, keeping Frank in our vision, we prayed as Lee led us.

"Great Father...Creator of the universe...Savior of the world...Yeshua. Make your presence known, send an army of Your Angels upon this land and protect us from this evil. Shine Your Light upon this darkness."

Frank squirmed as our words were like acid to soft flesh. He growled and moaned through clinched teeth, pacing in the sand, uttering curses and blasphemy. Just as we were about to continue, Frank dropped to all fours and crawled toward us like a crab, tight lips baring a mouth full of canine like teeth. He stopped about five feet from us and yelled, "You are worthless!! All of your sins are too much. You will rot in hell for all of eternity. There is no savior, there is a no god!"

"Be quiet spirit...I command you in authority of my Father Yeshua, the Great Creator and Spirit, the Savior of the world whose blood has set us free from the power of sin and death...come out of this man!"

"Noooo!" Frank shrieked and scrambled backward, kicking up sand and dirt.

"I demand you in the name of Jesus Christ and in the authority of His identity as ruler and King of the world and in my authority as Light of the World, to come out!" Lee said, breaking free from our grips and marching toward him with his hand outstretched.

"Aaaahhhhh!" Frank screeched and wrapped his bony fingers around his ears and began tugging and scratching until finally ripping one from his skull.

Blood oozed down the side of his head as stood to his feet wearing an awkward grin, remnants of his ear in hand. He stuck it his mouth and tore into it like a raged animal. Smacking and smiling as he did so.

Frank let out a roar that rattled my intestines as he then reached for his eyes with those same bony sharp fingers.

"No!" Rebecca yelled.

Frank chuckled as he tore at his eyes with both hands like an angry crab fending off predators with its claws. He plucked one out and reared back...he slung it toward us. We leaped to the side as it skipped across the sand.

Lee continued forward, Rebecca and I followed behind him.

"Stop! In the name of Jesus...spirit what is your name?"

Frank gave a childish laugh, continuing to dig at the other eye and said, "Of whom do you ask? Surely you don't think I abide alone? Could a child of god be that dumb?"

"What are your names!?"

In a deep raspy voice, "Kirkland!"

"Who else?"

"Ender!" he said in a quick burst, that sounded like a loud whisper.

"Are there more?"

Frank twisted his head side to side in violent fashion, his bones creaking and popping in protest of such unnatural movement.

"Are there more?"

Frank sat still, yanked his fingers from his face, eyeball in hand, the gapping sockets oozing blood.

Rebecca gasped and turned her head to avoid such a sight.

My gut knotted. I thought I'd heave. My cheeks puffed as that unfriendly feeling climbed up my chest and esophagus. Somehow, I managed to keep the vomit in check.

"Are there more!?" Lee demanded.

"Lucindaaaaaaaaaa!" Frank bellowed in a high pitch tone like that of a woman in distress. My ears rang as it felt like an ice pick being jammed into them.

"Kirkland, Ender, Lucinda, I demand you in the name of Jesus Christ and His Identity, come out! I command you come out of this man!"

Lee marched forward, repeating his words, motioning to me and Rebecca to join him. Rebecca still had her head turned, so I tugged at her arm and beckoned her to follow me as we strode toward the two. Rebecca squeezed my arm with enough force to seize the circulation.

"Pray with me...we need to lay hands on him,"

I looked to Lee then Frank.

"C'mon...pray with me."

Reluctantly following Lee's guidance, me and Rebecca stretched forth our hands and rested them upon Frank's shoulder as he sat upon his haunches in the sand, hollow eyes and bleeding ears.

"Come out of him unclean spirits, we command you on the authority of our Father in Heaven, by the Power of His blood, come out!"

The second our hands touched his shoulder, he jerked back like a dog after years of torture from its owner. He cowered and shifted across the sand shuffling his feet to propel him backward.

We followed him, still in earnest pray with outstretched arms. We touched him again and this time Lee repeated the prayer with a deeper sense of urgency and power. Rebecca and I repeated it with him.

Frank stilled as if hit with a tranquil dart from a biologist. His head drooped and in a slow sway, he dropped to the sand.

A soft jingle of bells and chains emitted from the woods to our left.

We shifted our vision. Breathing in short gasps the sight stalled my breath.

A beastly figure cloaked in black trimmed with bells and jewelry, stood less than fifteen feet away, dark face resting below a ginormous set of ram horns that spiraled toward the ink colored sky, void eyes glaring at us with a scowl.

Outwardly, my skin tingled and crawled, yet inwardly, my heart was firm and strong, knowing that my Father could not be threaten or defeated and neither could I. For just as Rebecca had said in the letter, "Even in the darkness, God is there."

The figure sighed and huffed out a scoff before turning and vanishing into the darkness.

Frank writhed in the sand.

The atmosphere shifted, the air seemed lighter, that warm embrace flooded my heart and soul.

"It's finished..." said Lee. "...we need to call Ray."

I dug my cell from my jean pocket and made the call.

He was frantic and asking more questions than I could keep up with. Ray split his time on the phone, between asking me questions and barking out orders to his men.

He had what he needed, we ended the call and waited.

That's when it hit me. Connor!?

"We got to find Connor!"

"What?" asked Rebecca in a short gasp, "You brought him out here with you?"

"No...he did," I said as I pointed to Frank resting on the ground, curled into a ball.

"Oh, my goodness," she said as she covered her mouth and looked at me with those heart stopping brown eyes.

"Stay here with Lee, I'll be right back."

"You sure James," Lee asked as he turned and looked at me over his shoulder as he knelt beside Frank, keeping pressure on his forearm.

"Yeah."

I bounded through the woods to where I last remember him holding Connor near the hole in the sand, which reminded me of someone yanking Lee into the ground.

My mind was spinning as I felt like I was in a movie. My hair stood on edge as I trudged through the darkened brush.

My feet caught on something in my path that my anxious eyes ignored. It gave like a pillow. I stumbled forward almost losing my balance. I looked to the ground. It was Connor.

"Oh buddy," I said as my heart throbbed at the gnawing thought of him being taken by Frank, then tossed to the dirt. Which also struck me with fear as I could only wonder about what must've happened at home? Did he—

God I can't go there. Lord...please be with Jason and Lauren and Starla. Oh God...please. My heart quaked as I scooped Connor into my arms, wincing at the pain in my shoulder as I struggled for my footing and balance before beginning my trek back to Lee and Rebecca. My adrenaline pumping stronger than a freight train

Thoughts of the evil I'd just witnessed bounded through my mind. The sight of that dark figure with those bells and jewelry...the sounds Frank made in those different voices flashed through my mind with adjacent memories of my childhood that I'd hidden for so long. Is Frank really my little brother Jessie? How could I erase something like this?

The thoughts flooded my mind as I stumbled onward.

As Rebecca's silhouette grew, hearing my trudging she raced toward us.

"Oh baby," she said as she took Connor form my arms.

"Guys we need to pray for Frank...I don't know if he'll last until they get here," said Lee as he glanced once more over his shoulder.

Rebecca and I made our way over to them. Frank moaned and shifted in the sand, mumbling, "Don't let me die, please God, don't let me die."

We rested our hands on his chest and prayed. The waves roared, the shells sang, and the sound of sirens travelling from the main land only added to the night song.

Frank cradled in a ball like a child, making soft whimpers as he continued to mumble.

Is this the man who'd rendered such fear in the hearts of the locals? Is this the man who'd committed such atrocity? Is this the GTK? The San Bernardino Phantom?

Here he lay as harmless as a whipped puppy.

It felt like we were stationed around a fire as the warmth of the Creator's embrace became more tangible with each uttered prayer.

Light flooded the atmosphere, driving away the darkness. God was here. Love was here. And no manner of evil could stand against such love.

Epilogue

June 2019

Five years after the encounter on the East end, I have yet
to been able to rid my mind of what I witnessed that night.
I knew then that evil truly existed. But you see out of that
came a comforting truth. If evil exists, then good must too.
If there is darkness, there must be light. If there is hate,
there must be love. Right? As I was drug along a journey
into the darkness, like a child snatched into a dark forest at
midnight, I learned the stark reality of the evil that exist in
this fallen world. On the contrary, I also learned the
staggering power of the Creator's light. His light is brighter
and stronger than the mere passing shadow of darkness,
the Creator's love is greater than any hate or evil that will
ever threaten me.

I'm so grateful I still have my family after that night,
things could've been much worse.

Jason and Lauren are now juniors and seniors at
Coastal Carolina. Lauren studying Marine Science,
following in the footsteps of her mother. Jason being the
business type that he is, chose finance and accounting.

Lily made a quick recovery and is now enjoying her job
and family in upstate Maine, where she works in

conservation efforts with the Department of Natural Resources.

Kelly took a bit to fully heal, but she's as vibrant as they come now.

Considering what we've been through, I'd say we've faired pretty well.

With Connor's birthday approaching, myself, Rebecca, Kelly and Connor find ourselves on our way home from Food Lion as Rebecca needed some tomatoes for her gumbo. Connor's favorite.

As we began the accent up the winding bridge to cross the ICW, I noticed a rip current snaking it ways out to the deep. I couldn't help but think of Jerry. He'd be proud to see we made it out of Georgetown and boy would he be worked up if knew what Ethan had done.

The stereo whispered behind the sound of the wind, Connor had me to turn it up.

I reached and twisted the knob.

"As you have all heard me tell of my journey from darkness to light, I'd like to have my best friend David end with something I had him pen in my journal not long after I was given a second chance at life. I like to call it, "The Beauty of Despair."

Another voice picked up,

'I've felt the dangers of hopelessness. I've felt the pain of despair. I know what it's like to dread another day of the same unfulfilling pattern. I know what it's like for the high of my day to be when I lay my head on my pillow at night. At least there, I can find some sense of comfort. At least in that state, I can escape the harsh reality of the cruel world. How do you find the strength to go another day? How do you find your worth when no one wants you, not even yourself? What do you do when the pain within becomes like a sickness you can't shake? First it was just a thought, then it became a feeling, but now it's a belief. My heart has left me. How can I find it? Where can I find it? What happened? Why? Why is it so hard? There must be a reason for the pain I feel.

'I've survived some of my darkest days. I've faced a million demons and slayed a thousand giants. I am a giant slayer. I've got scars to prove it. I've walked through emotional hell and lived to tell about it. I'm stronger than I think, loved more than I'll ever understand, if not by anyone here on earth, than at least by the one who has bled fought through far greater battles than my own. All in a relentless pursuit of my broken and battered heart.

'So where is my heart? It's in the palms of my Creator where it is being broken and reshaped to look more like his own. Because it's in losing yourself, you find the you that can change the world. The you that has been created and known by the Father before time ever began. In being broken you will be healed. In being lost, you will be found. In losing yourself, you gain the Creator and lover of your soul. It's in our greatest messes that the Creator accomplishes His greatest work. If He created man from dust and the earth from nothing, then how great of a story can he make with our messes, scars, and hardest battles?

'You see, nothing is ever wasted...that's the beauty of despair.'

"Thank you, David. You are never too far gone folks, no matter how dark your life may seem, the light is always there. No manner of darkness can stand against such light."

The crowd applauded and cheered as a booming voice came on over the song playing in the back ground. It'd become his new favorite,

"There's a hope for all who've gone astray
There's a road for all who've lost their way
There's a light that leads us back to Grace

Forever shines...never fades..."

"Thank you for listening to another episode of *Out of the Darkness* with Jessie Randolph and David Hoffman, tune in next week for another encouraging word from the man whose life was radically transformed from darkness to light."

The car was silent. I breathed through puffed cheeks.

Rebecca scrambled with a blind right hand in the center console for a Kleenex with her left bracing the wheel as we cruised down ocean boulevard.

I turned to Connor and Kelly in the back, their eyes red as well. Between the two of them sat Spirit, our white Husky.

I gave a comforting smile before turning and facing the front windshield.

"Man...if God can transform Jessie like He has...then they isn't no body too far gone," I said as I wagged my head.

"He's good, isn't He?" Rebecca asked as she turned and faced me for a brief moment Her long, wavy brown hair fluttering in the wind from the half-opened window.

I looked into those gorgeous brown eyes that still had their way of weakening my knees and said, "He sure is."

Investigation Today: Article 2, Vol 3

Thursday, June 27th, 2019

JESSIE RANDOLPH:

A JOURNEY FROM DARKNESS TO LIGHT

By Rachel Fuller

Having been a forensic psychologist and crime reporter for the past twenty-years, I've just about seen and heard it all. At least I thought. It wasn't until the fall of 2014, that I learned just how far us human beings can stumble into darkness.

I was a rising junior at Georgetown High in 1989, when I first heard the term: GTK. As the murder of a young couple shocked the local community, but as quickly as it began, it ended.

That is until a quarter of a century later, when the GTK returned. As you all likely recall, after the discovery of a series of bodies stretching from Coast to Coast, a nation wide manhunt in search of the GTK ensued.

These crimes had a significant impact on me as I felt a deep connection to the story as it all began in my home town.

Which is actually what sparked my interest criminology and one of the biggest reasons I'm where I'm at today.

After a series of cat and mouse chases between detectives and the Randolph family of whom found themselves in the crosshairs of the GTK's fascination, it all came to a boil less than five miles from the Randolph's home.

As Rebecca, the matriarch of the family, was taken captive and held against her will in a make-shift bunker on the far east end of Holden Beach, NC, her wit and determination enlarged her chance of survival as she spent a horrifying 8 nights and 7 seven days bound in the GTK's den beneath the sand.

After the heroic rescue by her husband James and family friend, Lee McGaha, the story...

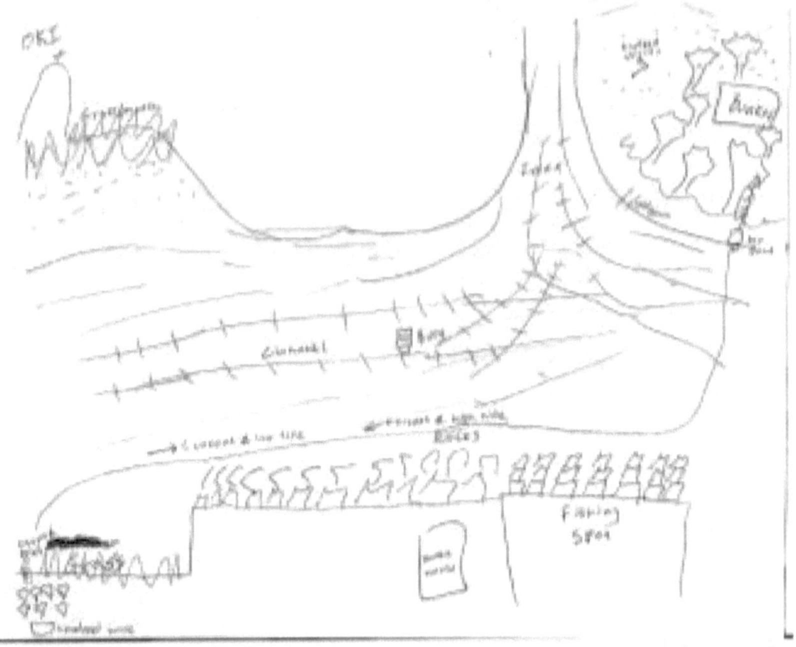

Sketched map of "Devil's Den" by Jessie Randolph AKA The GTK

of their encounter that night and the grizzly discover of what lied beneath the sand only yards away from where so many had undoubtedly taken a relaxing scroll along the beach, is enough to make you wonder how many times you've brushed shoulders with evil and was too naïve to notice.

Randolph could not have chosen a better location, as the roar of the waves was sure to cover any sound his captives may have made.

Randolph says he used a small Jon boat to travel back and forth to the bunker, only doing so at night. Often times between the hours of 2 am and 4 am. In the map above, which Randolph submitted to police after his capture, you can see the exact location of where he launched the boat and where Devil's Den was located, just around the bend from the popular landmark of the Kindred Spirits mailbox.

IT | 27

Inside the bunker, detectives found the remains of Lorraine Thompson, whose skeleton frame was secured to a wooden cross overlooking a altar which supported numerous mason jars full of human body parts. Everything from eyes, ears, lips, fingers, toes, and even the jagged remains of a nose.

Lying in the sand next to the wooden altar was the body of a middle-aged man who had suffered three gun shot wounds to the abdomen after a failed attempt to murder Lee McGaha. The body belonged to a man by the name of Robert Abercrombie. The older brother of Will Abercrombie, the young boy from Georgetown who has been missing since 1981, after not returning home from school just days before being let out for the summer.

According to the confessions of Jessie Randolph, formerly known as Frank Thompson, the GTK. Robert Abercrombie was a trusted accomplice.

Claiming Abercrombie helped to organize things while Randolph was away in Southern California. Digging the bunker being one of his biggest contributions.

Randolph says he and Abercrombie stayed in contact over the years and had been planning the murder of his brother James Randolph since 1999.

Randolph has since confessed to more than four dozen murders spanning from 1981 to 2014, with the total count believed to be 53.

Many of which were cold cases of missing people. In total, 43 were confirmed to have taken place in Southern California after Randolph fled to Palm Springs in 1989 just before being questioned about the murder of Melissa Berkeley and Stephen Rickles along with being held accountable for the gruesome accident at the Georgetown Papermill.

According to Randolph, he lived on the streets for his first two years as he blended into the homeless community, honing his skills as he took a dozen or more victims without being much investigation.

In 1994, Randolph secured a job as a local cable installer along with working odd handy man jobs in Beaumont, Banning, Yucaipa and Big Bear...

IT | 28

Small towns just outside Palm Springs.

Randolph says many of his victims after his days living on the streets in 1989, were customers he'd either installed cable for or had completed remodeling work for.

Using his jobs as the opportunity to scope out the lay of the house, he'd then sneak in after mid-night under the cover of darkness and take residence in the homeowner's attic. Often staying days at a time as he learned their patterns and habits, before finally relieving his twisted desires.

Detectives were baffled, as a series of homicides suddenly began taking place, in which they all seemed to have occurred from within, with no sign of forced entry.

Randolph continued this routine for just under two decades going completely undetected by authorities.

Randolph once stated in an interview by Time magazine, that he'd often claim 2 or 3 victims a year, through this process.

Saying in a good year, he might claim 4 or 5.

When questioned about the purpose behind his crimes, he stated it was due to his twisted theology which was ingrained in him by his Father (George Thompson) at an early age.

However, George Thompson was not his biological Father, nor was Lorraine Thompson his biological Mother. This is where the story of the GTK really begins.

In 1975, just weeks before reaching his fifth birthday, Jessie Randolph was on his way to a local playground with his older brother James, being 8 years his elder and a close confidant.

As the two journeyed along a wooded trail less than a mile from their home in Mt. Pleasant, little over an hour's drive south of Georgetown, the two brothers were met by a man as he protruded from the wood line. The man severely beat James, causing him to undergo a month long induced coma, and kidnapped the younger brother Jessie.

Spending the next six and a half years being brainwashed into believing George and Lorraine were his true parents, his name changed from Jessie Randolph to Franklin Ethan Thompson.

As the years went on, Randolph became introduced to George Thompson's dangerous and downright horrifying cult known as "For the Greater Good."

Randolph retold gut-wrenching accounts of animal and human sacrifice in which he was forced to take part in.

Even to the point of murdering one of his best friends from school, Will Abercrombie.

The missing brother of Robert Abercrombie who was found in the bunker at Holden Beach in 2014.

Randolph says Robert Abercrombie was apart of Thompson's cult and as repulsive as it is to believe, actually took part along with Randolph and Thompson in murdering his own brother.

Randolph claims Robert was even apart of a horrific murder that took place in 1976, in which a young man violently killed his mother and grandmother with a box cutter and attempted to murder his grandfather, Kirby Mooreland, before taking his own life.

Randolph claims, Abercrombie and Thompson were the ones who orchestrated the event as a means of initiation to enter their cult.

It wasn't until Randolph came home from school one crisp fall afternoon in 1982, that the appalling works of Thompson's cult came to an end.

In search of his mother Lorraine, Randolph ventured out into the barn where he horrifically discovered her dead corpse mounted to a cross as George Thompson knelt in the dirt, rocking in earnest petition.

It is here, Randolph claims to have murdered the man who'd stolen him from his chance of a normal life.

Burying the body under the home and setting the barn ablaze soon after planting two bodies from the cult's...

IT | *30*

sacrifices into the inferno.

Randolph says the reasoning for his murders in the coming years was all an act of pertinence for the suffering his mother endured.

As Randolph has given police details over the years that are far too graphic for publication, it seems we are slowly beginning to understand the reasoning behind the atrocious crimes of the GTK.

With Randolph's sentencing quickly approaching, the national debate of whether he should face the death penalty for his crimes is a topic which quickly breeds heated arguments among accusers and bystanders.

Having undergone a complete transformation according to Randolph and those closest to him, such as his brother James, Rebecca, the woman he held captive for 7 days, and a now close friend, Lee McGaha, Jessie Randolph has truly found redemption.

To further the point, Randolph along with the help of childhood friend, David Hoffman, who is now the Senior Pastor at The Good Shepherd Church of Shallotte, lead a Bible study and ministry in prison as he informs inmates of the true power of Redemption and Grace.

Finding parallel with the story of the radical transformation of Paul, the author of more than half of the New Testament, who underwent a similar journey from murderer to preacher.

Randolph spreads a message of hope and Redemption as he claims, "If God can rescue me out of that darkness and love me enough to not give up on me during my darkest times...than I'm convinced, no sin is too great for the Power of His Love and Grace. No matter how dark your life may seem...His light is always there. It may only be a faint glimmer, but I promise, it'll grow brighter and brighter as you begin the journey from darkness to light."

It's a controversial issue as many find it hard to believe in such transformation and claim it is just his attempt to dodge the harsh punishment for his crimes.

"Listen...I know a lot of people don't believe I've changed and feel I deserve to suffer for what I've done...

IT | 31

But you know it doesn't bother me what people think, because I know in my heart and soul...I'm a changed man. You can take it for what it's worth, and don't think for one second I'm not already suffering for the things I did. There's not a day that goes by I don't hear the voices from the ghosts of those I've wronged. And even though I can't physically see them as my earthly vision was taken the night of my deliverance, I still see their faces in the blackness of my mind. I'd do anything in this world to take it back, but I can't. I feel the best way for me to pay my dues is to tell my story in hopes it'll pull someone from that darkness I once was in. If my story of redemption can lead one person from darkness to light and stop them from wondering down that trail of evil, which only escalates into something bigger with each step, than I'd like to believe I've done my part in attempting to shine a light in the darkness. People often ask me, if I'm afraid of death and what might await me on the other side. I'm hearing that question more and more as my sentence draws near. I used to be, but not anymore, because I have discovered who I truly am.

I'm not a monster. I'm not an evil man. Did I do evil things? You bet I did.

But you see, I've learned along my journey of transformation, that...that's not who I am. My Father did not create me that way. He didn't make me that way, what kind of god would do such a thing? You see I was created to do good, but through my upbringing and the lies I was constantly fed, I became something I wasn't. Learning that the GTK is not who I am at the core has brought so much freedom as I continue along this journey. So, whether I'm sentenced to life or death in the coming days, I have no fear at what awaits me. I've discovered my true self, which is loved and cherished by my Creator and like a prodigal, I've stumbled home. Out of the darkness and into the light."

As Randolph continues to minister from his prison cell, his message even being broadcasted on local radio stations, one can only wonder how such evil could ever exist in the first place?

IT | **32**

Randolph preaching in Robeson Federal Prison

Furthermore, how many times have we encountered someone who perhaps was in the beginning or latter stages of such insidious evil?

Would you recognize it if it stood before you? Or would you unknowingly invite it into your home, like so many did in the early days of the GTK?

It's a reminder that evil does exist in the world and its not a matter of *if* we'll encounter it, but *when*. Whether it's encountering a GTK, like James and Rebecca did, or its simply bumping into someone in the store who happens to be on the same path as the GTK, sooner or later we are bound to cross path's with such evil.

My question to you is…will you even notice? Or will you unknowingly pass by another Devil's Den, like so many must have done at Holden Beach.

Upon exiting another of Randolph's sessions, with him ending in prayer, stretching forth the remnants of his arm, the words to a faith filled song titled, "My Liberty" by Christian recording artist Zach Williams plays in the background. I can't help but feel there is something different about this man.

As he speaks of love and grace, its hard to imagine he…

IT | 33

could have been capable of committing such crimes. Which leads me to believe, there must have been an underlying evil at work.

Over the years of my reporting's, I've discovered that evil can take on many shapes and forms, some obvious and others disguised as wolves in sheep's clothing. The latter which causes me to question my attentiveness.

But the question that continues to arise in my mind is this: If such evil does exist, than certainly there must also be an equal amount of good which is just as powerful. Correct?

There must be an equally powerful force of good to counter balance such evil. If there wasn't then cases like the GTK would be the norm and not the rarity.

Which leads one to believe that perhaps there is hope for humanity, even as depraved as we sometimes seem, there is comfort in believing in such a counter balance of good.

Just like every other form of polarity in our universe, if there is darkness, there must be light, if there is evil than there must be good. And one needs to look no further than Jessie Randolph to see that.

Having met with Randolph numerous times over the years and relying heavily upon my years of psychological study and training, I can honestly say, he seems to be a genuinely changed man. And if good can come from such evil, than I think there's hope for us all.

With America's attention now zeroing in on the coverage of one of it's most prolific serial killers since Bundy and Dahmer, one can only wonder if such redemption is possible. Perhaps miracles still exist and like the story of the transformation from Saul to Paul found in scripture and that of the GTK, there's nothing too dirty for Grace.

Story by Rachel Fuller, award winning crime reporter and senior journalist of Investigation Today

IT | 34

Thank you for reading *Devil's Den!* I hope you enjoyed it as much as I did writing it! If so, I would be grateful if you'd be kind enough to leave a review on Amazon as reviews truly are the life blood of any Author's career.

About the Author

I am a former college baseball player turned writer who thoroughly enjoys the outdoors, whether it be fishing, kayaking, hiking, and exploring new places, or watching a game of America's greatest pastime. I'm an old soul at heart, so I love old music (especially classic rock from CCR, Bob Seger, Bruce Springsteen, or vintage rock and roll from Chuck Berry, Muddy Water's, Elvis, etc) old movies and antique items. I own a Victrola Turntable in case you're not getting the picture yet. I'm an avid reader and writer of Mystery, Horror, and Suspense. I enjoy reading Stephen King, Ted Dekker, Frank Peretti, Thomas Harris, Steven James, C.J. Box, and James Lee Burke to name a few. I also enjoy a fun/inspiring Southern Story as well such as Where the Crawdads Sing. I was a top ten finalist in Inkshares 2018 Mystery/Thriller contest. I am a member of the Horror Writers of America Association. I hold an MBA from Coastal Carolina University and am currently practicing real estate in Myrtle Beach. You can find me on Instagram, Facebook, and YouTube to stay up to date with my latest work.

† RANDALL LANE †

Instagram: randall_lane31
Facebook: Randall Lane Fiction
YouTube: Randall Lane Fiction
Amazon: Randall Lane Fiction

Other Books Available

If you enjoyed *Devil's Den* then you'll likely enjoy my latest novel *The Reaping* as well. Available on Amazon! The book trailer is posted to my YouTube channel.

Synopsis: Something strange is happening in New England. Over the past 17 years, numerous children have disappeared after each of their parents were discovered brutally murdered and left with taunting notes. With rumors of the man in a black hood who roams the woods at night, to an escaped mental patient from Cushing Island, and a snake handling church with a dark past, veteran Homicide Detective, Laurie Daniels must work through this high stakes enigma to learn who the ghost-like killer really is. The deeper she goes the more she begins to believe the killer may be connected to her past. And a new, horrifying clue emerges . . . Daniels isn't closing in on the killer, but he's closing in on her. Can she catch him before he catches her?

I also have my novel *Omah*, available on Amazon too! To watch the book trailer, head over to my YouTube channel. (Randall Lane Fiction.)

Synopsis: After a string of mysterious disappearances and encounters in Northern California, Game Wardens are less than surprised when six-year-old Tyler Jacob's vanishes by the South Fork Eel River while fishing with his family. As the family is riddled with guilt and on the verge of losing hope, Native Americans from the local Yurok Tribe step in to help spread light on the recent events. While pushing through the vast wilderness and majestic Redwood Forest in search of his son, Randy Jacob's soon learns that what he once thought was just a Legend may actually be a living and breathing creature after all. As hours stretch into days and the clock rushes forward, can Tyler be found before it's too late?

Be sure to check out my collection of short stories titled, *Night Terrors!*

Includes everything from Ghosts, Aliens, Bigfoot, Werewolves, Skinwalkers, Strange Disappearances, and many other creepy mysteries.

OLD
GHOSTS
OF THE
VALLEY
A NOVEL
RANDALL LANE

1

Chapel Valley, NC

October 2023

3:33 p.m.

Carol Gore is a fifty-nine-year-old divorced mother of two, who lives alone up in the backcountry of the Blue Ridge Mountains. She has lived in the same house since the early nineties. She and her husband, Steve, moved to the area after he'd picked up a mining job in the town of Chapel Valley. It was also around this time that Carol learned of the Abbott cult. A co-worker from Piggly Wiggly wouldn't shut up about the sweet little Abbott family and its parishioners, so Carol finally relented and accompanied her to an event at the compound. That was all it took for Carol to become hooked.

As Carol thinks back to the moment she first stepped foot on the Abbott compound, she subconsciously rinses off a few glass plates from previous days meals. Skylar, her white Himalayan cat, is busy weaving in and out between her feet. The tickle brings her back just in time to hear the strange noise. Carol thought she'd heard something earlier but only brushed it off as a play upon her ears. Must be the house settling or something, she'd said to herself. Isn't that what we always say? Or at least what we always hope for, right? What if we're wrong though? What if we're not alone during all the times we think we are? What if someone or something . . . lurks within the shadows and watches without our knowing?

As Carol asks herself these questions, she hears it again. The sound is unmistakable this time. The creaking of a floorboard beneath a sturdy, unwelcomed foot. All day she had fought the eerie feeling of being watched. It seems a presence had been hovering just over her shoulder. She's being too paranoid, she'd thought. Things are different now. To think she's still being watched . . . well it'll just end up driving her crazy. She can't allow herself to go on thinking this way. They would end up throwing her away to the place where people drift along in white gowns, while being force fed medicine and whipped into submission. She'll never go back there. She'd made a promise to herself, and she's determined within her heart to keep it.

No amount of self-encouragement can eat away the growing feeling she has of being watched. It is stronger now than ever before. The home is quiet other than the running of the faucet, and the black and white film playing in the living room. Carol stands frozen with her back to the rest of the kitchen. She looks down to find Skylar staring behind her. Together they listen.

Creeeaaak!

Skylar hisses and enters in a low crouch, his ears flare backward, his hair stands straight. Carol feels someone in the room. She turns just enough, so she can scan the room with her peripheral. She goes over the China cabinet full of Grandma's dishes and scans over the kitchen table. Her heart leaps at the big shadow of a man standing in the kitchen's door frame. She gasps and drops a dish. The crash of the shattering glass fills the room. She fights the urge to look directly at the man, knowing that the chance of her survival will quickly diminish should she see his face.

Skylar emits a low growl and backs up to be between Carol and the sink cabinet.

"What do you want?" Carol asks with her words sticking to her throat.

A moment passes.

"You."

Creeeeaaaaak!

The dark man takes a step.

"Stop. Don't come any closer."

He stops.

She grips the sinks hard enough to hurt her fingers.

"Look at me."

She shakes her head.

"Carol."

Her heart sinks at the knowledge of this mystery man knowing her name.

"Carol. You have to look at me. It's very important."

She clamps her eyes shut and shakes her head again.

She hears him breathe deep. He holds it, then sighs.

"I don't want to do this Carol, but I'm afraid I have to. You're leaving me no—"

Carol snatches Skylar up and bolts through the side door of the kitchen for her bedroom. Heavy thuds pound towards her. She slams the door shut and engages the lock. She rushes to move a chest of drawers against the door.

The dark man slams against the door as soon as Carol slides the furniture into place. The door rattles hard on its hinges. She stumbles backwards with one hand to her mouth, and the other reaching blindly for the bed.

Her heart will surely explode any moment as adrenaline courses through her veins in an icy rush. Her legs meet the edge of the bed, and she bruises a heel against the metal railing below. She winces and bends to tend to the pain.

The door rattles hard once more. Skylar growls again before going into a frantic search for cover. Another hard thud pounds against the door.

As Carol rubs her heel, she begins to hear a faint but hoarse whisper coming from under the bed. The scratchy voice stalls her racing heart and sends her body freezing in place. Movement comes from beneath the bed. It sounds like something crawling across the hardwood floor. Carol jerks herself up and looks toward the window. A sudden thought hits her. What an idiot. Last week she'd nailed the windows shut after fearing someone was secretly entering in the night. In her efforts to keep someone out, she ends up trapping herself in. She must break it. She races over to a nightstand and begins to search for something to break the glass.

The whisper under the bed becomes more audible now. Between the thuds against the door, she can make out the words. It's saying, "Come near my dear."

Carol yanks open a drawer to her nightstand and pulls out a hammer she's used for hanging pictures. She tucks her face into the crevice of her elbow and takes a swing. The window shatters. She rakes away the shards along the seal and rushes over to the nightstand. As she begins to swipe away the clutter, lamp and all, the thing beneath the bed growls loudly. Carol catches a glimpse in her peripheral of a long, bony hand reaching out from beneath the bed, aiming for Carol's ankle. She screams and jumps backwards. The thing continues to growl. Its pale fingers fall limp to the hardwood. Its nails make a loud tapping sound.

Carol hurries and places the nightstand beneath the broken window. The door thuds again as she climbs upon the nightstand.

She wiggles through the window and falls to the ground. Her hip barks in protest. She grunts and manages to get to her feet. She hears her bedroom door burst open. She doesn't turn back to look but makes a break for the grove of pines.

Running and stumbling her way into the tree line, she pushes away the swipes of bony branches. Her tender feet scream with every poke and jab from the sticks and pine needles. Her lungs burn like they've been doused with gasoline and lit to a flame. Her breath steams into the frigid air. Running between the pines, she retrieves her cell. Moments later she finds the contact she's looking for and places the call.

Panting and glancing over her shoulder, she waits for her son to answer.

Tales from Uncle Joe
Mutilations
Randall Lane
Tales from Uncle Joe
It Roams At Night
Randall Lane
Tales from Uncle Joe
An Inside Job
Randall Lane

† **RANDALL LANE** †

Thank you once again for joining me on this journey through story. From one reader to another, may we all continue to find ourselves as we escape into the written word.

> Till next time!
> All the best,

Randall Lane